D. THOMAS GOCHENOUR

THE *Poet*

Contents

Chapter One

The Genesis of the Poet

Our hero made his first appearance in history at the precocious age of seven in the small Bashkir city of Ufa. He was sitting on a chair too tall for his short legs to reach the stage in front of a small crowd of proud parents and of schoolchildren dressed in white shirts and shorts. It was a hot sticky day in late spring, before Last Bell, when schools are let out for the summer. The point of this assembly is long since lost to Soviet history. But we know that also on the low stage was the head teacher from our hero's school, the mayor of the city, and the local first secretary of the Communist Party in Bashkiria, and they all made dense and ideological speeches so it was probable that a political message about the proper indoctrination of the schoolchildren was being delivered. But the highlight of the ceremony was when the head teacher called on our young hero to recite a patriotic poem, which was a traditional part of the yearly ritual of this ceremony although it was usually delivered by 12 or 13 year old students.

Now as I said, it was a hot and humid morning with an intense sun in the sky, and the mayor, who was a Bashkir man named Kanliyellov, who was sitting in his poorly fitting dark gray wool suit with a thick purple tie which had been loosened from his open collar so that he looked as if he had already been working for 14 hours, was sweating profusely. He could not pay attention to the proceedings at all because he could only think about water. But not because he was particularly thirsty at that moment—he had drunk a bottle of cold beer just before coming to this event—but because there was an overall water shortage in Ufa and the taps were everywhere dry. Even though Ufa is intersected by two lovely, green, broad rivers, the city's water supply which ultimately comes from those proud rivers had been contaminated and so the water plant had been shut. It seemed a particularly invidious contamination as well, as another petty bureaucrat, named Golovorezov, further upriver from Ufa in the next province had been tasked with disposing of some highly toxic PCBs which, for ease of disposal, meant that he had dumped an entire consignment into the upper reaches of the White River which then flowed straight down to Ufa. Dozens of people had been poisoned and died before the authorities, including Mr. Kanliyellov, had decided to shut off the water. And then when Mr. Kanliyellov had been tasked with buying water tankers to bring an emergency supply to the city, he had pocketed many of the funds, so that only a few tankers had arrived and they had been sent to only a few favored neighborhoods. And now there were no water tankers—not even a small orange one with its communal drinking glasses—standing there at the park where so many thirsty children and parents were assembled. He squirmed and sweated with worry, because this was just the sort of public failing where the assembled people could notice and raise a scandal. 'What, no water for the children to drink! In this heat!'

Then it was the turn of our hero, the young poet, not yet achieved. He slipped off his chair and brushed down his starched white shirt and walked—no really shuffled—over to the podium. The audience applauded softly for him. The head teacher adjusted the microphone's jib downwards to put it close to his mouth. And then silence, except for the soughing of grasses on the tall embankment just behind the stage which fell off to the White River far below them. Then he began to recite, from memory, the short poem "Homeland" by Michael Lermontov. His voice was small, but natural and musical without the stilted or strained emphases that student reciters usually employ to aid their memory.

I love the homeland, but it's a strange love!
It will not win over my mind.
Neither glory, bought with blood,
Neither full confidence, proud peace
Neither the cherished legends of dark antiquity
Do not stir me to have pleasant dreams.
But I love—why? I do not know myself—
Her cold silent steppes,
Her boundless forests quivering,
Her rivers in flood wide like the sea;
I love bumping along in the country in a cart
And slowly gaze piercingly the night shadow
Meet on the sides, sighing about accommodation,
Trembling lights sad villages;
I like the smoke of the scorched cornstubble,
In the steppe staying on an overnight train
And on the hill among the yellow fields
A couple of whitened birches.
With joys, many unfamiliar
I see a full barn
A hut, covered with straw,
and with carved window shutters;

And in celebration, on a dewy evening,
I look on until midnight ready
the dance with its stamping and whistling
By speaking of drunken peasants.

You have to excuse my English translation which removes the natural Russian intonation and rhymed couplets so brilliantly used by Lermontov. Our young hero delivered these poetic tropes so masterfully and naturally that he amazed everyone. It was a self-assured performance. Of course, he had memorized these verses, taught recitation by his mother's repetition. It was unlikely at his tender age with only one year of schooling that he could even read or fathom such a subtle paean. But he delivered it as if it was his sincerest feelings about his homeland. The adults in the audience were hugely impressed, this recital was the best performance of poetry they had ever heard and they applauded this time more forcefully than earlier. Even the schoolchildren in the audience were entranced. Our hero smiled smugly, looking straight out at the schoolchildren, who surely did not understand anything of Lermontov's verse.

The head teacher approached to pat his head and then lead him away, but he did not step back from the microphone. Instead he smiled again and put out his right arm as if to begin a declamation. And then he committed a major political blunder. He began to recite a short poem in the Tatar language.

> *"I love my homeland in which I stand,*
> *Blue cornflowers by the meadows are garland'd*
> *On the verges, the silver fields of grain abuzz*
> *With bees and crickets, and golden corn shifts in a stand*
> *The blue heavens overarch us and on the hills a golden sun*
> *Warms the oak and birch, and 'neath granite bluffs steep and dun*
> *Flow fresh clean rivers where splash perch and trout*
> *This beauteous land which was taken from us, I love as one*
> *Who has been robbed in the night by a cutthroat.*

And he then stopped and again with a smirk, stiffly bowed. Again no one in the audience, except the poet's father, understood what our hero had said. They were confused and again taken aback at this recitation in a foreign language, and they clapped this time softly and tentatively. Mr. Kanliyellov, of course, did not know exactly what was said, but being a Bashkir, he knew it was politically inadmissible and offensive to declaim anything in the Tatar language in the Soviet Republic of Bashkiria, especially as Tatars outnumbered Bashkirs. As there are so many similarities and cognates between the two languages, he recognized some meanings and that it was a pastoral, but it was the word cutthroat, which he understood and which set him off. A rage was welling up in his head causing his face to redden and he fingered his collar which suddenly seemed too tight, while reaching with his other hand for a handkerchief with which to mop his sweaty brow. He glowered angrily at the young boy as he returned to his seat. There would be consequences for this outrage, although no one in the audience seemed especially offended.

Just as his mother, who adored classical Russian poetry and was a poetaster of some limited renown in Ufa, had coached our hero in memorizing the Lermontov poem, his father—a Tatar speaker and a professor of literature in the local university—had taught him these two stanzas of a classic Tatar poet (perhaps it was a youthful work of Abdallah Tukai or a short poem by Musa Jalil). And there most definitely had been a political agenda in his father's act of encouraging his son to recite this short poem at this ceremony for the accomplishments of Soviet education in Ufa because speaking or using the Tatar language in official or public transactions was banned at that time. Much of Tatar verse is focused on the feeling of loss, dispossession, and of nostalgic love for a golden time before the Russians conquered their glittering capital of Kazan more than 400 years before and then wrested everything away from the Tatars. But our hero was innocent of all this. He merely understood the verse as a depiction of the summers he spent with his Tatar grandparents in a country house in a Tatar village where the countryside looked just as the poet described. And in his house and his grandparents' the Tatar language was spoken before even Russian. The head teacher was noticeably flustered and embarrassed by this impromptu performance at the end of the ceremony, and he clumsily declared the ceremony finished and thanked the students and parents for attending.

It was then, during the hubbub of the break-up of the audience—schoolchildren yelping with delight as they jumped up and chairs being pushed aside on the concrete, parents greeting and congratulating one another—that our hero witnessed his first vision, a miracle really.

The park where this ceremony was held is situated atop a high grass-covered bluff that steeply falls to the green White River (which in Tatar is actually called Athizel, which means the same thing). These bluffs were formed in a loop of the White River and the Ufa River (which both Tatars and Bashkirs call the Black River or Qarizel) and it was picked out for its defensive qualities by the Russians more than 400 years ago as the site of their fort when they conquered the region. (But contrary to what the local ethnic Russians would tell you, the meaning of Ufa does not come from the grunting sound of exhaustion that their conquering soldiers made after they scrambled up these bluffs.) There, on the highest point of the park, on a mound right behind the stage on top of a granite pedestal, there stands a memorial equestrian statue in bronze of the national hero of the Bashkirs, Salayat Yulaev (or Salavat as the Russians call him).

Now this statue is rather typical of decadent Soviet heroic style. The figure is of a heroic *batur* or valiant hero, who is a big, long-armed, very muscular rider—he is even a little distorted in his dimensions—with a riding knout dangling from his wrist like some dead serpent. This figure is mounted on a fiery stallion that seems to have been pulled up suddenly to stop at the very edge of this bluff and is barely under the control of Salayat. The statue was erected to the memory of the national Bashkir hero, who in fact lived most of his life in Estonia as a captive of the Tsarina.

But Salayat is an ambiguous hero. He certainly was not a batur, which derives from the name of the great Mongol-Turkic horse warriors. He was not big and probably not highly muscular—like some weight lifter it would seem from the sculptor's liberties. And he was probably not a pure Bashkir—his facial features depict a slighter face, without the Bashkir's broad cheeks and Mongolian appearance. And even his historic acts of heroism are somewhat dubious. He was in life the son of a landowner and local Muslim aristocrat, still quite young when he gained his brief fame. His father named him Salawat which is the

MuslimArabic name meaning prayers, because the son was the answer to his father's prayers, and because the local imam suggested it. Important for our purposes, Salayat was educated and literate, and he wrote poetry in Turkic and Russian, although nearly all of which is purported to be his is somewhat suspect.

Salayat's fame (or notoriety) began when he joined the Pugachev Cossack rebellion against Tsarina Catherine largely as a supporter and follower of his father Yulai. Yulai was undoubtedly a tarkhan, or aristocratic leader and military commander of local Bashkir and Tatar cavalry units, who had been swindled out of his land by a Russian merchant claiming a title given to him by the local Russian governor in Orenburg. A tarkhan was traditionally free of paying taxes, but the governor wanted Yulai to pay taxes, and further wanted to take more control over Yulai's military service. For these reasons and his grievance over the loss of his land, Yulai joined Pugachev's rebel forces as a local commander. Salayat also joined them. Salayat led many skirmishes over the following year, but he was arrested when the Russian forces took his wife and children hostage. Then he was led off to captivity for the rest of his life, where supposedly he wrote his laments and poetry which he sent in letters back home. The likeness and pose of the statue and even the facial likeness are a reproduction of the image created by a 32 year old Bashkir actor who was cast in the role of Salavat in a film some years ago when the Bashkir Soviet was desperately searching to establish its legitimacy and historical models. In sum, this Salavat accomplished little in his very brief heroic career, but he was adopted by Bashkirs later to represent a brave, freedom fighter who embodied the people's desires to resist Tsarist exploitation and slavery.

It was just as our hero was turning away from the crowds, just as Mr. Kanliyellov—his handkerchief now fully on his forehead mopping off sweat—was beginning his angry recriminations against the head teacher, that Salayat lowered his arm and turned slowly in his saddle—really just a numnah—to face our young hero. The horse lowered his forelegonto the pedestal and calmed down. Salayat had a benevolent look on his face and in a soft voice he said to our hero: "Young man, you will be the jewel and marvel of our people in this age. Yours will be the voice, and the music you sing out will lift our people with gladness and pride. Recite the poetry of our race. Be sure to continue with your studies of poetry and always speak as the poet does to the aspirations of our people. Look at this beautiful land, and how it is being despoiled. Look on the greed and grasping and denounce them. Tell the story of honest folk, our folk. And recite. Remember to recite."

Now Salayat smiled faintly and leaned forward on his stallion—which snorted with satisfaction—putting both hands on what the sculptor had cast as a pummel on this saddle blanket. Salayat was a giant—really larger than life, almost nine feet tall as the sculptor had cast him—and his movements on the back of his giant horse shocked our young hero. Then Salayat stretched out both arms, palms up to the heavens and began to recite:

> *I look at the chain of mountains in our gracious countryside*
> *And, awed by their spaciousness, I perceive God's mercy.*
> *The nightingale sings in the dale splitting the still evening skies,*
>
> *How the voice of the adhan rings out, praising God*
> *Does it not call to prayer the faithful Muslims*
> *and it accompanies me into battle like the dear banner of the Urals!*

Our hero wanted to say something to Salavat, but the shouting and tumult behind him was rising as chairs were being pushed back or thrown, some aimed at the head of the head teacher, while Mr. Kanliyellov was stomping off the stage and heatedly shouting and cursing and brusquely brushing off the arms of his companions trying to contain him and calm him down. Our young hero's mouth hung open, he was dumbstruck. "No need, young man, to say anything to me. But remember my command to you. Keep the poetry of this lovely land in your heart. And recite." And Salavat again stretched back only his right arm, the knout again fell limply down and when with his left hand he took up the reins his mount scuffed the ground with its hoof. Then both rider and stallion ossified back into their original bronzen pose to sternly gaze out over the green, White River and across the fields to the south. Teachers had rushed to pull our hero away from the scuffles, and were clucking over him like so many frightened hens, but our hero was standing as if in an isolation capsule, silent and unhearing. His mouth was still open in dismay and his eyes were so wide open staring at the statue of Salayat that some said they looked like the lidless saucer eyes of an owl. The teachers assumed he was terrified by the hubbub and dragged him by the arms down from the stage and across the open space of the park to under the shade of a linden tree where his mother was waiting proudly for him.

He was some moments lost in his amazement, saying nothing. His mother was heaping praise on him and thanking other parents for their congratulations. Finally, he pointed at the statue and said faintly, "Mommy, didn't you see that? Salayat spoke to me. Didn't you hear?" "No Slava"—for that was our hero's Russian nickname—"I didn't hear anything. What are you saying, my dear? You were so wonderful reciting Lermontov." "Salayat spoke to me, mommy. Just now." "What? No dearest, Salavat is not here. No one spoke to you. It's the heat, too much sun now. Let's get you a drink." "No, mommy, I saw him. There. He turned to me and he told me to recite." "No he didn't. You're just imagining things. Statues can't talk. Now let's get you a bottle of tarragon lemonade, if there are any left." And that was that. No one else saw Slava's vision, or heard what Salayat had said to him. How could they? They were all too far away, upset by the scuffle on the stage, bruised by the intense sun, and desperate to find shade and relief from their thirst. But what our hero had seen and heard was real, and was forever after in his brief life one of his strongest and most distinct memories. And the command of Salayat would stick with him.

As I said our young hero was called in Russian Slava, which means Glory. That's what his mother, Vera Belosnezhnikova, called him because she spoke to him exclusively in Russian. And that's what his school mates called him as well. But his official name was the Arabic Muslim name, Majid, which his father had given him, and which the local imam had suggested. It means Glorious. Majid Karimovich Khairullin, a Tatar name. For our hero Slava was half Tatar, half Russian, his father being a Tatar from near Kazan who taught literature at the Bashkir University in Ufa. His father, Karim, spoke to Majid in the Tatar language at home, and he always called his son Majid. Vera had from birth spoken to Slava only in Russian, and from the very beginning sang famous Russian lullabies to him. Probably, more than anyone else, it was Vera who from his earliest age planted the appreciation and seed of poetry in Slava (or Majid). Perhaps like the poet Khodasevich said of himself, Majid had imbibed his Russian poetic skills from his mother's milk. From the very beginning of his life besides Russian lullabies and nursery rhymes which Vera always sang to him, when he was a toddler she also read to him classic Russian rhymes and verses, rhymed fairy tales, and short well known poems by Russia's finest. So he first learned to speak in Russian and his ear was established from the earliest age. But in looks he was a Tatar boy with black hair, dark eyes and white, fair skin, slight and short—a beautiful little boy. And from his father and later his grandmother he learned to speak the Turkic Tatar language. Perhaps, his undoubted talent in Tatar poetry came from his Tatar grandmother.

In his home in Ufa, when Majid was growing up, there were always books and there was always poetry, because his mother loved reciting poetry all the time. His mother, a good-looking, mousy haired woman, had been a literature student of Khairullin's at the university and he had seduced her with poetry, and then married her. Majid was the product of their union and their mutual love of poetry. Of course he learned to recite poetry by memorizing the verses that his mother recited for him. This is one clue as to our poet's genius. He had a prodigious memory.

And he had a good ear—a musical ear for the arrangement of words in verse. You could say he had, like a good musician, perfect pitch. He memorized and was able to recite that poem "Homeland" by Lermontov in only two sessions of listening to his mother. He was only seven at the time. But even then after two sessions he understood the music of the poetic metrics better than his mother did, and when he recited it afterwards, he improved it over his mother's style of declamation. Vera read to him the poems of Pushkin, Akhmatova, and her favourite, Baratynsky. Of course these were all Russian language poets (Akhmatova was not really a Tatar although she had taken on the noble Tatar name of a distant ancestor, Akhmatov, meaning most praiseworthy).

It is not so unusual that memory is one of the poet's strongest tools. For centuries before the Greeks began to write their language poets recited thousands of verses of the *Iliad* from memory handed down from the legendary Homer. They of course used metrics, rhyme, alliteration, cadence and repetition as the chief tools of their powerful memories and could retain thousands of lines of verse. And Slava from the very earliest age showed everyone that he too had a prodigious memory.

The Khairullins lived on the fourth floor of a well-kept concrete kruschyovka located around a heavily shaded courtyard. It was just a short walk to Majid's school, but in a part of the city that was sheltered from the stench and noise of the oil refineries. It was housing meant for staff of the university, but of course, other less educated people lived there. Their neighbour on one side was a violent drunk, and often, through the thin walls, they could hear him on a bender or beating his wife. Another neighbour below them was a veteran of the Great War, who in fair weather would sit all day outside on a low stoop faintly singing patriotic war songs until the evening when one of his adult children who lived with him would fetch him back upstairs. But there were intellectuals and literary types in the building, and often Karim's colleagues would come by in the evenings and visit in their tiny kitchen, drinking tea, comparing news, reading reviews and even occasionally sotto voce reciting new dissident poetry and offering their critiques. Majid rarely attended these kitchen meetings, although after he became a teenager he was more and more encouraged by his father to join in these male social bonding events, especially as they were alcohol free. It was at one of these rare sessions that the near-15 year old Majid learned that he perhaps had been named after the famous Tatar-Bashkir poet (or Bashkir-Tatar poet depending who was in attendance), Majid Gafuri, or as they said in the official style Gabdel Mazhit Gafurov. As Majid was growing up there was increasing controversy about whether the Tatar-Bashkir Muslim names needed to be Russified with an ending of—ov, whether their family name should be Khairullin or whether it would be politically more correct as Khairullinov or even better perhaps Khairullov.

At school, Majid was teased a lot because he was small and so "pretty" and then later because he was so bookish. The straw-haired Russian boys who were all bigger than he at all ages teased him because of his foreign sounding name. Even though he was mostly called Slava, some teachers would still call him Majid, and when they did everyone sniggered. Now this teasing was strange as about half his school mates were either Bashkir or Tatar and all of those had similar Muslim names, but the Russian boys ruled the roost, so to speak, and were rough and condescending about it. The Bashkir boys were always willing to fight back against the Russian taunting, but that left poor Majid as an outsider, runt-sized and unprotected from the stings and arrows.

Majid was not outstanding in his studies in middle school, but on his own he avidly consumed books of literature and especially poetry in Russian. He was always keen to recite assigned poems, but not so keen on maths. When he was ten or eleven, and could read for himself, Majid again recited publicly for his classmates in a school assembly. This time it was Baratynski's The Skull, a soliloquy like Hamlet's over Yorick's grave, contemplating death as a sudden and permanent contrast to life's joys. This is a difficult little poem of eight stanzas with couplets that have an awkward 10 and 11 metric feet—a strange walking pace, not too unlike the awkward gait of the visitor in Mussorgsky's Exhibition. It ends sadly:

> *Let the living live! May the dead rot in peace. O Man, insignificant creation of the Almighty, finally recognize you are neither wise nor omniscient.*

> *We must have our passions and our dreams, for our being they are both food and sustenance. You cannot bring under the self-same rule the noise of the world with the stillness of the graveyard.*

> *The sage cannot extinguish his natural feelings. The grave will not give him a reply. Life give your joys to the living and Death himself will teach them how to die.*

His schoolmates were stunned into uncomprehending silence. They recognized from Majid's recitation the poem's gravity, but not its intent. His teachers were moved to tears.

Teachers also noticed that he had from an early age a remarkable vocabulary, and that he strove to know the proper name of everything, plants, machinery, birds, architecture, clouds, geographical features, trees, and so on. He enjoyed word play and puns, and as he was fluent in Russian and Tatar, Majid often played with making false cognates and homonyms. So it was no surprise when he began school lessons in a foreign language—it was French that was then on offer—that he excelled at that and soon was reading French tales and simple poems. He noticed the similar musicality between the Turkic Tatar language and French poetry.

In the summers Majid spent his time with his father's mother at a country house in an Urals village. This was a country house far up the blue Black River (the Ufa River) beyond the Pavlovka reservoir, over the first range of forested hills. It was a house in a small village named Golodnovo, which had a large garden plot, and milk goats and chickens. Majid went to live in it with his grandmother, Zineida, and his mother and a number of pet dogs and cats every summer throughout his childhood. Sometimes his father would join them on leave from his work at the university.

There are certain moments in our life when a scene, perhaps one that is often repeated, perhaps just a one-time event, passes in front of our eyes and becomes permanently emblazoned—almost cinematically—in our visual memory. Sometimes this memory includes birdsong or even more likely vivid aromas such as our first girlfriend's perfume which later through life elicit certain emotional responses. It was at this dacha, perhaps when Majid was twelve or thirteen, one high summer day that just such a moment entered into his memory and came to be an emblem of his summers at the dacha. It was a hot bright summer mid-afternoon when Majid was walking along a dirt track next to a meadow where a vast spread of rosebay willowherb (otherwise known as John's tea) were in full bloom. They painted the entire field in their purple hue which was also splotched by white corn chamomile, occasional red poppies and the wiry sky blue chicory. There was a drainage ditch alongside the track bordering the field and it was filled with ugly giant hogweeds with their white crowns of tiny flowers and underneath them spikes of cowparsley and the poisonous corncockle. There were larks, linnets and thrushes singing and flying through the field and the sun's glinting light seemed to reflect off the field's wild growth and onto a large copse of poplars and oaks standing on a slight rise at the far side of the field. The background music to the birdsong was a cacophony of buzzing insects and crickets and cicadas droning. Nothing special occurred as Majid idly strolled along this track but the sight stuck with him and he saw it in his mind's eye, almost cinematically, late that evening after dark, and he saw it weeks later, and he saw it often when back in Ufa. An idealized summer landscape recorded in his memory which meant life in the dacha.

Majid did not remember doing much in these idyllic summers. But he wandered far and wide through the countryside around the village. Sometimes he would swim in a stream that flowed down into the Black River, which was the Gold River at that place because it was well known that its sand held particles of the gold that had been washed down from the gold-rich ridges of the Urals only a few miles distant. Sometimes he would walk up to the woods in the hills several miles away. It was a land of wonder and beauty. Everywhere, he would ceaselessly ask after the names of the wildflowers, the trees, the insects, the birds—in both Tatar and Russian—and by this method he steadily acquired the rich distinctive vocabulary of the countryside around his grandmother's house.

And it was at this country house that he heard Tatar poetry recited, as his grandmother loved it and knew a lot of verse. From these summers he became equally enthralled by Tatar verse. His grandmother would often in the summer evenings read to him verses from a Tatar language anthology of poetry. And Majid would recite these verses back to her. It was Zineida who introduced Majid to the Tatar poem, the Tale of the Prophet Yusuf by Qol Gali. This poem was like the national verse of the Tatar people, and it owed its survival through more than 750 years to the many generations who memorized its quatrains and recited them to their offspring. Zineida liked it, had also memorized large portions of it, and she would recite one or another quatrain at almost any occasion where she thought it was warranted. She thought Majid was beautiful and so she recited about the beauty of Yusuf.

> *Among them was Yusuf on horseback in a gown of honor,*
> *He shone under a beautiful light and radiant halo,*
> *So exalted was Yusuf—*
> *He behaved nobly with all souls.*
>
> *The Egyptians saw him, they were enthralled,*
> *They said: "He's not of human kind—*

But is descended from archangels come down from heaven,"—
All bowed down before him in prostration

One summer when Majid was 12 or 13 she sat down with him over a number of evenings and recited to him from memory the entire poem of the Tale of Yusuf. All 1010 quatrains. (Perhaps she had occasional help of referring to a dog-eared copy she kept on a shelf.) There was a lot to the poem—its religious themes as it was after all derived from the Koranic story of the Biblical prophet Joseph—which Majid did not understand at the time, but the poetic structure of its rhymed quatrains—a form of rubaiyat—excited his imagination. And its simple rhyming scheme stuck in his memory.

Yet another poem which Zineida often repeated but which she never identified seemed to capture the summer idyll.

Under the deep blue dome of a cloudless summer sky, when the thrushsong was high, and the John's-tea put a blush on the fields ust as there was on your cheeks, we first proclaimed our love, my dearest.

But you have left me, and those bright hot summers by the great river have receded. Alas I cannot recover that beautiful land of my youth, nor my first love.

Majid learned it at once by heart, with its lilting Turkic hendecametric line and rich nuanced vowel sounds (so unlike Russian) and he would recite it back to her, whenever she hummed it. She was so delighted that she came to call him, 'My Most Praiseworthy', just like the name Akhmat in the poetess's name, Akhmatova.

During these summers of his childhood, Majid also learned from his grandmother the folk legends and tales of the Tatar people, told in the Tatar language. They left some impression on him, although he never recited them, because later when he was at university in Moscow, he typed them all up on his new typewriter and then unsolicited sent them to a publisher in Kazan, one who had also published some of his youthful Tatar poems. Only a small run of these tales were printed, and they did not sell very well. They have not been translated either into Russian or into English. It was only when Majid died that a literary researcher brought my attention to them.

As Majid grew into a teenager, Zineida's country house came to have another important role for the poet and his family. It became a significant supplier of the family's food, as the privations of the Soviet war in Afghanistan and a fall in world oil prices wrecked the economy and store shelves became spare of food. Zineida grew potatoes, carrots, cabbages and green onions and she supplied eggs and milk, which supplemented what little the Khairullins could buy in Ufa. People throughout Russia were doing the same where they had access to a country garden. At summer's end throughout the late 1980s Majid and his parents would go to harvest these food crops and put them down into storage under the house to last them through the winter and spring. So Zineida's house became the larder for the Khairullins in Ufa for a number of winters, even though her village was named, "the Hungry One", Golodnovo.

One year, after returning to Ufa for school, Majid's father, Karim, who also adored the poetry of Qol Gali, and knew that his son enjoyed it, took Majid to the university library. "I have a surprise to show you. One of our national treasures." In the library's dim cool vaults, Karim led Majid to the manuscript collection. The docent of the section brought out a large old book wrapped in a thick leather binding and spread it out on a table. He gingerly opened it vellum pages. There in front of Majid's eyes was an incomprehensible collection of squiggles written in brown ink with very elaborate and rounded hand strokes. It was clearly laid out as verses. Karim pointed to the right side of the page. "You see, you read it this way from right to left." he said in Tatar. And he began to read from the page with his finger hovering over the lines as he read. Once he had read a few lines, Majid knew without a doubt it was the Tale of Yusuf. He even recognized the part of the story he was reading from. "This manuscript is perhaps 500 years old. And we are lucky, here. It is one of the few surviving copies anywhere in the world. It was written in the Arabic script as all old Tatar literature was." It was the first time Majid had seen Tatar written in Arabic letters and it was puzzling and alluring at the same time. He had read Tatar only in Cyrillic script, from left to right. This old script made the poem so inaccessible and foreign. He was surprised to learn that his father could read it. (Although, truth be told, it was only much later that he learned that Karim did not know how to read old Tatar in the Arabic script. He had only recited a few quatrains from memory. His father's familiarity with Arabic script was very weak and he had acquired it from rare attendance at the local mosque, so that he could read out with difficulty some of the Koran's words.)

When Majid turned 15 two critical events occurred in the life of our poet. By that time he already was confirmed in his love for poetry and he read and studied prodigiously the works of Pushkin, Derzhavin, Tukai, Gafuri, Baratynsky, Blok, and Akhmatova, committing much of their verse to memory. Early that year, when the winter winds scour the city of Ufa and the skies are pale blue, Karim told his son it was time to go with him to the mosque and learn something about Islam. The experience was eye-opening for Majid, who learned in the following weeks that so much of the heritage of the Tatar language—his and his father's name and surname and the names of practically all Tatars— came from Arabic through Islam and through Turkish. This was a rich legacy and one which he immediately recognized for its elaborate language. He was put in the care of a young beardless imam who was scarcely six years older than Majid and whose converted surname was Gabdallah Aksakalov, but whose original Russian name had been Sergei Beloborodov, even though he was ethnically Tatar. At one session, as he kneeled on the carpets in an alcove and Aksakalov read to him chapters from the Koran, Majid was suddenly struck by what Sergei claimed were the words of the first revelation to the Prophet. So much of what

Gabdallah had read to him, in a droning voice with eyes screwed up in his head and his stresses stretched over long vowels, sounded to Majid like poetry of an ancient and very profound style. The first five verses—if you could call them that—had so much power. He asked him to translate their meaning for him. Gabdallah had an authorized Russian translation of the Koran with him and referred to it. He read:

Recite! In the name of your Lord who created,
He created man from a clot like embryo
Recite! Your Lord is the most generous one, who taught by a reed pen
He taught man what he did not know.

Majid was dumbfounded. The Prophet had received the same command to take up the prophecy and recite the words of God, just as Majid had received the command to recite the poetry of his Tatar people in a vision of Salayat. Thus in his fifteenth year Majid was introduced to but did not really accept Islam. But he did listen raptly to Gabdallah's readings from the Koran, and studied their translations. He learned about Muslim practices and standards of behaviour. He listened closely to the inner music and poetry of the Koran as it was recited (an action which is anathema and distasteful to a Believer). He went to the mosque a couple times a week throughout that year to attend the lessons, learned how to pray, which he seldom did after that year.

It was during these visits that he also met and befriended a young man from Kazan named Ganiel Faleyev. This tall young man wrote poems himself in the Tatar language and he introduced Majid to current poetic compositions either those which he had written and those by other poets. Ganiel was a member of the newly founded Society of the Lovers of the Tatar Word, a society in Kazan of poets, writers and literary critics who sought to promote spoken Tatar and elevate its literature freed of subservience to Russian. "You know, we founded this on the model of Derzhavin's Colloquium of the Lovers of the Russian Word. But we want to expel Russian words and their baneful influence from Tatar poetry and prose." Majid said he really liked the odes of Derzhavin. "Did you know that Derzhavin was actually descended from a Tatar noble family?" said Ganiel. "But he still wrote wonderful Russian verse." And Majid recited a short acrostic poem by Derzhavin.

The river of time in its mighty flow
Sweeps away all the works of men
And drowns all peoples, kings and realms
In the abyss of oblivion.

"It is an acrostic which says 'Ruin of Honour'. Quite good rhyme structure too. There are so many fine verses in Derzhavin's poems." "That's fine, Majid. But we are interested in only Tatar poetry. And Derzhavin didn't write any Tatar verse; he had become over many generations completely Russified. Like Anna Akhmatova or Bella Akhmadulina. In spite of their ancestry they are Russian poets." he pronounced this with some disdain in his voice.

During one of their meetings, Majid asked Ganiel to recite some Tatar poems for him. It was then that Majid realized that Ganiel was a poor reciter; he had both a lisp and slur of certain sounds, and he had no apparent talent in the musical intonation which makes poetry different from prose. Majid also noticed that Ganiel did not like to recite to him his own poems; he would instead give him sheets of paper with his handwritten poems on them. And strangest of all, Ganiel was shocked, dismayed and a little abashed when Majid proceeded to read them out loud in front of him. He was not accustomed to hearing his own creations declaimed. It even annoyed him. He found it funny, and of course when Majid read, it was not with the voice and sonority that Ganiel thought he had created and which he had captured on paper. Majid on the other hand was amazed that his friend did not mean for his poems to be sounded out loud. He found that odd. Poetry was more an oral performance than a written exercise to Majid. And to demonstrate this Majid would recite the Tatar poems of Tukai and

Gafuri he had learned by heart. Ganiel was captivated by Majid's talent. After hearing Majid recite Tukai's verses, he revealed that he had a project of transliterating Tukai's poems that were originally written in the Turkish modified Arabic script which Tukai had used. He would re-write them in Latin letters. He was also making new translations into Russian of these same poems, considering that earlier translators had done such a poor job.

Later Ganiel asked Majid if he had written any of his own poems. And that was when it occurred to Majid: It was a strange question, because Majid had never written down any poems on paper. But in his mind he had composed a number of poems, both in Russian and in Tatar, and had memorized them and had even recited some of them for his mother. But he had not committed any of them to paper. It was then and there—aged fifteen—that our hero resolved to be a poet. From then on he would compose poems and recite them to one and all. He knew that being a poet was a commitment to a style of life, a posture and response to the world around him, a way of living and thinking, and not a career. Oh how well he knew from his readings of the famous poets before him that being a poet was not a livelihood.

But first he would have to recite a few of his poems for his father, Karim. Majid knew that he would be Majid's harshest critic, and he feared that he would not approve. But with his new resolution, Majid would be brave. A poet is fearless, after all. So first he had to decide which poems of his to recite for his father—for he had already composed several which had been banging around in his memory for some months. He could recite a short poem, only a few stanzas long, in Tatar, and a longer more important poem in Russian which he had thought about a lot in the previous weeks and over the summer out at his grandmother's dacha. He decided the best occasion to introduce his father to his decision was at the weekly kitchen gathering of Karim and his friends and colleagues, which Majid had begun to attend sporadically in the previous year.

On the night when Majid finally decided to fulfil his resolution to become a poet, it was already deep fall, chilly and rainy. He had prepared a couple poems which he had composed some time earlier but had not committed to paper, but that afternoon, dreary and wet, he improvised a poem that fit his mood and the meteorological circumstances. He felt a little shy when he entered the kitchen late that evening. There were besides his father, a few men Majid had not met before, and two with whom he was barely acquainted. One was a Tatar literary colleague from the university, another was a relative—so distant that Majid had never been sure of how he was related to him—something like a nephew by marriage of a second cousin of Karim's. Everyone attending was aware of Majid's abilities to recite vast amounts of poetry from memory, but this was an "opening night", so to speak, as they had been told that on this damp windy night Majid would be performing some of his own verses. The kitchen was stuffy and humid from the small crowd sitting around a small dinner table set with a colourful oilcloth spread and glasses of fruit compote. Everything was illuminated starkly under a glaring light bulb hung high over the middle of the room. Majid barely fit in the door of this small kitchen and his mother, Vera, was right behind him because she was dying of curiosity to hear her only son recite his first public poem.

The group of men were at first boisterous with greetings and excitement. One blurted out, "Will it be in Russian or Tatar?" Actually our hero had prepared poems in both languages. "Where are your papers? Aren't they written out?" "No I know them by heart. But I have written them down too." "Don't be bashful. You'll have to speak up." But then the men settled down and all eyes turned on Majid. Karim's colleague then interjected, "What is the title of your first poem?" Majid paused, a bit taken aback. "I haven't given this one a title yet." In truth, he hadn't thought of giving it a title. So many of the poems he knew did not have proper titles. They were known by him only from their first line. "So I will begin." Majid—still looking like a child—stood more erect and looked out the darkened window. He recited in a calm small voice.

The slanting autumn rain causes
The yellowed linden leaves to flutter down
And clump in the flooded gutters
Under glowering skies, evening's early darkness
Tell us winter is nigh upon us.

Tires squeal on the slick streets, people rush home
In the deepening gloom and damp, dim street lights
Do not light the way home through the looming city.
The summer's bloom and brightness is all forgot
And harvest's bounty is stashed away.

The city dweller seeks his warm, dry quarters
But it is the light he seeks to piece the night
And fend off thoughts of winter's coming chill
While the farmer only wants to be done with the mud
And struggles to plant next season's seeds.

Winter there is merely cold and dark and windy
The storms of city society leave no mark
He puts the split dry wood in the stove which hisses
And sips tea as the wind howls over the roof.
Memories of warm spring's bloom lure him.

The earth's seasons roll from birth, florescence,
Growth, harvest, decline, decay and darkness,
But are repeated in cycles of rebirth and regrowth
So the advancing, black and chill clouds do not menace
Death, only winter's deep cold and still.

But man has but one cycle, birth through to death.
Enjoy your youthful blossoming, grow vitally,

Sow your seeds widely, exhalt your virility,
Heed the autumn rains, the maple's falling samaras,
Smell the acrid coal smoke from the guttering stove.

The cluster of friends remained quiet as the poem's dark message sank in. Majid's mother was the first to react and she was delighted. "Bravo, Slava. Well said." And she clapped, which prompted the men seated at the table also to clap. Karim was smiling, beaming with pride. "Son, I am so proud of you. It is a wonderful poem."

And indeed it was. I have in translating it, of course, completely discarded its wonderful rhymes and word play, and as well its metrical symmetry. But I believe it is better to capture the literal meaning and mood when translating a poem into another language, than to force it into awkward contortions to keep a rhyme scheme or to capture the exact metrics. In this case the poem was rhymed in an ABABC scheme throughout the six stanzas. And the metrics display a rare dactylic pentameter. I have tried to render this with eleven syllables in a line, but you'll have to forgive me if I have not been so successful in this. And the words he used are so precise and specific, quite mature really. (Again, forgive me here, as Majid used a word for a specific type of clay mud, which cement like sticks to boots and tools, whereas I have used the simpler English word, mud.)

"We'll have to get this published. Can you give me a written copy of it?" Karim continued. Later, the next spring, Karim was successful in getting the poem—titled as The Fall Season—placed in the university's literary journal where it attracted favourable comment. Everyone was amazed at how precocious the poem was.

But the poetry recital was not finished. Majid said there was more he wanted to introduce. And he proceeded to recite three more poems, all in Russian, and a fourth in Tatar. I have found one of them, which I reproduce here giving it the title that it got later in a first collection of his early poems, The Gate.

A formal garden lies inside the city park,
Fenced off, it is a floral sanctuary,
Where perfume of phlox and roses waft through the air
And seduce the weary visitor to quiet contemplation.

Entry to the garden is through a gate—
A green wood-panel gate, unlatched,
Set on a swinging hinge, with a light spring—
Which opens with the slightest push or tug.

Often on a summer's day I stroll to the garden
To meditate, thoughtlessly entering by this gate,
Giving no heed to my passage from outside to in
Where it seems I am entering into paradise.

Once I saw a large hound standing outside the gate
Waiting patiently for a passer-by to push it open.
How strange thought I that such a powerful creature
Cannot on its own barge through the gate.

With just a nudge with its broad paw or heavy snout
It could easily push open the gate for itself
And come and go in the garden as it pleased
To chase squirrels, root out moles, or dig up bulbs.

But then I thought how many of us stand in front of gates
Unknowingly capable of opening them
But dumbly, patiently waiting for some greater force
To push them open—so we might too enter paradise.

Gates which hold us back from a more elevated state
Hang blankly in front of us like a painted wall.
How little effort is needed to pass through these barriers?
But we wait to be shown how we can open them!

Presumably, the small group of poetry lovers were equally impressed. They were all literary connoisseurs, and had their own favourite Russian and Tatar poets. But they all were in agreement that these lines of verse were quite—even surprisingly—good. And with both of them, part of their enthusiasm was the way in which our hero delivered his poems. There was a natural music and rhythm which was alluring and pleasing to their ears. From all reports in the following years, it was especially Majid's deliverance of his poems which most enraptured his audiences and which established his fame.

Again this last poem had a mature form, an ABCA rhyming scheme with long metrically complex lines. It has a meditative, pensive mood. Majid had not thought of a title for this poem either at that time. Karim thought it should be the Hound at the Gate, but later the poem was named after its most salient image, simply, The Gate. He was to recite it often at his public recitals for several years to come, long after it appeared in his first published collection.

We don't have any written record of that evening's recital. Personal memories reside with the participants who are still living, and they all report the excitement and discussions which occurred between poems. They are all in agreement that our hero recited the two poems cited above and a third one in Russian which was longer than the first two, but about which there is no agreement about the title. It may have appeared in a later publication, but I cannot say with certainty which poem it was, or if we will ever know. He also recited a short two stanza poem, which was a cute satire of a local senior Bashkir politician in Ufa who had at that time awarded himself a gold medal for his truly awful poetry. Sadly this short poem also seems to be lost to us. It is a shame because later, after Majid arrived in Moscow, he became renowned for his biting satirical epigrams aimed at the corrupt or pompous or venal people who occupied every corner of Moscow life in that time.

The evening was getting late and the little party of poetry lovers were getting anxious, because although there was no official curfew in Ufa in those years, the police effectively operated one and residents knew that it was not advisable to be wandering home on the streets after 11 pm. Finally one of Karim's guests, himself a Tatar literary critic of some note in Ufa, spoke up. "Majid we have been overwhelmed by your exquisite poems in Russian. Can you recite any poems you may have written in the Tatar language?"

Of course he had, but once again he had prepared to recite a poem from memory and not any that he had written down, because at that early time in his career he still hadn't written any poems down on paper. Up to then he did not work graphically on any of his poetic ideas. He would later come to this "thankless labour" as he called it when he began composing longer poetic tales.

I see the mullahs dragged by their beards crying
As they watch the red-coat streltsy tearing down their mosques
They are banned from the Izel, torn from the faith.
I do not know why.

There's a broken down ulan on his trusty old steed
Back from years of service in the Tsar's foreign wars
His house and land forfeit, his family scattered and gone
I do not know why.

Then there is the pride of the Red Flower
Looking on at the Red Terror, flames in Kazan,
His young faith for a Red Tatar union dashed.
I do not know why.

I see the starving masses dying on the Izel plains
A commissars-engineered famine to solve the problem
Of national resistance and to eliminate the Tatar.
I do not understand why.

I see our youths press-ganged into the Red Army
To fight the Fascists at our door, and die far from home
Dead, lying in unmarked graves or Moabit cells.
I do not understand why

And now our boys are sent to far foreign fields
To aid in killing our Muslim Afghan brothers
To return in anonymous sacks or simple black coffins.
I must come to understand why.

Karim was so proud of his son, his cheeks burned red. When Majid finished his recital he jumped up and starting applauding. "Bravo, bravo!" The others also jumped up, and his mother was clapping and shouting, "My Slava! Wonderful, a miracle. My Slava!" (even though she did not really understand Tatar, nor the references.) Everyone congratulated Slava and proclaimed to Karim with much backslapping and handshaking that his son was a true poet. But promptly the visitors all had to clear out and rush home. It was then, only shortly afterwards, that these people began to spread the word that there was a prodigy and poetic genius living among them. Later, after similar evening recitals in the Khairullin kitchen, with other participants who also followed literary pursuits, Majid's poems began to circulate with much favourable commentary.

Our hero wrote down his Tatar poem and shortly afterwards went to the madrasa to find Ganiel to show it to him. Of course, first he asked Ganiel if he could recite it to him. After he did so, Ganiel felt amazed and ashamed too; ashamed that this young man could write a better poem than anything he had ever written. But he was enthusiastic in his praise and eagerly snatched the page on which Majid had written it down and read it several times closely, reciting it under his breath. Finally he looked up at Majid and said, "This is very good. I like it a lot. We'll have to get it published." "How can I do that?" asked Majid. "Don't worry. I'll submit it to the new Tatar literary journal in Kazan, the *Milli Yul*." This *Milli Yul*, or Way of the Nation, was a new journal at that time which was riding the sudden wave of nationalist excitement following Gorbachev's new policy of Glasnost, or Openness, which allowed greater openness in expression of national languages and national pride. In fact, only a month later, even before Majid's The Fall Season appeared in Ufa, *Milli Yul* published this poem in Kazan, claiming a new promising talent had appeared in the Izel (Volga Tatar) space. They gave it the title "I must know why". The established Tatar poets of his father's generation (born around the time of the Great Patriotic War) took notice (and were jealous—because they had all their lives struggled so hard to get their poems into print). I do not know the Tatar language, nor what comprises good Tatar poetry. I trust others—and a Russian translation of this poem which attempted to preserve the rhyming and metrics of the original—to tell me that this was indeed a very good Tatar poem, and it was especially good as a first poem of a young talent. Those in the know told me that it reminded them of the early poems of Gali Tukai, whom everyone admires as one of the leading voices in modern Tatar verse. I found an old copy of the *Milli Yul* with this short poem in it. And in the process of searching through the records I found later numbers with other poems by Majid Khairullin. Most of these are unknown to the Russian reading public as they have not been translated, and, as far as I can tell, our hero, the poet, did not give many public recitals outside of Ufa and Kazan in the Tatar language, so his following for these poems in Moscow is almost non-existent. (And by the way the references to the Red Flower, the Red Terror are to Musa Jalil in the early 1920s, and the reference to the Moabit cells is also to Jalil in the Nazi prison in Berlin where he wrote his best non-ideological poetry and where he later died a war prisoner in 1944.)

In the year that followed Majid started to "work" at poetry. He read copious amounts of poetry in Russian, Tatar, and French, and even some in English, and he committed large amounts to memory. At school he was only interested in his Russian literature course work, and often in other classes he would be composing his own poems, which his teachers uniformly interpreted as daydreaming. He began to notice girls too, but in general he was too shy to show them that they attracted him. His literature teachers knew that he was the student to call on to recite some poem by Pushkin or Lermontov in class work, and during the school year he again gave public performances of some poetry at school talent assemblies. He had wanted to recite some poems by Joseph Brodsky, but that was politically unacceptable, so instead he recited poems by Blok, Pasternak, and Pushkin for the school assembly. But there was never any question that he would be allowed to give a school performance of his own compositions. Everyone noticed that he was musically a natural—no droning, or false seriousness, or monotone declamations. And then at the end of the school year, there was a clap of excitement throughout the school when it was learned that his poem, The Fall Season, had appeared in the university literary journal. The teachers and students were all so proud that they had a real poet in their midst. Little did they know that throughout the school year, he had continued to give occasional recitals of his own poems at his father's kitchen soirees, which became more consistently Thursday evening affairs. What Majid recited were both poems in Russian and in Tatar. His output was steady and the subjects of his poetic explorations were broad and far-reaching. He continued giving his Tatar epigrams and short poems to Ganiel and the latter channelled them to *Milli Yul* so that, mostly unnoticed by his schoolmates, by the time he turned 16 at the end of that school year, five of his poems had appeared in the pages of *Milli Yul* in Kazan.

At one Thursday evening gathering in late spring, the conversation of the literary critics circle in Karim's kitchen turned to criticizing the poetry of one of the leading Communist Party bosses of the Bashkir Autonomous Soviet Socialist Republic. This man, Mustafa Safichov, had been a poetaster during and after the Great Patriotic War, but he became a Communist Party leader after the war. He had been admitted to the official Writer's Union at the age of only 20, but on the basis of what writings it is difficult to understand. His career as a poet in fact appears to be entirely the construction of his party affiliation, proper proletarian background, and his war record. The Bashkir Communists were looking to establish their national credentials and cultural legacy in the period after the war (which is why they also promoted Salayat to an early national hero) and chose Mustafa's poems to promote Bashkir cultural achievement because he wrote them in the newly literate Bashkir language. So he proclaimed himself a great Bashkir poet, and the Bashkir autonomous Communist Party leaders agreed and promoted him. But his poetry was just a young man's dabblings, nothing great, and really little more than a poetaster's drivel. And on this the members of the kitchen circle were all in agreement. Of course there was some jealousy in these views because Tatar poetry has a long provenance with many great poets writing memorable pieces through the centuries. Bashkir is close to the Tatar language, and if anything strikes the Tatar ear as rustic and uncultivated, even unpleasant to the ear, it is Bashkir. And Bashkir does not have a long literary tradition. But Mustafa Safichov was a "Big Wheel" in Ufa—so to speak—and although he had been a party hack and leading party bureaucrat for most of four decades, he still pompously promoted himself as "the national poet" and he had Lenin Prizes to prove it. As these kitchen conversations dwelt on the injustice and harm Mustafa's poetry caused to world literature, Majid composed another of his satiric epigrams there on the spot.

Mustaf writes his poems most carefully
He awards and praises them effusively
His rhymes are awkward, lines not terse
He often recites heavy, clumsy verse
That employs expressions which ignore all euphony, metrics, prosody,
*   and common sense.*

This little epigram captured the strange poetics of Mustafa's verse so aptly that the kitchen circle all erupted into laughter, and the conversation turned to more important literary questions. Majid showed again that he had a very sharp ear and a talent for improvisation coupled with satire. (Against my usual practice, I have tried my best to render this short stanza in a translation which captures the trite rhyme words, and portrays the mocking tone of the laughable last line with its deliberate stumbling metric.) A short improvised epigram by a 16 year old delivered in a private kitchen get-together ordinarily would disappear forever, except that it so struck the fancy of some of the participants that they took it with them and spread it around Ufa, causing mirth and sniggering everywhere. This is how this poem came to be preserved. Of course it caused great umbrage to the great Bashkir poet when he eventually heard it, as, being a senior party leader and a leading member of the Writers' Union, he would have inevitably discovered it when it was brought to him by the secret police and the local cultural authorities.

It was only a short time later, early in the summer of Majid's 16th year that his father, Karim, was killed. It happened late one Friday evening. Karim was walking home on a sidewalk in the city center, when he was struck from behind by the car of a drunken driver. This was odd because it was at a time when Gorbachev's "dry law" was still in effect and it was not at all easy to obtain alcohol other than home brew. It was also at a time when having a private car was not very common and street traffic of passenger cars after work hours was extremely low. Karim was hit and then dragged along under the white Volga car before his body was stopped by a lamp-post. He was dead by the time the ambulance got to him about 40 minutes later. The driver emerged unhurt from the car after it had hit another curbstone and slammed into the side of a brick building. He was too drunk to even recognize that he had hit a pedestrian, and he staggered around for several minutes before the police arrived to detain him. He shouted abuses at them as they tried to arrest him. It seemed he was claiming that he was too important to be arrested on the street. And he was right. He was Bashkir, and he had just come from a very important social get-together of the Republic's ruling elite. In fact, he was part of that elite being the grandson of Mustafa Safichov. And it later transpired that he was to escape all serious consequences or punishment for his manslaughter and public drunkenness. Karim Khairullin was just another insignificant victim of the system.

But consequences of Karim's sudden, premature death for the Khairullin family were catastrophic. First they immediately learned just how poor they were; how tentative their grasp on life was, how close to the edge of oblivion they were. Informing Majid, who was already out at Golodnovo, was very complicated and took much of the next day. Vera had to call a neighbour's house where the only telephone of the village was located, and the neighbour had to find Majid or Zineida and bring them back to his telephone to return the call. Then once informed they had to go together to the regional village, Novomeschanskovo, where they had to wait most of the next day to get the once a day bus to Ufa. The ride itself took more than six hours. They had to borrow a few roubles from Zineida's next door neighbour for their fares, because in the whole house they had only four roubles, and the two fares together came to just more than five. Zineida passed most of the trip sobbing and wailing over the death of her son. Majid was trying to conjure up in his mind the last images of had seen of his father only a few weeks earlier, also trying to remember his father's last words to him. But try as he might, he could not. Zineida's wailing was too distracting and his own emotional reactions were too confused and unfocused.

Vera spent all of those two days making arrangements for the wake, the funeral and burial and for the funeral dinner afterwards. It was all very difficult to register the death, prepare the ceremonies, and reserve a gravesite in the Muslim cemetery. Soviet rules for funerals had greatly modified Muslim funerary practices, so she had to ask one of Karim's closest friends, who was a Muslim, how things were properly arranged. There would be no cremation, the wake would be held in the mosque, but the shrouded body would not be displayed, and burial would occur immediately after funeral prayers conducted by the men alone in the mosque. She received financial help from the mosque which Karim had sometimes attended. But she still had to borrow some money from Karim's friends to prepare for the after burial dinner. She spent much of the second day trying to find and buy the food items but also a lot of her efforts went into contacting Karim's friends. By the time Majid and Zineida arrived that evening, Vera was ready to collapse and the full weight of grief only then hit her. No one knew what to do next, least of all Majid. Vera fell into his arms and starting bawling. As he was the only man in the household now he held her for the first time not as a son but as a comforting man. He felt it was a strange and new role for him.

The next day, the day of the funeral, was sunny, bright and warm. A brilliant deep blue sky illuminated the city and the florid green countryside surrounding it. The day had the feeling of joyful, resplendent early summer, without the repressive heat. Majid stepped through the motions and rituals of the day, with which he was totally unfamiliar, as if he were an automaton. His father's friends and colleagues, people he by and large did not know, continually came up to him with sad faces, offered their condolences, rested their hands on his shoulders, tried in vain to express the sorrow of their loss and how hard that loss must be on Majid. It was in the mosque during the prayers for the dead when all the men were kneeling on their haunches between prostrations, on the sour smelling carpets, that Majid saw another of those scenes which became permanently embossed on his memory. Unlike the summer scene in Golodnovo which he had encountered many times, this scene was completely and utterly new and unique to him. There in front of his eyes were the two score or so men in the midst of prayer, kneeling on the industrial oriental carpets in a large room, with the shrouded body of his father laid out in between them and the mosque's mihrab. The day's brilliant light broke through the dimness of the mosque in shafts from windows set back in the upper walls. And around the body were candles. In this sudden photographic vision, Majid noticed one of the candles was guttering and sending up a thin plume of white smoke. And then the candle flame sputtered out and the thin curl of smoke rose up in the air and disappeared. This scene stayed with him for the rest of his life, it became emblematic of the transience of life and its abrupt disappearance, mostly unnoticed just like the final white curl of smoke. The other men, continuing with their prayers devout and focused, did not notice this moment when one candle burned out. Throughout the rest of the day, the procession to the cemetery, the burial and throwing clods of dirt over his father's body, the memorial feast at their apartment, this scene stuck in front of his eyes. The other mourners of course concluded that Majid was numb with grief. But in fact he was already searching out ways to convert this "cinematic still" into words and verses that would convey the metaphor and bring in some of the emotional impact of that moment. A poem emerged from this reverie and image, and our hero included it in his first collection which was published about three years later when he was in Moscow. It included the lines which have since become famous

> *Death is the robber who creeps up on us unawares*
> *In the silence of the night and cudgels us from behind*

and

> *Life is that flame on the top of the fireplace extinguished*
> *By a bucketful splash of water leaving behind*
> *Bitter ashes and wisps of pale smoke which curl and*
> *Disappear into the uncaring sky or offend the nose.*

Karim's sudden death and the great dislocation of moving into Ufa to attend the funeral, as well as the very hot summer weather that year, proved to be too much stress for Zineida. Over the coming month she suffered two small heart attacks while Majid was living there. There was little Majid could do, and the only doctor available came from Novomeschanskovo and arrived both times too late to give her much therapy. He could only suggest rest, which was all she could manage in any event. Majid tried to take care of the animals and the garden, but was not successful. He really had not paid much attention in summers gone by to all the measures that were necessary, and did not know how things were done. Milking the goats for him proved especially difficult, but also paying attention to the laying hens was harder than he expected. But then before he could begin the vegetable harvest, Zineida had a final massive heart attack, uttered a last cry of "Oi, God forgive us", and collapsed in the center of the wooden floor of the large room in her house, dropping a vat of milk as she fell. Majid who was outside harvesting summer green apples, heard a faint crash and rushed into the house to find a terror stricken Zineida gasping for air, her eyes wide open but unseeing and her hands unable to grasp his. She died in agony a couple hours later, long before the doctor could come to administer any pain relief. The doctor arrived in the mid-evening, shook his head as there was very little he could do, but he promised to file the certificate of death in the local administration center. He also gave Majid instructions of how to prepare the body for burial and how deep to dig the grave. He promised to telephone Majid's mother Vera in Ufa to tell her of Zineida's passing.

That night Majid, for the first time, slept by himself in this old four-roomed wooden house. Zineida's body lay on a plastic mat in the center of the main room, covered in a white sheet. Majid only half slept, as he was kept awake by noises and sounds he had never noticed before: a creaking which seemed to come from outside, shuffling movement of claws in the crawl space overhead, a general low groaning of the entire house frame as it seemed to be mourning Zineida's death, which was punctuated several times with a sharp snapping sound, alarming shuffling slithering sounds seemingly coming from under the floor boards, the gentle rubbing sound from the roof which was probably birds, and occasionally in the quiet that made his ears ring, the sound of mice scampering around the kitchen and the larder, their little claws scratching at something. Throughout the night he kept remembering Zineida reciting to him stanzas from Qol Gali's Book of Yusuf, her good humor, and her cooing over him. But in the darkness of that night there were no sounds of snoring or grunting coming from Zineida as was usual when she slept fitfully in her bed, although in her death there was a new, unfamiliar smell in the house.

> *We are made of mud and a blood clot of the first seed,*
> *And when, at our appointed time, the last breathe leaves our bodily frame*
> *And our soul expires, to the swamp mud we return and*
> *The foul gases which churned through us, begin to escape from our remains*
> *Inflate us and distend our features and invite ants and flies to suck out*
> *The fermenting remains of our vital juices, so we become ready for the*
>   *earth.*

The next day, thoroughly haunted, tired and fearful, Majid asked for his neighbors' help in burying Zineida. The work was too strenuous for Majid by himself. He could barely move Zineida's body it was so heavy and lumpy. But digging a grave in the raw clayey rocky soil, proved much too much for the still frail teen. But in this village only old men and women lived, and so several old men came with shovels and picks to dig out the grave, while the neighboring widow sewed a shroud. They were finished by late afternoon. The five people of Golodnovo and Majid placed Zineida's body in the grave and performed the prayers for the dead, and for the second time that summer, Majid found himself throwing clods of soil onto the shrouded body. Afterwards the neighboring women—the *babushkis*—prepared a cold meal for Majid and clucked and fussed over him, trying pointlessly to console him and encourage him to eat at the same time. That night our hero slept very soundly and did not hear any of the complaints of the house or its other occupants.

Meanwhile over the summer Vera had been busy making arrangements to move back with Majid to her childhood home in Kazan to live with her parents. This entailed getting permission to transfer her propiska—her residence permit—from Ufa to Kazan, although in typical bureaucratic bungling her childhood Kazan propiska was still valid. She also had to get a propiska for Majid so that she could register him for school in Kazan. And it required her finding a new teaching job in Kazan. All of this took a lot of effort and humiliation, as such things were not usually done without sizeable bribes. Vera had luckily been at home when the doctor called with the news of Zineida's passing. She still had to go to Kazan to make final arrangements and move some things to her parents' house, so she was more than 10 days delayed before she could get out to Golodnovo. A neighbor and friend of hers in Ufa had driven her out in his tiny red Lada all the way from Ufa, more than 140 miles away. It was late August, but it was still warm summer weather when she arrived, too early for the potato harvest or for the cabbages. Some of the apples were ripe, but there was not much produce ready to harvest and take with them. Settling for what would become of the house and its gardens was a rather more difficult issue. There was nothing Vera could do, herself so recently a widow and her inheritance rights still not established by the administration in Ufa, so they were obliged to abandon the house when they left for Kazan.

The next two days Majid was too busy collecting and packing food and other valuable items into the car to even notice that the vision of a brilliant summer day in this lush countryside which had been frozen in his memory like a photo no longer existed here. It had become an abstraction which existed only in his memory; it belonged to another age and time. As the heavily laden car pulled away, Majid looked back at the wooden house surrounded by its vegetable garden and a sky blue painted picket fence, not knowing whether he would ever see again this dear sight of his childhood summers.

The trip to Kazan was long and uncomfortable—it took two days as it lay more than 400 miles to the west and Russian roads are bad—and Majid was in a daze and benumbed when they arrived at his grandparents' house on Gogol Street. He had not seen his maternal grandparents since he was a toddler, and it was the first time he had come to their house in Kazan. They lived in a communal apartment on the top floor of a three storey nineteenth century brick house near the intersection of Gogol and Maxim Gorky Streets, a very appropriate literary address. It was small and tight; only two small rooms for the four of them, with a shared kitchen and bathroom. Also in the communal apartment were a couple who, from the bruises on the young wife's face, it was clear that her husband beat her often, an elderly couple who made no noise at all, three widows in their rooms quietly tending their mementoes, and one older man, a war veteran who was regularly drunk on homebrew vodka. There were no children in their apartment. They were all ethnically Russian, while the occupants of the second storey communal apartment were all Tatar. In this apartment there were seven children aged from 2 to 17. Relations in their communal third floor were cordial and cooperative, but there was no joint cultural life, and there was no room for visitors to hold literary evenings as Karim used to hold in Ufa. There was little or no food filching, because there was little or no food kept in the kitchen or in the refrigerator as this was the time when finding food became so difficult and whatever stocks the residents could find were safeguarded in their private rooms. Still in the two years that our hero lived here he didn't like being in the apartment and tried to spend as much time as he could outside visiting or staying at other people's apartments. On nights when he was there, Majid shared the one small bedroom with his mother who slept on the other side of a curtain that divided the room at night. Vera found a position as a school teacher on the far side of the city, so that she left the house early and came back late and exhausted by her long day and commute. Majid's grandfather, an ethnic Russian, was a stern, reticent man who outwardly seemed to be seething in anger. In fact he was. He was a veteran of the Great Patriotic

War and now worked in the property department of the city where he had worked for more than 35 years. He had lost a lot in the war, and he had the medals and ribbons to prove it, and he felt that he was owed something (which never came). He barely tolerated Vera and Majid and usually did not join them in eating dinner. His grandmother was also quiet. She was a Tatar and a retired school teacher who reminisced a lot about her youth during the repression years. Grandfather always hushed her when he heard her carrying on. Her pension was entirely consumed by their food bill and she spent most of her time during the day, every day, waiting to buy food.

Although home conditions for Majid were more difficult in Kazan than they had been in Ufa, our hero's time in Kazan was a very fruitful and much more comfortable period in his life, especially because at school he no longer was harassed by Russian bullies and because he got a teacher who admired and encouraged his poetry. The school he attended was populated almost entirely by ethnic Tatars and Majid did not stick out in any way—that is until the teachers and students discovered that he was a published poet, but that took some time. Ironically he was universally known as and called Slava in this school, and he did not object. The minority ethnic Russian boys were still trouble makers—they were noisy, undisciplined hooligans who, because of an inability to pay attention or to read and because they were abused at home and desperate for attention (I think we call it attention deficient disorder these days), were poor students who often fought with each other and mercilessly harassed the girls. But they did not bother Majid because of his name or modest size. Slava or Majid did not encounter them much either in the hallways or in the classrooms because they had been segregated out of the classes Majid attended and into classes for the hardened problem students. The school was in any event a Tatar school, that is, Tatar was the spoken language of the students in the corridors before and between classes and on the playground or in the lunch hall, while Russian was the language of instruction in the classrooms. Majid quickly fit in to this pattern. During these two years Majid first became attracted to the pretty girls in his new school. They were Tatar girls, slender with willowy figures, they had fair complexions which contrasted with their dark hair, small faces—not the broad Asiatic cheeks of Bashkir girls or the broad course features of Russian girls—and they had dark, mysterious eyes, and their bearing and natural behaviour was demur and sweet. Majid found them very alluring and he often sighed for their attentions. But he did not have any girlfriends in this time, because at first he was too shy to show his affections.

Majid was discovered as the poet that he was by his teacher of Russian language and literature. This man was named Osip Buterbrodsky—in fact he still lives and teaches in Kazan—and he fancied himself to be a poet of sorts, but after he learned that Slava—what an amazing stroke of luck a student in his own class—was a published poet, and after he read these few samples, Buterbrodsky realized he had a student with real talent and he virtually adopted him. Over the course of the first year in his class, this teacher discovered that Slava not only had published that handful of Tatar and Russian poems, but that he had composed a large number more and he kept them in his memory. He also discovered that Slava was an avid student of poetry and he studied and memorized vast volumes of whatever Buterbrodsky recommended to him. In class work, Slava was always the one selected to recite the works of the poet who was being studied at that time. Most of the time that meant Majid recited poems by Pushkin—as he was the single poet that was most acceptable and recommended by the Soviet curriculum. But that did not upset Majid, because he adored the works of Pushkin. But there were also other poets whose works were acceptable and which Majid recited in class for the other students: Lermontov, Gogol, Mayakovsky, and the other poets who promoted proper Marxist-Leninist ideals. Buterbrodsky was a liberal however and as a poet himself, interpreted the literature curriculum liberally—in the *glasnost* sense—and included works of many poets who were otherwise prohibited, for example including works by Baratynsky, Blok, Pasternak, Akhmatova, Mandelshtam, Tsvetaeva, and Okudzhava and even some Tatar poets such as Jalil and Akhmadulina (which anywhere else in the Soviet Union, even in the age of *glasnost,* was something totally unheard of and scandalous and probably if any parents had complained at that time would have resulted in Buterbrodsky's dismissal even there in liberal Kazan).

It was only a few months into the new school year that Buterbrodsky first invited the teenager to his home after school for the evening. It was the first of many evenings that Slava spent with the Buterbrodsky's. At this apartment Slava met Buterbrodsky's still young wife, Anna Gorchitsenko, who in addition to being very familiar with lots of twentieth century Russian poetry, and in addition to cooking tasty hot meals for the two men, also played the piano and on occasion would play settings to verse on the small upright piano they had in the main visiting room. The couple were childless and although they behaved as if they were close to each other, their marriage seemed to lack affection, certainly there was no signs of physical affection while Slava was there. The real highlight of that first evening—and all of those poetic evenings which followed—was the recital round the kitchen table. Slava would recite the poems that he was in the process of composing, and Osip would read from poets that he admired but could not present in his classroom. On a few occasions during these poetic evenings, Slava would actually improvise and compose verses, or the beginnings of what would later become a longer poem. It was in this way that Slava composed his most famous early poem, named *Metamorphosis* in most collections, although it is unlikely he gave it this title.

(You know the one, with the famous lines:. *It is not the gods who make us wild asses, our own stubbornness and ugly spirit make the transformation, it is not from other powers that we become cruel and savage as tigers, it is our viciousness and greed that motivate us to eat our companions.)*

Several other poems or themes also took shape during these evenings over that first year. After reciting, the two would discuss the features of the poem that they especially liked, the turn of phrase, the metaphors, the rhyme scheme, or the rhythm and intonation. Osip was a very perceptive analyst of poetics and had something that few poetry lovers, and even poets, possess; he had real taste in picking out poems and poetic voices. Anna would contribute as well, and she too had a particular acute ear for the music in a good poem. As the winter continued their evenings became more often, sometimes twice or three times in a week. Occasionally, the three of them were joined by one or two other young men who also would add to the discussions insights into the current literary trends. Sometimes they would also discuss politics. It wasn't too long during that first winter in Kazan before Slava would stay overnights in the small Buterbrodsky apartment, sleeping on a pull out couch next to the piano, which afforded him more privacy and space than he had in the shared room with his mother. In fact, Slava couldn't help feeling that Anna reminded him of his mother—in her looks, figure, voice, gentle manner—and he felt strongly attracted to her; she was so solicitous with him.

It was Osip and Anna who introduced our hero to orchestral music, more precisely vocal music with orchestral accompaniment. Anna especially thought that as musical as Slava's normal speech and his verse were that he would like hearing verse set to music. One frosty December evening, Anna had as a surprise bought two-rouble tickets for a concert at the chamber music hall in the Kazan Conservatory named after Zhiganut. This conservatory was located only a few blocks from Slava's home on Gogol at Gorky streets, and he had often walked by and heard piano music streaming from its windows. The program comprised a collection of what are called Russian romances—poems of Balmont, Blok, and Gippius set to music by Myaskovsky, Prokovief, and Shoshtokovich which Anna thought Slava would especially like. The evening was a big surprise to everyone. Slava hated it. His ear could not accept the musical interpretation of the poets' works by the composers. There was something askew and clumsy he found in all of them, something which consistently missed the internal music of the poems. Osip was especially surprised as he thought that Myaskovsky's settings of Balmont's romantic verses were very fine. But Slava objected. Later that evening at the house of Osip and Anna, he looked up the poems of Balmont and Blok and recited them out loud. This confirmed him in his view. The accompanying music was jarring and significantly off the correct intonation written by the poet, so in his view it did not add to the meaning of the original poem, but rather detracted from it. Osip and Anna were both amazed by the young poet's insights. Slava concluded that music and poetry were two art forms that were not entirely compatible, although they were closely related, and that they each addressed meaning in different ways. On the whole, thereafter, he did not care for classical music and did not attend concerts. But also he refrained from trying to sing his own poems. For him his own voice and intonation was music enough. It was more than ten years later, when he was convinced to go see a performance of Tchaikovsky's opera, Eugene Onegin, with the famous Pushkin verse that he was ready to concede that there were possibilities in joining music to verse. But even then, even though he liked that opera, he concluded that Tchaikovsky had not entirely succeeded in capturing in music the unique rhyme scheme, *AbAbCCddEffEgg,* and the special intonation that gives such a dynamic life to the verse novel. This still does not explain our poet's wonderful ear for the Russian line of verse. As a lot of fans of his said, he had a very musical lilting tone when reciting, something magical and hypnotic. But this did not come from an explicitly musical talent.

It was over his seventeenth winter that Majid got a letter from Ganiel, who was still in Ufa. It told him that Ganiel was coming on a visit to Kazan and that he wanted to see Majid again. When they met at a tea stand in the train station, Ganiel looked so pleased. He had been looking for Majid for the previous 8 months, and it was only by accident that he found his new address. He was coming to Kazan on a short visit to some friends to participate in a poetry circle which was active in the city. And he wanted to take Majid along to join this circle.

Majid was warmly welcomed by the members of this circle which met regularly in the late afternoons in a side arcade of the Marjani (red coral) mosque in the old Tatar district between the Kaban lake and the Volga River. It was an awkward looking building, almost appearing like a German style rathaus with a minaret tower over the central peak of the sloped roof which looked more like a clock tower except for its small balconies for the call to prayer and the golden crescent moon on its upper mast. It was one of the few mosques in Kazan which had continued to operate as a mosque throughout the Soviet period until those days when Majid first went there. The nationalists, greatly encouraged by glasnost, had chosen it for their occasional meetings, and so had the Tatar poets who were hoping that the nationalists could deliver to them greater freedom to conduct life, compose and publish poetry, and get education in the Tatar language. The poets' circle was a small group, no more than eight or nine people were sitting around on cushions on the floor when Majid and Ganiel arrived there. The aim for this circle of young men was Tatar poetry of course and they showed no interest in Majid's Russian poems. But they had been tipped off that he had already published five poems in the *Milli Yul* and they very much approved of them. The circle was led by a bohemian looking man in his late thirties named Gabdallah Chulpan (but his registered family name was Kapustin, which means cabbage). He had a distinctly hungry look to him—probably because he was hungry, poetry in Kazan does not feed its proponents—a lean face, unkempt hair, and shabby clothes. But Gabdallah had intense dark eyes and his ear for a poetic turn of Tatar was very sharp. He could improvise verse almost on any topic in an instant and this frequently provided entertainment or winces from the other participants. The meetings were conducted in the Tatar language, which Majid had not spoken much since his father's death but he quickly resumed his fluency. Majid immensely enjoyed these sessions. He was exceedingly proud to be treated as a poet equal to these older practitioners. Immediately after his first meeting with the poetry circle he began the composition of his most famous and longest to that date Tatar language poem, *Idel* (meaning Volga River). He completed this poem after only five weeks, in time for his third meeting with the group.

> *Oh mighty Idel, we call you the father of waters*
> *You who have two powerful sources in the far north*
> *You who carry the blood of the Tatar people*
> *Your rippling currents are like a boundless sea*
> *You have given us your name and your fame*
> *And from antiquity your strength carries us onward through history.*
>
> *Standing on your banks, we can hear your deep resonate voice*
> *Telling the countless stories of armies and kingdoms*
> *Of conquest and loves, of glorious cities and minarets on your banks*
> *And of the unceasing questing and trials of our people*
> *Your waters have been our lifeblood and highways through all time*
> *And from your rocky, big-shouldered bluffs we see both dawn and dusk.*

This poem of 20 stanzas reflected a growing dichotomy in Majid's output. In the Tatar language he wrote overtly nationalistic poems, which increasingly were highly critical of Russia and Russians and became more politically challenging. While in Russian he wrote a wider range of poems, themes, and styles, sometimes also nationalistic. It is difficult however to put exact timing to the development of his diverging Tatar and Russian verse during these four years as none of his works were dated unless they were published in *Milli Yul* or later when his first collection of Russian poems was published in 1990. The last stanzas of *Idel*, give some idea of the voice he adopted in his Tatar verse.

Russia has tied the arms of the yellow Idel and salty Chulman in iron chains
And for centuries it has sought to strangle our broad river to submission
It has not been enough to enslave the straining bargemen on its banks
In their Sisyphean labors, Russ has tried to starve and kill our people
By killing the life waters of the Idel with the poisons
From ten thousand factories, dams, and concrete barriers.

She steadily squeezes off the mighty flow by large lifeless inland seas
Piled high behind earthen dams, just as she has pressed our hearts,
Fished its waters empty till only bones are left floating
At its final estuary in the distant gassy, salty south
A rubescent sheen glistens everywhere over your surface
Trailing sadly behind a vast fleet of smoking nameless cruisers.

These poisons are seeping into our hearts and killing our young
And as you slowly die, O Idel, we also die with you, from sorrow
And bitterness and a life cut off from its source waters.
We see our future—bound so closely to the Idel's stately flow—
Ineluctably siphoned off to feed the greedy Russian
Who will not stop until all are slaves and the Idel flows no more.

This poem, when Majid recited it to the members of the Tatar poetry circle, caused a huge stir of excitement and wonder. As was our hero's gift, he recited it entirely from memory, all one hundred and twenty lines as he had not written it down on paper. His cadence and rhythm was magical. Gabdallah began to try to mimic it—to recite it from memory at that first hearing—but he could not. Ganiel was not there to hear this first performance, but the others immediately cried out that Majid should recite it a second time, there and then. Just as Ganiel had, they insisted that Majid produce a written text and that it be published in the *Milli Yul* as soon as possible. Majid wrote it out later and distributed the poem among the members of the circle, a sample of his first piece of samizdat. I got this poem in a Russian translation which was made from one copy of this samizdat, only a few years after it first appeared, but I am told that the Russian version does not give justice to the marvel of his Tatar diction and rhythm. I've been assured by Tatar speakers that it is a modern Tatar masterpiece on a par with anything by Gabdallah Taki.

This poem was the first to cause Majid to have a run-in with the authorities. This happened some months into his last year in high school some months after *Idel* appeared in the Milli Yul. It appeared that what actually caused the problem was a short political poem of his that had appeared only a short time before *Idel* was to be published. It should have been censored or banned altogether from publication, and by the time this oversight was caught by the censor, *Idel* had already been submitted for publication. Majid was in class one day when a school monitor interrupted the teacher and told Majid he was to come at once to the head teacher. Once there, the head teacher looking very sombre and upset explained that Majid had been summoned to go the office of the head censor of Kazan, one Mr. Ivan Chelikdishov. Majid was astonished. It had never occurred to him until that moment that there was still such a thing as a censor inspecting poetry and vetting it. This was the first time in his life that he had fallen into trouble and it shocked him. It was agreed that Osip Buterbrodsky would accompany him.

At the bureau of the cultural affairs office, they found at the office of the Cultural Compatibility and Standards Conformity Chief Inspector,—in other words, the head censor—that the unpaid editor of the *Milli Yul* was also there for the same meeting. Mr. Chelikdishov's office was a small, very cluttered, windowless cubby hole where every surface was draped with loose papers, newsprint, and magazine pages. Mr. Chelikdishov stood up and after clearing a pile of papers off of one chair and shaking their hands, he ordered a secretary to bring two more chairs which barely fit into the room. He stubbed out the fag end of a Belomorkanal cigarette, clearly a perk of his position as cigarettes at that time were already getting to be hard to find, especially the higher quality ones. Then he turned his rheumy, pale grey eyes onto Majid and stared hard at him for some time without saying anything and finally made a deep audible sigh. "So young man, who put you up to writing such subversive swill?" Majid did not know what to say. He noticed that the censors fingernails were stained orange from cigarette tobacco and that the creases in his fleshy face were highlighted and darkened by smoke stains. With his shock of white hair, and a pair of brown thick rimmed glasses hanging on cords around his neck, he had the appearance of an elderly, mousy, overworked librarian in a state archive. "Are you going to answer me? You seem to feel quite free to say things that are shameful and even prohibited in your verse. Or are these poems really yours?" And he held up a clipping of one of his short Tatar poems from a page of a recent issue of *Milli Yul* and a typed page of *Idel*. Majid answered him in Tatar. "They are really mine." "Speak to me in Russian. It's enough that you insist on writing this ethnic incitement in Tatar. You don't think we understand these verses? What do you mean to be claiming that Russians are greedy and spread poison everywhere they do? Why do you state that Russia kills Tatars. That is a criminal offense you know. Spreading hatred between the equal fraternal nationalities of the Soviet Union." Majid balked and switching to Russian said in a soft voice. "They are not false claims. They are statements of fact, stated poetically." "Nonsense, more insurrectionary rubbish. Like everything that *Milli Yul* publishes. And when have you become an authority who can state what is fact or history? You're only a schoolboy, unqualified at anything. And for that matter you're not a poet, who can freely publish whatever drivel or inflammatory verse you please. You're not in the Writer's Union, are you?" Majid shook his head. "But still I am a poet." "Not a sanctioned one, and not likely to be sanctioned if you continue to write like this." Mr. Chelikdishov then turned on the unfortunate editor. "And you should know better. Nationalism is a form of insurrection seeking to break up the Union of Soviet Socialist Republics. It is sedition and it is a very serious political crime. You know that don't you?" The editor nodded his head in consent but kept his eyes downcast. "Fine then, we are all in agreement. The offenses that you have all committed are serious and will not be repeated. The verses are offensive and should not appear in a publication with open distribution." Mr. Chilkdishov with a flourish then held up another long page of paper to display to them. "Here is the acceptable version of *Idel* for your nationalist paper. If you publish anything else, we will put out an order to deny you access to the printing plant." The page he held had the last six of the twenty stanzas crossed out in red pencil. "And furthermore for printing this first untitled poem, which should have been banned, I will start an administrative protocol against you which will result in a 1,000 ruble fine against your paper. That is all. I hope I don't have to call you all here again." He gave the marked up copy to the editor.

The three upbraided visitors stood to go. Mr. Chelikdishov did not shake their hands this time. As they were turning to go, Mr. Chelikdishov whispered something to Majid in Tatar. Once they were at the checkroom getting their coats, Osip asked Majid what the censor had said. "He said that I wrote very good Tatar verse for such a young man and that I shouldn't waste my talent with subversiveness." The chastened editor muttered that he could not continue this way. He said he would appeal to higher authorities in the Tatar administration who wanted Tatar language and cultural output to continue to be promoted. But as he said this he was thinking instead that he hoped he wouldn't be dismissed from his regular day job because he needed the money. "It would be better not to publish it at all," said Majid calmly and defiantly, "than to publish it in the chewed up form that Mr. Steel Teeth requires." But that is not how things turned out. In early 1988, the first fourteen stanzas of *Idel* were published in *Milli Yul* and four years later after the Soviet Union dissolved, the complete unbowdlerized poem appeared a second time. By then the samizdat version had already been widely circulated in Kazan and even had appeared in Russian translation. And Majid had also some vindication when several months after the poem appeared in its abbreviated form in *Milli Yul* in accordance with the censor he received an invitation from the Society of the Lovers of the Tatar Word to give a recital of his poems, including *Idel*, at a public performance where he would be the sole poet to recite. In spite, of the name of the sponsoring society, Majid agreed to perform his Tatar language poems only if he could also recite a few of what he considered to be his better Russian verses. The Society relented to this and the performance was held in a small drafty hall in the cold spring of his final high school year. A few score poetry lovers attended including his mother Vera, Osip Buterbrodsky and his wife Anna, and Ganiel, and Majid remembered vividly the sounds of the chairs scraping and screeching on the wooden parquetry and how those sounds echoed around the hall, and he remembered the aromas of mustiness given off by the hall. He was able to recite *Idel* in its original form without the censor's red pencil and it was very enthusiastically received. At the end of the recital, Majid was mobbed by members of the audience who were seeking to know where they could get printed copies of his works.

That was the first of what were to become many public recitals of Majid's poetry in the coming years. It occurred in the final months of Majid's schooling, almost two years after the death of his father and the move of Vera and Slava to Kazan. Our hero's poetic development continued during this brief period quite rapidly. He of course had had the encouragement of Osip Buterbrodsky and he had joined the Tatar language poetry circle. He composed a fair number of poems in both Russian and Tatar and several of latter ones appeared published in the pages of *Milli Yul*—which was just scraping through as an economic venture. In school he had begun studying English when he first had arrived in Kazan and he had focused his literary appetite on both French and English poetry, in addition to his enormous appetite for Russian verse (carefully nurtured by Buterbrodsky).

Over these years during his visits to the poetry circle he met a Tatar veteran of the war in Afghanistan named Ildar, a still quite young man who was darkly scarred by the experience. His harrowing recollections of the fighting in Afghanistan left a profound impression on Majid. Ildar told him stories of the mates he knew from his unit who were killed by sniper fire or by night-time marauders and how they were put in black bags and shipped back home where news of their death was suppressed. He had also been involved in a number of fire fights where their Afghan allies abandoned them and left them to perish were it not for the air force. It was through this acquaintance with Ildar that he met a number of other returned veterans and spent some evenings listening to their stories of life in the war zone in the previous years. All of these veterans from Kazan were bitter that their experiences in Afghanistan had to be kept secret, that the funerals of their comrades had been hushed up, that the war was continuing and was largely ignored in Russia. These contacts led Majid to compose one of his more famous poems which was also to cause him troubles later. This was a poem in Russian and it appears it was intentionally political at a time when there was almost no open political questioning of the Soviet war in Afghanistan. It is a poem that starts with the lament:

Why do our boys fight and die in Afghanistan?
So many dead, so many scarred, so many lost.

The poem is 80 lines long. It continues with an attack on the Soviet leadership who had originally authorized the war in 1979, but who by 1988 had all disappeared. This part of the poem—more of Majid's "subversiveness"—entered into Russian political dissidents' discussions in the following years:

Beetle-browed doddering old men in the Kremlin
Dreaming of the Red Army's faded glories of their predecessors
Hoping to turn back their years of impotence and decay
Ordered killings of a faraway people in a faraway land

Relying on the advice of generals more accustomed
To stacking piles of paper than making war or using guns

They who were more accustomed to stacking bodies in truck backs
Trained as they were to throw away young men like detritus on the battlefield.

Fraternal support was the battle cry but support for whom?
Afghans did not want to fight or lead, it was our lads who
Had to traipse through the mountain heights and the deserts vast
To be picked off and shot like wingless birds in a pit.

Also at the Tatar poetry circle he met a fiery Tatar nationalist, a woman named Bairamova, who actually spoke of the promotion of the Tatar language as a vehicle to seek independence for the Tatar Republic. But she was also a Muslim activist who equated Tatar nationalism and independence along with Islam as the state religion and a fundamental identity. Majid was not too convinced with her ideas and he remained sceptical of Islamic activism. He could not equate Tatar identity as being primarily a Muslim identity. He felt Islam was only one aspect of being Tatar. He objected to Bairamova's insistence that the road to greater Tatar independence was for greater adoption and devotion to Islam in the Tatar speaking regions. Bairamova was the only adult Tatar city dwelling woman he had encountered who wore a headscarf not only in the mosque but all the time on the street. It struck him as old-fashioned and backwards, like those Asian Muslim women of Afghanistan or the illiterate village women in the Caucasus, the Urals or those poor Central Asian Soviet states like Tajikistan.

Although Majid spent a lot of time away from home in these two years, and he started spending nights at the apartment of the Buterbrodskys, he did go occasionally to the apartment in the old brick house on Gogol Street at Gorky Street. One early spring evening he came back late and found that one of their neighbors in their communal apartment was standing on the landing outside the door of their communal apartment. She was sobbing and she had a welt on her eye. Her husband had obviously not long before beaten her. He did not want to interfere, but he noticed that the thin cotton t-shirt she was wearing was torn at one shoulder, and that it was clear that she was not wearing a bra. It was the first time he had taken such close notice of her and he was immediately aroused by her. She was attractive and sensual, and the sobs of a young woman in distress appealed to him. They made effort to try not to acknowledge each other, just as they did as the waited in robes to go into the shower, but still he noticed for the first time that she had a beautiful wide forehead. His strongest instinct was to retreat into the communal apartment and pretend he did not notice that it was his near neighbour suffering. Only a few days later in the early evening he was coming home when he saw his neighbor's husband standing outside by the main entry door, smoking a cigarette. Every other time he had cautiously paid him no attention, the man was a mechanic about 10 or 12 years older than Majid and bigger and quite obviously stronger. This time however Majid spoke up. "Why do you beat your wife?" The question caught the neighbor, who was called Vlad by the other members of the communal apartment, offguard and he reacted with surprise. "What did you say?" Majid a little less assertive repeated his question. "What do you mean I beat my wife? What makes you say that?" asked Vlad aggressively. "I saw your wife the other night with a big black eye. So you hit her. It wasn't the first time I noticed. And we hear you beating her through the walls." Vlad tossed off his cigarette butt. "Fuck off, you little prick. Mind your own business, and I'll take care of mine. Besides I don't beat her, I only scold her." Majid noticed when Vlad threw off the butt that Vlad had a small tattoo on his hand in the crotch of his thumb and forefinger. He had noticed this tattoo around Kazan on Russian men a lot. "But why do you have to beat her? What has she done to deserve that?" Majid continued. Vlad sniggered. "It's a manly thing. You see, little boys wouldn't understand. Why don't you run upstairs and let mommy wipe your nose and your ass." Majid didn't move. "I said get out of my face, before I pound it to a bloody pulp, and you understand what a beating is." And he lurched at Majid, who quickly side-stepped and went up the stoop and into the entry way.

It was at about that same time, when Majid received a shock. He had been out late talking poetry with the Buterbrodskys when he decided to go home. When he got to the communal apartment, it was dark and quiet, it seemed everyone had gone to bed already. He went to the room he shared with his mother. When he entered, from behind the drawn curtains where his mother's bed was, he heard what seemed like loud wailing from his mother interrupted by her short aspirations and gasps, and at the same time, a rhythmic steady, slapping humping sound which caused the bed to creak and shudder on the floor. It was clear from the heavy breathing that there were two people in the bed. Majid stood on the other side of the curtain, in the dark, listening to what he had never heard before when his father was still alive. The sounds of his mother's lovemaking shocked and surprised him, because like many young people, he had never imaged his mother having sex. She seemed so virginal and sexless to him. After a few minutes the louder noise and movements subsided, and Majid very quietly undressed and got into his bed. But he could not sleep for some time. He was both aroused and alarmed by what had happened. His mother had a lover and this came to him as a complete surprise that he was so uninformed of her intimate life. And he thought that this was improper coming less than two years after Karim's death. His mind was racing with ideas of what this lovemaking could be like. At the same time he felt a little guilty, being an uninvited witness, and listening in to two peoples' passion, so close to him he could practically touch them through the curtain. Finally he fell asleep, but he was awakened not long after as the man heavily and clumsily got up from the bed and searched for his slippers and shorts to go to the toilet. Majid saw only a dark shadow of a big man leaving the room, and shortly afterwards coming back in and slipping back behind the curtain. He then fell asleep.

The next morning, when he awoke, dressed and went to the kitchen, there was his mother, Vera, sitting at the small table with a large middle aged Russian man in rumpled clothes and wearing thick black glasses, eating a piece of buttered bread and drinking a chicory coffee. Vera tried to introduce them, but Majid avoided her eyes and started the kettle on the stove for his tea, slipping around the kitchen in the spare spaces without making eye contact or paying attention to them, just as it was commonly done in communal apartments. About the only thing Majid closely noticed was the man had enormous feet encased in scuffed black dusty shoes. "Slava, this is Artyem. He works with me at the Institute. Slava, shake his hands." He did not respond. He took his cup of tea and went out into the communal corridor. "Slava, darling, don't be rude." Vera imploringly whined as he went back to his room to get his school bag. He was feeling hot, and his eyes were burning with shame. He felt as if he had been finally disowned by the last of his family. He quickly left the apartment and ran off to school. He didn't go back to his apartment for the next week. But Artyem hadn't moved in to share their communal space. He was only a lover to Vera and not a new potential mate or husband, because he was still married with a family of his own.

This situation made it further awkward for Majid to continue living with his mother and grandparents. He became an occasional visitor and not a resident, spending most nights at the apartment of the Buterbrodskys. He would call ahead to see if his mother and her boyfriend were planning on spending a night of romance together, or whether he could quietly pass the night there. At this time it also became clear that for Majid he needed a little more quiet space for him to compose poems, space he did not have in the communal apartment. At Osip's apartment he was given a small room where he would sleep and change clothes. It also had a small desk and there he could do his school assignments, if he had any, read, and think about his next composition. Not every evening was devoted to poetry evenings with Osip and Anya and their occasional visitors. Oftentimes Majid after eating dinner with Osip and Anya would retreat to his room and do his studies or work out a rhyme, but above all he would read and recite poems. It was as if Slava had been adopted by the Buterbrodskys who did not have any children of their own. It was in the late fall of his final year of school after he had started reading the French decadent poets and had been very impressed by their symbolist images that he had another of his visions. He had been going already for several months to Osip and Anya's apartment and staying for most nights of the week.

It was a Friday or Saturday evening and Osip proposed a party. He bought some samogon, the potent, sometimes dangerous, moonshine of Russia's underground economy, as well as some party food, and he invited some other friends to come over to join them. Two couples, like the Buterbrodskys also in their 30s, came to the apartment with kolbasa—smoked dried sausage which was hard to get by this time in the USSR—and marinated mushrooms and other vegetables and the party started, like most, in the kitchen. Majid had not before in his life drunk any samogon and he was reluctant to start. In general he neither drank alcohol nor smoked, but not because of any religious objections. He was initially given fruit juice to drink at the protective urging of Anya. Osip did not push the drink on him, but one of the guests was very insistent and became more so as the toasts began to mount up. Osip it seemed quickly began to act drunk, as did the guests. They ate lightly, pickles and crisped bread with cheese mainly, but drank hard, knocking back the shots of the fiery water in one gulp.

After a little while Osip suggested that they move to the sitting room (where Majid normally slept) where there was a divan and a pull out couch as well as more chairs. There was another toast, but this time Majid agreed to sample a shotglass full of samogon. He instinctively did not like the burning sensation that immediately burst out in his mouth and down his throat and he coughed several times, Osip patting him on the back. And then it began.

When Majid looked at the room of partyers he felt he had a ridiculous rictus on his face which was blushed and burning up. It felt as if his hair was standing on end and the room was spinning round. He looked to Osip who had suddenly become naked and was massaging Majid's back. The others were undressing. And Anya was standing on the couch bare to her waist and completely bathed all over in a strong chartreuse light. Above her head, which now had viridescent long black hair was a pale green shining halo. In a moment Anya looked to Majid like his mother Vera, only younger, much younger—except that Majid had never since earliest childhood seen his mother's naked breasts. But that wasn't the strangest thing: she had suddenly grown large diaphanous wings sprouted from her back and her eyes, her eyes were a burning orange spheres gazing hard at Majid. This green fairy continued undressing until she was completely naked when she began to bounce up and down on the couch, her breast bouncing and jiggling lively with her jumps. In the meanwhile the other couples began copulating on the floor. At the next moment Osip—but he was no longer Osip at all for now he looked like the photographs of the young poet Verlaine, balding and with a copious rufous beard—was with one hand smoking a pipe of a noxious smelling weed and with the other proffering his erect penis to Majid. Anya, still all in bright green and now completely naked, fluttered in the air over to Majid who was still standing in a daze and with her pubic hairs thrust into his face she bent over and began to pull off Majid's shirt and then she unlatched his belt letting his pants fall off of him. As she was bending over him, he instinctively raised his hand to touch one of her pendulous breasts hanging down in front of him and he was surprised by how soft and hot it felt to him. He had a new sensation: he looked down and saw that he was erect with his pants lying on the floor around his ankles like shackles. Verlaine—or at least he looked like Verlaine although his voice still sounded like Osip's and he was still speaking in Russian into Majid's ear—was shouting out some verse:

> *Oh beautiful adolescent, poet of a man's perpetual dreams*
> *Be my infernal bridegroom, induct me into your inferno*
> *Or heaven if that may be for a night.*

Know that we together should break all the conventions
Indulge in all the senses and all the vices in extremes
Make love, drink the magic liquors, smoke from the oriental sotweed

Derange all the senses, let all the words come tumbling out
Struggle with the words in our drunken excesses and
Transcend all earthly bounds to become the poet of all time.

Meanwhile Anya, the green fairy, was whispering in his other ear. "Stick your tongue in my mouth so that I can taste the sweet words of genius. Kiss me so that I may know pleasure." And she put her mouth to his and forced open his lips and put her tongue in his mouth in a rapturous kiss. At the same time she took in her hand his erect member and began to massage it. The room was definitely spinning in Majid's senses: At one moment Verlaine was in front of him copulating with one of the male guests at the next he was behind him rubbing against him while Anya, the green fairy was trying to put his penis inside her and shouting. "Inspire me! Pleasure me! Take me to the Elysean fields of delight!" The other two women were wriggling together giving pleasure to each other, while the third man was floating up on the ceiling laughing and laughing, looking at one moment like a devil and the next a furry black cat. And then Majid felt intense pleasure exude suddenly, hot and fervid from his loins.

Next thing Majid fell over in the overstuffed arm chair. Anya—looking more and more like his mother, Vera, except for her green color and flaming orange eyes—flew up gently onto his shoulders, her fairy vulva full in his face. "Now with your tongue insert your poetic words into my vagina and make me come! And I will be your eternal muse and lover." He seemed to taste a sour salty excrescence on his tongue but his eyes could no longer tell where he was. It was suddenly noisy and loud, and the four guests were reclining on around or intertwined with Verlaine who was lying propped up on cushions on the floor. They were nipping, caressing, or licking him on one part or another of his naked body. And there were wisps of opium smoke whirling around them from water pipes which had come from nowhere. They together looked so much like the statue of the Laocoon fighting with the serpents, but in this case they were horizontal and the serpents were wisps of opium smoke. Anya, still sitting lightly on his shoulders, now was laughing wildly and even cackling with delight more like a witch than a fairy when Majid noticed Verlaine standing naked next to them with an old revolver type pistol pointed at his chest. Verlaine shouted at Majid, "You don't love me anymore, you ingrate!" And he shot at him two times. At that very moment Majid passed out and the vision ended.

When Majid had to get up because of an urgent need to urinate, he found he was still seated in the armchair wearing only a pair of undershorts. Osip was on the floor mostly naked and asleep in the arms of one of the male guests from the evening before. While Anya lay on the couch—fully naked and distinctly not glowing green and without the long black hair. She was asleep and curled together with the man's wife who was also undressed but partially covered with a light blanket. It was still dark and his head was throbbing. But there was no revolver and when he looked there were no wounds, he had not been shot anywhere. His mouth was dry and gummy. He got up painfully and went to the toilet and then had a glass of water before coming back to sleep. No one had moved. For some time he stood looking closely at Anya's nakedness and felt pleased. She was so beautiful and shapely. After a while he pulled out some blankets and covered the sleeping bodies and wrapped himself up and went back to sleep on the armchair until dawn.

It was in the next week when Majid discovered that perhaps it was not entirely a vision that he had seen, although it had been vivid and magical and other-worldly and it clung to his memory. That night he had gone to bed on the couch in the big room at Buterbrodskys' apartment, and only an hour after the lights had gone out in the apartment Anya, dressed only in a skimpy short green nightshirt, tip-toed into the room and slipped under the blanket with Majid. "Love me, Slava. Kiss me."

she hissed at him. But making love was not something Majid knew anything about. He was then a virgin and he was intensely embarrassed and completely baffled by everything involved with copulation. It was not love making at first, but efforts to couple that evening and the many evenings that followed which came to be an important part of his weekly routine. That night they fumbled and awkwardly thrashed about. And he was completely ashamed of the result. But Anya was satisfied and wanted more. She became his teacher about how to make love, and she taught him tenderly and passionately. And so they became regular but silent sexual partners throughout the winter and the rest of Majid's final school year. He even began to enjoy it immensely and to look forward to Anya's coming into his room. Sometimes they would have sex two times in one week. But they did not become lovers, they did not turn on that wild chemically imbalanced state of passion that drive ordinary people wild and insatiably craving for more and more sex, and acts of affection. Anya did not have orgasm with him although she clearly drew great pleasure from Majid. He in turn loved the sex and came to feel like a real man. He also came to understand that Anya and Osip were not sexual partners or lovers any more (if they ever had been) and, although they appeared to have affection for each other, Anya was starved for physical love. Over those next months, Osip continued to show his affection and admiration for Majid and did not display any outward signs of jealousy. He continued to have poetry evenings with Majid and they would talk about poets and recite poems as if nothing had changed between them. During waking hours, Majid and Anya continued to behave toward each other as they always had, affectionate like a mother with her teenaged son. It was only at night that they became partners in intercourse.

During that same period, Vera's married boyfriend, Artyem, moved in to the communal apartment with Vera and took Slava's place in the shared bedroom. Even the separating curtain came down. It became nearly impossible for Majid to go to the communal apartment at all and by that winter he was spending every night at the Buterbrodskys'. He saw his grandparents once or twice, but they also felt offended by the unwanted presence (and bulk in such cramped spaces) of Artyem in Vera's life.

During these final months of his schooling, Majid suddenly became a top student. His prodigious, powerful memory, which he had always employed for poetry, became the tool of his scholastic successes, as Soviet schools of the time put the highest premium on rote memorization of lessons. He intensively conducted his studies in all his course subjects, although he was most focused on literature and especially poetry. On exams, where he could quote pages of memorized text, he was unsurpassed. Some suspected he had a photographic memory. But it wasn't that at all. His memory was entirely aural. He could hear the many pages they were assigned to read for exams. He could hear the lectures his teachers gave, and reproduce verbatim the words back that had been said. He was reading Shakespeare in English and Baudelaire in French. And when he read them he read them out loud to himself. During the last five months of his schooling he also became enamoured of the Russian poetry of Alexander Blok, which Osip introduced him to. He was especially attracted by the iambic tetrameter that Blok employed to such devastating musical effect. It gave him an even greater appreciation for Pushkin's iambic tetrameters. One day in studying Blok he came across an epigram of Blok's that stayed with him for years afterwards: *"A poet does not have a career, a poet has a fate."*

By this time he had reached his full mature adult height: he was short and slight and not given to sports or athletic activities of any sort. He had dark wavy hair and white skin and the girls in his school class thought he was beautiful and very attractive. But he did not reciprocate their advances, he ignored their flirting eyes, although there were several very cute, mature looking girls. His attitude toward the girls in his class was largely shaped by his regular love making with the much older and shapelier Anya. Majid thought all the girls were immature and flighty, skinny and too childish for him to pay them any serious attention. The girls naturally interpreted this as arrogant vanity and even narcissism. If only they knew. None of course suspected Majid of his affair with Anya, wife of their literature teacher.

It's not clear when or if he composed a poem to Anya or their love. In his first collection of published poems there is nothing that suggests his feelings about those five or six months when he was having sex with Anya. But he did publish a poem only a few months before his accidental death which seems to refer to this affair. It could well have been written at this time. A poem which he held apart, but it is not noted anywhere when he wrote it. This poem could have referenced another lover, or it could be entirely a work of imagination. But I think Anya is the subject of this mysterious love. I quote it here in my clumsy translation because I think it belongs here.

> *So is this what we might call love then?*
> *Her soft brown curls brush against my face*
> *Her face is contorted with pleasure, eyes shut,*
> *A salty drop falls her forehead on to my lips*
> *Our warm sweat mixes over our bellies, in a love cocktail*
>
> *She pulls and claws me, she nips me with her teeth*
> *Her kisses mark my body, and she asks for more*
> *Her legs wrap tightly round my loins*
> *Until my gush of passion drains me*
> *And her hot breath and sighs become rhythmic wails.*
>
> *Her soft pendulous breasts hang above my face*
> *Her arched back is moist and glimmering*
> *She is hot all over, her teeth shine white through a tight smile*
> *She murmurs occasional instructions to me*
> *Then her eyes roll up and she gasps and barks.*

I hear her heart beating madly, louder than my own.
My heat is dizzy and my sight unclear
Could this be my mother's hands groping me, her teeth clinching?
Am I but a toy for her to insert into her dark corridors
And when she's had enough, was it truly enough? And for me?

She has taken me and is transported
In one night of passion she is carried to perfumed gardens
Am I really capable of giving her such pleasure
Will then she truly love me in the morning?
Should I hide in shame? So is this love then?

In the final months of his schooling in Kazan, it wasn't only the girls in Majid's class who noticed his increasingly open arrogance. Osip noticed that Majid, up to then a reticent youth who rarely offered any comment on his own, became more outwardly critical of public statements by politicians and especially of contemporary poets and their works. Now if he disliked the public recitation of a poet he would condemn it in the strongest terms, comparing the poet to himself in negative terms. At this time he began composing a lot more of short critical epigrams about the state of poetry in this time when the Soviet Union was in advanced decay. He was especially critical of the "officially sanctioned" poets and the poets which the establishment admired. This arrogance was also noticed by the members of the Tatar poetry circle in the Marjani mosque, where Majid became more assertive. By his last spring in Kazan, he was no longer merely a youngster attending the circle's meetings to learn about and discuss others' poetry, he was their foremost poet and his poetry the best, and he let the other members know it. He also was highly critical of the assumption that Tatar language poetry and Islamic themes were inseparable. He argued forcefully against the nationalists who insisted that Tatar identity was first and foremost a Muslim identity. He even argued this against the formidable Bairamova, improvising sarcastic verses to mock her arguments.

Not long after he gave his public recitation of *Idel* in that drafty hall for the Tatar speakers of Kazan (but his mother attended too), he also gave his last poetry recitation at his school's assembly. This recitation was in Russian and it comprised a poem by Lermontov, one by Pushkin, and a short poem by Blok. The Lermontov poem was *The Sail*, that famous short romantic creed which Lermontov set up for himself as a model as a romantic hero. This was a time in Majid's life when he was beginning to see himself as a romantic. The Pushkin was the short poem dedicated to Chaadayev, which Pushkin wrote at about Majid's age. And the poem by Blok, *The Singing Girl,* is an exquisite example of the Symbolist poet writing in iambic tetrameter. But Majid was allowed this time to include a recitation of one of his own poems. It was a short poem which two years later appeared in his first published book of poetry. As had been his practice since the start, he recited all of the poems from memory, again displaying his formidable memory.

Majid's mother, Vera, had been able to take time off from her school work to attend this performance and as always she was ebullient and proud in respond to her son's performance. But Majid, or Slava to Vera, did not see her this time. After the applause died down, the other students were marched out of the assembly hall, and Majid was led backstage, so Vera could only go to the cloakroom and get her coat and return to her school. She tried calling Majid that evening at Osip's apartment but the unreliability of the telephone in their communal apartment and the waiting line to get to it meant that she did not reach him to tell him how wonderful his poem was and how certain she was that his career as a poet was going to be successful. And it was not long afterwards that he received a quite unexpected confirmation of his future progress in this career. He had sat for the entry exams for the Philological Department of the Moscow State University (the famous and extremely prestigious MSU), and just a week after his recital he got word back that he had been accepted as an outside student, in other words, a student from outside of Moscow. This was at that time quite a rare achievement, as only a very few outside students were allowed to go to Moscow from the provincial cities or the ethnic republics of the Soviet Union. It's difficult to know if there had been some political intervention on Majid's behalf. Osip had pleaded on his behalf, we know, and Osip had a good friend and old schoolmate who was at that time a Vice Rector of the department in Moscow . Perhaps that had been enough for Majid to gain admission, but I suspect there were some Tatar nationalist politicians who had been convinced by the poetry circle to support and press for Majid's admission as a representative of the renaissance of Tatar language and poetry. Otherwise his admission appeared to be almost miraculous. But it happened.

Vera was ecstatic when she received the news from her Slava by telephone, and at the same time she was able to tell Majid how much she enjoyed his recitation. Vera immediately thought about how she could send money to Majid for his expenses in Moscow. She didn't earn much, but she knew that life was expensive in Moscow, and he would need an allowance. Majid was of two minds about the development. On the one hand he felt very pleased and giddily proud to have been admitted. On the other he felt it was only what he deserved in life, that there was nothing really remarkable about getting admitted, as he thought it was a foregone result due to his superior intellect and potential. It was his fate, regardless of being a Tatar, provincial boy with no political ties or links to the ruling elites. Osip, however, knew better. He was very proud of Majid and was sure that he would do very well on the entrance exams, but he knew that intermediation had been most likely the preponderant decisive factor in the case for Majid. Osip felt it was almost the accomplishment of his own son, and he was sure that being a student at the MSU would bring Majid recognition and success in his career as a poet. Anya, however, was distressed by the news. It meant that Majid would be leaving them at the end of that summer. And as much as she had tried to avoid and deny it to herself, she had come to love Majid as a mate and a lover. She tried in May to hide her anxiety about the coming separation, but it made her seem tense and bothered, and during the days or evenings in their apartment she began to show more openly her physical affection, and at nights she clung tighter to him when they were in bed together after sex. She wanted more and she feared losing Majid. Majid appeared oblivious to Anya's concerns and began thinking up new poems and poetry projects for the summer months before his departure.

Last Bell came and went. The ceremony and festivities were emotional and jolly, but Majid, having joined this class of graduates only two years earlier and having become an arrogant, posing, self-appointed poet, felt excluded from the excitement. He briefly thought of his father, Karim, and felt the keen pain of his absence. If his father had still been alive, his graduation celebrations would have been in Ufa and not in Kazan. His mother attended, but he felt no longer close to her. She had bought new clothes for him for the occasion, a starched white shirt and black slacks. He avoided her during and just after the celebrations, and when he was with her he felt intensely embarrassed. Osip and Anya did not pay him any attention because they were very busy involved in conducting the formal parts of the ceremonies. He had no girlfriends among his classmates, even though there were several very attractive Tatar girls who fawned adoringly over him. He danced with some of them awkwardly, but neither his feet not his heart were in the gaiety. He did not attend all the parties outside of school, especially the parties at classmates' homes. The class party at the Black Lake city park he found to be boring and without much direction—the boys were looking for ways to get alcohol, and the girls were trying to smooch with their boyfriends, if they had any, otherwise they clung together in feminine groups giggling, shouting, and chirping. Besides after only two hours a dark cloud blew over and a sudden downpour put an end to the festivities.

It was about that time that he composed a short poem in iambic tetrameter which poked fun at Pushkin and Lermontov and the entire

Romantic movement. It seems he first performed it sometime in that summer or around the time of Last Bell in early June. It appeared later in his first collection of poems some two years later, where it was called "Clouds".

> *A poet is not a cloud, so much should be self-evident*
> *He doesn't float in the air, for one*
> *And clouds don't pout although they do spout*
> *And clouds do not trail sorrows when they're spent.*
>
> *Poets have some free will, and make much clatter*
> *Clouds are buffeted by winds, sun and dust*
> *And they come and go, and evaporate as they must*
> *They are rarely solitary but not social either for that matter.*
>
> *In truth few are the clouds that show any emotion*
> *But we poets assign to them our own feelings*
> *The wretched aching of our passions, our yearnings*
> *The twisting of our tongues and life's daily commotion.*
>
> *And if a poet were to stand like a cloud, in a tower*
> *He would find himself pinched in by a vast indifferent crowd.*
> *He'd look like a buffoon with long trailing scarves*
> *And his hair'd be pushed up on his head in a pompadour.*
>
> *And then there is nothing quite so evanescent*
> *As a cloud. Even the poet's words ring out and*
> *Echo through time and are not burnt by the sun,*
> *And a poet may be history's fool or ass when his time is spent.*
>
> *No one really remembers yesterday's clouds.*

You'll have to excuse me as I have tried to render this poem in a translation with rhyme and meter that reproduces the humorous tone and intent of the original. It had word play and alliteration, part of his repertoire of literary tools.

In late June that year, Osip and Anya invited a group of the recent graduates and Majid out to the countryside on the right bank of the Volga (the Russian side) to participate in a celebration of St. John's Eve, for John the Baptist, but really for Ivan Kupala (John the bather), a much beloved pagan folk holiday marking the midsummer eve. This holiday was one that the Orthodox Church and then the Soviets had tried vainly to eradicate. But it had persisted in secrecy and among a select few, because it was so much fun, being as it were a fertility ritual that was an excuse for an open air all night debauch in the woods, involving water and fire, and of course some drinking of samogon. Majid did not know what to expect exactly. Osip told him to read the pertinent scene from The Master and Margarita, but as this was only available in samizdat, there was no time to get a copy and read it before they assembled and left the city.

The group of school leavers with Majid and Osip and Anya and a few other adults arrived in several cars at a clearing in the woods on a back road. It was a brilliantly warm clear summer afternoon and everyone was dressed lightly. The girls twittered with excitement. They all carried several baskets of food and drink further into the forest and stopped at the side of a very large pond at the forest's edge next to a fallow field which sloped gently away to a distant riverbed. The field was ablaze with birdsong with the droning of crickets acting as a harmonic line. There they spread out large ground sheets and sat down for a group picnic with sandwiches, hothouse tomatoes, and pickled vegetables and fruit drinks. Then the girls and women in the group went altogether into the field and began collecting late spring flowers, while the boys and young men started collecting kindling and fallen branches for the fireplaces. It was clear the place had been used before because the remains of several fire sites lay in different locations, and one, in the shade of a towering dark fir tree, was very large as if for a bonfire. Once the women had returned, they began weaving garlands and wreaths with the flowers, the adult women showing the younger girls how to weave the round garlands with cornflowers, purple mallows, blue chicory flowers, and yellow asters and dandelions. In the long evening the first ritual began, when the women all decked out in their yellow and blue garlands or wearing flowers in their hair went to the edge of the pond and carefully lay the wreathes on the water and sent them floating to the middle of the pond. They sent them off with their wishes for a happy husband and for a loving coupling and a big family. Then they all scattered into small groups or couples to search for the magical fern which flowered only on this night. This search was pointless of course as ferns do not flower, but then the entire holiday is about miracles and rituals that enhance magic and ward off devils and witches. Shortly after the group reassembled, hot and sweaty and covered in sticky spider webs, everyone undressed and jumped in the pond for a festive swim and much splashing. Majid's classmates, especially the girls were initially shy and reluctant, but Majid was no longer ashamed or embarrassed by his nakedness and he plunged right in with the other adults. Once in the water he curiously looked back at the girls who were formerly his shy classmates to examine their little breasts and especially their vulvas. He did not see too much, as there was too much commotion. And the waters of the pond were black and inky and soon it was too dark to see much clearly. The girls shrieked from stepping down into the oozy soft mud on the pond bottom and everyone soon was covered in mud and duckweed. After washing off amid lots of splashing and some swimming, they all emerged from the pond and, after drying off and dressing again, they lit two fires to warm themselves and then to cook some supper. The adult men brought the samogon out and began to pass jugs of it around. A guitar was brought out and after a little while everyone began to sing. They sang mostly pop songs, but a few songs by Okudzhava—the poet and protest folk singer—were also sung. The full moon rose above the field sending its white light into the clearing where their fires were.

Summer night comes late to this part of Russia and it was near midnight then before it was completely dark and the moon at its most brilliant.

It was time to light the big bonfire and begin the next ritual of the celebration. The fire went up in a huge ball of flame that nearly touched the fir tree boughs and sent them bouncing. The group of revellers gathered round. And again the women first stripped down to their waist, baring their breasts to the light of the flames, encouraging the girls to follow their example. The men followed suit, and some of the women, including Anya, undressed again completely. Then when the flames died back and were lower, the women picked a mate and hand in hand began to jump over the fire, giggling, although some would recite a short verse, "Fire, clean me of my impurities, take my yellow and give me your red." Anya who was a little taller than Majid came around the fire and took him by the hand as her partner and invited him to jump with her. It was the first time any of the others in the group, beside Osip, had seen or guessed about the relationship between Anya and Majid. Osip had in the meantime taken as his pair another young man that Majid did not know or recognize. All four of them stood in line behind other pairs until it was their turn to jump. Anya whispered to him, "Come on now, Slava. Don't let go." And they began their run to jump clear. But over the flames, their hands separated and they landed apart, clear of the flames and embers. Anya, who had all evening long had the look of excited anticipation on her face looked at Majid with disappointment in her eyes. It was inauspicious for them that they could not jump over the fire with their hands conjoined. It meant they would separate soon—as she too keenly was aware already—forever. She took his hand and told him they would jump again. And through several more attempts they held their hands together as they jumped over the low flames of the bonfire. He thought it was an especially funny feeling as by holding tight to Anya's hand and the way she jumped meant that he flew closer to the center of the fire and he had the distinct feeling of scorching his bare bottom as he flew over. As the couples continued to jump, the party continued to undress until eventually everyone became entirely naked and the shadows of the fire dancing on yellow bodies, limbs and bouncing body parts wove a magical tapestry in amongst the trunks of the forest pierced by the white moonlight. When everyone was thoroughly purified and tired, the couples all ran over and again jumped into the pond. Then after again splashing and squealing, the couples emerged from the water and found their towels and blankets and went off into different parts of the forest to sleep together. Anya and Majid did not sleep at once, but once they lay down on the blanket out of sight of the fire on the verge of the field, they began to make love, the first time they had done so under the open sky. Anya was choked on the idea that she was near the end with Majid, while Majid was just beginning to feel that perhaps he loved Anya and that she was his woman. Neither gave even a moment's thought to Osip. They remained wrapped together all night under the blanket as it became much cooler in the early morning twilight, which began around 4 o'clock. After climaxing with Anya, he fell almost at once into a deep sleep, most likely the result of the samogon. He dreamt of naked witches flying through the air on broomsticks, of giant bullfrogs turning into professors, and serpents slithering together in balls in the pond waters, and he over and over dreamt of being unable to fly up to Anya who circled around him and sang to him inviting him to fly away with her and her coven of witches. But the cool morning air woke him and he was surprised to see it was so bright, even though the sun had not yet appeared. He peered deep and close at Anya's sleeping face, examining the fold of her eyes, the slight reddish tint in her brows, her brownish thin lips with bits of lipstick still on them, closed tight together, the fine fur on her ears, the arch of her white neck, her rising bosom as she slept—she was still clasped close to him—and the dimple in her shoulder. He could not later remember how long he studied her on that morning, but her close sleeping face and figure was a vision that stuck with him throughout the rest of his short life.

Chapter Two

The Poet Becomes Known

How splendid and magnificent was Moscow! Majid was amazed and dazzled by the mighty city and its big-shouldered vistas. After his arrival he spent long hours walking around its historic center, the Kremlin, dumbfounded by the scale and the pomp and power of the city. From the university he stood long admiring the view of the city from the platform atop the Lenin Hills overlooking the whole city. Everything was so much grander than he had imagined. His first impressions were that Moscow was even more splendid than Leningrad, contrary to everything that he had read or heard. He was even charmed and bemused by the small Moscow River looping around the city center. In comparison with the Volga, the Moscow River was a narrow, lifeless stream.

In the days before his classes started and throughout September, he made a point of visiting the monuments to Moscow's literary greats to pay homage to the poets. First among them was the homage he paid to Pushkin standing looking forlorn and pensive on his pedestal in the eponymous square and park in the center, looking at the pretty young women in their light summer dresses walking under the linden trees or by the splashing fountains. It seemed to Majid that the sculptor had made Pushkin too tall and too muscular. He had imagined that Pushkin in his lifetime was of a stature more like Majid, slight and short, not powerful, although unlike Majid he was swarthy. He spent more than an hour there, looking at the master, while reciting just under his breath poems that Pushkin had written and which Majid especially liked. A passerby saw that Majid was religiously singing Pushkin's praises and pointed out to him that Pushkin was not really a Moscow poet. But then he suggested that he go to the Pushkin house museum, one of the many places where the illustrious poet had spent some days while he had been visiting Moscow. And then he pointed out to him the way to walk down to Arbat and to find that museum. When Majid finally did visit the museum he was astonished to see among the many artifacts, actual handwritten notes and verses of the Master. He could imagine him scribbling out these verses with a feather quill pen in a dim garret room with only candlelight to guide his words onto paper.

In the same manner Majid stopped in front of both statues of Nikolai Gogol, the triumphant, tall almost heroic one of Gogol which Stalin had ordered and had preferred to the sad and depressive, seated Gogol which more fairly represented the artist's actual bipolar character and his loss of hope later in his short life. Majid noticed that this latter statue had been hidden away out of view in a small permanently shady courtyard belonging to the house where Gogol had lived while in Moscow. The sculptor had been careful to give Gogol a large nose and befitting a position in a deep sunless courtyard, Gogol appeared to be quite cold. Majid was intrigued by Gogol because as a youth he had grown up speaking and writing both in Ukrainian and Russian, not unlike his own bilingualism. And although everyone seemed to treat Gogol as a prose writer, his greatest piece, Dead Souls, Gogol had offered up as a 'poem', he had thought of himself as a poet.

It took him some searching around the city to find the monuments to Lermontov and Yesenin as they were well hidden away from the center. Of course, both of them, like Pushkin, had been only occasional visitors to Moscow, and were really St. Petersburg based. Lermontonov's statue was not even anywhere near the small wooden house that he had stayed in near Cook's Street. The same could be said about Yasenin, but Majid learned that there was only a plaque to this popular poet on one of the houses he resided in briefly. Majid also visited the monuments to Griboyedov, Turgenev, and finally Leo Tolstoy. These later two had had houses in Moscow which had been preserved and which had carefully cultivated house museums located inside them. But Majid was disappointed by them as he was unable to find any indications from the houses or the collections inside of what motivated the writers or how they composed their work. It is noticeable from his itinerary that our poet deliberately skipped a visit to either the monumental statue to Vladimir Mayakovsky or to the shrine that the Communist Party had made out of his house. It was already clear that Majid despised the bombastic and ideologically loaded poetry of the Futurists and especially of those like Mayakovsky who had become propagandists for the Bolsheviks. Perhaps he also did not like Mayakovsky because he resented that he had been a tall and ruggedly handsome Russian figure, given to overly dramatic declamation of his poems. The prominently featured statue of Mayaskovsky in Triumfalnaya square would have certainly offended Majid's sensibilities even more.

Majid enrolled in the Philology Department, with his focus on the study of Russian and Western European literature. He was placed in a dormitory room in the main Stalin tower which after it had been built had become the symbol of the university throughout the Soviet period to that time. It was in effect a 10th floor walk-up room with communal toilets and bathrooms. He had as a roommate a third year student of poetry from Ukraine and a sometimes poet too, a young man bearing a name almost as rare as his, Innokenti Anonymski. They grew to be close friends and Innokenti became something of a mentor to our poet as they spent long hours discussing how poetry should be written. In particular Innokenti was critical of the romantics and the mystical writings of the Symbolists. Innokenti was, like Majid, highly critical of the bombastic school of poetry declamation which was so widely practiced in that time. He introduced Majid to recordings of Bulat Okudzhava reciting publicly some of his earlier works of poetry to demonstrate that there still existed in Russia an alternative to Soviet declamation. Innokenti also felt strongly that the poet's art was to express his ideas in words that were crystal clear and precise. Out of this view, Innokenti attacked the works of contemporary poets who used vague language and the language of the street, as imprecise as that was. It was from Innokenti that we have the only first-hand testimony of how Majid composed his poetry. He often watched him at his desk in the university dormitory reciting verses just under his breath and then writing a few lines down and continuing. Sometimes Majid would stand up and pace around the small room repeating a few lines and waiting until he got the right rhyme and metric. In his first two years of studies, we know that Majid would recite his new completed poems to Innokenti, still only from memory. He would write them down after Innokenti gave him his comments and suggestions.

Classes themselves were not much of a challenge for Majid. The professors who gave lectures seemed completely bored of their subject, and their insights into poetry were few and banal when they had any at all. Far too often their literary insights were rote repetition of the "politically correct" interpretations which the Communist Party had contrived over the years. Sometimes their analyses of literature were even exact quotes of the critiques written by Zhdanov 40 or even 50 years earlier when Communist authorities were striving to establish the norms for Soviet art. Many of the students in the lectures, when they did not actually skip them altogether, slept or carried on conversations with each other in the back rows. There was little classwork and almost no homework; all the students' efforts were focused on taking oral exams at the end of each term. When not in the classrooms or lecture halls, Majid spent most of his time either in the library or at the student cafeteria where he had his only hot meal of the day at lunchtime. The meals were subsidized, meaning he did not pay for them. But the cafeteria—like the canteen where coffee and tea were served—was a grim, greasy, gray place with grimy windows, broken chairs, and weak lighting. The canteen was one of the few places in the university where students could congregate and talk freely for much of the day or evening. But the coffee was thin and poor and the snacks on offer were ordinary and never enough. A black and white TV ran day and night, usually on a news or information channel. After a certain hour the snacks in the canteen, especially the sweet ones, were always sold out for the rest of the day. The canteen always closed at 10 in the evening and the biggest drawback was that, although very inexpensive, Majid had to pay cash out of his own pocket for whatever he had there. Usually he had a cheese pastry and strong black tea from the giant samovar which perpetually steamed, gurgled and bubbled in the center of the room. He found that it was warmest place to stand in the room once the winter started. Lunch was subsidized, but there were no facilities for dinner and breakfast he had to have either in the café or in his room (even though single cup electric water coils were supposed to be banned from dormitory rooms everyone had one to boil water for morning tea). Money was always a problem. His mother had committed to sending him 25 rubles a month for his "extra" expenses, which meant mostly food but also transport around the city, but after a few months it was clear that she was not always able to send him these funds on the same date, and in his first and second year occasionally he didn't get any funds from her for an entire month (it was still difficult to send money at that time). As a result he was always very hungry by the time the cafeteria opened for lunch. Through that first autumn in Moscow when he felt he had enough money in his pocket, Majid would take the metro to the center and spend his afternoons walking around the center, sometimes visiting museums and sometimes going to an art film. There were at that time a few small shops serving either blini or meat or cabbage pirozhkis with milky coffee where he could afford to eat and stand at a small round table for an hour or two, but otherwise there were very few places downtown to "hang out". There were no cafes or tea shops in Soviet Moscow. Public places to congregate, meet with friends, drink a coffee or hot chocolate while reading a newspaper were mostly banned. Most of his visits to Moscow center therefore were perambulatory and this practice fell off as the winter grew especially cold.

He wrote letters to his mother and to the Buterbrodsky's with his impressions of the city. They wrote back to him telling him how much they missed him, and reporting only a very little bit on their own continuing life. This group had all seen him off at the train station in Kazan in late August. Majid with two small scuffed up suitcases in his hands, Vera bearing food gifts wrapped in small parcels, Osip and Anya presenting him with a new winter overcoat. They had arrived early and stood around on the platform a long time. All were a little embarrassed by the suddenness of their upcoming separation. It was the first time Vera had met the Buterbrodskys. Both women were jealous of the presence of the other, although Vera had no idea about Majid's relationship with Anya. By the time Majid had boarded the train and settled into his sleeping compartment, he was heavily burdened with goods. It had been an overnight train and there were thieves on board according to the wagon's conductor. All night long, instead of sleeping he had kept close watch on his things from his perch on the upper bunk, while his compartment mates after drinking heavily fell asleep, snoring. Unknown to Majid when he left Kazan station, Anya was already pregnant. She had known of her conception for almost two months. Contraceptives at that time were expensive and hard,—no nearly impossible—to obtain which was why the most common contraceptive methods were abstinence or abortions. After Slava's departure, Anya told Osip and said as well that she would prefer an abortion. But Osip would have nothing of it and insisted that she bear the child and it would be their only child whatever the outcome. About this neither Anya nor Osip wrote even one word to Majid. She delivered a healthy normal little boy that next March. He looked like Majid, but Majid did not learn of this little boy—his only son—until he again visited Kazan almost nine years later. Osip probably knew in his heart of hearts that the child was not his, but he adopted him as his own and embraced him and loved him as a proud papa. The boy was named Evgenii.

In his strolls around Moscow, he soon became struck and even amused at how bland and utilitarian were the names of places, things like Pharmacy Number 16, Infants' Food, a shop called Household Chemicals, Bread Roll store number 11, House of Books and so on. Streets and intersections seemed to be all named after old Communist, Bolshevik or other political heroes, not unlike the pattern in Kazan, but all names of founders or imagined names for stores had been wiped out. The original identity of the city had been erased and in its place a colorless and even stern pattern of names had been imposed on it. Of course this made for some very ugly neologisms, names like Frunzenskaya for a metro station, Komsomolskaya Prospect which connected the university with the city center, Kalininskaya Street, or Orzhonikidzski Theatre. There were a few exceptions and he did encounter some relics. Lermontov's house was located off of Cooks Street, a name he found attractive whenever he was hungry and amusing because it was situated right next to Knife, Tablecloth and Bread Alleys. He wondered if there had ever been a Cutlery or Soup Spoon Alley. But of all the names of the city that most attracted him, the Arbat district was most intriguing. Perhaps it was the slight suggestion of an Arabic origin, perhaps it was the place where Muslim traders congregated to offer their wares in the middle ages, or perhaps it was the love that the poet Okudzhava heaped on the neighborhood, which was both his home and the home to many activist dissident artists and thinkers. But even in the Arbat stores had such plain names as Milk (no number, no word or what it was whether a store or shop, just as sign proclaiming Milk as if that were a traffic signal proclaiming itself). And finally he laughed at the "produkty" or Products store as a name for a grocery, stores which were always empty in those days. He found only one real such store, and it retained its glorious pre-Revolutionary name, Yeliseyevsky Gastronome on Gorky Street. It retained its founder's name and the word gastronom of course indicated what a wonderful place it was, a functional name but one with many layers of meaning. On days when Majid was especially hungry he would go there to breath in the aromas, to ogle the meat pies and smoked dried sausages, to marvel at the pineapples and brightly colored oranges and bananas, to wonder at the wines and imported spirits, and to think of the days when such luxuries might be available to him. During the middle of his first year at the University when he was reading Bulgakov's masterpiece, The Master and Margarita (a copy printed abroad from the complete unburned manuscript), he followed the itineraries of Bezdomny (The Homeless One) around the city from Patriarch's Pond to Woland's golf tee atop the Pashkov House on the street of the moss gatherers, from the Griboyedov House to Ostozhenko Street.

Dawn and sunrise on the calm Moscow River
All is quiet and the great city sits on perched on its banks
Like a ravenous predatory bird.

The bricks of the Kremlin walls become bloody red
In the soft morning sun, the city begins to bustle
And its proud people shake their heads.

Just as the terrible Ivan looks over the parapets
At the victims of the execution mound on Red Square
Traders begin to hawk their wares.

Unbowed Napoleon looks down from the "Bow Down" Hill
On the quiet wooden Moscow and its still, sparkling river
Where he waited in vain for keys.

The city is humming with its industrial strength
Just as the implacable Man of Steel looks out
Over his towers rising high.

*In awe I look down from the Sparrow Hills on the city
In full afternoon sun, its peaceful river glittering.
It is an indomitable, beautiful city.*

Majid continued to compose poems in Russian throughout his first two years of studies. However he mostly ceased composing Tatar poems and instead he began translating Tatar poetry, both his own and others, into Russian. He had a hard time finding the means of giving a recital of his poems and he no longer had the support of the Tatar Poetry circle which he had had in Kazan. But eventually he found a medium. He saw a flyer announcing a poetry recital at the Maxim Gorky Institute of Literature located not far from the gaze of Pushkin on his plinth, in the house where the early socialist revolutionary Alexander Herzen had been born. The recital took place in a small hall at the Institute in the late winter of Majid's first school year. The hall, unlike most rooms in the center of the city, was insufficiently heated and most of the audience remained in their coats. The hall was packed full—standing room only and many stood in three ranks along the walls—and the audience rapt by the reciting of three young poets—all of whom were students at the Institute. After the performance, which lasted two hours, there was a reception in the former ballroom of Herzen's father's estate house. Majid introduced himself to the three poets. But he had liked the poetry of only one of them, a graduate student at the Institute about seven years older than Majid, who was named Victor Krivonosov. Majid introduced himself in a small rhyme, a manner that he often spoke in ordinary talk. "I'm called Slava, though my name's Majid, I'm a published poet from Kazan, Perhaps you have time, I can read you some of my verses. I won't wander on. They're nothing from Parnassus." Krivonosov perked up his ears and took notice of Majid at once. The two at once liked each other. They arranged a time to visit together when Majid could introduce Victor to some of his poems. In Moscow over the next several years, Krivonosov took Majid under his wing, in the same way that Ganiel had in Ufa, and he became an important conduit to publishing and introducing Majid's poems. He also invited Majid to join him in his informal, unofficial literary association, a LITO, which was a group of young struggling poets which met irregularly to share their works and to discuss and analyze poetry in general.

In that first winter he made a cherished acquisition when he got two foreign ballpoint pens (Bics no doubt) which were still rare, cherished items in those days. This enabled him to write clearer finished copies of his poems on paper, without the smudging of soft pencil lead or the blotches of ink from old cartridge pens. In his second year he made another much sought after acquisition, a working typewriter. It may have been registered with the secret police, but it was an old German made model maybe 35 years old which had been heavily used and had been handed down from student to student through many generations. The only problem with it was that the ribbon was nearly exhausted, and it took him lots of time to find a replacement ribbon (although the replacement was also used). But the acquisition marked the beginnings of the furious work, which lasted the rest of his life, of typing out the poems which came to him almost continuously.

Majid only slowly got acquainted with his classmates. This was not easy. He discovered that they were socially completely different from his schoolmates in Kazan. The overwhelming majority of them came from Moscow meaning that most of them were sons or daughters of the sallow faced, anonymous bureaucrats, the *chinovniki*, who actually ran the Soviet Union. A very large proportion of these came from the social elites, the *nomenklatura*, the communist party members who were the top administrators of the government and party. As such they were the scions of the highly priviledged ruling class, and they appeared toward outsiders, such as Majid, as vain, egotistical, competitive, condescending, self-important and distinctly unfriendly. In other words, he quickly appreciated that he had landed in a closed shop. In fact as many of these students had gone to the same schools together before university, they were familiar with each other and often had already ready-made cliques which protected them from the outsiders. This first semester was also the first time Majid had encountered such a highly cosmopolitan society. In his school in Kazan, the students had been mostly Tatar with some few ethnic Russians, some few of mixed ancestry, and some who were from the non-Tatar native peoples of the Kama River basin. While in Moscow he encountered for the first time a wide variety of peoples, mainly Russians, of course, and other Slavic peoples, such as Ukrainians and Belarusians, Baltic peoples, Caucasians, such as Armenians and Georgians, and Jewish students, and a few Turkic students from central Asia. Outside of the university, Majid also became aware of Koreans and Azerbaijanis and other Caucasians, especially in the open food markets. Those from outside Moscow were true outsiders, like himself, but he came to learn that the Jewish students, as well as the Caucasians, even if they were from Moscow, were also held apart as outsiders and felt unjustly spurned. He had never met a Jewish person before he came to Moscow, and he observed them with interest and curiosity, just as they watched him. This blend of peoples among his classmates and professors meant that there were many different face shapes and hair colors than what he had grown up with or seen before. There were far more fair-haired and blonds in his group than he had ever seen before, and he found in the girls that this was quite attractive, but he could not understand exactly why. (Perhaps it was the subliminal ideals of beauty projected by the stars of Soviet films which he had seen.) And those who were from the *nomenklatura* were also noticeably better dressed and fed than the others, and especially than Majid.

The first Jewish classmate he got to know was a short red-headed young man who was always wiping his nose with a stained linen handkerchief. (This perpetually runny nose intrigued Majid and stuck in his mind for the rest of his life, as first impressions often do.) His name was Avram Katzenellenbogen, but he was called Ari. He was outspoken, well- informed, nervous, and ambitious, and not particularly good looking or well-kept in his dress. Unlike nearly all his other classmates,

Majid noticed that Ari seemed to be current and well informed about world affairs, and he also seemed to care about what was happening in the rest of the Soviet Union or in the outside world as it had an impact on life in Soviet Russia, events which were usually not covered in the public media. He spoke about the war in Afghanistan and its winding down, about America and its presidential elections, about Israel, about riots in Baku, about the terrorist bombing of the Pan Am flight above Scotland, or about the catastrophe in the Armenian earthquake and how the state was unable to help the survivors. He had already well formulated ideas about literature and especially poetry, and he was quick to tell Majid about them. He said early on in their acquaintance, "You know, Slava, what is the point to poetry? I can understand it as a private activity, like writing diaries or memoires. So then keep it to yourself. But as a public activity it seems all rather senseless and antique, like the ancient Greek poets who publicly recited in the agoras and who created literature, a precursor to public drama or ritual singing and religious chants." On another occasion, after Ari became familiar with Majid's poetry—which he liked by the way—he said: "Slava, a famous poet said that in Russia a poet is more than a poet. He must've meant that the poet is the otherwise unspoken conscience of our people in confrontation with the state." "Ari, I don't think of myself as the conscience of any people. I'm only my own conscience. And I'm not unspoken, although not many have heard me yet." Ari laughed at him, "That's right, you are only outspoken, and without a conscience." Over the months of his first two years of study, Ari was the first person that Majid had ever encountered who openly expressed his contempt for the Soviet state (instead of obliquely or sarcastically), and who said that the only solution for an individual caught in such a society was to emigrate. Majid occasionally improvised short epigrams for Ari's amusement and would recite them to him in the hall ways or in the canteen after classes, in response to some critical remarks that Ari made about life in Russia. Ari used to boast teasingly about knowing Majid in front of others. "You should know my first Muslim friend,

Slava here. He's a poet in two languages. And what's more he's not an Azeri nor a Chechen."

Ari was also the first to claim that the secret police were listening in on the students. He even claimed that they had planted their agents amongst them, pretending to be students. "You see that one there? He's not 18 or 19. He's more like 25 or 26. He never says anything to anyone, but he's listening to everything. He claims his name is Leonid. You can almost see him taking notes on everything that's being said. Of course he's a secret police agent. So watch what you say around him." He also was the first to tell Majid that some of the teachers and professors also were reporters for the secret police. One day in late winter after the withdrawal from Afghanistan, when they had been discussing this spying on the university campus, Ari turned to Majid and said, "Slava, you know that the KGB spies on us, because we're potentially troublesome. But the authorities will never let me emigrate, because I'm Jewish. Ironic isn't it? They want Jews to be expelled, but then won't allow it when it comes to a concrete application."

You'd better watch carefully what you say
I'm always telling my sharp friend Ari
What he says is incendiaryand it burns the bugs of the Kay Gay Bay.
   (That's how KGB is pronounced in Russian)

In the middle of that first winter in Moscow, Majid turned 19. It was the time when he had to register for the conscription board of the Red Army. His mother forwarded to him by post, the notification from the draft administration and the documents he needed to submit for registration. Ordinarily he would have to be registered and then drafted into the Red Army for 2 years of conscription service. That meant at the very least going back to Kazan. Throughout the 1980s that also usually meant serving in Afghanistan for at least six months. But not long afterwards, after he had sent the documents for registration, he was sitting in the canteen on an especially cold dim winter's afternoon when his eyes were attracted by a special TV broadcast which was especially different than the usual fare. He looked closer at the grainy picture. It showed a large trestle bridge in a bright treeless country and a Red Army officer. In the video this officer saluted someone, received a Red Soviet flag from someone else, and he turned his back to the camera and marched onto the bridge where there were some armored personnel carriers waiting. They all together slowly moved away from the camera across the bridge. There was script running across the bottom of the screen. "Lt. General Boris Gromov, commander of the 40th Army of the Soviet Red Army leads the final withdrawal of our troops across the Friendship Bridge back to the Soviet Union, ending our fraternal support for the Afghan regime of Mohammad Najibullah against the Muslim mujahideen and the foreign supported insurrectionists." The video coverage switched over to what was ostensibly the other side of the bridge, showing the armored vehicles arriving in Soviet territory, flying red banners and manned by camouflaged troops who were smiling and looking rested in their clean uniforms. It was finally over. The Soviet intervention in Afghanistan which had lasted most of Majid's young life was finally over and Soviet TV was showing it, not live but with very little delay, to all the populace. This cruel war which had cost the Red Army nearly 100,000 casualties, among them young Tatar men he had met in Kazan, was over for the Soviet Union and Majid was not going to go there. As it was then, as he was a university student he was now eligible to receive an exemption from conscription. As he watched with others in the canteen, students who by and large did not understand the consequences of what they were watching, a great gladness rose up in his heart. He was not going to Afghanistan to fight for communism. At the same time he felt again bitterness at the huge waste and pointlessness of the war and all the suffering and lost lives which had occurred in that miserable country. He quietly watched the TV screen until the end of the transmission on Afghanistan. His classmates who watched distractedly and who were mostly Muscovites, seemed indifferent even dismissive and mocking to the news story and all it carried with it and it caused him a contrary feeling of rancor toward them. The truth was, Majid came to learn, his Muscovite classmates were indifferent to such news because they were almost totally unaware of the full horror of the war in Afghan. They had been uninformed and untouched by the war. It had not concerned them, and over the years of their youth they had not paid any attention to what little information had been made available to them, spoonfuls at a time. In fact, this was a general attitude of the Soviet people of that time: to put their heads down and not pay attention to what was actually going on in the world around them, for knowing would require reacting, taking a position, which was in Moscow always a difficult and dangerous thing to do. Majid had a long talk with Ari about the incident in the canteen. Ari had not had much contact with the war. Unlike Majid, he had not met anyone who had fought and suffered there, he had not listened to the stories of the returned conscripts. But he was not surprised by Majid's insights into the indifference and ignorance of their classmates of the events culminating in that mid-February photo-op on Friendship Bridge. "They are all people who are informed by their parents and grandparents—the same kind of people who participated in the decisions which caused us to invade Afghanistan in the first place."

The girls in Majid's classes were mostly slender and well dressed. In the final months of autumn when they were still lightly dressed and without heavy coats he was especially attracted by their figures. He was surprised to notice that contrary to the claim of Pushkin that a shapely leg was not to be found in Russian women, there were a lot of very shapely female legs in his class, clearly shown because dresses only fell to the knee as was the fashion then. (It was not yet the time when the women in Russia all switched over to wearing jeans or stretch pants, although those who could get them wore blue jeans smuggled in from the West.) He didn't find attractive many of the Russian girls' faces however. So many of them had broad high cheek bones and large almost bovine features which reminded him too much of Bashkirs, whose looks seemed to him too Asiatic, too Mongol. But there were still a lot who had thinner faces that he found very pretty, especially those with their long narrow almost straight noses having a slight turned up ball at the end. He liked the girls with small lips but wide mouths, but he noticed that the girls in his group were much less prone to smiling, than had been his schoolmates in Kazan. There were many who had light green-gray eyes, and mousy colored hair. There were also a lot more blond haired girls than he had ever encountered in his life, although he was only much later to learn that many of these were not natural blonds but instead had dyed hair. He also was surprised to see for the first time in his life young women who wore a little bit of lipstick and jewelry, mainly simple earrings, but also chains and brooches and sometimes amber necklaces. In short he encountered for the first time in a large sampling of young women, all the traps and snares they employ to attract the young men. But unfortunately for Majid, during his first year in Moscow University, these young women who were his classmates paid him not the slightest attention. Much of Majid's time at university, it seems, was given over to the observation of female pulchritude. And he wrote several poems about this study in these early years.

While Majid felt attracted to many of the university girls, he quickly realized that they didn't pay him any attention. Through the first winter he began to understand that Moscow girls were dour, self-infatuated, vain, and unsmiling, and uninterested in a short, dark-haired Tatar boy. They rebuffed his advances and sometimes even cut him dead when he tried to introduce himself. When he approached them or tried to introduce himself, they would, as they say, 'strike the third position', (a ballet position) that is, they became rigid and haughty in their bearing toward him. This aloofness to him by the pretty Muscovite girls (as well as his male classmates) contributed mightily to Majid's feeling of isolation and depression. As the first winter at university bore on, Majid's initial awe and wonder with Moscow began to shift to a darker view. His walks around the center, although much less frequent than in the fall, began to reveal to him the decay and general dilapidation of the city. It must be said that Moscow in the deep winter is a grim, murky unappealing place, but Majid was put off by a large number of discoveries about the city's sad state. At first he could not believe it, but then it caused him great consternation as he began to see that decrepitude and almost non-existent maintenance was a widespread condition of the city. Everywhere there were to be seen buildings shedding large patches of their plaster, with broken windows, cracked walls, peeling paint and rusted or broken pipes or iron railings. Some of these decrepit buildings were abandoned some derelict but many were still in use and many were even within the shadow of the Kremlin walls. Even the majestic Great Stone Bridge over the Moscow River next to the Kremlin's Water Pump Tower was missing large stones which had fallen from the underside vaulting and on the sides of the bridge cement façade work had crumbled in many places. The winter long nights were not illuminated by streets lights, which were dim, flickering or broken. The city in deep winter in any event looked dirty and shabby, with befouled or blackened snow piles everywhere, mud puddles filling the streets, trash bins were uncollected and overflowing, and the trees loomed overall bare, black and scrawny. But the dimness of short winter days could not hide the overall decay and neglected condition of the inner city. Even around Red Square and the Kremlin, the chief monuments were in dire need of new paint. And in many of the small alleys around the Kremlin there was a strong smell of this decay, the smell of mildew and rotting emanating from basements. The city more and more impressed him as a place that was slowly dying. The people of the city also lent to that impression as in the winter almost everyone wore black clothes, black coats or leather jackets, black fur hats or caps, with only a very few wearing dark brown or deep dark gray jackets—as if everyone was slouching off to funerals. Riding around on the metro in packed over-heated cars he also became aware that the residents of Moscow that winter smelled dirty. It was a smell of dirty unlaundered clothes, mothballs on coats and jackets which had hung in closets over the summer, and the fetid smell of sweaty people who could not afford to wash themselves often enough. The metro riders all around him not only smelled bad, they also noticeably had unwashed hair. And on especially cold days that winter there was also the intensely offensive odor of the drunken homeless men, (those who were called in particularly ugly officialese, bomzhe) who invaded the metro and sometimes even slept and urinated in the metro cars. He had never paid much attention to the economics of hygiene, but in the crowded spots of Moscow he realized that people could not afford soaps and detergents, nor they could find them in the shops if they could afford them. The combined smells of dirty clothes and the commuters in the metro made for an irritating cocktail of offensive smells which Majid conflated with the decay of the city above to further turn Majid's attitudes of the city to the negative. He began to realize that contrary to all the public pronouncements, the Soviet Union was neither youth and powerful nor rich, but it was mired deep in poverty and despair, even in its showcase capital city.

In was in this mood—the combination of feeling isolated and rebuffed at the university, the increasing awareness of the decrepitude of Moscow, and his increased sense that the Soviet society was bankrupt and rudderless—that it seems likely Majid wrote one of his early successful poems, which has been given by others the title 'Old Man Russia'. It seems he composed it late in the spring of 1989, at the end of his first year in the university and it was included in his first published book of poems which appeared late the next year.

> *I see him standing there under a crumbling arch*
> *All hope drained from his rheumy gray eyes*
>
> *Slowly he takes a wheezy breath*
> *Raising a cigarette to his lips, he stares unfocused.*
>
> *No dreams does he see there, no futur*
> *He has dispensed his life in violent throes*

To see no result and now his energy is spent.
He never once did anything of his free will.

They gave him a rifle and said "Kill!"
And he killed faceless invaders

Sprawled in frozen mud while all
His mates around him were dying

They gave him a trowel and hod and said "Build!"
And he built walls which leaked drafts

And tilted and not long afterwards collapsed
But he had no house at the end of his building.

They gave him a shovel and overalls and said "Drive!"
And he shoveled coal into the dynamo and rushed through the smoky air

They gave him a woman and said, "Make a socialist family!"
And he took her and fucked her and beat her

He squeezed out of her two children, like
Squeezing water from a mop, but then he lost them.

They did not give him food, nor any vodka
But he somehow ate little and drank a lot.

Now they command him nothing more and say, "Keep quiet!"
And he does, having nothing but a wrinkled shirt and faded overalls.

His face is deeply creased, he's missing a finger
And his hands are tattooed, he's known the prison yard.

He has no dreams, never had any, and as he watches
The sun slips below the horizon, he wonders if he'll see another

Sunset, but then he sees little anymore, only a clouded horizon
Not sunrises nor sunsets, not family nor

Happy proletarian society—he is alone and sullen
He smokes his cigarette to the bitter fag end.

A lone car drives by, splashing gutter water
On his dirty cracked boots. He shifts his feet

A slip of plaster falls off the house where he stands
And then the city is dark, only dim streetlights flicker weakly.

I see this man everywhere in every town and city of Russia.
He is not free to dream, to think, nor even to die.

After Majid first performed this poem in public it attracted a lot of attention, mostly the critical kind. Many despised the negative view of a Russian man, saying it was too glum and unfairly harsh. Then there were those who correctly read the poem as a metaphor for the state, and not a portrait of an actual man. These critics were extremely harsh in their attacks on Majid. They were especially enraged that he was able to get it published, saying such anti-Soviet pabulum was criminal, defamatory, and would have been cause for imprisonment in earlier times. None of the critics remarked on the quality of the verse. But—let me say in spite of my clumsy translation, that it is a brilliant work of poesy, in rhyme and metrics. And those that heard Majid recite it says that he delivered this grim message with an intonation and cadence that was moving. Some said he was a new "physician" for the sick soul of Russia, with great insights in his diagnosis. There were cries of 'Bravo!' and 'Slava!' (which means glory) from the audience when he finished reciting it at one venue.

There is an interesting story about how Majid published his first collection of poems. Over the winter our hero the poet made several trips into Moscow to visit Krivonosov. On the first visit, he prepared several poems to recite for him. The more experienced poet was very impressed, but he had a poor ear and he could not really enjoy and fathom the richness in these poems without reading a printed text. His response to a poem came out of textual study, he did not really fully understand the phonetic meaning, the cadences, or the metrical and musical qualities. He simply did not understand those facets of a recited poem. So on his next visit to Victor Krivonosov's garret, Majid brought a few of his poems written out on individual sheets of paper (with his BIC ballpoint pen). Krivonosov could see that he was in the presence of a poet of real talent and quality. After perhaps his third or fourth monthly poetry circle meeting in the spring, Krivonosov proposed to Majid that he should publish some of his poems in a book. "How many poems do you have to put in a first collection?" he asked. "Let me think. I've never counted them." "Do you think you could put together 30-35 finished poems?" Krivonosov asked a little sharply half expecting that Majid would not have so many. "Oh, I probably have composed in Russian five or six times that amount." This was an answer which nearly bowled Krivonosov over. "Of course the problem is that I would have to select which ones would best go in the first collection and I would have to collect them." "Have you a large number printed already?" "No, that is a problem. I have these four poems, and maybe another four or five that I have handwritten out back at the dorm room. The rest are in my memory." This last statement completely took Krivonosov by surprise. "Are you serious?" "Well of course, I memorize all my verse. Can you think of anything worse, than having printed copies burned or stolen?" Krivonosov was dismayed and left speechless for several minutes. "How can that be?" "It's not so unusual. In her last two decades Anna Akhmatova memorized all her poems because she was afraid the authorities would take her written texts away and destroy them. And you know she was always able to recall her own verses." Krivonosov continued to stare in disbelieve at our hero, his mouth hanging open. He had completely underestimated Majid. It suddenly occurred to him that the few samples of handwritten verse in his hands were a very small portion of a considerable oeuvre, and if they were representative, they were a sampling of many excellent poems.

"At any rate, the poems you select would have to be typed when we choose which ones to publish. And then they would have to be edited and re-typed. Do you have a typewriter?" "No, how can I get one?" "We'll find you one here at the Institute." And that was how Majid bought his first typewriter. His friend Ari helped Majid finance it. He lent Majid most of the 35 rubles (an average monthly salary in Moscow) that it cost and Majid paid him back in installments over the next year. Of course he had to learn how to type as well, which is not at all straightforward using the Cyrillic keyboard, and learning to type on his own. When he first got the machine, he of course was a hunt and peck typist, but slowly he learned to type more and more quickly and accurately. Still it took him months to type out 40 of his poems, well into his second year at the university.

In the meanwhile, Innokenti excitedly came to Majid early in the second university term, which would have been in the Fall of 1989 according to my estimates, and said he had bought tickets for both of them to attend a concert recital of the great bard of Arbat, Bulat Okudzhava and that they would just have to go, as such opportunities were rare. Indeed it was a rare event. Okudzhava was already in his mid-sixties at that time and acted old and sick, (this was just about the time that state authorities announced that the average life expectancy of a Soviet male had fallen to 60, an announcement which caused a scandal in a society which projected youthful vigor and activity in its official propaganda) and as it turned out he gave only a very few more public concerts in the remaining years of his life. The concert was organized by 'Yunost' (which means youth) the literary journal for young people and they had advertised it. As a result the hall where Okudzhava performed was packed, young poetry lovers stood lining the walls around right up to the apron of the stage where more sat on the floor crowding around him. The hall was a small one. The séance had been organized by the Soviet literary magazine for young people (which was called appropriately "Yunost" or "Youth") and, although the featured performer was already an old man by Soviet standards and so many of his songs related to the 60s, most of the audience were comprised of young people, plus a few tired looking middle-aged dissidents also in attendance. The only celebrity Majid recognized in the audience was the famous clown, Yury Nikulin, and that was only because he had featured in many popular movies. Majid and Innokenti had seats about 12 rows back, and it was difficult to see the performer because a tall Russian man was seated directly in front of Majid. But he could perfectly hear Okudzhava in his thin, weak voice chanting his poems of life in Arbat, of resistance to oppression, of times past both sad and contented accompanied to the few simple chords on his guitar. He realized that Okudzhava was not a musician who set poetry to music, but really a true poet who recited his own poetry to the spare accompaniment of a guitar which really only provided cadence and some emphasis to the metrics and the words. Majid was deeply impressed by the performance. Okudzhava seemed to perform out of a feeling of great pain and suffering—his songs were not joyful—his expression remained dour throughout the two hour performance. The concert was more a social event than anything else and it generated tremendous excitement in the crowd who applauded vigorously at the end—even then Okudzhava did not even faintly smile. It was a social event of the small dissident crowd, the young liberals and cultural "oppositionists" to use the term so often used then. In the audience there were other dissident poets. Innokenti pointed some of them out to Majid. Majid saw Victor Krivonosov standing and leaning against the wall toward the front. When he caught his eye, they waved to each other, and Victor signaled to him to join him when the concert was over.

After the crowd got to its feet Majid and Innokenti squeezed through to the apron of the stage where Victor was standing. He lead them onto the stage and behind the rear drapes to a small room, which was already filling with devotees and fans of Okudzhava, who was smoking a cigarette and mopping his head trying not to make eye contact with anyone. He was looking pallid and thoroughly exhausted, but relaxed.

Next to the fans and those bearing adulation and seeking to boost their self-importance by getting a word from Okudzhava, Majid felt that he was standing in the presence of a spent poet, one much abused by his society. So he stood aloof. But Victor seemed to have already made the acquaintance of Okudzhava and he pulled Majid forward. "Bulat, as always we are overwhelmed by your words. I especially liked your new song returning to the theme of Speranza." "It is not new." "Are you going to release any poems soon?" "The song about the lost young man was a new song." "Any new published works?" "I have a novel ready, but they still won't let me publish. There are some new records that have come out recently." "I want to introduce you to a new young poetic talent, Bulat. He's from Kazan." "Really? People think I'm from Georgia, but I'm from Moscow. Glad to meet you." Majid paused, and said, "The pleasure is actually all mine. But I'm an orphan via Kazan from Ufa. I thought your singing was fine, but your poems remind me of those of Rafi Mustafa written late in his time." Majid spoke these words with a distinctly poetic inflection, with rhyme and cadence. Again Victor noticed again how when Majid spoke he almost naturally was reciting verses. Perhaps Okudzhava also noticed at that time, but no one will ever know. Then Majid continued much more straightforward, "Do you know how I can get some poems published? Will 'they' let me get published?" Okudzhava turned his dark eyes on Majid for a moment and then turned away and took another suck on his cigarette. "You should ask my friend from *Yunost*. He's over there. Andrei Dmitrievich, talk to this young man." And like that passing them onto the editor-in-chief of *Yunost*, Okudzhava dismissed them from his court of adulators.

But Andrey Dmitrievich was more welcoming. Majid and Victor spoke to him and arranged to meet him at his editorial offices to see if Majid could get a poem published in the journal. And Andrey Dmitrievich was more than a mere manager and editor. He also was an accomplished and published poet whose poetry had a cheerful, hopeful, and positive outlook on life reflecting his own generous, gregarious personality. When Majid met him in his offices near Pushkin Square, he showed interest in Majid's texts, read one of them quickly, and although he was rushed, he introduced him to several members of the editorial staff and passed around the sheets of paper on which Majid had hand written three poems. Everyone seemed enthusiastic and welcoming. Several months later, the poem appeared. They had not even informed him before then that they had accepted this poem for publication, nor that it was to appear in the November issue. It was Ari who discovered it when he read an issue of *Yunost* and recognizing his friend's name as the author he rushed with the journal to show Majid. Majid looked at the page for a moment or two, struck by the uncanny way that the printed word on a page appears so different from the image of the spoken word he held in his head. He put the journal down and recited the short poem more for himself than for Ari.

She moves as lightly as the dewfall over the grass
Her quick coy smile invites me
Her youthful slim beauty enchants one and all.
She inspires, arouses, attracts all eyes
She is a beautiful goddess bearing cups
Of a magical wine that intoxicates the senses.
Her alabaster skin glows, her small breasts heave.
I can only think of love when I behold her.
She bids me to drink from her golden beakers
Then laughs softly and flits on to another.
Sister of the Muses she no less incites my words
And rouses in me a lifelong devotion.
I can only dream of her sweet kisses.
I could sing for her but my hearts beats too loudly.
Then just as the sun melts off the dew from the lawn
She—our goddess Hebe—is gone without a sound
Perhaps slipping behind bowers of fragrant jasmine.

The journal had given a title to the poem which Majid in his fashion typically had not. They had named it Hebe. Ari listened intently and nodded his head with approval when Majid finished reciting it. After a moment's pause he asked, "Was there any girl here that you were specifically addressing in this poem?" Majid looked at him strangely and then said "I'm not sure there was. Perhaps she was a composite of many of the pretty girls in our class. I did see a photo of a marble statue of Hebe at the time, and I recognized in her some of our prettier classmates." Ari smiled impishly, "Oh so you've seen a number of our girls with no clothes on?" Majid shook his head. He thought back about the portrait he had created of a beautiful young woman, and he added, "But perhaps I was inspired last year by a painting I had seen by Modigliani of the young, nude Anna Akhmatova, his lover for a brief time. Modigliani spoke of her as his inspiration." Ari did not know what Majid was referring to and the exhibition in the Pushkin Museum where this painting had been on loan had since closed. "Maybe not. She was not so terribly beautiful of course—I mean Anna—and in most of her photos and painted portraits she never smiled. And I can hardly say with truth that Anna Akhmatova has been my beautiful Muse. Besides my Beauty in the poem is standing, perhaps in a garden. Anna was lying on a couch, perhaps waiting for the painter to mount her. As for the inspiration, my Beauty is classical and ethereal, whether or not she is dressed or naked. Anna in that pose captured by Modigliani was carnal."

Although Ari had noticed this poem and made the connection with its author, few on the campus or in his classes made the connection, or perhaps even noticed the poem in Yunost. But that was not the general reaction. The journal got a strong favorable response to Majid's poem and inquiries about its author. So keen was the response and positive comments that Andrey Dmitrievich had begun to search for Majid and he inquired from Victor Krivonosov on how to find Majid. Victor told Majid all this the next time he went to the Gorky Institute to attend Victor's LITO. At that meeting Majid had taken with him a few more poems that he had written out and he recited them for the small circle of poetry students who regularly attended. At that meeting, Victor also read out a poem of his own from a typed sheet, but his style of reading and declaiming was poor, made worse perhaps by his poor vision and the fact that he could not recite his poems from memory but had to read them, as if it was a school reading of a foreign poet's work. They discussed the poems that Majid read for the circle and decided on which ones were best to submit to Yunost. A few days later, Majid went again to the offices of *Yunost*. Andrey Dmitrievich was once more very welcoming, enthusiastic and glad to see Majid. Again he quickly glanced at the pages that Majid had brought with him, two of them typed on his recently acquired typewriter, and just as before, he called in some of the other editors to also look at them. They also quickly perused the texts and looked up at the editor-in-chief, looking satisfied and approving. Andrey Dmitrievich blurted out, "Why is it Slava, that you don't give titles to your poems?" Majid thought for a moment, then slowly answered. "I happen to think that it is pretentious to give the poem a title or name. That takes away from the listeners the pleasure of determining for themselves what the real objective of the poem should be, and even giving it their own title. In older cultures, poems were not named. They were referred to only by their first line." Everyone accepted that, and Andrey put aside the pages on his desk. "Fine, we'll think about where we might print one or more of these poems." Then out of nowhere as if he suddenly remembered the most important news, Andrey said. "Oh and by the way, Okudzhava told me he liked your poem and he told me that the publishing house where he used to work might be willing to make a small print run of a collection of your poems. Wouldn't you like to put together a collection of your poems for printing?" What had happened in the interim is that Krivonosov had gone back to Okudzhava after his last concert and had asked his help in getting Majid's poems published, and the older bard had gone to his former employers and convinced them that they should publish Majid's verses. It was true also that Okudzhava had liked the poem that had appeared in *Yunost*; something in it made him reminisce about his own difficult and painful youth and his first loves. There in the editor's office Majid was over the moon and he agreed to put together the collection as soon as possible. He spent the next several months slowly but feverishly typing out the thirty or so poems that he had chosen with the assistance of Krivonosov to publish. He wasn't ready with this collection until the middle of the next winter of 1990.

That winter was not very cold. Or perhaps it would be better to say that it was very cold, but only for a very short spell. For the entire month of February there was a major thaw when the temperatures allowed only for chilly rainfall which turned the uncollected snow piles around the city into huge puddles in the streets and dirty slushy expanses on the sidewalks and in the parks. Cars would careen around the city sending great waves of brown filthy cold water onto those unfortunates near the streets and staining the walls with a grimy mess. But for the whole month it was still cloudy and gloomy and the scene added to Majid's wintertime depression. Moscow came more and more to represent in his mind a murky, oppressive city. The first bright sunny day did not come until early April and spring as is its wont did not really arrive until mid-May.

In that winter semester he began a course on Shakespeare. The professor lectured in Russian, but the material examined was in the original English. Majid had studied now enough English that he could read and recite the texts, with some improper accents and pronunciation, of course, but he was trying to capture the sound and cadence of English metrics and during the late winter he applied himself to this effort, just as he had with French. His teacher of English language was very helpful in this regard. An Englishman, he was more interested in teaching his students spoken English than absolutely proper grammatical rules. Outside of class time, this Englishman, who had a thespian background and adored Shakespeare, would help Majid with the proper stresses and pronunciation of Shakespeare's works included in this course. The last third of the course focused on Shakespeare's sonnets. These sparked intense interest in Majid and beside studying them and memorizing them in the English originals he began a practice that he followed through the rest of his life with other poetic forms, he would try translating them into Russian poems.

It was also during that semester that he met and began hanging out with Larissa, or Lara, as she was called. She was a student in the history faculty and Majid had first glimpsed her in a peculiar light when she was standing one inky black late winter night under a yellow street lamp on the campus. The scene was painterly. She had been standing perfectly still for a long time when Majid first noticed her and started looking at her. Her face was turned to the left and her gaze was cast down, almost wistfully she seemed to be studying something on the ground. The weak yellow light etched her face in deep shadows, and dressed in a long dark navy blue coat. She wore a black knit cap which let her long inky black hair bulge out and curl over her shoulders and around her chin. Majid walked up to her and asked if she had some difficulties and if he could help her. She turned very slowly toward him, but still not focused on him, as if some unwanted noise had jolted her out of a reverie. He then introduced himself and asked again if she were looking for something. He asked if she were cold standing so long in the winter air. Still she did not say anything to him but looked toward him but her eyes looked through him as if she were still far away. She had the most beautiful almond shaped eyes, a long nose, thin lips which appeared in that light to have purple lipstick on them, and a lovely heart- shaped face. She was taller than Majid and she again cocked her head to one side and looked down at him almost as if she were a curious owl looking at a mouse that had spoken to her. He asked her if she would like to get a mug of tea, to get out of the cold. And she consented with only a faint 'yes' that was almost like a small groan. He led her to the canteen almost taking her by the elbow because she walked with a slow stuttering and deliberate gait over the snow. There in the canteen not far from the samovar which heated the middle of the room under the flickering fluorescent lamps they talked for two hours about nothing in particular. Under her heavy coat and scarf, she was wearing a long knit dress which clung to her figure, accentuating her curves. She was indeed beautiful, curvaceous and slender, languidly beautiful. She eventually told him her name was Larissa, or Lara as everyone called her, Lara Antipova. It was some months before he began to learn about her story on that cold night, but from those hours in the canteen, Majid felt close to her, and felt that she wanted to be close with him. But from then on she remained a mysterious presence in Majid's life throughout the remaining years of his life. After he left her at the metro station that evening, he wanted desperately to see her again and asked if they might meet again. Her answer, as always as he was to learn, was obscure, but basically she said 'Maybe they would.' He would slowly learn little bits about Lara over the next two years only in riddles and incomplete sentences. In those early years, she remained a mystery who kept her personal story and secrets wrapped up in conundrums (a very Russian thing it has long been known).

They met thereafter in the canteen, sometimes between classes, and in the library where they sat near each other as they studied. As the mild winter melted away they met more and more often. As the winter turned to spring they would take long walks around the huge area of the university campus, or out along the overlook on the palisade atop Lenin Hills. Eventually they kissed and embraced, and after those first tentative kisses Majid was immediately hooked on her. In late April, she consented to climbing up the ten flights of stairs to Majid's dorm room, and they made love all through that night. They did several more times, but Lara did not like the long climb up the stairs to his room, and having no alternative places to have sex they stopped. She was very particular about their love making; she dictated strict rules: sex only in a darkened room, he must not touch her nipples, no biting or leaving love bruises, she didn't like him to see her completely naked or to look closely at her private parts, and likewise she was not interested in looking at his body or genitals, no beating or smacking her, and she did not want to talk with him after they completed their copulation. But she did want the sex, she did luxuriate in the short verses her composed for her and recited in her ear, she did want to achieve orgasm with him but she was indifferent to his own orgasm, and slowly but steadily she began to react affectionately to Majid and his caresses. She loved his poetry and especially how he declaimed it. Over time he began to realize that while she enjoyed his companionship and just being close—she definitely would become very aroused in her passion with him—she did not love him. But he felt that he was falling in love with her, he was strongly attracted by her dark mysterious character and her languid personality, and the slow, measured way that she doled out to him her affections. But he did not come to know her very well. Around the last time they made love that spring in that tenth floor room, she told him—almost as if she had considered it a mere curiosity, a trifle that changed nothing—she had been married—to a man named Antipov— and divorced already even though she was not yet 22 years old. (Majid never did learn her maiden name.)

So it was, as part of his exercises in writing and translating sonnets in the style of Shakespeare, that Majid composed a trial sonnet (one of many it seems which were directed at Lara) which later became known and was published several years later in the Russian decade. I give it here in English in my stumbling effort to reproduce the sonnet form and rhyme of our poet hero (who after all cannot object to my lame efforts because he is no longer with us in this world). I don't think I stretched the English sentence structure too much to make this a passable translation of what Majid wrote in Russian. I ask the reader not to be too harsh with my translation:

> *For my sweet Love, I took a proposal*
> *Thinking of the happiness we'd have together*
> *Of holding her in my arms in her bridal*
> *Dress of silk, of hearing her heart a'flutter.*

I dreamt of our future moments of passion
Of our fond embraces and making a family
Our joyous outings and loving I'd envision.
She'd speak to me sweetly or smile at me shyly

Thus I scribbled for her tender verses
Of love, rushing to her my troth to bring
Sadly, my Beloved turns away, her brow creases
And she frowns and says "Take back your ring."

"In truth my poet friend I'd most welcome
If in my presence you'd scarcer become."

I have never been able to find out if this sonnet reflects an actual incident which occurred between Majid and Lara in the early spring of 1990. If there was such an incident he remained silent about it in the following years. I am sure even if I were to find Larissa, she would not tell me either. So was this sonnet, which he did not name but which in Shakespearean fashion he gave the number four, merely an exercise or was there something between them that happened at that time which prompted him to write a sonnet addressing the incident? I'd like to believe that there was. But we'll never know.

These events of the early and late spring were not the end of Majid's relationship with Lara. They continued being companions for strolls and presumably lovers when during the next university year—her last at the university—Majid moved to his own room on the fourth floor and they resumed sleeping together. It was only many years later that he learned that Lara had been raped by her step father when she was a young teenager living in a small apartment in Novogiriyevo with her mother. Through her teenage years her step father would have sex with her in one room and then beat her mother in the next room to cow her and keep her from protesting too publicly. Once she let slip out that she had married Antipov as a mistake, as a way to escape her brutish stepfather. Antipov and she had both been not yet 19 when they wed.

They remained married only two years, and she found after she began studies at the university that he was nearly an imbecile and insufferable. These were parts of Larissa which Majid learned much later than 1990. It seems probable that Lara calculated that she needed a comfortable and safe shelter so she moved in with Majid in his fourth floor room during his third university year. She hated and feared the idea of going back either to her parents' apartment or to the apartment of Antipov's parents where she had fled when she had been married to the brutish Antipov. To her part of the cost of taking shelter with Majid was having sex with him. But they did not become like a domestic couple, a married pair. She stayed with him the last two years of his university course even after her graduation. After that she slipped away just as inscrutably as when she had first entered into his life.

It was in that late spring of 1990 that his first collection of poets appeared. The printer made 2,000 copies of this small book called simply 'Verses from my youth'. But it is hard to say that they were published as the printer made no effort to distribute or market them. Instead they delivered to Majid several dozen bundles of the small format books wrapped in brown paper and string. He asked Andrey Dmitrievich if *Yunost* might advertise them and sell them, and when they agreed he left four dozen of these bundles at their offices. Each bundle had twenty four volumes in it. Needless to say, he did not sell very many. He tried to convince the Moscow Book Store (its name again banally simple) to offer them for sale, but they said that as he was not a member of the Soviet Writers' Union they could not. The printer sold only about 150 copies for a small amount of money. He sent a copy with a long letter to his mother in Kazan and to the Buterbrodskis he sent four copies. They sent him back letters in reply gushing with praise and amazement. They also inquired when Majid might be coming back to Kazan to visit with them. The book did not receive any review or comment in the press. Even *Yunost* did not comment on it, even though it advertised it and sold it. In general these books are now hard to find in Moscow.

You might if you're lucky find a copy in one of the used book stalls on the Arbat. I myself was very lucky to be able to acquire an unused copy a few years later after I first learned about this poet and attended one of his recitals.

The coincidence of the appearance of his first published book of verses and his first public recital which occurred in May that year was almost too much to think that it was anything other than providence or the divine intervention of his muses. He had spent some time early in that semester trying to organize a recital within the faculty of philology and literature and he finally got approval to give a public recital in one of the university's auditoria on the upper campus if he agreed to share his performance with one or two other poets from the department. Majid found one other through the recommendation of Innokenti, who himself did not want to perform his own poems. As it was, this other poet wrote some interesting ideas into his verses but in the latest style: that is, using street language and slang, unrhymed verses, lots of insider references which only students of contemporary modernist Western poetry understood, and full of loud declamations, anger, and expletives, and in short he declaimed rather bombastic poems. To Majid's advantage this latter's recital style was impossible to listen to: ugly, unmusical and unmodulated, and with a falsetto bass and tenor voice like the one that Louis Armstrong used and Vysotsky adopted as his signature. In short this other poet was difficult to understand, and his versifying was awkward and often hard to hear and the audience did not care for him. By contrast, the audience—which comprised mostly young women including Lara, but also including Viktor Krivonosov and his friends and disciples as well as some of the editors from *Yunost* and some other literary journals—were very responsive and pleased to hear Majid's declamation of his poetry. You could even say they were in raptures. His performance included several of the poems which had appeared in his book, including Hebe, My Father's Voice, The Muse, and Beauty, as well as four of his sonnets. It was a performance of poetry about love. And the applause at the end of the recital, after Majid finished (for he had gone second), was long and loud. He had thought of bringing along with him several bundles of his brown paper wrapped books. The result of this warm reception was that there in the auditorium as the crowd of girls pressed around him with their adulations, he was able to sell more than 50 copies of his newly minted book (at seven rubles each, it was the first time that Majid had ever earned or held a lot of money). This first public performance in Moscow was Majid's breakthrough and the real beginning of his public career. The word around town spread that there was a new poetic voice in Moscow and it was one of a genius. Even a review appeared in one of the literary newspapers. Majid learned that evening that his natural audience and consumers for his poetry were young women. His good boyish looks helped him in this respect greatly. He would not forget it in the future. It's hard to know when Majid composed the poem entitled Beauty, but it appeared in his first collection and apparently he recited it without embarrassment at his first public Moscow recital. I quote my translation of it here because it was to be a regular and popular poem which he recited at future recital performances. It was written in rhymed iambic pentameter with an added half line, in an ABBAC CDDCE scheme which I have modified to try and give some sense of the rhyme of this poem.

> *From across a stadium lost in a crowd*
> *Her beauty is list in the faceless blur*
> *But standing in the middle of the field*
> *Already her shapely figure is clear*
> *Her hair is brown and shines proud.*
>
> *Standing closer still now on the next platform*
> *It's obvious she is a beauty, a queen.*
> *She had the ideal proportion of waist to hips*
> *Her hair glints in the sun, now I spy*
> *Her joyful eyes, a pink smile sits on her lips.*

Across a small room she is most beautiful to me
A goddess of fair figure, slender sculpted legs
And now inner beauty sparkles in her eyes
The skin on her face is smooth and white
Her bust is gently round and curved like her thighs.

At arm's length she is Venus rising from the sea.
I am seduced by her glowing beauty
But I note a mole on her lip and her cheek
Her blue eyes are not quite the same size
Her lovely breast like marble but not symmetrical.

Even closer still in tight embrace a landscape
I espy that is hard to say is the beauty
Of a woman. Small bumps rise on her arm
Blemishes next to reddened, wrinkled skin
Now all I see is a freshly plucked hen.

Intimate now my view focuses close
Like Donne's lucky flea, my eye now wanders
Through a dark forest of bent pine trunks
Standing in the soft soil of Venera's hill.
Do we call this secret landscape beauty still?

So we call her beautiful but tis hard
To say that she is such, when from afar
Or intensely close in. She is a beauty
In the mid-range of our view. Too far
We lose sight, too close blemishes appear.

How strange then that our words do not capture
The degrees of beauty as she draws near.
Is she then most beautiful at a distance of five feet?
Or as poor Gulliver learned, is she most
Hideous when pressed up too close?

After the June exams, Majid said good-bye to Innokenti. He had graduated and as he was a Ukrainian from outside Moscow, he did not have the propiska (the residence permit) to continue to live in Moscow so he returned to Odessa, his home town. It was a sad moment for Majid as Innokenti, with his impeccably good taste and a sharp ear for rhyme and metrics, had been an invaluable and tireless and constructive critic of Majid's poems. Innokenti was one of the very few who witnessed the poet in the act of creation. He noted that Majid would become very detached and focused and would recite verses barely out loud, sometimes repeating lines until he had the right meter and rhyme to accompany an earlier line. He also listened carefully to Majid's open recitals and offered insights that Majid usually found to be very accurate and helpful. Innokenti especially harped on the importance of alliteration in poetics and on many of Majid's verses he offered suggested changes which incorporated alliterative words. He felt that alliteration, especially of consonant vowel combinations, was as important as rhyme. Majid valued Innokenti's comments and counted him one of a number of important mentors of his work. They maintained an active correspondence in the following years, but Majid did not see Innokenti again for more than 10 years. After his departure Majid some time later came to feel that although Innokenti had a wonderful ear for the music of poetry, he had nothing really to say and that was why he composed so few poems. Innokenti now teaches literature at a university in Kiev and he has written several articles about Majid's poetry and his contribution to Russian verse. I have spoken with him at length and he too considers Majid to have been the major Russian poet of the late 20th century.

Not long after Innokenti's departure, Majid himself also left for a summer camp in the Crimea. He spent seven weeks at a camp for university students from around the Soviet Union. It was located in at Koktebel (the Blue Height) in the mountains above the sea not far from Yalta. The camp had structured activities, mostly sports and play, regular trips to a beach, some drama programs, and visits to historic sites. Most important for Majid at that time, there was ample food at the camp which included in its program three full hot meals a day and afternoon tea. It was the first time in two years that Majid was not always hungry. It was during one of these visits off the camp that Majid met some young men who were Crimean Tatar. He was surprised at how easy it was to communicate with them in his own Tatar language—the two languages are very closely related. These young men he met were recently returned from the exile that Stalin had imposed on their parents and grandparents. Many of them hung around the camp's entrance offering tourist services to the tourists who drove by, such as leading horseback rides or grilling kebabs, or selling trinkets and handmade mementoes. After Majid met a few of them, he would sometimes leave the camp and spend some time talking with these young men. None of them were old enough to remember the expulsion, but they remembered the miserable lives they had led as outcasts and politically undesirables in harsh steppes of Kazakhstan or Uzbekistan. They with their parents had moved back, illegally, to the Crimea when Soviet controls had weakened in the last years of the 1980s and were just scraping out a living. One evening Majid went "AWOL" (for in fact he had to be accounted for at morning and evening roll calls and could not leave the camp premises without permission which was rarely ever given) so he could meet with some of these young men who took him that evening to their homes in the newly rebuilt Tatar settlement of Ba'chasaray, which had once been the capital of the Crimean Tatars. The settlement still looked like a squatters' or refugee camp;, small unpainted carton shaped cinder blocks houses uniformly spaced and separated from each other by narrow dirt lanes. They all had just one window and one door but they were distinguished one from the other by their roofs, either flat or slightly sloped finished with hammered galvanized iron. The evening Majid arrived in this settlement which was located outside the historic town of Bakhchisaray which the Soviets had cleared of all Crimean Tatars and had partially restored as a tourist destination he was taken to one of these non-descript houses where he was introduced as "one of ours".

He was taken to the main room, which was small but furnished only with cushions and floor mats so that it seated a large number of people comfortably on the floor. Tea was brought for Majid with some small savory cookies and fresh figs. Then over the course of the evening men of all ages came to meet and visit with Majid each telling his own story of exile and return or of the difficulty of reestablishing their lives in Crimea. Around the end of the evening twilight an older man came in and he was introduced as Karim Ozanov, the community poet. Majid told him that he too was a poet, but he composed poems only in the Volga Tatar and Russian lanugages. Ozanov was impressed and invited Majid to recite and for the next hour the two took turns in reciting their verses entirely from memory. Majid was surprised at how much he understood from the older man's verses even though linguists considered that the two languages were distinct and derived from different tribal sources. Finally around ten o'clock that night, Mr. Ozanov offered to tell his own long ballad epic, which was called 'The Ballad of the Tatar Ghazi'. This ballad was not in fact Ozanov's but was a poetic epic of four or five centuries age which had been handed down through the generations from one minstrel to the next, each who spent their youth memorizing it. Everyone in the room strongly urged him to recite it, and some even encouraged him to recite certain sections of the ballad before others. Majid had never heard an epic ballad recited before and he too encouraged the poet to commence. But Ozanov excused himself and said the hour was too late that he could only recite four or five of the twelve adventures that night. Everyone was agreed. Ozanov reinforced himself with some tea and pastries and he started. Over the next two and a half hours he must have recited about 3,000 lines of verse, all from memory. Majid often lost track of the meaning, but so did many of the other listeners in the room, as the language was archaic and elaborately poetic and the material culture that the ballad described was mostly unknown to all those in attendance with its rich references to types of sabres, daggers, scimitars, and bows, horses and their saddles and their accoutrements, and dishes of food all of which had long ago disappeared from Crimea and the steppe lands around it. Ozanov was visibly tired when he stopped, but his auditors could have stayed for more. Majid was immensely impressed. He was especially impressed by the repetitive metrics and cadence that Ozanov employed to declaim his verses. Not even the Book of Joseph was so long or elaborate. This night was another one of those sharp impressions that would stay in the visual memory of Majid for the rest of his life. It is very possible that Ozanov's performance of this ballad is what planted the seed in Majid's ear to write his own long ballad some years later, The Ballad of Salawat, or the Ballad of Eldar as it is also known.

In his third and fourth year at university Majid continued studies of Russian, French, and English poetry. He took courses on the poetry of Pushkin, Blok, Baudelaire, and Mickiewicz as well as a survey course on English poetry. He was interested in studying contemporary Russian poetry. But the university at that time reflecting the views of the cultural authorities in the communist party was still very conservative (and it should be said anti-Semitic) in its offerings and had almost nothing to offer which the communist authorities found subversive, anti-revolutionary, or objectionable, which meant nearly all of the outstanding Russian poets of the 20th century were officially banished from the curriculum. That meant Akhmatova, Pasternak, Khodasevich, Nabokov, and especially Mandelstam were non-persons with no record of poetic achievement acknowledged by the university. It goes without saying that the living and working poets of that time, most of whom were critical of regime, like the popular refusnik poets such as Gangnus, Vozkresensky, Okudzhava, or Akhmadulina, were especially anaethema. Their works could only be studied surreptitiously in samizdat copies in student organized gatherings after hours outside the formal curriculum.

Majid during these two years also continued to compose his own poems, which now he would type out once he had finished composing them and had recited them, and he also spent long hours translating foreign language poems into Russian, including many of his own verses that he had written up to then in Tatar. Lara moved in with him not long after the start of his third year and became his sexual partner, although their relationship was still not one of love and wild passion. She remained secretive and aloof from him, and she demonstrated little affection for him outside of their bed. Perhaps worse, she did not appreciate his poetry at all, or at best was mostly indifferent to it. He wondered if she even understood it at all. It was clear to him that she had no "ear" for poetic speech. This was probably due to her overriding sensibility which was dominated by a constant striving for material gain and tactical advantage in her interactions with people. After living together for about 18 months one day she just wandered off without any break- up or farewell, and eventually she moved in with a new boyfriend who owned a nice apartment in the city center as well as a new black Mercedes, an emblem of real power and prestige in early 1991 Moscow.

In these two years Majid also gave more public recitals of his works. He arranged and organized these recitals himself. Two were held in auditoria at the university but one he tried to arrange at the large lecture hall in the Polytechnic Museum on Novaya Square. In this he was not successful—it is a very large hall and his renown at that time was not sufficient to convince the managers that they could fill the hall for a literary evening based only on Majid's poems. The manager there in turning him down exclaimed to Majid that even the dulcet tones of Orpheus probably could not fill that hall in those impoverished days, even though in earlier times, Mayakovsky, Yevgheny Gangnus and Okuzhava had performed in it to large audiences. It was in going there that Majid stumbled over the great Chekist police master, Felix Dzherzhinsky—or to be more accurate his colossal statue, Iron Felix, which at that time stood in Lubyanka Square with his back to the Polytechnic. He was struck by the angry, even bloodthirsty look on Felix's face. Then following Iron Felix's glare, he saw the big sign across the square, Detsky Mir, or Children's World, and it immediately struck him as a vile joke. For Iron Felix was glowering at Children's World situated across from the historic headquarters and capital of fear, torture, murder, the Gulag system and general relentless repression, the former Lubyanka prison and seat of the Cheka and then the KGB. Ironically as well Iron Felix had his back turned to the Polytechnic which was the symbol and exposition of Russian science and engineering accomplishment. Of course it does not take much technology or scientific achievement to run a system of terror and repression, thought Majid, so Felix could afford to turn his back on science. The irony of the situation he saw in the square that day inspired Majid to compose a poem, which he began on the metro ride back to the university and he thought about it over the next two days. While he was formulating this poem, as whenever he was composing his verse, he did not pay any attention at all to Lara those two nights.

Behold there in the square at Lubyanka
Iron Felix glowers at Children's World

From his high perch overlooking the square
A look of hatred pours from his steely stare
At those bourgeois children, innocent and pure

They should be taught the truths austere
Of our glorious revolution, the Red Terror,
The bloody piles of our slain enemies.

They should turn their backs to meretricious'
Toys and take up their guns, salute Lenin
And behold! Just opposite, is Adults' World.

The Lubyanka—my realm—now quake with fear
For there they can learn the real lessons of this land
Or play with the instruments of torture.

In Adults' World my spirit lives on
And it should fill them with loathing and dread
So children's laughing will be expunged from the world.

This poem, which Majid recited publicly in late 1990, became more timely and was picked up and repeated widely about a year later when angry crowds, tired of the Communist party and KGB regime, pulled Iron Felix down and hauled the statue off to a graveyard of Soviet monuments. This was a period when Majid in his last year at the university was becoming more politicized. It corresponded with a particularly hard time in Russia and Moscow when the economic crisis was so deep that even basic food supplies were in short supply and long lines of people stood slumped in the weather waiting to get whatever was on offer. People were genuinely hungry, and once more Majid became aware that he seemed to live from one afternoon dinner at the cafeteria to the next. Even finding his staple of bread rolls and tea had become hard. Gorbachev's reforms were not working and the system was breaking down.

During one dark December night in that time, he was in the canteen trying to keep warm sitting near the samovar with a large mug of tea and a sweet roll when the perpetual television screen changed its usual fare. On came a strange sinister fleshy face with a grim expression and the bottom headline saying it was the face of Mr. Kryuchkov, head of the KGB. He was the so- called Comrade Hook. Majid along with a few others in the canteen turned their attentions to his words and realized that in his strange, convoluted bureaucratic style of speaking, Kryuchkov was declaring that the economic crisis and failure of reforms had caused a state of national emergency. It was unclear from what he said what consequences this statement would have and Comrade Hook did not make any appeal to the people of the Soviet Union nor did he lay out any steps or measures that would come into effect as a result of this declaration. He was in a veiled way not addressing the people, but instead he was publicly addressing Gorbachev and his political supporters. But it all sounded ominous at the time. Majid began at that time to look into the strange politics of the failing Soviet Union and to try to interpret the meaning of the declarations, issues and goals of the key players. The first noticeable crisis, which glasnost had revealed, was the rise of liberation movements of Union member states. Over that winter the Baltic states declared unilateral independence from the Soviet Union.

And over that winter semester of 1990-91, Majid completed not only his course work but he also composed a small assortment of poems concerning the political failures of the Soviet system and its cruelty and oppressions. *Yunost* published in three separate issues two of these "political" poems as well as one of his love sonnets. In April he gave a recital in one of the larger auditoria of the university. It was well attended and his new poems about the sufferings of the people were well received. There even appeared a review of his recital in one of the newly published liberal newspapers. Of course this review was mostly about the political currents of the time and was advancing Majid's poems as examples of the support of its liberal reform agenda. But the reviewer also put his finger on one of the characteristics of Majid's poetry which set it apart from that of his contemporaries. It was Majid's voice, and his musical delivery. He did not declaim like the refusnik poets of the 1960s and 70s, shouting and spitting out his words, expressing great rage and vehemence, dramatically. But instead he recited his verses with a calm, magical voice, almost hypnotic, with a regular and musical intonation that rose and fell, slowed and accelerated as the meaning changed, at one time noble and proud and at another quiet and full of pathos. His intonation was never monotonous or droning. Like many of the great poets, his verse was better in live performance than when read off the page. (Of course there have been in the recorded age of the last century many acclaimed poets in the West whose declamation and voices were poor even objectionable vehicles for their own poems, men like T.S. Elliot, V. Nabokov, C. Milosz, or W.H. Auden for instance.) For those lucky enough to attend one of Majid's performances, all would agree his greatness lay in his performance and they all seemed to feel uplifted by their attendance and by hearing his magical voice. They often left and for long afterwards repeating the words they heard, one or two lines which stuck in their memories.

In that last spring at the university, at the suggestion of Krivonosov, Majid applied for and was accepted for graduate studies at the Gorky Institute of Literature. Now at that time, this Institute still had a brilliant reputation for developing budding poets and writers, although admittedly its reputation was perhaps overstated as its output of graduates were not leading poets and writers at all, but in the late Soviet period it put out officially approved writers, hacks, and members of the establishment. Its role had shriveled to a school for the children of the elites which pretended to teach these students how to write poetry and fiction. But Majid did not know that at the time, although he should have suspected something just from the rather conventional and sparse output of his mentor Krivonosov. In fact, one of the school's major activities was teaching its students the art of translating literature and especially poetry into Russian. The most immediate effect of this change was that Majid had to move from the majestic (although crumbling) Stalin skyscraper on Lenin Hills high above the city to the distinctly dilapidated and modest buildings of the Institute located in very center of Moscow only a short walk from the pensive statue of Pushkin. The main hall of the Institute was built in the late 18th century and used to be the manor house where Russia's most famous early revolution Alexander Herzen had been born and raised as a youth in the early 19th century. It was in shabby ill-repair and Majid when he first entered it was impressed by the old floor boards and the plaster flaking walls of the old house. He also was taken by several photos hanging on the wall of the young and probably most famous of the Institute's alumnae, Bella Akhmadulina, giving recitals in front of massed microphones in the 1960s. She was still living at the time of Majid's admission although she was much less productive in poetry and more a celebrity and translator than anything else. What struck him then, was how beautiful she had been when she was in her early twenties and just after she left the Institute, breaking into the poetry world. At that time, still quite young she had married the Institute's other leading light, her first mentor, Yevgheny Gangnus. (although the Institute did not hang his photos on the wall because that was politically incorrect—Gangnus had dropped out and later became a refusnik and somewhat a critic of the Kruschev and Brezhnev regimes). The images in these photos stuck in his mind's eye—the pretty young poetess with the long arching neck declaiming—and soon he became equally enamored by her sweet light poetry. Those images bore him up when he sat in his tiny attic garret room at the Institute working at his poems.

But almost at the same time that Majid made the move to the center of Moscow a great national event occurred which finally illuminated the dire warnings of Comrade Hook nine months earlier. The KGB and its State Emergency Committee (Goskomchrep) tried to take over the state from the Communist Party, they said in trying to preserve the Soviet Union as a police state. The August Putsch against Gorbachev and his reforms and desperate efforts to save the Soviet Union and its economy. On the night of the announcement of the coup, troops invaded the city in tanks and troop carriers, and from all corners, people poured out into the streets and converged on the White House down by the Moscow River. Majid was among the crowds for those three days in mid-August 1991, sustained only by the excitement and the wild confusion. With some of his classmates Majid rushed down to the White House on the river early on the morning of the 21st, where they joined in the throngs of people milling around scores of tanks. He had never seen the city streets so crowded and animated, and even when there was shooting and high caliber bullets were whistling around overhead there was the feeling and excitement of a giant street party in the air. But no one knew what was happening, or which side was prevailing. After the first nighttime standoff at the White House when the tank troops and their officers changed loyalties it was not clear what had happened until some days later. One group rushed off to seize the Communist

Party budget office, then at another time a large group rushed off to seize the television tower, and yet later a large excited crowd converged on Lubyanka Square and proceeded to topple the statue of Iron Felix, which was not at all easy. One of the few casualties of the coup was a demonstrator who fell from the statue early in the process of trying to pull it down. Majid actually witnessed this. Along with the serious business and the potentially deadly confrontation, there were everywhere scenes that appeared absurd and comic. At one time, papers flying out of the upper windows of the Communist Party headquarters in the inner city as it was sacked, at another an army truck that was stopped by the crowds and upended spilling its cargo of thousands of handcuffs onto the cobblestone streets. The most surreal vision of all was the sight of buses and trolley-buses stacked up against tanks. He was in a crowd that turned to looting one of the Communist Party's elite food stores, the so-called Birch stores which, compared to the rest of the economy, were richly supplied with foodstuffs and delicacies even then in the depths of the economic hardship and shortages. This immense political crisis abruptly ended when the soldiers sent to suppress Yeltsin, then President of the Russian Republic within the USSR, and his supporters decided they did not want to shoot and kill their countrymen (or at least not too many of them as the only way to impose the will of the Goskomchrep was to kill scores, maybe even hundreds, of unarmed young people in the center of Moscow and then of course to go on to kill hundreds more in the small soviet republics which had declared independence from the Union of Socialist Republics). The feckless leaders of the Goskomchrep—the Gang of Eight—were arrested and shown to be sniveling, drunken wrecks; images which had been widely broadcast over the television when they first claimed control. Comrade Hook, as stern as he looked, it turned out did not have to the stomach to slaughter so openly and mercilessly so many unarmed citizens in the streets in front of television cameras. On his way to prison he prayed that his mentor Andropov in heaven would forgive him his weakness. Over the following three months into the autumn the chaotic events of August became clearer as the television replayed videos of the confused events and provided explanations. The crisis caused by the putsch wound down, again behind the scenes, as Yeltsin and the local political leaders of the other major soviet republics arranged for the dismemberment of into the near supine body of the Soviet Union and Gorbachev powerlessly escorted it in its demise.

But even before the crisis was resolved and Gorbachev restored to the head of government in Moscow, Majid had composed a short poem, tried it out, then typed it and sent it to *Yunost* for publication. The editors wanted to publish it in the mid-September issue, but although the grip of the Communist Party and the KGB on power had been shaken to its core by the putsch, the apparatus of state control had not been. The censor stepped in and banned *Yunost* from publishing the poem. They were so alarmed by the wording of the poem that they shredded the paper copy that Majid had submitted and they sent police inspectors to Majid's garret room to search out and seize other copies. They did not find any, not even a carbon copy, but they did assure themselves of a successful punitive raid by seizing other paper texts of different poems. They aimed to frighten Majid, tearing the place apart, looking closely at the typewriter and threatening Majid all the while with dire punishments or even banishment for writing anti- Soviet subversive verse. Fortunately nothing came of that. And also fortunately for us, Majid preserved the poem in his memory and not long afterwards he wrote it down again and also performed it at a recital three months later, about when the Soviet Union became the Disunited Soviet Republics. It has never been published and I found a copy which I have translated and reproduced below:

> *Eight scorpions crawled out from under their rocks*
> *From out of their bunkers*
> *Where they presided over the frozen gulags*
> *And spied on the people,*
> *Stinging those who spoke out,*

Casting fear in one and all.
Although they stood guard over the regime
And were the scaly henchmen who had enslaved us
They mistakenly believed they should govern too
Thus they tried to seize power and
Sting those who sought to liberate us.
But they could not bear the bright glare of the sun
They could not command those who were pledged to defend us
They had no words to explain
Nor manifest to outline their goals
In front of the people's will they lost their nerve
And their stinger tails waved about frightened and confused.
They tried to scamper back under their rocks
Or taking shelter in strong spirits
But the people's outrage kicked away their shelter
And they were burned by the sun of liberation.

Now I will be the first to admit it is not one of Majid's better poems. But it is an important first step in his political activism. It was the beginning of his conjuring up monsters to represent the secret police of the KGB and its successor the FSB. Here the Gang of Eight are portrayed as scaly poisonous scorpions. In another poem written a few years later, he represented the secret police agents as *oprichniki*, the historical, cruel and unrestrained enforcers of the reign of terror of Tsar Ivan the Terrible. But to heighten this cruel image, Majid referred to them as driving around the city in black Mercedes sedans with not the heads of dogs hanging from their horses' pommels but real human heads draped in net bags hanging from the cars' antennas. This vivid image became a widespread watchword for the secret police that people used in chat and computer social networks ever after it first was uttered.

This was certainly an exhilarating tumultuous start to our hero's new studies at the Gorky Institute. The entire student body was energized by this sudden political clap of lightening, and filled with enthusiasm at the prospect of freedom. But after only his first month of studies, shortly after the raid on his room by the police, Majid was called into the office of Dean Nenovatorov and given a stern warning—the type which goes "I really should be expelling you, but…" and which ends with the threat "we will be watching you to see that you behave". But the dean was not sympathetic to the censors' actions nor to the political conformism and conservatism of the bureaucratic apparatus and the police. Nenovatorov had long considered himself a poet and litterateur of some merit, but he had not written anything in years and he had also gotten his appointment not for merit but for his political connections with that same bureaucratic apparatus which he reviled. But he feared scandal. His upbraiding of Majid was merely an attempt to cover his back and preserve his propriety in the eyes of the bureaucratic world that he worked in. The dean dismissed Majid with those threatening words, but it was also the last time Majid saw him. Nenovatorov was dismissed as dean in early 1992 for a corruption scandal. It seemed that he had been taking funds directed for the tuition and boarding costs of the non-Russian students (that is students from those non-Russian republics which had declared independence from the USSR in late 1991) thinking that no one would notice.

In spite of the dean's early warning, the course of study at the Institute was anything but conservative, especially when compared to the Moscow University. It was a liberal curriculum, even perhaps progressive, when Majid first arrived. Krivonosov had strongly recommended Majid to join the Institute because of this liberal curriculum. And the new dean made the Institute even more so. Majid studied the works of poets who were unheard of (or more accurately had been omitted from the curriculum) at the University, names like Yesenin, Brodsky, Pasternak, Akhmatova, Mandelstam, and Voskreshensky among Russian poets. He also continued learning and studying the French poets of the late 19th century, and the verse dramas of William Shakespeare. At the Institute he was introduced as well to the verse of William Butler Yeats, to Czeslaw

Milosz, and to Robert Frost and William Stevens. He worked hard at his studies and even worked harder on his own compositions. Other boarding classmates record that Majid would be up many evenings pacing his small room and reciting out loud in English, French or Russian the poems he was learning. They sometimes peaked in because at first they thought a foreigner was visiting. But in spite of the big work load he seemed to have a huge appetite and enthusiasm for these studies.

Majid's two years at the Institute were marked by the changes occurring around him in Russia. Of course, the dissolution of the Soviet Union was the biggest change; one that was accompanied by a subtle revolution that occurred over 1992 and 1993. It was not a violent revolution in Russia itself, although there was a great deal of violence in many of the republics which gained their "independence" from the Union of Soviet Socialist Republics and from the hegemony of the Russians. But there was a revolution nevertheless as Yeltsin's regime aimed to dismantle communist economic administration giving people many new rights and freedoms including the right to own property and strove to introduce democratic and market conventions. Guaranty of freedom of speech of public assembly and of movement were three new rights brought in which had never really been allowed the Russian people. There had never really been a civic society; when Majid was in university in Moscow, there were no public places where people could meet, talk and socialize such as pubs, public restaurants, or cafes. On the streets it had been the practice if three or more people collected together and started to talk or visit with each other, whether in an arranged meeting or not, within minutes an agent of the police—either in uniform or a plainclothesman—would be sure to appear and drive the group apart with threats and sometimes even with blows from a baton. For instance, Majid's Institute was located close to one of the shining symbols of this revolution, the recently opened McDonald's hamburger restaurant, the first of its kind, and a first in so many ways for Russia. This became instantly a magnet for large gatherings of people—usually people waiting in line to make an order for the new fast, high quality food, but then also sitting for as long as they wanted eating and drinking their orders. Majid himself couldn't afford McDonald's fare while he lived at the neighboring Institute—often hungry and short on cash—but many of his classmates, especially those who were Moscow residents, could and did on occasion eat there and of course did socialize there. Majid instead when he wanted to eat more than the two meals which were offered at the Institute cafeteria, would go to a nearby small canteen that served up blinis with cheese or meat and weak coffee for a very low price. There were no seats in this canteen and its clients had to eat standing at the bar installed on the wall and leave straight afterwards. As private ownership of businesses became allowed private shops, restaurants, and kiosks began to appear on the streets and they brought with them color and lighting into the otherwise drab streets of Moscow. Early in the spring of 1992, a time when the streets were still wet and filthy with piles of old snow and cigarette butts and the city was often still gripped by winter's dim, overcast and chilly weather, Majid was surprised to learn that Ari had opened a small coffee shop and had started to sell imported quality coffee. Ari contacted Majid by the communal telephone at the Institute and invited him to come see him in his new business. "See what I am trying to do?" said Ari as he welcomed Majid into his closet sized shop. "With these new freedoms, I'm trying to convert Russians to drinking coffee instead of tea. I'm using private enterprise. Isn't that amazing?" Also an early sign of the revolution was the appearance of kiosks selling brightly colored fruit and flowers—things which were at that time still rarely available in the state-owned food stores. Majid on his walks around the streets of the capital also could not help noticing that many of these kiosks were owned and run by people from the Caucasus, Azeris, Armenians, Chechens and sometimes Georgians. In those years the city began slowly to festoon itself with colored neon lights and illuminated store front signs.

The year 1992 for Majid started as part of this overall revolution. He was actually invited to give a recital in a public theatre in the center of the city, a paying recital! Someone in the cultural establishment had heard one of his past performances and had read poems from his first book and had taken a liking to them, and on his own had proposed to the management of this small theatre that they arrange a date for him to give a recital. His argument to the managers was that Majid's performance would sell a lot of tickets and make money for them— something that was a new concept in Russia for theatres which had up until then been state- owned and financed through the budget. This man who acted as a self-appointed agent was actually Vladimir Pozyn, a cosmopolitan, a television journalist, and a celebrity of some repute in the former Soviet Union as well as in the US. He had once before been invited by Krivonosov to attend one of Majid's earlier recitals while the latter was still a student at the Moscow State University. Unknown to both Krivonosov and Majid, Pozyn had also been a graduate of the Department of Philology and had worked on and off in the secret intelligence services, but nevertheless he was a highly cultured man of the world who recognized superior poetry when he heard it. And he had been very impressed when he first heard Majid recite, so much so that he searched out and found a copy of Majid's book of verses, which impressed him even more and convinced him that Majid was a major talent. This connection turned out for Majid to be extremely fortuitous as Pozyn continued to be a sponsor of Majid's poetry through the rest of his career. It was not too untypical either as Moscow functions not as a big impersonal metropolis but through word of mouth and personal connections and recommendations of friends, classmates, lovers, and neighbors where everyone seems to know everyone else—in short it operates socially like a large village. As it turned out Pozyn was right: the recital sold a full house of tickets and Majid's performance of twenty of his poems was resoundingly well-received. It was at this recital that Pozyn introduced himself to Majid, who from the time of this performance to his death professionally was introduced as Slava.

Both were impressed with the other: Pozyn by how mature and soft spoken Slava was, and Slava by the brave almost brazen openness of Pozyn. Pozyn—who was in his 50s and was an aggressive, outspoken, no-nonsense man of the world—was later to confess that he too felt the lure of Slava's way of speaking; that he found it was hypnotic and utterly convincing and it seemed that when he spoke he continued to speak in verse metrics, unrhymed verse or alliteratively. This was the beginning of a new mentoring relationship in Majid's life. If life is unfair and good young poets as well as poor ones—just as composers, writers, or painters—are often merely lost in the shuffle of life and forgotten and their works neglected and then lost, so it can happen that a career is "discovered" by a significant cultural figure who hails it, promotes it and brings it inescapably to the attention of the public. A sponsorship by a cultural leader has often made all the difference in Russian history. One has only to think of the invaluable role of the critic Vladimir Stasov in the 19th century in shaping and sponsoring the musical careers and fame of Glinka, Mussorgsky or the artistic career of Ilya Repin. This is what in effect happened with Majid—that is Slava the poet—Vladimir Pozyn took his works and artistry and launched him and assured that Slava was not lost to the world.

At this recital, Slava recited a new poem that he had composed sometime that spring between all his course work. This of course was his important narrative poem about a serf and freedom, often entitled "The Composer". It tells the story of Vanya Ivanov loosely patterned after the story of the life of an actual 18th century serf-musician. The poem recounts how Vanya was taught to play on the clavichord and violin as a child and then was moved indoors to become a house serf and a musician in the palace of the Moscow nobleman Sheremetyev. As Vanya grew into adulthood—while still a serf—he gained more and more personal freedom as he turned to composing music. The poem tells how Vanya came to think of himself as a freedman only when he was composing. And he composed a lot. He had to give concerts twice a month from the household orchestra and most of what was performed he composed himself. He was the first to take up playing the new fortepiano in Russia and even learned of the career of Haydn and proceeded to play some of his music with the orchestra. It then tells of how the old Count Sheremetyev had promised him many rewards and even emancipation, but that when he died, his son, Pyotr reneged on the promise. While composing for the house orchestra, Vanya fell in love with another serf, the famous Praskovia the Pearl who sang opera and arias with the orchestra.

> *On to the stage came a radiant vision, like an angel*
> *It was Parasha in her operatic raiment*
> *And when she sang her voice swept out like a crystal harp*
> *And all hearts before it, the audience wept*
> *She was truly a gleaming Pearl and Vanya fell in love with her.*

They came to feel love for each other and his heart would beat wildly as she sat at the keyboard where he gave her lessons on the clavichord. Except in a turn of harsh fate, Pyotr Sheremetyev the son of the old Count, stole in one night and seduced the still young singer while she was in her bath and he took her as his morganatic wife. This crushed Vanya who composed even more, feeling ever more freedom as he composed music.

> *As he sat at his spinet and he listened to the sounds*
> *Welling up inside him, as he played a phrase,*
> *And scribbled the notes down on his lined paper*
> *As the harmonies swirled in his head*
> *He came to se the world through the eyes of a swallow.*

> *All worries and set-backs lifted off his shoulder*
> *And the day's travails were forgotten, he became free*
> *His spirit flew upward unshackled by the world*
> *O'er the brilliant golden domes and glinting river*
> *O've the brick and plaster'd cities and their grand concert halls.*

The poem ends as it describes Pyotr taking Praskovia with him to St. Petersburg and with the composer demented with grief, fleeing from the estate where he had lived all his life, to Moscow where he dies a truly free man but plagued by hunger, illness, cold, and heartache, clutching the unappreciated manuscripts of his scores which he had put together over the years. The entire poem of about 400 lines is a masterpiece told in rhymed iambic pentameter. The audience loved it. It addressed what was one of Majid's major themes throughout his life's work, enslavement and the nature of freedom in Russia, or more correctly the lack of freedom in Russia. This recital was a success for Slava in another way too. It was the first time he had ever received payment for performing his poetry (although admittedly it was not very much at the time, but when there was general poverty and hunger stalking the city, it was a very good sum which Slava the poet had not been expecting when he began the evening recital).

The year 1992 was the very nadir of the economic hard times in Russia. Shops were bare—the Soviet system of distribution had completely broken down—and companies and ministries were finding it hard to pay their employees. People in Moscow were often hungry and those who could spent the summer out in their country gardens cultivating potatoes and vegetables. The city looked its very worst; its budget was also severely short of funds. Buildings had gone for many years without painting or re-plastering and their level of decay was quite apparent. The city streets were rutted and filled with potholes which went unpatched, and they went unswept all year long. In that winter snow was not collected, and in the summer all the meridians and parks around the city were overgrown with weeds and dandelions and gardens were unplanted—all because there was no money in the city's coffers. Even the state budget ran short of funds. The post office stopped transporting and delivering mail because they were unable to pay the postal workers, some of whom resorted to throwing sacks of undelivered mail in ponds in protest. Government services everywhere broke down for more than a year. In the boulevard park next to the Institute Majid had noticed when he first arrived in August 1991 that the local residents would walk their dogs, and often large black dogs in one of the few free activities still available to them. By the end of 1992, he noticed again a shocking sign of the times—the vision of omission— there were no longer any dogs being walked down the shady lanes of this boulevard park. People could no long afford to feed their pets and had been forced to let them go or to release them to run wild in the streets. The big black dogs disappeared altogether from Moscow. The government adopted "shock therapy" to the economy and embarked on privatizing many operating companies. The new private companies operated for some time afterwards in disarray and even in insolvency. This meant many affiliated companies, schools, nurseries, clinics and canteens were closed and many people were laid off from their jobs. The hunger and economic uncertain led to even more drinking and a higher death rate as the poor elderly merely gave up on living. Another thing which Majid noticed on the streets of Moscow for its being absent at that time was that he saw no pregnant women anywhere in the two years that he lived in the very center. At that time he gave a lot of thought to the phenomenon of becoming aware of what was noticeable only for its absence.

The Institute had long been a special center for students from the non-Russian republics of the USSR who came to Moscow to study Russian literature and to start a career as writers or poets. Needless to say these students represented the elites of their ethnic republics and they were well educated and spoke excellent Russian. Coming from out of town, they were also residents at the Institute. Majid found that socializing and mixing with these classmates was easier for him than it had been at the conceited Moscow University. In the 1992- 1993 school term, Majid met one of these students, the beautiful Irina Bykova, from Uzbekistan. And he fell in love with her, almost from first meeting. She was half Uzbek, half Russian with pretty almond shaped dark eyes, long straight black hair and an alluring, gentle smile. Like Majid, she admired the poetry of Alexander Pushkin and knew lots of it by heart. Irina always smiled at Majid and would often sit with him when studying, and over that winter she went on long walks with him down the snowy lanes of the boulevard park. But she never reciprocated his love. Majid dreamed about her, in daytime reveries he thought of her and her lithe figure as she languidly strolled through the winter landscapes—in short she occupied his imagination for most of that year. But they never kissed and never became more intimate because she never came to love him. She thought he was sweet and very talented, but not really very sympathetic or attractive, because he was often too concentrated, too focused on himself and his work. But he never understood why she rebuffed his affections. Throughout the winter, Majid received what he interpreted as signs of her attraction to him. Irina continued to flutter her dark eyes at him (he thought coquettishly but he didn't realize that her rapid blinking was due to her wearing contact lenses and she blinked uncontrollably as she refocused on him), and she continued to demurely smile at him (a sign of her self-consciousness not of her affection for him). On many little occasions, Majid wanted to tell Irina that he loved her, but he never could find the words or the right timing, and so he never did. As winter melted into spring there was a convergence of his love and attraction to her and his reading of the early poems of Boris Pasternak. Those early poems were concerned with Pasternak's love for an unnamed beauty in the time of the first European war. Majid was overwhelmed by the detailed physical world of these poems, the music of its alliterations, the role of nature in the poet's emotional outlook, and of the aching feelings of the poet for his beloved. He conflated that heroine with his own Irina in the present day. Out of his unrequited love for Irina he composed a number of poems which sought to capture those brief moments that he spent with Irina over that winter and spring using the technique and voice of Pasternak.

The snow crunched beneath our feet, a hard winter day
Our frosted breath rose up like smoke intertwined
To the dark lattice of bare linden branches.

The cold constricted my heart—
I so much wanted to tell you
That it burned me even to breathe—and find the words.

The light was dim under a blanket of cloud
Your gaze was cast down on the path, half hidden
By a fur lined hood. I took your hand.

Perhaps the glint in your eye, like a glittering chip of ice, bespeaks your
  love for me.

As it happened in that late spring when Majid graduated from the Institute, Irina was forced by the deep economic crisis (which had hit the former Soviet Republics as hard as it had hit Russia) to withdraw from the Institute and return to Tashkent. They parted friends, but Majid never saw her again and after a few letters exchanged never heard from her again after she got married later that summer. The vision of her lovely face and figure stayed in his memory for the next decade. And we have six poems which record his love for her in that winter and spring and remain with us as a portrait as achingly beautiful and distant as Dante's Beatrice. At the train station, upon Irina's departure, Majid slipped her a folded piece of paper on which he had written a few lines of verse. *Don't disappear, my love. Your departure removes only your physical presence. In my heart your smile, kind voice, and spirit will live on with me, like the memory of the morning sunlight. Don't disappear. Stay a while longer so that we may face life together as unified souls.* Irina tucked the paper in her purse and did not read the verse until after the train had left the station. But she did give Majid an intimate long embrace and the most passionate kiss he had ever received from her. When she was seated at the window seat in the train Irina's hair in the sunlight looked to Majid like shining blue-black coal. The sour smell of the station's coal smoke stuck in his nostrils all that day and night. He was crushed.

For the end of the semester as part of the graduation celebrations there was a tradition at the Institute of making a presentation of the best poetic compositions of the year by the Institute's students, both graduating and continuing, in a juried recital. Usually all of the students attended along with the teachers and professors, and the students themselves selected the best poets to represent them. Majid was selected to declaim a poem that he would compose especially for the occasion. It was requested that it be neither too long nor political. He was told that the old poet Yevgheni Gaponovich Gangnus would be the head of the jury (perhaps there was some irony in his selection, as Gangnus had dropped out of the Institute and never completed his studies there, although there was always suspicion that the authorities forced him out). Majid thought it was unjust that Gangnus would head the jury and not Bella Akhmadulina, whose photos graced the entrance to the Institute. He did not especially like the poems of Gangnus. They reminded him too much of those of Mayakovsky, and he imagined that like Mayakovsky, Gangnus—being of German descent—was also probably tall. The event was held in a small theatre not far from the Institute, as there was no auditorium with a large stage at the Institute.

On the day of presentation itself, Majid was still trying to complete a few lines that didn't fit in with what he had already completed. He was distracted by thoughts of what he should wear. His own wardrobe was shabby and in poor shape, being regularly unlaundered and never pressed. Finally a classmate who was also an out-of-town resident brought him a long dark jacket. Majid laughed. It looked like the cut and fashion that would have been acceptable in Baratynsky's day, 150 years earlier. But there was nothing else to do. He was not a Romantic poet, but his looks were on that day; his white almost sallow complexion, his dark eyes and black wavy hair worn long, and this long jacket worn over his slender shoulders. Ironically, at the same time that Majid was fretting about what to wear the elder poet Gangnus, who had gotten up late, was worrying about the same thing. The night before he had "hit the tipple" too hard as the saying goes, and he was looking for the "hair of the dog". He had in recent years gotten the reputation for being an outlandish dresser,—many said, a clown—who alone in almost all of Moscow wore brightly colored clothes with hot patterns and unmatching and uncomplimentary combinations—plaids with paisleys, stripped with barred shirts, ties which were too wide and did not fit in with anything. But on this morning, Gangnus had a huge hangover headache and actually thought that he did not want to be a "performance artist". And besides it was not an occasion where he would be the center of the day's program and he did not want to draw any undue attention to himself. He was afraid of what the students of poetry would think of him. He was especially afraid he would fall asleep on the stage and confirm to everybody in the audience that he really was an old man and spent force. He found a pair of clean blue jeans and tried on a plain white shirt with oversized collars, but then he threw that off and matched his jeans with a sold pale pink shirt without a tie and then he put on a coal gray-black jacket that he could no longer button up. But he really desperately craved a shot or two of vodka. He went off to the theatre near the Institute cursing his bad fortune and hoping that the ceremony would not last too long and that the poetry he heard would not be too execrable. He took the metro to Pushkin Square and walked from there. Majid completed his poem with some last adjustments and two inadequate lines, a couplet of alexandrines, which he hoped no one would either notice or object to. He also rushed off, cursing his bad fortune and hoping that the ceremony would not last too long and that his poem would not sound too appalling.

The theatre hall was filled, mostly with students but also with special invited guests, friends and family members of the poets of the day. Majid had to walk through the audience and up onto the stage on the wing stairs. He was lead to one of the six chairs arrayed for the poets of honor. The jury was on the other side of the stage seated behind a long table that was draped with a green cloth. There were three jury members already there, but Majid did not know or recognize any of them. Gangnus was missing; his chair at the jury table was empty. The event moderator stood in the center of the stage befuddled, looking like a deer caught in a car's headlights, not knowing what to do. The audience quietly mumbled but otherwise were patient for the first 15 minutes, but then their noise became louder. Then about 20 minutes after the time when the program was meant to start Gangnus barged into the hall from the back, and proceeded loudly up to the front and the stage, a gangly unbalanced swagger of arms and legs. Gangnus was drunk: he had found his vodka and imbibed until he felt calmed and restored. The moderator helped him to his place, and he fell into his chair, shouting out that he didn't need any help from anyone and that he was finally there so the program could start. The first young poet got up and declaimed a noisy poem in blank verse that was dramatically accompanied by the vigorous waving of arms and filled with the vile and obscene prison slang which is called *blat'* and which is usually not considered appropriate for any sort of polite society or where women are present. This poet declaimed in one tone—anger— and his shouting and waving went on for much too long, finally he ended with a loud repeated unrhymed couplet of six anapests strung together. This was followed by very brief applause from the audience and highly exaggerated deep bowing from the poet who finally was led away by the moderator while he was still bowing. The next two poets were rather more typical of student poets. They read their verses from printed pages they held in a monotonal droning that only at the end of each stanza had a slight rise in the voice. The first of these read a poem in rhymed iambic hexameter with inserted repetitions of the first line at the end of each stanza. He received more applause from the audience than had the first poet. The second read the same way but an unrhymed verse with no regular metrical structure. By the time he was ten lines into his declamation, Gangnus was already nodding off;

he was dreaming of being on a small wooden stage in a large stadium waiting interminably for Voskresenky to finish his declamation. More polite applause from the audience aroused Gangnus. Then it was Majid's turn. He was introduced by the moderator as Slava Khairulin. When he stood up from his chair, short but in his long jacket, with his long dark wavy hair, he looked very much like a Byronic hero. As usual he recited his poem entirely from memory, and his intonation moved up and down the scale of emotion. From his first words it was clear he was a lyrical poet with well-structured metrics and musical intonation and rhythm, but he did not sound old-fashioned. He made minimal use of his arms. Starting quietly and slowly increasing his volume, Majid immediately caught the attention of the audience and Gangnus woke, sat more erect, and started to pay close attention. Majid recited for a little more than 14 minutes, long alexandrines in iambic feet, ending the final lines with a rising voice and emphasis, and shortened metrical feet. Unfortunately this is one poem that we do not have any complete copies of. Only parts of it are available as Majid never did type out this poem; students in the audience scribbled out parts of it as best they could either there at the time on scraps of paper, or later from memory trying to piece together the parts they liked most. These are some of the lines that I have been able to collect and translate, gathered from these recollections and circulated by samizdat by fans of Majid's work.

Am I a public poet? Do I not recite to people?
I do not compose verse for my private amusement
To recite in the privacy of one's own room
To declaim to the wind which never listens anyway to man's words
And whose booming voice ensures that no one else can hear.

Am I recognized as a poet? I cannot. Have people heard me?
No one appointed me a poet,
I do not have a certificate of poetic legitimacy
No, I do not ask permission to breath in the air around me
Or a license to sit in the sun and bend my face into its brilliance

And so my voice is an endowment unto and to myself
And my songs rise out of me just as the acorns
Sprout from the fallow soil without asking 'by your leave'.

Is the public poet a moralist? Must he have courage?
Yes of course, and the honesty to declaim in words most precise
Just what he sees and life's many hypocrisies
But the ancient bard was not a philosopher or sermonizer
More likely he was the preserver of ancient wisdom
Dispensed freely on the street corner or in the market square …

At this point Gangnus thought faintly that Slava, this new young poet, might be addressing and criticizing him. But he could not follow the verses close enough, he only heard indirect quotations from his own distant past.

And in dissenting the poet's songs challenge the elites, the rulers,
and all those who would enslave us in conformity and silence
But these poets only cast stones in the authorized directions—

Poetry is a youngster's special realm. The art slips away from the middle-aged
And the hoary, honored and much decorated old man.
Homer spent the greater part of his life as an old man telling yet again
His great stories of war and love in a verse long after copied
But he was a poet only in his strong youth, when the spark of rhyme
And meter and his singing wove the structures which we re-tell today …..

The stern air of poetry require words—are words not sounds?
Do they need the inky frames of printed page?
I think not. Court proceedings require printed words
Although their judgments always stumble
dumbly over the sounds and meanings—

I sing the songs of outrage and love, sorrow and beauty
Because it is my in my nature,

Because I hear the music of my own throbbing blood
Because I am at one time both to sing by command and at my liberty
Can you prevent water from being wet and cold
Or from running downhill to the salty sea?

Majid ended with that slight flourish and a sweep of his right arm, and then fell silent. There was at once strong applause and hurrahs from the audience when Majid finished. Gangnus jumped up from his chair and shouted out excitedly:

Now here is the next great one, to Pushkin an heir
A mighty voice, a sincere song, his words thrill the air!

He tried to get around the table to rush over and embrace Majid, but his arms and legs got in the way and he bumped into the other jury members and the table, spilling a plastic bottle of water. Meanwhile Majid had offered a quick curt bow and left the stage behind the curtain to the back stage wing.

Shortly afterwards, Majid joined the crowd of students and audience members standing on the sidewalk outside the theatre. It was a warm afternoon and the sunlight twinkled through the leaves of the tall popular trees in the boulevard park opposite the theatre. It was one of those odd days in warm May when suddenly the air looked as if it were snowing: the cottonwood poplars were releasing their huge sacks of "cotton fuzz" (or *pukh* as it is known in Russian) which floated through the air and fell thickly on everything. When this cotton fuzz falls most heavily you have to be careful to keep it out of your eyes or nose, or mouth. So the clusters of people after the recital were standing around talking and waving their hands to sweep away the fuzz. Majid approached one group and suddenly he noticed that in the middle of this cluster was the familiar face of Bella Akhmadulina, the lips of her closed mouth drawn down sharply to the right which made her look extremely sad. She was no longer young and looking upwards as in all the photos in the

Institute. Majid wanted to introduce himself to her, but Akhmadulina saw him and immediately smiled and reached for him. "Slava, I'm so pleased to be able to meet you. I adored your poem just now." And she made to give him a friendly kiss on the cheeks as is common between good friends in Russia. "Call me Bella, short for Isabella." They spoke for several minutes, about nothing but occasionally about poetry. "I was so glad to hear you rhyme nature with liberty, and blood with love, and prince with mud. So few poets are able to do that so naturally." Once she began to smile, Majid thought she was beautiful again as in her photos from almost 30 years before. She looked like his mother. Before they separated, Akhmadulina gazed at him with affection and said, "You'll have to come visit me at my house out at Peredelkino." And she brushed off some cotton fuzz which had stuck to the shoulder of Majid's borrowed long jacket.

Chapter Three

In the five years following Yeltsin's shoot-up at the Russian White House (and the promulgation of the new constitution which Yeltsin's disposal of the Soviet legislature allowed for), the revolution in Russian society really took off. The 1990s was a period of rapid changes in society as people throughout the country took advantage of the new freedoms which had seldom been available to Russians in all its history. In this period the economy although still suffering from widespread poverty rapidly became dominated by consumerism. There was a rush to buy imported, quality goods which had been denied the population in Soviet times. Things like large screen color TVs, imported quality cars—especially German cars—label fashion, sexy lingerie, perfumes and cosmetics, top of the line Swiss watches, personal computers all flew out the door of newly founded shops peddling the new consumer goods. Companies were founded by entrepreneurs working in fields that the Soviet planned economy had never allowed for: private banks, media companies, restaurants and cafes including fast food eateries, branded gasoline filling stations, telephony, night clubs and casinos, computer software, supermarkets, private high class hotels, share brokers. Marketing and sales and human relations managers became professional occupations employing the ambitious and driven. Advertising appeared and grew rapidly. And the gems of Soviet era production associations were sold off in politically driven privatizations: oil production, coal mining, steel bashing, aluminum smelting, minerals mining, heavy industry, car manufacturing. These were snapped up by the new financiers; those who were later called the new elites, the oligarchs as they came to direct Yeltsin's government. People in their millions who had never been allowed to travel abroad in Soviet times now got their first foreign travel passports and flew abroad on vacations, on shopping trips, on cruises; travel abroad for holidays where the pasty complexioned could lie in the sun on warm beaches and or travel even just to conduct business. They could see for the first time, first-hand what the Soviet authorities had always denied; namely that life in so many European countries was really better, people in these countries were richer, that Soviet-made goods were truly distinctly inferior (when they had been available at all).

These new freedoms and changes in society manifested themselves in so many ways in the life of Moscow. Sometimes it was difficult at first to notice the changes but steadily they occurred and spread. People relentlessly buying cars lead to traffic jams where none had occurred before. Noise levels increased along the roads, pedestrian fatalities rose as cars came to dominate the roads at the expense of those on foot. Parking became a problem; cars parked everywhere, in courtyards where ice hockey rinks had formerly been, on sidewalks, a grass verges, in short anywhere where there was available free space. And increased car traffic resulted in an increase in car emissions, dirty and muddy roads, and pollution. Nearly all of the decorative shrubbery died from the fumes— the beautiful lilacs bushes in the parks around the center and the small horse chestnut trees lining the New Arbat all had disappeared by 1999. The appearance and growth in advertising saw the city festooned by outdoor colorful bill boards and neon screens growing out of seemingly every available space. The Stone Bridge in the middle of the city was apparently renamed the LG Bridge by its corporate sponsor. Two huge billboards seemed to re-christen the Lenin Library, the Yves Delorm and Samsung Library (you could take your pick), and the Tretyakovsky Museum prominently situated on the banks of the Moscow River proclaimed itself the Museum named Lipton Tea. It was only a marvel that huge advertising flyers were not hung from the red walls of the

Kremlin. Color and neon light increasingly lit up the previous dim, shadowy gray city. One politically connected entrepreneur made himself a fortune by getting a city contract to supply architectural lighting on the outside of nearly every building on the main avenues and thoroughfares of the city center—this made nighttime walks around the center less intimidating and frightful, and further encouraged a growing public nightlife that was active even later than the 9 pm virtual curfew which had been imposed by the Soviet authorities and which had dictated the ending time for concerts, films, and plays. The new nightclubs and casinos dressed in their gaudy neon light displays (as well as the strip tease joints and brothels) encouraged a new nocturnal activity and liveliness in the city never seen before—all-night flower stands, cafes open 24 hours, liquor stores and kiosks selling beer and cigarettes open to well past midnight. On the streets and in public foyers there was an increasing presence of banking teller machines next to garishly lit slot machines and electronic one-armed bandits.

Even though the years of 1992 and 1993 were the very nadir of Russia's economy and economic hardship affected everyone, beginning in 1993 there was a steady and dramatic economic growth in Russia which gradually came to appear as an economic boom which did not let up until the crash in late summer of 1998. This boom attracted a huge influx of migrants and economic refugees into Moscow from all parts of the Russian Federation as well as from the now independent states that had left the Soviet Union. One day in 1997, for example, when our hero Majid went on one of his rare visits to the central mosque in Moscow he was surprised to see that its population had changed since his previous visit when he had first arrived in Moscow from Kazan. At that time, in early 1989, the majority of worshippers using the central mosque were, like him, Tatar migrants living in Moscow, but when he went again eight years later he noticed that the Tatars had been almost entirely replaced by Muslims from Chechnya, Azerbaijan, Krasnodar, and other places in the Caucasus. At the same time there was a big influx of foreigners seeking to cash in on the newly emerging economic opportunities in Moscow. In 1996, Majid was also surprised to see a St. Patrick's Day parade marching down the center of New Arbat Boulevard, manned almost entirely by Irish expats resident in Moscow. He also saw advertisements for American Fourth of July parties which were to be held at one of the city's parks and which were sponsored by global American consumer brands. Then there was the dramatic increase in the population of Tajik and Uzbek street sweepers, road builders, and courtyard and sidewalk cleaners. But they did not have the money nor the political connections to organize the public celebrations of their own national holidays.

These physical changes to the city brought about by the growing economy also led to cultural changes. The Russian language began to change as its material culture became open to the west. Throughout those years scores of new words appeared in the Russian lexicon, some which were useful, some which were offensive to the Russian ear, and many others which became established neologisms which were adopted and assimilated into Russian just as Dutch, German, and French words had in the previous three centuries. Majid sometimes noticed these invasions as they occurred—new words like Speed for AIDS, supermarket, *veep* for V.I.P., gamburger for the McDonald's hamburger, manager, okay, ouch and wow (called neoyorkisms as they were carried by young Russian emigres returning from New York), mobile for mobile telephone, marketing (with the stress on the second syllable), *lanch* in place of the traditional *obed or* midday meal—and sometimes he would be surprised by whole realms of new words that had snuck up and built up a constituency. Words such as *coffeinaya* for coffeeshops, HR, bankruptcy, meeting for a public demonstation, *gipermarket*, swaps and options, chat, networking, konsulting and kompaniy, sandwich in place of the well-established open face German *buterbrot,* surfing, snickers and *snikersi* (for the candy bar and the sports shoes) hacking, *biznesmen,* programmer, *bankomat* for ATM or teller machines, *raiderstvo* for racketeering attacks, password, sushi and sashimi, e-mail, *rolliki* for rollerblades, post (as in to put on your social network), and of course oligarch was a neologism to describe the small group of men led by Boris Berezovsky who took over the crown jewels of the Russian economy and became filthy rich and politically powerful in the process. There were many words which sounded ugly to Majid's finely attuned ear, but some were admittedly irreplaceable as they stood for totally new things or concepts. Some words sounded to Majid amusing or merely silly. He noticed also in this decade the spread of silly sounding names, especially the names of banks. There was a "sticky" bank (Lipky), a Most bank and Mor bank which in English begged the presence of a Less Bank (which did appear also), but in it meaning was Bridge Bank a place where he could get a bridge loan? or a Flight bank (for flight capital?), Tar Bank, Absolute Bank (for depositing vodka perhaps?) and his favorites Svetlana Bank and Bank Tatyana, with the former represented in advertisements by a shapely blond scantily dressed model inviting people to come make a deposit. For those in doubt about the meanings of the names of new banks there was also a bank named simply Bank' Bank. Worse on the ear however with the proliferation of private banks which were linked to the new companies there emerged the very Soviet practice of forging compound words which were cumbersome and ugly with names like MezhSviazPromStroi Bank or InterRezhDepoKhozTov Bank, and many others with similar clumsy combinations.

On the streets during this period people, especially young people changed their fashion and dress quite dramatic in the years after 1993. This change in how people dressed was highly stimulated by new markets, strong pent up demand and desire for decent looking clothes, and a huge influx of imported goods. Right after the shoot up at the White House, November was one of the coldest snowiest months in many years. Immediately there appeared new impromptu markets all over Moscow for *dublovki*, the suede-leather fleece-lined coats and jackets in vast arrays of colors, with or without hoods, with buttons or toggles, made in Greece or Turkey or China. Women wore them because they were warm and impervious to the wind in spite of how dumpy they looked in them. Men wore fashionable black ones or fleeced-lined smooth and shiny leather jackets. These markets were always temporary and set up in under-used large warehouse spaces which were built in public buildings which were no longer functioning. They were run by shady organizations—often Caucasian men—that had no intention of investing in regular stores or staying long in business. Within a few years these same impromptu markets switched to selling inexpensive fur coats of mink, ermine, rabbit, and fox. These coats were inexpensive and sold like hotcakes—it seemed that in just a few years every woman in Moscow had either a *dublovka* or a full-length fur coat, or both. Of course at the same time women en masse seemed to have abandoned the dress and skirt for pants and leggings, most often jeans. This sartorial switch became very obvious by the summer of 1994. Majid was amazed by the transformation. Young women especially began dressing in ways that would most attract attention or reflected the latest fads in Western Europe, whereas in the past everyone would dress in ways that would make them most blend in with the masses and not attract attention to themselves. One year the fad was to strut about town bra-less and in thin white tee shirts, another summer, it was to wear low cut jeans and tee shirts that exposed waist and belly, and yet another was to wear dark thong panties which were displayed brazenly on the bare middrifts. These fads did not last long. Young men in this time adopted baseball caps and sneakers. Later in the period there was a fad where young people would wear all black, dye their hair inky black, apply kohl around their eyes, wear heavy black Dr. Mertens boots (imported from Germany), wear silver jewelry and ear piercing studs. They called themselves Goths and patterned themselves after western goth rockers or Marilyn Manson, although it was never clear to the outsider what musical tastes they had. They dressed this way to attract attention to themselves and to alarm people. In their numbers were many teenagers, and Majid often wondered if they went to school dressed like Goths or if they went home first and changed into these grim costumes. They would congregate in large groups loafing around at well- traveled spots around the city. But they were not preaching and hardly anyone really noticed them besides the police who were convinced that they were all drug-heads and thus harassed them constantly.

This period in Russia witnessed a flurry of new economic activity, hyperinflation, high unemployment and misery and great uncertainty, although there was also strong growth. This all was accompanied by public displays of breathtaking greed, criminality, and violence, including murders. Among the new entrepreneurs the drive to snatch whatever assets possible at the lowest possible price was irresistible and made for endless news stories of the greedy Noveau Russians and their struggles against each other. The oligarchs were especially prominent in these battles for assets. Hucksters thought up imbecilic swindles to steal thousands of rubles or privatization vouchers (stock shares basically) from unsuspecting pensioners and made themselves millionaires overnight. This was a period when it seemed everyone was demanding bribes, policemen stopping people on the road for $20 worth of rubles (this sum changed frequently), bureaucrats refusing to do their assigned tasks without lubrication, and it was this time when protection racketeers became widely famous. In early 1995 Majid went to look for the coffee kiosk his friend, Avram, only to find it was locked up and closed. When he finally caught up with Avram, he found that his friend was packing up and getting ready to emigrate. "Well, of course, what do you expect? Russia doesn't want Jews here. Russians hate us, even if most of the oligarchs are Jewish. Better to chase opportunities in Israel or the United States. I closed the kiosk because racketeers were always threatening me for protection money. I paid protection from racketeers, and paid other racketeers for protection from the protectors. There was no one I could pay for protection from the *chinovniki* nor from those greedy bastards at customs, who by the way seem to be especially fond of coffee. There was no way I could do business and come out ahead, or even whole." Not long after that Avram did immigrate to Israel while the opportunity to do so was still available. He had run his coffee kiosk for less than three years, but closed it before the huge fad in opening coffee houses started in Russia. Avram was an entrepreneur before his time in Russia. This was also the period of the so called bankers' wars when more senior bankers were assassinated than even the oil men who were murdered. For a couple years, it seemed a banker—usually the owner of a non-descript little known bank with ties to a shady company whose business was unknown to everyone but thrived only through bribes—was murdered every month, often at the armored door of his bank but sometimes in the seat of his expensive car at home. There were other murders as well. Assassination attempts occurred against the oligarchs—limpet bombs planted on the roofs of their armored cars, or high powered sniper rifles shooting at them usually killing only the bodyguard—and investigative journalists and news readers also fell victim to these killings, even governors of distant resource rich oblasts were gunned down. None of these killings were ever solved, and the professionalism of the assassin suggested that the secret police were involved or unemployed KGB hitmen assassins were the the culprits. Most Russians only read about these in the press, but some killings occurred in broad daylight in front of Moscovite witnesses. The citizens by and large carried on as if nothing serious had happened, and it seemed most Russians believed that the target usually deserved his fate. Of course, this killing wave led to an increase in the number of armed bodyguards and even police escorts who worked for the new entrepreneurs and oligarchs, even small time chinovniki were seen escorted by a detachment of beefy armed bodyguards, who were universally identifiable by their all black costumes and expensive jackets which fit them poorly. One afternoon as Majid was walking along New Arbat, Majid ran into a vision of one of these small oligarchs, an oil general stepping out of a jewelry shop. The door was opened for him by a bodyguard dressed like a 17th century *strelets* guardsman wearing a red peaked cap, a long black (instead of red) heavy felt coat, orange felt boots and he was wielding a short *bardiche* or poleaxe and waving his sabre. Out hopped the petty oligarch dressed also as a medieval boyar in a long purple, fur-lined felt tunic with gold braid and buttons. Three more *streltsy* body guards dressed similarly followed their master out of the shop where a distressed looking jeweler looked out the door. The four of them-towering in height over their lord and master—then formed a close circle around the petty oligarch and accompanied him to his war horse parked on the side of New Arbat, all the while waving their sabres at the passing pedestrians. They then mounted and all galloped off toward the Kremlin. This vision of a deadly serious medieval costumed party occurred to Majid only once, but the whole city frequently saw the same thing time and again, only instead of horses these characters rode top of the line armored, black Mercedes equipped with blue flashing lights and dark tinted glass and instead of swords and *bardiches*, the bodyguards carried Uzis and high powered pistols. It was a period of low-grade warfare conducted on the streets of the city. This public warfare became embodied in new racketeering "mafias" who came to control whole sectors of the new economy, like the port of St. Petersburg, for example. They received a tremendous amount of press coverage, especially as these new mafias established affiliate offices overseas and in Russia set about killing the former Soviet era "thieves in law" the latter who had discreetly run more traditional criminal activities under the KGB's careful watch.

The new, promised freedoms from the Yeltsin constitution also led to violence in other ways: the war for independence of Chechnya, the Chechens felt they had the right to secede from the Russian empire. In fact there were steps taken elsewhere in Russia to gain independence from the newly formulated Russian Federation (which even pared down was still an empire, although a broken down one), in Tatarstan for instance. But it was only in Chechnya especially that open warfare broke out and well-armed Russian troops fought with large bands of well-armed freedom fighting guerillas. And it was a bloody, messy affair that often pitted Russian officers against former Soviet army and special forces officers. This bloody savage war broke Majid's heart. Of course he did not see any of it, but there was extensive coverage in the news and on TV about the fighting and lots of discussion about the high casualties of the poor Russian conscripts (although no one reported on the high Chechen casualties). To Majid, it was a repeat of the Soviet invasion and war in Afghanistan: the powerful Russian empire pitted against a poor, Muslim land for reasons which were hard to know and which defied all logic and strategic sense. The war among other things caused a noticeable increase in the displaced Chechen population of Moscow, and everywhere they seemed to be visible. They drove the streets in run-down Ladas offering their services to anyone who was hailing for a ride as curbside pick- up taxis, the so called *jihad* taxis. There were rumors even that they formed their own mafia in the city, running certain sectors of the open air markets and dealing in drugs and arms, but the violence seemed to be restricted to Chechnya itself. Majid followed news of the progress of the war and wrote several short poems expressing his revulsion at the loss of life there and the senseless violence. He was especially upset by the careless leadership of the Russian forces which resulted in needlessly high casualties on the Russian side and atrocities against the Chechen non-combatants. The war was settled through negotiations led by a gruff, battle tested general, Alexander Lebed. But the ceasefire came too late to restrain the rise of a violent Russian nationalist movement which promoted hatred and violence toward all of Russia's "negroes" as they called the Chechens and Caucasian peoples. By 1997, there were regular assaults and murders of Azeri and Chechen youths throughout Moscow and other Russian cities.

The new freedoms which came into force in 1993 were what allowed Majid to remain in Moscow after he graduated from the Gorky Institute. A classmate at the Institute, named Igor Formico, told him of an available room in a *communalka* apartment which was located not far from New Arbat and the river. In late July with the help of Igor and another friend who owned a beat-up Lada they moved his belongings to this new residence. Most of his belongings fit in two boxes and a large beat-up suitcase, but he still had 12 cartons of the unsold books of his collection of first poems which he had printed three years earlier. He did not need to get a propyska to live in that apartment. It was however an inauspicious residence. The residents were the usual collection of misfits trying to survive in economic hardtimes: an Armenian family with three children lived in one room, a middle aged childless couple lived in another although the husband often disappeared for days at a time on vodka binges, there was another room occupied by a young couple who disturbed the rest of the *communalka* by alternating bouts of angry furniture tossing or of sudden violent noises of what seemed to be either rowdy sex or intense shouting matches and beatings, and there were two rooms occupied by old widows both of whom slid around the apartment's public spaces like wraiths trying to avoid notice. In his first spring there he noticed that one of these old widows would go around the parks and clip off the panicles of flowering lilacs which she then sold in bunches from a plastic bucket at the entrance to the metro or she would bring the unsold flowers back to her room. So there were hardships in the *communalka* when Majid arrived. But even more unfortunate for the residents were the concussions of tanks shooting and the stray bullets which zipped around their building (even broke some windows and brought down several chunks of plaster) during the October shoot up at the White House, not 350 meters distant, which for several hours terrorized everyone in the building. The residents of the *communalka* spent the worst night of this coup huddled in the central corridor with the lights off and the doors to the rooms shut so that bullets would not penetrate the house through the windows. They survived unscathed fortunately and on the morning of the 5th of October when all the fighting and shooting seemed to be over, they emerged into the transformed city warily searching for food.

In the summer of '93, after Majid moved out of the Institute and before the fighting over the White House, Majid did take up Bella Akhmadulina's invitation to visit her at her dacha. It was a hot August day when the summer skies turn ashen white and the streets seem to melt under the heat and the city moves quietly at a turtle's pace, and those people, who can, escape the city center for the shade and coolness of their summer dachas in the forests of the countryside. Bella said she was planning a get together for literati and she would love to see him. She even offered to have one of her invited guests, a poet that Majid should get to know, to drive over and pick Majid up to take him to Peredelkino, the famous writers' colony located in a woods just outside the city. In the early afternoon on the appointed day, a white old model Volga drove up to Majid's building where the young poet stood waiting on the sidewalk. Stuffed into the front seat of this Volga, as if he were a pillow jammed into a jelly jar, was a bespectacled smiling, very heavy, young man. He popped out of the car with some difficulty appearing at first to be a creature made of all legs and arms and an oversized head. Straightening himself out, he then appeared to be not pudgy and overweight as he appeared to be in the car seat, but very tall and gangly with a huge shock of mousy colored hair and black horn-rimmed glasses, proffering Majid a long-fingered hammy hand. "My name's Leonid. You can call me Leonya. It always has seemed strange to me that a car like this Volga has so little space for the driver that I have to stoop double over to be able to see out the tiny windshield! So you're Majid, the latest poet marvel? Glad to meet you." "Call me Slava, if you like," said Majid as he arched his neck back to look up to Leonya's face as Leonya's hand swallowed up Majid's small hand. "Well, no need to dawdle here when the day is so beautiful, and the heat so stifling. Get in." Majid had never ridden in the front passenger seat of a car before, much less a large one and he marveled at the leg space he had. But immediately he became amused by the efforts and grunts made by Leonya as he folded himself awkwardly back into the driver's seat—the steering wheel pressed against his middle torso, the shift stabbing his ribs, his knees folded high up almost behind the wheel, his shoulders stooped over forcing his elbows out both sides, his head crooked to one side and down and forward so he could look out the windscreen. Once in, he started the car with a roar and sped off. He first drove down the short alleyways and he had to make several sharp turns which he achieved at enough speed so as to squeak the tires and to throw Majid against the door or the shift stick, each time Leonya exclaiming, "whoa, glad there are no pot holes there!" These maneuvers were to move the car around several blocks to be able to get onto the main thoroughfare out of town, New Arbat which they entered at a point only fifty meters or so from where they had started. "I've very much liked the poems of yours that I've read. I've never heard you recite, but I hope you might recite a few verses today. There'll be other poets and I expect they'll recite today. They always do." Leonya drove fast, carelessly, and he weaved through the traffic on the broad Kutuzovsky Prospect, shouting and snarling at the other drivers he passed. This was the very first time for Majid to be driven through the streets of Moscow in all his years there and it scared the wits out of him, he thought several times that their car was certainly going to side-swipe one car if not tail-end yet another. He held tightly onto the dashboard until his knuckles were white. But they did not have far to go, in only 12 minutes they had escaped over the "new" city walls which are called the Outer City Ring Highway and passed into the suburbs. After only a few more miles Leonya turned off the tree lined highway and onto a small poorly finished road that was hidden in deep shade and soon after crossing a small stream the Volga slowly drove past a gate emblazoned with the name Writer's dacha cooperative Peredelkino. The road deteriorated further into a gravel lane between towering dark pines beneath which lay large wooden houses with glassed in terraces in leafy yards surrounded by green picket fences. Things looked orderly but in need of fresh paint and some repairs. "This is a marvelous place, Slava. Founded at the recommendation of Maxim Gorky himself. All the literary greats have lived here. You see over there, that was the house of Ilya Ilf when he lived here. Boris Pasternak lived here year round for many years after the war. You'll see his place probably today." Majid had never been on a literary tour before and he was bemused by Leonya's comments, as if he were a tour guide.

They arrived at a plot surrounded by a pale green fence with a gate which hung askance with a rusted hinge. There was a fairly good sized two story brown wooden house which had white trim and large windows on a front terrace. In front of the house there were several Russian made cars parked in a front yard which was planted with some poorly growing grass and several slender birches creeping up against the pines. There was one patch planted with pansies which looked like they needed watering. Leonya parked and then proceeded to dislodge himself comically again from the driver's seat. The temperature was perhaps five degrees cooler than in Moscow and the air was refreshingly breathable. Once inside the house, Leonya proceeded to introduce Majid around to people who were arranged on the terraces and in different rooms. He introduced most of them as poets, but he also pointed out some as painters or literary critics. Nearly all the visitors, perhaps 13 or 14 of them were men. There was nobody that Majid knew by name or reputation. But as Leonya made introductions, there were several who responded enthusiastically to him "At last, the Poet has come." Finally they came to a door room hidden in deep shadow where Bella was seated in an overstuffed chair. She sat next to a few other older people. "Sasha, I'm glad that you could come. Good boy, Leonya." she said without really smiling while standing up. She immediately stretched out her cheek to him for a greeting kiss as if they were old friends, as if she was the queen who expected her subjects to show their deference. In fact, she was the queen of the day and her guests at the house were her court which regularly met to pay respects and homage to her. Sitting around her in that room were her husband, a painter and set designer, and her contemporaries—members of the Moscow's 60s generation, dissidents and victims of the regime of that time—which included the poet Roger Rozhdestvenko, Bella's third husband, Kuliev, a straw haired novelist, Vasily Aksennikov, who just then was visiting from the US, and the bombastic poet, Arkady Voskreshensky, who shook Majid's hand warmly but almost immediately made to leave, saying he had to go. "If you haven't already heard him in recital, Sasha" said Bella, "you have to whenever you can. He's unforgettable—an artist of the first order using the paintbrush of words." Elsewhere in the house were middle aged and younger men whom Leonya later introduced, nearly all of them as poets. They were seriously discussing poetry, sometimes reciting a line or two, current politics, especially the crisis emerging over the passage of Yeltsin's program for the new constitution, or merely gossiping. Majid noticed that there were hardly any women in any of the rooms or chairs. Bella's court comprised men, those who would fawn over her, pay attention to her, those she found sexy, those whom she could mother, those who would flatter her and pretend that they found her still sexy and would flirt with her, or would praise her poetry and would overlook her sad grimacing smile. But there were some women. One beauty in particular Majid noticed as she flitted from terrace to room to room and would then duck down a long dark corridor lined with hanging coats only to return with a tray of drinks or canapés. He was instantly attracted by her deep alluring eyes. "Who is that lovely one?" he whispered to Leonya when he continued his tour through the house. "Oh, that's Bella's daughter, Liza, Liza Bellanovna, she's a poet too, of sorts. She's always here but we don't hear her recite anything." "That would explain her wonderful eyes. She has her mother's."

The entire group gathered outside around a long table set for luncheon, sitting on a jumbled array of different chairs—some antique, some metal frames—stools, and benches. The mood was jolly and the table was well provided for. Liza and another young woman were bringing out bottles of juice, wine, and mineral water followed pitchers of fruit juice and berry juice. This was a special affair, and in all his life Majid had never seen the likes of it, a feast, a royal banquet. Plates of sliced cured meat and tinned fish lay on the table next to many plates of salads in mayonnaise and sliced fresh vegetables alongside salted cucumbers and marinated vegetables and sliced salamis. There were serving plates of stewed meat in aspic, along with small dishes of red-dyed horseradish, radishes, fresh parsley and dill, butter in little bowls, baskets of bread, and small dishes of black caviar. For a young man who had passed most the previous six years in perpetual hunger because of the scarcity of food, he could barely believe his eyes, and he certainly couldn't contain his appetite. He ate heartily and tried and tasted everything on offer. And those were just the starters. After about forty minutes, the girls cleared away the dishes and then brought out a large cauldron of boiled potatoes followed by platters with sliced boil beef and carrots along with and a plate with small grilled minced meat which they called lulei kebabs. Majid ate more at that one sitting than he had at any meal before or after in his lifetime. It was a spectacle as well as a saturnalia. The wine was cold and sweet and someone kept filling his cup, but he wasn't as interested in the wine as in trying all the foods.

"So who says lyricism is dead? There's still a lot of life left in classical poetic forms." This was a challenge thrown out by a mustachioed middle-aged man with a cigarette, sitting not far from Majid. "Bella is still the queen of lyrical poetry. And the newly crowned king is our exiled hero, Brodsky." "Easy for you to say that when all the declaimers of dramatic show poetry are not represented." "You mean those who perform 'word art'? Bella cut in, "It's not that I didn't invite them. Voskreshensky couldn't stay and no one can ever invite Rev Lubenstyen, he's too dogmatic. Besides some of Arkady's poetry is dam good and even quite classical in form—it's just that his recitation is even better." "You mean, very dramatic." Another chirped in, "It has to be dramatic if it is going to pack in a football stadium and be heavily amplified." "No it has to be histrionic, and dramatic, if it is going to convince people that blank verse is poetry or if it is going to interest anybody in the future." Another person cut it, "Has anybody here seen videos of American nigger hip-hop performances? Well it is poetry, but of an awful sort. There's a dance that goes with the words—which are mostly profanities—and of course it has a background of sexual music, that is a grinding, persistent bass line played over a 'boom box'. Of course no one in America considers what is being recited to be poetry; they market it as music. Nevertheless it shows the death of poetry there. And with this new 'word art' and blank verse performance poetry, we have the death of poetry here as well."

Majid finally contributed to this conversation. "As for performance art poetry, I haven't seen any." "You should see that silly old scarecrow Gangus perform," someone interrupted seeking to curry favor with Bella. She frowned. "It is pathetic. And he still pretends to be a dissident." Majid continued, "But I think there is probably good blank verse and poor blank verse, although most of what I have heard or read seems pretty poor and unpoetic to me. The real threat to poetry is the poetry written for solely for other poets, with obscure references to past poetry, internal commentary and oblique critique on others' works, having a contrived ideology which is only a temporary fad and possessing unpronounceable metrical contrivances. It is poetry meant to be read or dissected by a small handful of specialists and academics and never meant to be recited. This is the real death threat to poetry. No one will want to either hear or read such poetry in the future and the craft will be irrelevant and die out. And, you know, I think video filming will also hurt poetry and could be fatal. It removes the live experience of the words and the internal feeling and emotion of prosody from the listener, and it makes poetry just a poor competitor to other films and cinema. And that is a competition that poetry will always lose. Movies hardly require that listeners think and feel about what they hear, and soon video recordings of poetry being recited will do the same thing." Another young person at the table said, "Yes, can you imagine computer readings of poetry recorded on video—awful. It will spell the end for sure. They have already computerized readers of prose works—I've heard some and they sound laughable, disgustingly mechanic. Like some science fiction robot. Can you imagine Pushkin being recited by a robot?" Everyone laughed.

After the dishes were cleared away, and as Liza and the other girls were bringing in tea cups and mugs, Bulat Okudzhava walked around the corner of the house and approached Bella. There was a swell of approval from the acolytes seated at the table and Bulat smiled a little smile out of embarrassment. He came up to Bella and stooped to kiss her cheeks. "How is my beautiful one, my darling doing? I'm sorry I'm a little late." "Everybody, if you don't already know, this is my neighbor and lifelong friend, Bulat Okudzhava." Then she proceeded to introduce the people at the table, excepting her husband, the regulars and the more established poets. Bulat politely, almost shyly bowed his head to each person. "And there is the lovely young bloom, Liza. Hello my darling." When Bella came to introducing Majid, Bulat smiled with recognition. "I have already had the pleasure of meeting the young poet and even hearing him perform. I'm so glad to see you again in such august company, Slava." A chair was brought up for Bulat and he sat next to Bella. The girls brought in fruit and berry pies, followed by baskets of fresh fruit. Bulat reached for a slice of berry pie, "I'll have one of these. I have a sweet tooth for Bella's pies."

Bella then stood up to make an announcement. "I have reached agreement on publishing a new collection of poetry. The book should come out later this year or early next." There was a small cheer around the table, then a call for a toast to Bella's new verse, the clinking of wine glasses. "And now, as is our tradition at these summer get-togethers I will regale you with a new poem I have composed. You'll be the first to hear it. And then you will have to recite for us one of your own recent compositions." She then proceeded to recite a poem without a title, which everyone seemed to know was about Anna Akhmatova. "*I envy her, so young and slender, like a galley slave, more ardent then some alluring harem girl, her golden eyes burned and looked out over the waters of the Neva as if together two dawns burned. This name, by which she was called and which she herself had wanted, was a violation of her features and limits and the East of the uninvited authority, which like the lilac suggests imminent death. But her name and mine fundamentally sound alike…"* It was a sad poem recalling a time already more than 30 years earlier when she was a young woman starting her poetic life and encountering the grand dame of Russian poetry who barely acknowledged her. It is a poem acknowledging Akhmatova's poetic strength and evergreen youthful quality even after a lifetime of suffering. But Akhmatova had not taken on Bella to include in her circle of young poets to mentor and cultivate as she had Joseph Brodsky. And after Bella sat back down, two others stood up and recited short poems one after the other, but they were memorable only by being so hack and unmemorable. Majid paid them little regard; he was luxuriating in the warm sunlight and also staring at the curvature of Liza's breasts behind her snug-fitted white blouse. Liza was by then sitting right across from him. Someone at the table called on Okudzhava to sing one of his works. But he declined, saying "I came unprepared as I don't have my reliable old guitar with me. It's in Moscow. And as you all know I cannot sing without my simple guitar. And perhaps I cannot sing with it either." Bella spread her arm towards our hero. "Slava, I invite you to declaim for us one of your poems, recent or otherwise." said Bella. "I would love to, but perhaps we should hear something by Liza first." Liza looked up in alarm and shook her head emphatically, "No, no. I don't want to. I haven't any verses prepared." The other guests at the table urged her and begged her to recite, but now looking embarrassed she continued to object. "I don't know my poems by memory, I need to read them." And then she scowled and she went into a pout. And that is when he realized that he had seen Liza before. She had been a second-year student at the Maxim Gorky Institute during Majid's final year there and on occasion he had caught glimpses of her in the corridors. Once even after seeing her pass by he had thought that her alluring eyes reminded him of someone and seemed very familiar. But he had not realized until just then that she reminded him of the very young Bella portrayed in the large photos of her hanging in the entry foyer of the

Institute. The alluring eyes but without her mother's depressive grimace in those turned-down lips. That afternoon he fell in love with Liza. But then it was Majid's turn to recite something.

"I'll have to improvise my contribution this afternoon. Excuse me if it is not up to standard."

Sunlight shimmering through the tops of majestic pines
Cast a yellow light—the light of love—on a summer garden
Where the Beautiful One holds court over her circle of acolytes
Teaching them versification as an age old craft
While her daughter blushes in the aroma of peonies.

A chill wind bends the pines in the thin grey light of the Finnish Gulf
There is the buzzing of clouds of mosquitos—grey light is for the grief
Of Anna as her circle of young poets learn the words
Which capture the terror, the bloodshed, and loss.
One young man promises to build the next rung on her ladder.

The guttering of lamps casting blue shadows across Ivanov's door
Allow only a dim pale light—the light of apprehension
Where a group of acmeists gather searching out
Words to replace symbols. But one dreams only
Of mimosas, hot savannahs, and the torrid light of Africa.

The sun's searing white light beats down on umbrella pines
In a land of exile—where white light means death—
Only forget-me-nots resist the bleaching—Sappho leads
Her daughter to recite the exquisite verses—
Soon to be long lost—as she climbs the cliffs.

The group cheered and applauded when Majid was done. The mustachioed man jumped up and shouted, "Bravo, a new lyric champion!" Bella even smiled bashfully, as it seemed some of the references were to her and her daughter, who rushed away from the table blushing.

(This poem has never appeared in any of Majid's published output. I was fortunate in the details of this visit and in getting a copy of this poem to receive the report of Leonya, who copied this poem down from memory after the events of that afternoon. He was impressed and I gather from the samizdat of this poem of some of the other participants that he was not the only one. I have to admit that in trying to translate this I became even more in awe of this masterful poet. To think he improvised this poem—the references, the compressed languages, the rhyme scheme of ABCBA, the perfect metrics, and, I imagine, the intonation of this poem were all perfect. What genius. I found it tremendously difficult and tricky to translate and had to resort to a strict literal translation. But clearly he thought it a work in progress and he never did polish it or attempt to have it published! I believe he in referring to Sappho and her daughter, he was addressing Bella and Liza.)

After the poetry circle was finished and the coffee and dessert dishes were cleared away, Bella invited her guests to take a walk around the leafy lanes of Peredelkino. The entire group set off at a slow pace; clusters of the group discoursing on inflation, on gossip, on new plays or poems that had recently appeared in Moscow, on the economic hard times, and some, very guardedly, on politics and Yeltsin's difficulties with the communists. "Over there, that is the dacha of Boris Pasternak. Some of his descendants still live there." said Bella. "And just around the corner here is the dacha where Isaak Babel was staying when the secret police came to arrest him and afterwards shot him." A hundred yards further on and Roger Rozhdestvenko waved his arm at a small run-down looking dacha. "And this ladies and gentlemen is my humble abode. I will leave you here." And he swept through his gate and turned around to wave to the clusters of the group as they shuffled by. "Bella won't tell you, but that is the dacha/home of her first husband, Yevgheny Gangnus." said Leonya in a whisper to Majid. "She tends to wipe him from her memory and barely acknowledges him. He rarely lives there anymore." Bella continued the tour. Majid kept trying to walk next to

Liza. He thought he detected lavender scent wafting from her. "And that is the house of Arseny Tarkovsky. He worked on *Solaris* while he was living here." Not long after this when the group turned to another lane, it was the turn of Bulat to wave goodbye; he begged off returning to Bella's dacha saying he was feeling weak and unwell and he slowly walked off. Bella resumed her tour talk. "It was Maxim Gorky who suggested setting up this dacha settlement for the literary community. Just like he set up the World Literature Institute. During the purges it was of course convenient to have all the leading writers collected in the same place. It made it easier to collect them and silence them. It was named Peredelkino after the nearby pre-revolutionary estate, which has long ago been removed. But the name is ironic as *peredelen* means amended or re-done. And so we have had it through the repressions of the Soviet era. The works of the artists and poets of this settlement could only appear if they were amended, rewritten, or re- done—or they would not appear at all. It was like the condition of being able to live here. Amend your works to our standards or leave." Some of the group separated and walked off to the train stop so that they could ride back into the city. The rest walked on another twenty minutes and Bella pointed to another house, which was marked as a cultural center and museum. "Even the children's stories by Korney Chukovsky, who lived here for many years, had to be amended to suit Barmelei's whims." (She used the term that Anna Akhmatova had assigned to Stalin and his henchmen, but she was of course referring to all of the Soviet authorities, censors, internal spies, secret police, bureaucrats right up to those times.) Those remaining with the group returned to the garden, now lying in the deep shade of late afternoon, and they either had tea or made movements to begin to leave. As the early evening set in, the last remaining guests of Bella gradually slipped away usually after long repetitive farewells were said over an elaborately ritualized departure routine. After Leonya was finished with this formula—which took only fifteen minutes—he grabbed Majid and packed himself back into Volga and the two drove back into the city. Majid was lost in a cloud of contentment; a large delicious meal and daydreams of Liza shrouded in lilac perfume. After that summer feast, Majid would regularly go out to Peredelkino to visit Bella, to discuss poetry, and to exchange ideas. Usually twice every summer, he would go when this large circle of Bella's followers and friends would gather.

As it turned out, Majid was also to publish a new book of his recent poems in 1994. This all came about because of the efforts of Igor Formico who had taken on a self-appointed role in promoting Majid and his poetry. He was just that way. It was hard to tell what Formico did to support himself, but he very much busied himself by supporting his friends. He was not a poet, but a poetaster, but he was not really that. He had studied six years at the Gorky Institute where he had met and befriended our hero, and he was one of many in those years who recognized the genius and masterful output of Majid. It would perhaps be best to call him, following the pattern of the Russian compound word for musicologist", a "*poeziyaved*" which normally we would translate as "poetry-ologist" or prosody-ologist" but which literally means a "poetry-eater." He would run around town mediating contacts, "networking" (before there was such a functioning concept in Russia), making introductions, and connecting ideas, compositions, or productions to publishers, theatres, or musicians, literary magazines. And of course he attending all sorts of cultural presentations; poetry recitations, plays, opera, musical recitals, contemporary composers nights. Majid could never figure out how Formico managed it all, especially the expense of buying all those tickets, or the effort of keeping up with the program schedules (at that time there was no internet nor any weekly journal publishing the programs of all the scheduled upcoming cultural events so that being informed was very challenging). But Formico did. And he would call Majid frequently on the chipped telephone in the corridor of his *communalka* to tell him of a poetry reading he shouldn't miss, or an interesting upcoming performance of *Winterreise* to hear Schubert's musical setting of Wilhelm Mueller's poetry, or a lecture and discussion on state of Russian art at one of the cultural institutions around Moscow. And it was Formico who called him during those intensely cold and snowy three weeks in November of 1993 when people stopped going outside to stay warm indoors. He had discovered a publisher who would print a new collection of Majid's poems. "When can you have a new collection ready?" The major work was not the composition, for Majid had composed perhaps 120 poems of varying length since his first book had appeared three years earlier. No, the real work was to review in his mind an appropriate selection of the better ones and to type them up to be able to give a manuscript to the printer. Majid estimated it would take him three months at the barest minimum to type up 30-35 poems and have them ready. Formico said, "That's a deal. March then to deliver them." And he hung up leaving Majid perplexed. As it was, it took somewhat longer than that. Four months longer in fact before he presented a typescript of about 110 pages of his verses to the printer. When he met Formico in the street on the way to the printer's, the latter took the pages in his hands and the first thing he said was this. "Did you use carbon paper, Slava? Do you have two copies of these?" Majid of course had not. It was not yet his habit to work with carbon paper. He still had enough trouble with working the typewriter. "Don't worry. Let's go down to the xerox shop down here around." At that time these were new businesses that were sprouting up everywhere, and were changing the entire nature of *samizdat*—at least the looks and legibility of samizdat copies. Majid was amazed how clean and simple it was to make two collated copies of his original typescript. He was even more amazed when Formico paid the rather exorbitant cost of xeroxing. He couldn't imagine having so much spare money, nor could he think Formico had so much. Money in those days was scarce for everyone it seemed, especially for an unemployed poet. Formico showed Majid how it was done over that winter when he took him to the conservatory to attend the performance of *Winterreise*. He went to the box office and asked for and got two special entry student tickets for the upper balcony. They were complimentary or counter-mark in the local language. He had also gotten him a text of the German poetry by Mueller which Schubert had set to music so that Majid could read the poems and dissect them and learn their inner music in advance of the performance. Igor was very concerned to demonstrate to Majid that composers could set good poetry to music successfully. Majid was convinced. The emotional "sound" and mood of the music complemented the verse just as Majid thought he understood and he was impressed. He thanked Igor for proposing and arranging this concert. Igor shrugged it off. It was not a favor, it was something that Majid needed and he knew how to make it happen. It was just the way Igor Formico was.

Money was a particular problem for Majid in the year after he left the Institute, in fact it was going to remain a problem for him through the rest of his life. He never had enough. He did not have enough at that moment to be able to attend the *Winterreise* concert out of his own sources, if Igor had not shown him out to wheedle a counter-mark ticket out of the system. He was not working at any regular job. He received some sporadic pocket money for translations that he did for the literary journals, and he still received money from his mother, although inflation in those early Yeltsin years had badly eroded the buying power of the ruble and prices of food ran away from his allowance. He was at any rate very abstemious by nature; he never played the role of romantic poet sitting all day in cafes, drinking aperitifs or coffees or smoking cigarettes (he didn't smoke) as he simply never could afford to do this. And he did not have the numbers of friends from whom he could borrow money. Nearly all the people he knew from his university years were from out of Moscow or were also barely scraping by. In the late winter of 1993-94, he got word from his mother that his grandfather had died, so Majid bought a train ticket to Kazan to visit her and attend the funeral. He arrived only just in time for the farewell service at the morgue. Snow still lay all around the streets and parks of Kazan. At the morgue he found that his mother was now accompanied by her partner,

Artyem, the same man that as her lover had driven Majid to move in with the Buterbrodskys. His grandmother was not there—apparently she had died a few years earlier and his mother simply hadn't told him. Grandfather's body was on display in a coffin buried under flowers. It was shrunken and shriveled up and Majid did not recognize him at all. He felt a great sadness that those mortal remains of a family member appeared to him to be those of a total stranger. But then as the funeral services wound on, and continued to the wake dinner, his mother looked so much like a stranger to him as well. Admittedly she had lost weight, the skin on her face was drawn tight in a way that he had never seen, and her hair was beginning to turn white, but when she stood arm in arm with Artyem her partner, he did not recognize that she was his mother of his memories at all. She was no longer the bubbly, sweet mother, champion of his efforts at poetry, the poetry lover who used to recite to him verses, both classic and children's favorite rhymes, from his earliest childhood. All of that character had ebbed away. She even received a copy of Majid's first collection of poems with an indifference that hurt him more than he thought possible. Even at the funeral dinner afterwards she was distant and only limply responsive to Majid even though she did not show much outward grief. The day after the funeral his mother was all business. She was going to receive all of her father's ruble savings as well as the two rooms in the *communalka*, which had been privatized only shortly before his grandfather had died. She baldly said that she could no longer afford to send him monthly allowances. Her salary had not grown one kopeck in the previous four years and inflation meanwhile had eaten it down to nothing. But she was expecting a large inheritance from her father and after she got that she offered to send him a one-time payment of 200,000 rubles which would have to do for him until he got his own income. There would be no more after that. The sum was not large (At that time when they met it amounted to a little over $600, but by the time he got it, it was worth less than $500. Inflation had killed his grandfather's savings in the previous three years.). Majid had not been counting on anything from his grandparents, but the promise to cut off his allowance was almost too much for Majid to bear, even if in real terms it amounted to only a few dollars a month. It was as if she were for the final time severing her relationship with him. She bought him a return train ticket when he left, but he felt devastated on the ride back, as if she had died and departed.

The Buterbrodskys, on the other hand, were overjoyed to see Majid again after more than seven years' absence. They were all hugs and kisses and shouts of happiness when he arrived at the front door of their small apartment. Anya looked at him with adoration in her eyes. She looked as beautiful and shapely as he remembered her. Osip had grayed a bit, but the youthful ardor was still in his expression. And their apartment had a new addition, their son Alexander Osipovich, a small six year old dark-haired boy, who looked a lot like Majid had when he had been the same age. Alexander, or Sasha, once he got over his initial shyness was demonstrably pleased by Majid, was quite chatty and precocious and he tried to attract his attention all through their visit. Unlike the cold grief and aloofness of his visit with his mother and Artyem, Majid's reunion with the Buterbrodsky's was all joyful talk and excitement; he could feel the warmth and affection pouring over him. "Our Slava, the poet", they would coo all day long. He presented them with a copy of his first printed collection of poems, and Osip was so pleased that he right away cracked open the small book and began reading out loud several of the verses. Besides catching up on their news—the Buterbrodskys insisted that nothing ever happened to them and there was no news, except of course recalling the constant developments and accomplishments of their young Alexander—Majid would recite a short poem or two for them or regale them with the stories of his walks around Moscow, or reciting for Yevgheny Gangnus or his first summer's day visit at Bella's dacha in Peredelkino.

When Majid had left Moscow, he was hoping to re-establish his poetry contacts in Kazan. So he took with him one carton of his first published collection of poems and he copied the telephone numbers of the editor at *Milli Yul* and of his Tatar friends from the poetry circle, including Gabdallah Chulpan. When he was in Kazan, he found that *Milli Yul* had closed and although he reached Gabdallah, the poetry circle at the Marjan mosque had long since ceased to meet. He met Gabdallah and found a depressed shrunken man from what he had remembered. The mosque had been taken over by a more fundamentalist group of Muslim worshipers and they immediately banned the poetry circle from the premises for being too blasphemous and profane. After that the circle of poetry-eaters and poets found it hard to meet; public spaces where they could hold meetings now wanted rent or were inappropriately located or just not available. And then there were the conflicts that arose in the group between those that felt that Tatar poetry had to reflect and promote Islamic values and those who wanted to write more contemporaneous, secular poetry in the current idiomatic forms of the Tatar language. At the same time the public media were demanding nationalist Tatar language literature. Gabdallah could not resolve these disparate schools and the disputes had grown bitter so the group had dissolved, everyone going their own way. Only as an afterthought did Gabdallah ask Majid if he had any new poems in Tatar. Majid couldn't bear to tell him that he had almost entirely stopped composing Tatar verse. And when he offered him a copy of his book, Gabdallah took it disinterestedly. When they parted, Majid had, for the first time in his life, the certain premonition that he would never see or hear of Gabdallah again. It was a strange sensation, one that he was to have more often in the coming years. There were no further errands to run in Kazan. It no longer felt like home to him. He felt like leaving Kazan that day was also going to be for the last time.

But in the morning before Majid left Kazan, Osip took him to a downtown bookstore where they negotiated the sale of the remaining twenty copies of his first published collection of poems. They went for cheap (equivalent to about $4.00 each), but he was surprised that the manager was willing to buy them at all (the manager planned on selling them for $6, which was still expensive for a small book of poetry in those days). The real selling point which Osip stressed was that Majid was a Tatar poet and that he was already acknowledged in Moscow as an up and coming champion of contemporary poetry. The bookshop buyer promptly suggested that he would be even more eager to sell any book of Tatar poetry that Majid had ready for publication. This led Osip to propose to Majid that he collect all the Tatar poems he had composed and he would find a Kazan publisher to print them. Out of this Majid got a pocketful of large denomination ruble bills (hyperinflation had caused the growth in ruble denominations) when he hadn't really expected any money from Kazan. (Four years later in 1997 Osip's project came to fruition when a small volume of Tatar verse, some 23 poems, appeared with the title (in translation) "The strong wind blowing in my youth" printed in Latin letters. It sold out but was not re-printed because the Russian Federation declared that Tatar had to use the Cyrillic alphabet.) Later that afternoon, when he left the Buterbrodsky's, they insisted that he write them more often and come visit them now and then. Anya gave him an intimate, prolonged kiss, while Osip had his arm around the young Alexander. Unlike for his mother, Majid felt a real love for these generous warm people who had taken him in when he was lost. In contrast, his mother's send-off at the Kazan station was cold and stiff. She bought him the ticket and accompanied him to his wagon and then left with just a peck on the cheek, almost no words at all. It seemed like a farewell. But only a few weeks after returning to Moscow, Majid got over the sadness of departure and resumed writing letters to his mother, along with letters to Anya.

So what did our hero do with himself in that year and half after he graduated from the Gorky Institute until when he started working in the public relations firm where he got his first job? He worked on his poetry, and he worked hard, either composing new poems, or typing them up, reading vast amounts of poetry in Russian, and in English and French, and translating foreign poetry into Russian verse. This was the time when for the first time the Russian poetry of Joseph Brodsky was being published and distributed in Russia and his works were being consumed ravenously by poets and *poeziyaveds* and poetry lovers of all stripes across the country. Brodsky's works were like the discovery of new lands across the ocean, like finding unexpected hordes of treasure and recognizing it as your own inheritance. It caused a stir in all the literary circles of Russia, an eagerness to explore his works, and amazement and wonder that this national hero had been expelled and had become virtually unknown inside Russia for more than 25 years—virtually a lifetime. Majid discovered Brodsky's newly published works in the Moscow House of Books one of his regular destinations on his walks around the city. It was a comfortable warehouse of books where a serious bibliophile or *poeziyaved* could pick out a book and find a seat and stay for hours reading. In those years it was beginning to carry more and more previously banned poetry and literature in Russian or translation and there was a tremendous thirst for this literary heritage. Majid avidly studied Brodsky's works as each volume was published, reading to himself in the Moscow House of Books or reciting poems out loud as he paced back and forth in his room, memorizing verses that particularly enraptured him. His neighbors in the *communalka* were at first worried by his constant pacing and reciting, hearing this through the thin walls of their apartments, they initially assumed that Majid was a madman or one possessed by demons, just as they assumed that the young couple were wild cats constantly mating and thrashing. Once they understood that he was a poet, they were bemused and concluded that he was indeed mad. He also continued his long strolls and exploratory walks around the city center, and now he added a new destination. He would walk over to the Institute and search out Liza in the hallways or corridors. It took him several such trips before he finally "bumped into" her as if by accident. She was as coy and attractive as he remembered from that summer first meeting. But she seemed at that time pleased to see him again, and she agreed to join him on one of his strolls after her classes. They made arrangements to meet after that and he got her contact telephone number. Once when he had scraped up enough cash, he even asked her to join him at one of the new cafés for a tea and pastry after one of their walks. It was in these years when he also included regular visits to the fine art museums to spend hours studying their permanent collections and special exhibitions. The Pushkin Museum collection of classical sculptures particularly attracted his attentions. Even if they were mostly reproductions, he would stare at the masterpieces of Roman and Greek art, the human curves, the expressions, and the ideal proportions, and he read about the background stories of the goddesses, nymphs, heroes, and half-man-half creatures there on display.

It was in mid-1994 that Igor Formico came to him once and proposed to him to give a poetry reading at one of the smaller theatres on the Boulevard Ring. Igor would make all the arrangements, and he did so brilliantly, as it turned out, because the booking occurred only two weeks after Majid's second volume of poems was published and appeared in the bookstores. The publisher had given a title to the book, *The Spring Voice of Orpheus*, loosely following the meaning of one of its poems, and this book is much more readily found today around Moscow than his first collection. Following their appearance, Formico also went to *Yunost*—knowing that *Yunost* had already printed several of Majid's poems in the past years—and convinced them to write a review. Other reviews appeared in other literary journals, most of them were positive in their view of Majid's poems, but there was one, which appeared in *Moscow's Union of Communist Youth Clubs* newspaper, which was decidedly negative, attacking of all things Majid's old-fashioned lyricism and his negativity toward Russian life of that time. Formico even notified the public television station *Kultura* that they should mention Majid's recital in its news section on upcoming cultural events about town. They agreed to and mentioned his recital four times in advance of the date. The result of this favorable timing—whether the newspaper reviews were negative or not—was that more than three hundred paying poetry lovers came to the theatre to hear him. And they received his recitation very enthusiastically. Most of Bella's circle of young poets came, as well as Bella and Liza, even though that June was the first when it appeared that Bella was beginning to have difficulties walking on her own. In fact, it turned out that much of the audience was already well aware of Majid's poetic genius and entrancing declamatory style, you could say they were fans of his already from earlier recitals at the university or Institute. He gave a program of entirely new poems, including many that had been printed in his second book, which lasted more than an hour and half and then faced ten minutes of sustained applause and a cascade of flowers proffered by young women. And then true to form as the evening wound down and the clapping stopped, Majid was thronged by those who really enjoyed his poems around the skirt of the theatre, new fans who wanted to touch him, to speak to him, to get him to autograph his new book, or to share their new found emotional enthusiasm with him. He found that this happened each time at the end of his recitals. He would stand around awkwardly with a bouquet of flowers in his arms listening to the adulation or inquiries coming from a crowd around him. Members of the audience, usually women, became so emotionally aroused by his recitation that they sought an immediate intimate contact with him after the reading. He burned with embarrassment from all this adulation. Igor Formico hovered around Majid, like an agent/impresario, answering some of the many questions, handling some requests, giving out some information about Majid, and directing his attention to important people in the throng. This was when Majid first met Anna Yadrova. She managed to introduce herself and congratulate him in just a few words, but she was smiling at him with love and affection like any devotee of a rock and roll star. And he was immediately taken by her. In the memory afterwards of the audience, and the adoring crowds after the recital, Majid kept seeing the smiling face of the young Anna Yadrova. In reviewing the evening, he also came to realize that the vast majority of the audience was comprised of women—young, middle-aged and gray-haired matrons (They were cruelly called dandelion puffballs because of their similar color and because of their ephemerality—one puff and they were gone. They comprised the core group of audience members attending poetry readings or classical music concerts.); admiring, fawning, heads inclining toward him, adoring, some even sighing with delight. The evening was for him an entirely unexpected triumph and it spread the name of Majid around the town. He even made almost $200 (in rubles) for the night—which was a fair amount of money in those hard-pressed days. The reviewers in the press in the days after the recital acclaimed him and continued the bravos.

The voice of Orpheus in the spring
Seems to coax the lilies of the valley out of their shy hoods
Shames the nightingales' riverside courtship song
Instills in all a great joy, a happiness
As if eternal life and youth should prevail.

His springtime melodies bend the mountains
Down to him, overlays the sirens' allure who
Drown in the waves trying to reach his boat;
All who hear Orphee's dulcet tones
Want to cease their labors and smile at him.

The voice of Orpheus in summertime's heat
Stills the angry hearts, batters down the gates
Of Hell and lifts up the weeping Eurydice;
The very rocks crack and the stars streak from
The inky skies in praise to his singing.

His songs are quietly beautiful, refreshing
They led Jason's men into lands of fear.
On his harp, the words cause the mute to sing
The lame to dance, the barren to bear child
The doubting to build castles and theatres in the air.

Orpheus' autumnal voice sounds of the divine;
One and all celebrate his verses, sing a liturgy,
The miller and milliner, the spider and the bee
Direct their works to an eternal goal
Singing across the ether to the distant stars.

Through all time, his songs resound with love,
The sound is truer than the words' meaning
His words more powerful than steel swords
And his refrains live in us all through eternity,
Lifting us out of the clayey earth to the heavenly stars.

The winter voice of Orpheus evokes such passionate love
That the virginal muses beat their breasts
And desperately vie to possess him, with such fervor
That they tear him limb from limb all to
Grab a piece of his body to sate themselves.

But Orphee's singing does not cease
As his sweet voice sing out from his severed head
Floating down the river of life to the river Styx;
The passion for his songs cannot be assuaged
We seek out Orphee's progeny through the eons.

In those days and weeks following that recital, however, Majid's "courting" of Liza did not go so well. And this was at a time when the weather improved to such a degree that long outdoor strolls were very comfortable and pleasant, except perhaps for the cottonwood fluff flying through the air. But Liza was not responsive. After the first couple of strolls, they arranged others by telephone, and over the phone it was much easier for her to decline to meet for one reason or another. She did not always want to go out with him and when she did she did not talk with him very much at all. Surprisingly on one walk she said that she actually did not want to be a poet, it was her mother who pushed her in that direction. And besides she added she was not very good at poetry, she liked poetry and she liked Majid's poetry, but poetry did not really turn her on or inspire her, and she said she had not the skill at putting verses together. Unlike Majid she really did not like long strolls, and she needed to sit down occasionally. On one stroll he tried to take her hand, but she lent him a limp hand and after only a short while she shook off his hand. When they walked, he felt keenly that they did not fit together. Their strides were quite different in length—she was bit taller than he—and they walked with a different cadence. She also sensed that. And she realized that Majid did not have any money, so she felt awkward suggesting to him that they sit in a *kafe* (which is not a café such as a coffeehouse, but actually a type of simple restaurant) for a coffee or cake or a meal, because she did not want to offend him by offering to pay for both of them. The truth be told she undoubtedly was not very attracted to Majid, and she was embarrassed by his shows of fondness for her. But perhaps in thinking about Majid she also remembered the unhappy story of her mother who while still at the Institute as a young poetess she had married the brash, successful poet, Gangnus, who had dominated her and overshadowed her and gave her little credit, and Liza did not want the same thing to happen to her. As the summer began, she moved out to her mother's house in Peredelkino. So for that summer he did not see her at all, neither in Moscow, nor much to his disappointment at Peredelkino because she also skipped out from the next meeting of the circle of poets when Majid again went to Bella's dacha. It was at that session that Bella spoke to him at length about translation of poetry and how important it was for keeping one's own poetic skills sharp. She herself had been long engaged in translating Georgian poetry, the music of which had fascinated her when she had spent a long summer vacation in Tiflis and Khaketia a decade or so earlier. She inquired if he were translating any verses then, and encouraged him to make it a regular practice to translate great foreign poetry into Russian.

But while his lame romancing of Liza petered out that summer, Majid found another romance. Or is it better to say it found him? One afternoon during that summer of 1994, one of his neighbors knocked on the door to his room to tell him he had a phone call. The receiver was lying on the floor. On the line was a mellifluous voice that he did not recognize (and which was somewhat distorted by the old telephone equipment and lines), asking gently, "Is this Slava Khairulin?" He was charmed by the voice. "Yes, the self-same. And who is this?" "My name is Yadrova. Anna Petrovna Yadrova. I was at your recital a few weeks back and I introduced myself to you afterwards. You might remember me. I was wearing a blue patterned dress." He didn't really remember the dress or the name, but he recalled some very attractive faces in the adulatory crowds that evening. He was intrigued by this unknown female caller (she sounded young over the telephone line). "How did you get my telephone number?" "I asked Igor Formico for it, and he gave it to me willingly." Now his curiosity was thoroughly piqued. It turned out that the caller was proposing to him a date; she wanted to see him again. Majid was amazed and reluctant. But when Anna suggested that they have a dinner date—food being still very important and enticing to him—he agreed. And what was she proposing? He even told her he could not afford going to a restaurant. But she told him in as tactful manner as possible that all of that would be taken care of, and if he would accept, she would come on such an evening in her chauffeured car and pick him up to take him to that restaurant. He agreed again, now quite keenly curious. But he said he would stand outside his house at the appointed meeting time, because he was ashamed to let this stranger and admirer see his dingy *communalka* or his bare room. On the appointed evening, a black S class Mercedes drove slowly up to his house and stopped next to where he was standing on the sidewalk. Out of the car emerged Anna, gracefully and with dignity. She was wearing a yellow dress with thin white sweater and she fairly gleamed when the evening sunlight hit her. Majid at once remembered this vision of beauty and grace, and his breath was taken away. She came up to him offering her hand to shake. "Let me once again introduce myself: Yadrova, Anna Petrovna." She was slender, a little taller than Majid, with large, brown friendly eyes, a broad forehead, a straight nose with a slight upturn at the end, upturned pink lips with a sincere smile, and nut brown short wavy hair. She was beautiful, just as he had thought the first time he had seen her. She seemed also to be a little bashful with this first meeting, but she knew what she wanted and went boldly ahead with her plan. They drove across town to the restaurant called Sirens. Anna asked him if he liked seafood, but the truth at the time was that he had never before in his life tried any kind of seafood, neither shellfish or sea fish, not mollusks or crustaceans. Seafood had never been available when he was growing up or it had cost way too much money when it had been available. He was quite willing to try it. He had liked fresh water fish when he had eaten it. The restaurant was one of the earliest privately owned, professionally run, first class restaurants in all of Moscow and Majid was astonished by the décor and the layout. At the entry they stepped over a glass panel in the floor which revealed a large, colorful aquarium underfoot. Inside the restaurant had light wood paneling with paintings of naked lithe young sirens and mermaids either in the water or sitting on the rocks singing to distant sailing boats. And in the center of the restaurant—something Majid had never seen before—there stood a large display of fresh fish and mollusks arranged in crushed ice as if in a fish monger's store for the customers' choice. It goes without saying that all of the creatures on display were unknown to Majid. Anna saw this and even before they were seated she guided him through the silver, orange, blue, red, and white fish and gave them all their common names and then she introduced him to the names of the mollusks and crustaceans arranged in the ice alongside the fish. It was a breathtakingly beautiful restaurant; for Majid a little overwhelming. With the paintings of the sirens on the wall singing their alluring songs, and the smiling, sparkling attentions of Anna, Majid became aroused. She started their conversation by telling him about herself: that she was 28 years old (actually she was

29 but didn't want to confess that), that she had loved poetry since she was a little girl, that when she first went to a poetry reading of Pushkin's verses, she felt that she had been seduced by Pushkin and that it was one of the most memorable events in her life, that she had gone to Moscow State University and had studied poetry there, and that yes, she was married (Majid had noticed a sizeable diamond ring on the ring finger of her right hand and had asked) and she had been since she was 19 but she hadn't any children, and that she wasn't rich but she did not have to worry about money. Most important after this long introduction Anna confessed that she had fallen in love at once with his poems and the way he declaimed them. He chose to eat a sole and two crevettes, marinated and grilled over charcoal, and they were delectable. But he was distracted from the delicious food by the clear affection that Anna was ladling over him throughout the meal. It was difficult for him not to reciprocate, and he was effusive and flirtatious in return. She was so charming and attractive that he could hardly pay any attention to his plate. She was so delicious to his eyes and sugary to his pride that he knew at once that he loved this woman and wanted her right away. He was so enamored of Anna, he came to think that after only a 40 minute conversation he had known her well for years.

Then before dessert, when the table was bare, Anna said, "I was particularly struck, Slava, by a beautiful couplet in your recital. It stuck in my mind, although I cannot remember the entire poem it came from. It went: *'Love is when the passions and affections of two people attracted to each other become subsumed into a separate entity, a union, which is held together by a adamantine bond unlike any chemical bond.'* That's really sublime. I have wondered if you were thinking of this kind of love out of some memory of falling in love with some actual woman in your past."

Majid was immensely embarrassed, taken completely off guard. There was no concrete lover in his past who fit that definition and sentiment. (Perhaps there may have been one or two women whom he would have liked to have had such love.) He cleared his throat with a little cough, "No, I would have to say that there's been none such, but then there is always hope." (Artfully he answered her in a rhymed couplet.) Anna clapped her little hands, and then turned flirt, "Oh, wonderful. Then I too can say there is always hope. For neither have I had such an adamantine love." In a sudden rush, Majid felt that he had fallen in love with Anna. But instead of acting on this impulse or declaring his sudden burst of love, he carefully answered Anna that the point of the couplet which she had quoted was in the context of a scolding of the romantic poets, and maybe Lermontov especially, who confused love with their insatiable desire to seduce beautiful and attractive women, and who in the process never really knew of the real power of such a union. Just as he was saying that he realized that Anna was wearing essence of lilies of the valley. It was one of his very favorite spring aromas in his youth in the forest verges east of Ufa. She was smiling at him. Dinner was over. But Anna had a program. While they were still seated at the table she asked him if he would be able to come to her apartment late one afternoon soon for an afternoon tea that she was giving for a number of her girlfriends and if he could recite a few of his verses there. She was thinking that he had exceptionally long eyelashes and how cute that made him seem when viewed up close. She said he could pick any program of verses but needed only recite for an hour or so. Majid had never participated in such an event and he consented to do so, largely to be close to Anna again. Outside the restaurant as it was still bright and warm from the 'white night' of high summer, Majid suggested that they continue the evening by taking a walk. They were not in such an attractive part of Moscow, and he proposed that they cross the Garden Ring and walk down to the Boulevard Ring and then over to the so-called Clean Ponds (of which only one green, dirty and littered pond remained). Anna agreed and asked her driver to meet them after an hour and a half at their destination. Majid was so glad she did; he quickly appreciated that they fit together as they walked. They talked, but he did not remember, just of this and that. The rest of the evening of this first date rushed by. Anna dropped him back at his house, but did not even make an attempt to go up to his apartment with him. But they did share a light kiss on the sidewalk in parting.

He had fallen in love. *Out of such happiness, the lover cannot sleep.* He was breathlessly thinking of Anna all that night and for some nights afterwards. He kept in his mind's eye her lovely brown wavy hair, her limpid green-gray eyes and their sparkle, her dainty hands, her slightly turned up nose, the way she smiled at him, her beautiful pellucid skin. He counted each moment until he could see her again. Each day seemed too long. He was in such disarray that he could not think or compose any verses. Words and their music failed him for almost ten days and then he had to call her. He proposed that they meet, anywhere in the center, to take a walk, to enjoy the summer air, perhaps have a milkshake at one of the new cafes. Anna agreed at once and proposed to meet that very evening at the Hall of the Columns next to the next parliament building for a summer concert. It was sweltering hot, but Majid agreed at once. They could stroll in the late evening twilight after the concert. The evening confirmed him in his attraction for Anna and seemed to confirm her affection for him. The concert hall was stifling and the music dense and hot as well. The big hall and corridors of the Hall of Columns did not have any air and the hall smelled of sweat after only a few notes from the orchestra, and in the quiet moments of the music the fluttering of paper fans could be heard throughout the hall. He thought that the hall was splendid and grandiosely beautiful but it was built at a time when in summers all the windows were meant to be full open. Anna wore a loose fitting but near transparent yellow dress which outlined her underwear and emphasized the curves of her shapely figure. He again noticed the fragrance of lilies of the valley rising off her neck. One of the concert pieces was a set of songs by Berlioz with lyrics by Gautier. *Come sit with me on this mat of mosses to speak of our love and with your sweet voice, tell me, 'Forever'.* He fell in love with the strange music—sung by a slender sad looking soprano—and Gautier's verses were perfect for his courtship of Anna. He made a mental note to find the poetry of Gautier, which he had never before encountered. After the music, they took a long walk, hand in hand. Their talk under the quaking linden leaves was about nothing but meant everything: they agreed to have the "tea and poetry" at her apartment in the next week. He returned to his bare room so excited and sodden from the heat that he stripped off his clothes and began composing love songs. Now he was sure she loved him too.

Anna had told him that she wanted to hold the "tea" on a Thursday late afternoon in the next week. Her apartment was located in the "elites" neighborhood of Frunzenskaya down on the Moscow River. As the date approached, Majid suddenly realized that he did not have any decent suit of clothing. Everything that he had was old and a tad shabby; his shoes were scuffed and the heels worn down, his shirt collars were all frayed. He recalled that all three times he had seen Anna she was so well dressed with fashionable imported clothes. He was most ashamed that before the date of his presentation he could only scarcely rectify his situation. He could only afford to buy a new white shirt, imported from China, at one of the many open air markets run by Azeris that had sprung up all around the city. So he went in his old pair of jeans, his black scuffed shoes, and a new white shirt. With Anna's address in hand he went to a monumental red brick building about 8 stories tall on the riverside entry through the deep cool shade of poplars and elms. The afternoon was sunny but not too warm or stuffy. The building was very imposing and grand; Majid had not imagined that there were such monumental houses anywhere in the city and he was surprised to see them and a bit intimidated. At the archway entrance into the inner courtyard there were several memorial plaques of past Soviet residents of this apartment block. He did not recognize any of the names. There was no concierge but the entry door had a call box and when he entered the code numbers, some unseen person rang him in to a large entry foyer of red sandstone tiles with a grand staircase at the back. On the third floor, Anna was holding open her apartment door. She was wearing a white blouse and blue skirt but the first thing that Majid noticed were the pair of diamond earrings dangling from her ears. She kissed him on the cheeks as she ushered him in, and he caught again a whiff of that heavenly fragrance of lilies of the valley. She was lovely, and she acted very excited to see him. She led him into the large main room which had been arranged with a dozen chairs set in a circle around the center of the room, each chair had a small serving table set out in front of it. On one side of the room, a large sofa-divan had been pushed and on the opposite side a table with a white table cloth had been set up with a samovar, tea pots, silver spoons and a selection of small open face sandwiches and pastries. The room was very large and dark, with 3.5 meter high ceilings, dark wood paneling on all of the walls, and light colored wood parquetry. This main room had three large windows which provided only a dim light as they were partially blocked from the outside light by an overhanging balcony and by the tall trees opposite them. Majid had never before seen such a luxurious set up in a private house for a private party like this one. The room struck Majid as a strange setting; like a gay summer garden party set in a funeral house or law offices. Already gathered in the room were ten or so women dressed similarly to Anna in light colored dresses, who also trilled with delight while greeting Majid. Anna introduced him to her mother whom Anna greatly resembled, even down to the clothes and jewelry. As she made her introduction, Majid noticed that now Anna was wearing a diamond wedding ring in addition to her gold wedding band. And she says she is not rich, he thought. "My husband is in Africa on long-term assignment. In Angola I think," she told him almost in a whisper. When the last of the invited women arrived shortly afterwards, Anna introduced the assembled women to the poetry of Slava saying a little on his background. Then she invited everyone to take their tea and resume their seats so Slava could begin his recital. There was a momentary confusion as it was unclear whether it was better to deliver his verses standing or sitting; he was seated next to Anna, quite close. After a little discussion, it was decided it was best for Majid to remain sitting. He declaimed five poems, three short ones, and two long ones, but altogether the recital took much less than an hour. The women clapped politely after each poem, and then sipped at their tea. One was a poem that he had written down several months earlier, but he thought it was even more appropriate; *To say she is beautiful* has been the title given to this poem.

To say she is beautiful is not to say
She has the stern lifeless beauty of Persephone,
Who administers the curses of men
From her chill nether world home.

To say she is beautiful is not to
Compare her to the beauty of the golden tansy
Or the toxic belladonna
Which make the heart rush before they kill.

To say she is beautiful is not to say
She has the erotic beauty of
Helmut Newton's nudes strutting their misery,
Sadder than a lifeless manikin.

To say she is beautiful is not to say
Her beauty has the banality of
Advertizing; forced smiles and
Superficial promises of happiness.

To say she is beautiful is not to liken her
To the cold marble statues of Venus
With their blank looks into the future
And smooth but pitted and cracked surfaces.

To say she is beautiful is to affirm
That she shines a love that warms a room
And her smile, sincere, reflects a
Light that brightens everyone's life.

To say she is beautiful is to say
Her skin is vital and pellucid and finer
Than the clearest onyx or marble
Which bespeaks perpetual youth.

To say she is beautiful, and I do so say,
Is to say she has the beauty which
Inspires the genius of poets, enduring
Long after the paint peels or marble cracks.

To say she is beautiful, and she truly is,
Is to affirm her creative beauty.
She is the source, like mother earth,
Through which our seed is born, fruits, and thrives.

This poem elicited gasps of approval, and gentle polite clapping from the attendees. A short epigram which he declaimed also caused all kinds of delight. (Both of these poems appeared in his second collection of poems which had been printed earlier that year. Should we assume that the beauty he was referring to was some specific young women, perhaps Liza, whom he had tried for almost a year to win over?) Majid noticed that during his recital, Anna's mother was looking rapturously at him with her eyes wide open. He could not really notice Anna, because she was sitting too close immediately next to him.

In a field of grass round an old apple tree
I remember forget-me-nots' pale blue abundance
Floating like low smoke over the garden ground
But this year they grow less profuse, their color dissipated.
Perhaps they have forgotten us?

The audience reacted very enthusiastically after Majid completed his recital. "Bravo!" "Adorable!" "Charming!" "Genius!" "Entrancing!" He looked to Anna to catch her reaction. She looked lovely and was smiling brightly at him. Then Anna again took charge of the proceedings. She suggested that everyone should get some more tea or pastries and re-take their seats and perhaps if they had any questions about the verses Slava had recited to ask him to elucidate them. Majid took some green tea and a small portion of a cake which he had never before seen and which looked delicious. It was called bird's milk cake and he enjoyed the wonderful incongruity of the name almost as much as he loved the cake. Growing up he had never eaten such rare delights. The women then wanted to ask him some questions. 'Who is your favorite poet?' "You mean after Pushkin?' 'What is your favorite flower?' 'Hard to say, maybe each is my favorite in its own season. When I was young I loved lilies of the valley, in Moscow I've come to love lilacs and chokecherries.' 'How did you think to rhyme love and blood?' 'Oh that has been done all the time.' 'Can you rhyme a word with life (zhizn)?' 'I think I would rhyme it with prism.' 'What was that unusual meter in the first poem you read?' 'Alexandrine. Invented by the French.' 'What was that interesting and attractive metrical device you used in the third stanza of the first poem you read?' 'I think what you found so attractive is the internal alliteration.' 'What are the sources of your ideas for a poem?' 'Poems are not built up out of ideas, they are built up out of words. They have sonic and phonic meaning. And of course the sounds of those words and how we combine them together creates the metrics, which have further meaning on their own. It's why we can remember without any difficulty the lullabies of our youth, lines of our favorite songs, or advertising jingles.' 'How do you write a poem?' 'That I am afraid it impossible for me to say, because I do not know. But I hear the sounds and intonation of a verse in my head, and then I say them until they sound right. And I continue like that.' 'Is this beauty you wrote about, your real muse.' 'I love looking on beautiful women, it is true. Women like you.'

'Do you rely on inspiration to think of your verses?' 'No, if you mean divine inspiration. But of course I too need to breath and I take breathes all the time.' (Here I have to note that he was playing on words, as the word for inspiration derives from the word to inhale.) "That's enough for now," said Anna still directing the course of the tea party. "Slava has brought copies of his first two collections of poems that you can buy right here right now if you liked what you heard this afternoon." And of course everyone wanted to buy a copy of each of the little books. The exchanging of books and money was clumsy and embarrassing for Majid, but eventually everyone was served. He noticed that each woman in her turn made a move to touch him, caress his arm, or pat his hands, or perhaps to put their hand to his cheek, and some even tried to give him a formal chaste hug and give him a kiss on the cheeks (Anna's mother most of all). Slowly the girlfriends of Anna made their leave, squealing their pleasure at being able to attend such a wonderful event. Parting such parties in Russia takes a long time and has an elaborate order and ritual, formulaic statements and repeated farewells. Last to leave was Anna's mother who again tried to take him into her arms and give him kisses on both cheeks. And as she parted through the door, she caressed Anna's arm and nodded to her approvingly as if the two had some agreement together.

Immediately as the door to the apartment closed, Majid felt as if the apartment had suddenly shrunken, he was standing near Anna, and there was no space between them and no place around them to flee to. She was looking intensely at him, her eyes fluttering. He hopelessly loved her lovely face and nut brown hair. She loved his long dark eye lashes and his cute face. "You Anna are truly beautiful." "And you Slava are a genius. You're also quite beautiful." He repeated this line again after he had hugged her, kissed her, undressed her and lay down with her. She was indeed beautiful; narrow shoulders, small round breasts, a supple figure, smooth white, unblemished skin, and shapely legs. She was completely naked except for her expensive jewelry, a gold necklace which clung to her chest, and her pendant diamond earrings, which made a tiny clicking sound. And so they made love in the big room, dark paneled and now growing dim, on the big divan. But their act of love was not successful, not passionate, not satisfying or a joyful act of bliss. It's difficult to know what happened exactly as Majid was the only source of the story in a letter he wrote. He did write coarsely and vituperatively, "I screwed the girl the other day." But what was the clear outcome was that he left the apartment later that evening feeling angry and humiliated. Perhaps Anna was frigid and unresponsive. They did not share a passionate climax; they did not achieve the affectionate thrill and breathless peak of a sexual coupling of two lovers. After the act, Anna slipped away from him covering herself quickly with her clothes picked up off the floor. And then after they both had dressed, there was almost a resentful silence between them. Until finally Anna said that he should go. She was not pleased either, but about what, he would never know. As he got ready to go she went to her room and brought back a wad of roubles. She had from the start planned on paying him for his recital regardless of the outcome of their romance and sexual encounter (which had been perhaps desired but not planned). It was a lot of money (about equivalent $110). "Here," she said, "this is what you should earn for your performance, I think." Majid was amazed, insulted, and hurt and he refused to take the money. He had loved her, and thought she had loved him. But she had not and she apparently tried to insult him as well. As if he were a gigolo, as if he were a poet trophy that she had bagged! He left in a hurry. And he never went back to see Anna again. He refused to take any of her phone calls in the coming days. After ten days she stopped calling, and he never saw her or heard from her again. After some years he wrote down two poetic interpretations of his love encounter with Anna Yadrova.

Sometime later that year Igor Formico called Majid and invited him to an event organized by the Moscow Writers' Union at the House of Journalists. It was to be a panel discussion on the current state of poetry in Russia, with contributions of several widely recognized new younger poets. It was an evening program in late fall when the seven o'clock starting hour was already deeply dark. The building was dim and poorly marked and was hard to find, even though it was near the very center of Arbat. There was no admission charge as Igor had told him, but Majid could not find the hall right away and entered shortly after the program started and had to crawl along the wall to get to a free seat half way down the room. It meant that many in the audience of about 200 people noticed him when he came in. There were five people identified by name plates sitting at a table erected on the podium at the front of the hall. One of them was Majid's old friend Victor Krivonosov who was already looking bored with the proceedings. The others he did not know by name or face, but none of them looked young, they all looked to be in their fifties and lean, gray, and underfed. The first speaker sat down to polite applause. He was a critic named Mr. Cedar and he had been lampooning bombastic poetry that imitated Western styles of poetic expression especially from the American 'beat generation'. The next speaker got up, a Mr. Kudryavshin, a poet, who looked a bit like Osip Buterbrotov except he was bald, first giving a short talk about the need for words to reflect the silences around them and the requirement for a poetry that was more like Japanese *haiku*. He then read three very short poems where nearly every word was repeated twice, sometimes more, and the metrical lines were very short (although the poems in their entirety were longer than haiku). He sat down again to polite applause. The third speaker was a Mr. Konoplyanka. It was then that Majid noticed that all five speakers' names started with the letter 'K'. He wondered to himself if Mr. Konoplyanka's poetry was inspired by eating too much cannabis (as his name indicated one who harvested cannabis). But when Mr. Konoplyanka started to speak, Majid was sure of it. Mr. Konoplyanka gave a long talk, but he delivered it in machine gun style with a rapidity that truly stripped away any meaning from the auditors in the audience. Majid—and he was sure no one else in the audience either—had never in his life heard anyone speak so fast. It was dizzying and remarkable, scarcely understandable, but in spite of his speed in diction every word every syllable was clear, not slurred or elided. His long talk would have taken others 40 minutes to deliver; perhaps he completed his in 12 minutes. It took the audience's collective breath away. When Mr. Konoplyanka sat down, there was no applause, the performance had been too spectacular, too fast to understand. You could hear the collective blinking of eyes and whirring of minds as audience members struggled internally to catch up with all that he had said. Then the moderator announced that they had received a film of Joseph Brodsky reciting some of his poems in Venice so they would intersperse this film into the program. The film was about 30 minutes long and in it Brodsky read four of his poems, none of which Majid had read or studied before (at that time only one volume of Brodsky's Russian poems had appeared in Russia—others followed in the coming years). Majid listened fascinated to the great exiled poet, the poet who had been cultivated by and knew Anna Akhmadova personally. He had never before heard Brodsky declaim his own verse and he was stunned by his incantatory style. He recognized that here was a truly great poet, but he was amazed at how similar Brodsky's droning monotone style of reading his own verse resembled nothing more than an Orthodox liturgy with long recitation between breaths. In the four poems read Majid noticed that Brodsky had only two voices and that his intonation was very stable and unchanging, neither ascending nor descending, neither crescendo nor decrescendo, neither louder, nor softer. Majid was disturbed and very disappointed and he could not understand how Brodsky had arrived at such a style. The Brodsky poems Majid had read up to then seemed to him to be quite receptive to a great and quite musical intonation, but the author himself ignored that. This film presentation kept him pre-occupied and pondering through the rest of the program. So much of a poem's meaning comes through the aural reception and interpretation of the words uttered. As Majid saw it, Brodsky had a radically different interpretation of his own poems than what Majid had read and tried to re-create. After the film, Krivonosov had nothing new to say, and he recited two poems that Majid had first heard almost five years earlier, and the final speaker, a Mr. Kargo was again a critic and literature professor who mumbled in an addled manner about how one should analyze the poetry of the past three decades and what innovations had appeared. But Majid was still thinking of Brodsky reading his verses in an empty Venice church. He almost came to the heretical thought that he did not like the sound of Brodsky's poems, even though he had admired them when he himself read them and tried to recite them out loud for himself. He again noticed that of the "young contemporary poets" promised by the program none were younger than 45, and if you included Brodsky, the majority were born in the war generation. Majid tarried in leaving and as he emerged into an entry foyer adjoining the House of Journalists he saw Pozyn talking animatedly with another man, his arm around the other man's shoulder.

"Ha, Slava I'm so glad to see you. You're just the person I was thinking of just now. I noticed you when you entered the hall. I'm glad you didn't sneak out. How are you by the way? I'm in New York most of the time nowadays so I don't see many people here anymore. Here, I want to introduce you to my friend Pavel Jastrzebski. Pavel Maciejevich this is Majid Karimovich Khairulin, or Slava. He's our great hope in Russian poetry." The two of them shook hands. Pavel had a sharp narrow face, one could almost say a hawkish face with intense eyes and heavy glowering brows. "Victor was just telling me that you're a very fine poet. And that you're from Kazan. I'm very glad to know your acquaintance." said Pavel. "We have to talk, Victor Vladimirovich said that you could help me." "Slava," Victor addressed him in his flawless American accented English, "do you speak English well?" "I do not know how good my English is." Majid answered him back in English. "I do not have the opportunity to speak it often enough. I only speak when I read English verse." "That's just fine. You speak better that 90 percent of the English language graduates from schools I meet here. Quite understandable and accent free." Returning to Russian, Majid addressed Pavel, "I would be pleased to talk with you, at any available time, Pavel Maciejevich. You name the time and place, and I will attend you." It was scarcely noticeable because of the way he stressed his sentence, but Majid's answer was in a rhymed couplet. It was nonetheless mellifluous to the ear. They agreed to meet at Pavel's offices in the next week. Pavel gave him a business card, the first Majid had ever received from anybody, and another sign of the social revolution that was progressing in Russia in those days. "Great, that's all settled." said Victor. "Now I too would ask you, Slava, to come visit me while I am still here in Moscow. I finish filming at the end of next week. And here's my card too, to add to your collection."

It turned out that Pavel Jastrzebski had founded a public relations firm to serve politicians and the newly formed, publicly traded corporations which both had the completely new requirement to communicate with the press, with constituents and with investors and shareholders. It was an entirely new business that had never before existed in Russia, not before the Revolution and certainly not during the Soviet period of the clamp downs on any public information or any accountability. Pavel was interested in offering Majid a position working as a consultant PR official based on the strong recommendation of Victor Pozyn. Of course, Majid did not know anything about the skills or requirements of such a position, and he did not know anything about the functioning of publicly traded corporations and he knew little about the public communications of Yeltsin era politicians. But Pavel was not too concerned about that. The important thing for a PR man presenting a politician's or corporation's message was the delivery. Pavel's firm was called *Yasnost* or clarity, which not accidentally rhymes with *glasnost* which had been one of Gorbachyov's great political reforms in the 1980s. The point of *Yasnost* was to make clear presentations of information that needed to get across. And Pavel understood in no time that Majid possessed the rare ability to make convincing locutions, that when Majid spoke, he was hypnotic, entrancing, lilting, soothing, comforting. His spoken Russian was correct, clear, elegant, rhythmic, reassuring; all the things that a public spokesman needs to be able to convey. Not long after Majid joined the company, Pavel was appointed the top PR job in the country, namely as the Kremlin press secretary for Boris Yeltsin.

So in the beginning of 1995, Majid, our poet and hero of this story, got a career job; an income to support his poetry occupation. And this enabled him to step up a notch in life. The most immediate change in his life was that he was able to afford to buy food. And so for the first time since he had been a little boy in Ufa he was able to eat adequately and not feel hunger day and night. He did not splurge, as he didn't have a clue about how to cook and he did not feel he could afford to go often to restaurants. But his eating routine remained mostly the same as it had been during his university years; the midday meal taken at the company canteen was his main meal of the day and he would buy bread, cheese, cured meats, yoghurts and fruit (all items then available in the groceries of the Yeltsin market transformation) for his morning and evening meals at home. And home life changed dramatically too. After a few months working with the PR firm he had saved enough money to move to a much nicer apartment that was not in a *communalka* and which had had a thorough reconstruction and refurbishing completed by its owner, which meant he had his own kitchen, telephone, toilet and bathroom. It was for Majid spacious; a one bedroom apartment which meant it had a stand-alone main room, a bedroom and a kitchen off the entry corridor. It was located in the center of Moscow on the outskirts of the Arbat in the neighborhoods that he was now familiar with, not far from the park-like expanses of the Boulevard Ring closer to the Moscow River. His neighbors were now a little more distant than his *communalka* bunch and a little better off as they lived in their own independent privatized apartments where they had also done refurbishment and of course had already bought large new color television sets (the best-selling item of the 1990s). Interestingly he had found this apartment by a contact he had made with a local Tatar who had many years earlier moved to Moscow and stayed. He had introduced him to the landlord who was a man, who, like him, was half Russian and half Tatar, who had moved to Moscow to study, married, divorced and then had moved to an even nicer newer apartment in one of the leafier bedroom neighborhoods of the city. Once again Igor Formico helped him with the move of his goods to the new apartment, which comprised primarily a growing library. Majid was very pleased by his new living arrangements. He had never in his life enjoyed so much personal space. The apartment was very comfortable and the toilet and bathroom had been completed redone with new ceramics and new tiles on the walls. But while impressed by the clean modern refit of his apartment and aware that all of the other apartments in his entry had also gotten 'Euro-remont'—as the refurbishments were called—Majid was puzzled by the condition of the entrance stairway which served all the apartments. It remained dim (broken or missing low watt light bulbs), dirty, and especially smelly. This entry was even smellier than the one where he had stayed in the *communalka*: Majid noted it had the perpetual overwhelming aroma that was a foul mix of cat piss, rotting cabbage, naphtha from the old paint, cigarette smoke, dust, and sweat. He wondered why the neighbors who had spent so much money on re-doing their apartments did not spend a little money on cleaning up and repainting the entry. After he got to know his neighbors, he asked one of them why this situation persisted. The neighbor bluntly put it: "Who can trust anyone else? If we contribute money to one of our neighbors to organize and conduct the clean-up, repainting, and replacement of lighting, how will we know that the money won't just be pocketed and the works won't be done? Besides, the city (which still owns the entrance-way) is responsible to clean it up and restore it." So that attitude effectively meant that nothing would ever be done, and nothing ever was done through the rest of Majid's life while he lived in this apartment. He embarked in the second half of 1995 on a long, slow process of furnishing his apartment and some of the earliest things that he bought were a new large bed and mattress and a desk and chairs. In the next year he bought himself a computer and printer, which pushed aside his treasured typewriter and the carbon paper and spare ribbons which came with it were tucked away forever after. The apartment was already furnished with a large divan and plush chairs in the main room, and, most important, a kitchen table with chairs and a new refrigerator in the kitchen. Eventually he was able to receive guests (which meant people coming over and visiting in the kitchen for hours in the evenings). One of the neighbors on the entry staircase was a very pleasant elderly man who was a professor of archeology who had specialized in the ancient nomadic peoples of the Central Asian steppes. He was very interested in Majid's background as a Tatar from Ufa as he had spent lots of time digging in the kurgans around Bashkiria. But Majid did not have long to get to know with the old professor and his wife. The professor had decided that he was underpaid (as he undoubtedly was as he was supposed to be retired) and that interest in his field had completely evaporated after the Soviet Union dissolved, so in 1998 he emigrated to take up a well-paid lectureship in archeology in the U.S. Majid was amazed that the old man had so much drive and devotion to his studies in his field that he would take such a huge risk and plunge into a new life in a foreign country to continue to practice it. But the old professor on one of their last meetings together over tea told him, "It is not so much of a challenge as a new opportunity. And it is an escape from the boorishness and hostility of Russia. Recall how many literary giants also chose exile to be free to practice their calling rather than be oppressed here. Men like Bunin and Nabokov, Balmont and Khodasevich, Tsetayeva or Brodsky and Solzhenitsyn. I could go on, but don't forget the scientists and composers and other intellectuals—perhaps less famous—who have felt the need to leave to escape oppression and go into exile. I'll be just one more." He sold his household effects and apartment—at a loss—and moved off with his old, confused wife saying 'no regrets' as he bid farewell to Majid.

Of course working for Yasnost meant that Majid had less time for poetry. But he continued to compose and polish his own poems in the evenings as well as to read and to translate others' poetry and he kept to an assiduous work schedule. His compositional work style also changed from this time. He started to carry a notebook with him all the time and whenever some ideas or verse or particularly nice rhyme would occur to him during the day at his office or his client's he would jot them down in the notebook and afterwards elaborate on them. His day-time job with Yasnost in the first year took him to different cities of Russia as Yasnost got PR appointments with oil companies in Tatarstan and Siberia, and with the metal smelters in the Urals. This was the period when the oligarchs were taking over the high points of the former Soviet economy and wanting to convert their cheaply acquired assets into publicly traded companies that would attract outside investors, especially foreign investors. This work exposed Majid to one of the issues which became a predominant theme of his over the next few years, overarching greed. He saw it everywhere, from the deputy finance minister who deflected the payments for a huge arms transaction with a foreign country into his own pocket, to the oligarchs who acquired so many of their assets by putting a low assessment on them and then fixing the auctions held by the government, or who then demanded tax breaks for their companies while escaping personal taxes on themselves by pushing on their political connections, or managers who put out purchase contracts which included in the sum a percentage given back to the manager. This was the time when politicians discovered the way to riches was by demanding kickbacks on any of the government or budgetary work they let out. As he visited corporate offices in remote provincial cities—often one-horse cities that relied exclusively on the activity of the sole industrial company in the city—places like Surgut or Cherepovets, Almetyevsk or Nizhny-Tagil, he came to appreciate how different Moscow was from the rest of Russia. How much his upbringing in Ufa more accurately reflected life for the vast majority of Russians, those living outside Moscow. And he noticed over and over again that so many people lived in circumstances of run-down, dirty even squalid housing with little or no hope, no prospects, often with no employment, and with no direction in their lives. By contrast, the owners of the industrial companies that animated these provincial cities—the oligarchs and the senior-most managers—lived very comfortably but concerned themselves most of all with how they could get even more assets or, perhaps most important, how they could get more than their rivals.

In 1995 Majid wrote and published in the *Novy Mir* literature magazine a poem that sparked both admiration and outrage. It also caused Majid a lot of trouble. It was all about the First Chechen War, which is rather a misnomer as Russia fought the first war in Chechnya over 30 years in the mid-19th century which, after much misery and death, Russia claimed to have won. In this case, Chechen activists declared independence in 1993, trying to extend to themselves the reasoning of the breakup of the Soviet Russian empire in 1991 and having not signed the federation treaty after 1991. By late 1994 President Boris Yeltsin could no longer abide by this situation—especially as ethnic Russians were being expelled and discriminated against in Chechnya and general lawlessness there prevailed—so he declared that a quick military takeover of Chechnya would 'restore the constitutional order' in less than a month once Russian forces invaded the country. But this did not happen. Instead the badly prepared, demoralized Russian forces got stuck in a vicious guerrilla war which became more and more savage in the months of 1995. News stories were initially open and reported the debacle and carnage, but very soon in 1995 they began to try to control the political criticism and damage and began to apply censorship and controls on journalists' access. Nevertheless Majid closely followed the progress of the fighting with an increasingly heavy heart. He wrote this short poem shortly after the news of the massacre at Semashki hit Moscow's newspapers and he sent it for publication. It was promptly printed not so much for its artistic merit but for the political sympathies of the editors who opposed the war in Chechnya.

> *Two frightful beasts stalk the hills and mountains,*
> *Towns in the land called 'redoubtable'*

One is noisy, mechanical, deadly and diurnal.
It booms and shouts, bombs and kills, shrilly;
Its tanks driven by scared, underfed boys.

The other is pantherlike and vengeful.
It prowls, murderous and nocturnal
With long knives, like claws, it slits the throats of young officers.

These two beast, war and hatred,
Scour the land called 'frightening'.

Knocking down doors and walls, houses and mosques,
One kills the poor, the miserable, girls and boys.
The other sends dead conscripts in black bags
Back to 'Mother Russia' as a warning and
In turn the other then murders grandpas and young wives in their gardens.

The beast of war rules the skies and the day
Emitting terrorizing sounds and screams,
No one is safe in the land of 'the terrifying'.

The beast of hatred devours the timorous
Minions who cannot sleep nor rest by day or night
No Russian man is safe in the land of 'the horrifying'.

The old instructions of Alexei Petrovich still apply
'Eradicate them all' he said.
'My name shall terrorize, brutality's my mark.'

The locals seek freedom and revenge
They buy their arms from Russian troops
And then turn them back on them, murdering and maiming.

There can be no hope, nor peace—
Only death and destruction, fear and flight,
In this the land of 'the fearsome'.

> *How many dead in vast unmarked graves?*
> *What needless killing is caused by such rage?*

(In translating this I have used the various meanings of the Chechen capital Grozni which our poet has used repeatedly to create a dreadful effect. He does not actually say Chechnya anywhere but leaves the meaning clear by citing 'land of the fearsome', the land of Grozni, the capital of Chechnya. I do not know and have not found any mention anywhere that Majid ever recited this poem in front of an audience.)

Not long after this poem appeared in *Novy Mir* Majid got an invitation from the secret internal police to report to them at their offices down at Lubyanka. Majid with some trepidation went alone and sought out the indicated office which he found only after long waits passing at many security check points and document inspections and walking down many corridors into the bowels of the security headquarters. He was escorted to the small windowless office of Mr. Nikolai Pytka (this unnerved Majid as the man's name meant Mr. Torture and he wondered if it were a pseudonym) which was furnished only with a steel file cabinet, a small desk and two chairs one on each side of the desk. On the wall were hanging a large portrait of Dzerzhinsky and a smaller portrait of Boris Yeltsin. Mr. Pytka was studying a newspaper page when Majid entered the office. "Are you Majid Karimovich Khairilin from Ufa and Kazan?" "The self- same." "What is your profession?" "I am now employed as a consultant by the public relations firm, Yasnost." "So you are a public relations professional?" "I have only just started there." Majid was still standing. "What training do you have to be a public relations specialist?" "I studied philology and literature at university and took an advanced degree at the Gorky Institute." "And that qualifies you to be public relations specialist or a press spokesman?" "I do not know what studies are required to work in public relations." "So you are not qualified nor certified in public relations." "No I suppose not." "Tell me where you have lived and the addresses for the past six years." Majid told Mr. Pytka who was being gruff and unpleasant but in a soft low voice. "Are you the author of this poem without a name which appeared in the 3 June 1995 issue of *Novy Mir?*" and he showed him the page he had under his hands. Majid acknowledged it as his. "Why doesn't it have a title?" Majid did not know who to answer him and trying not to sound flippant he said, "I did not give it one, I guess because I did not think it was needed. Most titles I think are presumptious." "When did you write this poem?" "Two months ago I think." "Are you qualified to write a poem?" "I am a poet." "Who authorized and appointed you to be a poet?" "I did not know that anyone had to do so for me to be a poet." "So you are not by profession a poet, are you? By what right do you call yourself a poet?" "I am a poet by outlook, upbringing and my formation. It is not a profession. By what right do I call myself a human? I am a human and a poet by self determination." "You're not a member of the Writers' Union, are you?" "No. You do not have to be a member of the Writers' Union to write poems." "Sit down there please, Mr. Khairulin." And Majid sat down. "Why did you write this poem?" "I was expressing my outrage at the killing that is happening in Chechnya." "It's none of your business whether there is killing in Chechnya. Who are you to judge what is happening there? Do you support the Chechnya Islamists insurrectionists?" "No." "But it sounds from your poem that you are a sympathizer for them." "Yes, I sympathize for those who are unjustly being killed all the time." "You know you committed a serious seditious crime in writing here that the Chechen insurrections buy their guns from the Russian army?" "No I was not aware that saying so was a crime." "You were giving away secret national security information. How did you know that any such absurd things were happening there?" "The press have reported such stories quite often in recent years." "The treasonous press?" "The Russian press." "You then claim that you did not receive any of this information from the insurrectionists from informants or enemies of the state?" "I did not." "Do you communicate with the insurrectionists in Chechnya?" "No." "But you are a Muslim." "Not practicing, I was born to a practicing Muslim, my father, but that does not mean I inherit being Muslim automatically." "Yet we have information that you have often gone to the mosque." "I have over the past ten years rarely gone to the mosque." "How many times here in Moscow have you gone to the mosque?" "Perhaps six times." "And you say that you are not practicing?" "That's right." "And did you meet in any of those six times with any Chechens?" "No, I do not think so." "You are aware the Moscow mosque is overrun with Muslim separatists from Chechnya?" "I have become aware that there are Chechens in the Moscow mosque, but I have not met with nor communicated with any of them." "And then how did you get information on the instructions of what our forces were supposed to do in Chechnya?" "What do you mean the instructions?" "The eradication instructions! Your lines here." "Those were words supposedly uttered in the instructions of Yermalaev for dealing with Chechnya in the 1830s, not current instructions." "I see, but those are still secret instructions to our troops." said Pytka. "So you do not acknowledge that you have committed a crime in publishing this poem with this information in it?" "No I do not believe I have broached any laws nor disclosed any information which was not in the public's possession." "You are not being cooperative Mr. Khairulin. I have no choice but to put out a publishing ban on all of your works. Now I want you sign here an agreement wherein you acknowledge authorship of this untitled poem and the seditious nature of its contents and that you disclosed state secrets which could imperil the national security." And Mr. Pytka pulled a typed page out of a drawer of the desk. In this you agree not to write or publish any more verses or texts about the events occurring in or around Chechnya. We will be watching you in the future and looking out for any future publications by you." Majid spent the rest of the day negotiating the agreement and insisting that he had not revealed any state secrets nor had he been in receipt of any information from the insurgents that would have given him the information he had implied in the poem. When he left the offices of the secret internal police, he was shaking both from exhaustion and from anger and irritation.

Only two weeks after his visit to Mr. Pytka, events in the Caucasus again caused him to compose a poem. But on this occasion he did not seek to publish it. It was the season when the boulevards in the center are enveloped by the sweet subtle perfume of the blossoming linden trees, the sign that summer has at last arrive. But it was at that time, the horrible news clanked into Moscow like a load of tanks being dropped in a central square. There was a raid and hostage-taking conducted by a band of Chechen separatists under Shamil Basayev in the town of Budyonnovsk in the Stavropol district about 70 miles outside of the borders of Chechnya. The news media covered the events of five days closely. Almost from the start of the hostage holding, after storming the police headquarters and town hall, innocents were killed in the hospital. Shamil especially insisted that the press show the entire crisis and so they filmed the storming of the hospital by Russian special forces, a series of unsuccessful attacks meant to free the hostages but which were incompetently conducted and only managed to kill more innocents in the crossfire. The crisis ended with negotiations and a negotiated release of the hostages after Shamil's band safely returned to Chechnya. This is what Majid wrote in the final days of the crisis.

Oh, what an act of contemptable cowardice!
What evil have you endowed on this earth,
Shamil, in the name of a spiteful faith?
Can you ever triumph by pointing a gun at a child's head?
Or killing the infirm and immobile or young mothers in delivery?

Is such a despicable act ever justified to gain peace?
You have sunken to the lowest of the low, vengeance is not gained
You are worse than the left-handed one who eats and wipes his ass
With the same befouled hand, your prayers can never be heard by God*
Better you should rape your mother for the disgrace you spread in the world.

There can be no cure or palliation for this evil deed,
It is proper that your name will live forever in infamy

And those who hear your name spoken will spit on it and curse
For surely if there is God given justice in the afterworld
Yours will be the eternal punishment of hellfire.

(This poem did not get published until almost eight years after the crisis at Budyonnovsk. I put it here to show the correct chronological sequence in Majid's output. *I note that Majid insult's Shamil by making a twist on Shamil's name which is Arabic in origin meaning comprehensive or inclusive. Majid takes another word that is nearly the same spelling but which means 'left' and plays on the Muslim contempt for a left handed person because the left hand is used for cleaning one's excrement and is banned for eating with and is thus ritually unclean, virtually a kafir. This is a very considerable insult, an insult worthy of killing in revenge. Shamil probably never was aware of it as he was killed only shortly after this poem became public.)

At the end of 1995, the top managers and owners of a giant metals and mining firm, which was a client of Yasnost, decided to have an investors' meeting and presentation in Vienna, Austria and they needed their PR representative, one Majid the poet, to join them and help convey the messages. Of course, Vienna is not the best place in Europe for investor conferences, and just before Christmas is a particularly terrible time to get any fund manager anywhere in Europe to break away from their Christmas parties and spiked punches to attend investment conferences or any kind of presentations, most especially those for high risk, little known Russian companies located in God-knows-what-kind of city somewhere in Siberia or the Urals. And that of course was just the point that had decided the managers on giving their presentation at that time and in Vienna, which they had heard (from a company director who had spent some wonderful years in Vienna in Soviet times as the KGB bureau chief) was a delightful place for Christmas parties (and warm weather too) and for generally enjoying the fine food, beautiful prostitutes, fine wines and schnapps, and eating all kinds of the chocolates and Christmas goodies. The city was decked out in its sparkling best, and Majid found it very beautiful and quite rewarding for strolls. It was his first trip ever outside of Russia and he approached it with both a little trepidation and excitement. He was nervous that he could get lost, and he did not know what to do if he lost his traveling companions, or if he were locked out of his room, or if he could not find his way back to their hotel. But he prepared for the trip by looking up and doing some research on the cultural treasures of Vienna and its poetic output. The flight on Austrian Air was thrilling and frightful at the same time—pressurizing, leaving the earth's surface, the clean, bright plane interior, the noise, the pretty stewardesses in their tight uniforms, and then tracing the clouds and the landscapes as they flew over them—it was all magical. They stayed in a grand hotel directly on the Kaertner Ring, the heart of the city. Ah Vienna, much nicer and *gemuetlicher* than London, it has to be agreed.

It turned out that there was very little work that Majid actually had to do at this conference. The conference was organized by a local Austrian firm which made all the arrangements as well for the parties. There were an entire posse of Russian to German translators, who spoke German (and English for that matter) much better than Majid, and besides they knew well the financial terminology which he was still only just getting his mind around. One night the organizers arranged a night at the Wiener Staatsoper for a glittering operetta befitting the season, but that left Majid with one day and one evening free to roam the streets. And on his free day his roaming took him to the Belvedere Museum on a hill just outside the city center. And there he discovered, literally was bedazzled by the collection of masterpieces by Gustave Klimt. He spent a couple hours studying the glittering magical canvases in the white-washed and crystal bedecked halls of the palace. Undoubtedly it was this afternoon at the feet of Klimt and his polychromatic portraits of women that Majid composed this poem which is sometimes given the title "Der Kuss" after the best known of Klimt's works, but it most likely represents a composite, the idea of gilded love.

They are lovers—the artist and the madame
Just released from love's passionate embrace.

She has entered into the most delightful raptures
She shimmers and throbs with luminous pleasure
Like an electric station humming
From the warm glow and throbbing emanates
A golden nimbus, twinkling like stars
She is encased in crystal drops of sweat
Refracting her bright light even more
As if she emits her own sparkling halo.
Her face shows a dumb look of utmost contentment
He has brought her to such a climax.
Ah, this is love's miraculous moment.

He sees his lover encased in dazzling armor
Of gold leaf, sparkling gemstones, brilliants.
It is an aura as if she is a goddess
Descending on shafts of the most blinding sunlight
Her shining comes not from a silken robe but
From her gilding, the finest chrysalis made of gold.
He can catch only a glimpse of a rose pink
Areol on one breast or of her magical Venus mount.
He wants to kiss her or bite her tenderly once more,
But is afraid he'd break his teeth on the gemstones.
Ah, this is love's miraculous moment.

This poem was not published until almost five years later and it then became very popular. (I have as usual made a hash of translating it, because it is alliterative and has a lilting metrical scheme, and sadly in translating the exact meaning I have made it clumsy. Also typical of Majid he did not give it a title, but everyone calls it "Der Kuss".)

Not long after his visit to Vienna, the news reached Russia that its greatest living poet had died, died alone in exile, prematurely. The news took Majid by surprise and grieved him and disturbed him because there would therefore never be any reconciliation, any culmination to Brodsky's life work and love of the Russian language, never any repatriation, never any final public reclaim in Russia of its greatest poet in two or maybe even three generations. Majid had not paid much attention to Brodsky's verse before his encounter with the filmed recital in Venice he had heard several months earlier. Part of that was the relative unavailability of so much of Brodsky's opus inside Russia. Ardis Press in the West had only a few years earlier begun shipping editions of the poet into Russia and they were not widely distributed. As Brodsky had been a Leningrad (or St. Petersburg) poet even his samizdat works were more in circulation there than in Moscow. And while he was two years at the Gorky Institute not long before, Majid somehow had not made the acquaintance or attended workshops of the poet/professor Mark Reiner, who was also "an orphan" of Anna Akhmatova and friend, contemporary, and promoter of Brodsky's verse. But Majid had started closely studying Brodsky's poetry after his visit to the House of Journalists in late 1994 and he had become much closer to feeling the peculiar genius and pain of the man now dead. He could still not figure out Brodsky's voice, how his locution was appropriate for what he read or recited, his intonation, but he was immensely impressed by the collections he was able to find. He found Brodsky's verse precise, classical, concrete and without the ranting, bombast, hysterical declamations, and political attitudes of so many of Moscow's famous poets such as Gangnus and Voskresenksy. His poems were more profound and thoughtful than those even of Akhmadulina. He perceived that Brodsky, as he felt about himself, was most pre-occupied with the word, with language and the phonetic conveyance of meaning. He was an instrument of language, which was what had made Brodsky's exile so oppressive to endure, just it had Nabakov, or the other famous poet in exile, Ovid. Majid also discovered much to his delight that Brodsky was a prolific innovator of rhymes putting together words and combinations of words in a way that was thrilling and amusing to our hero who also experimented with new rhyme pairings. It was clear from what he was able to find and read that Brodsky was the leading and greatest Russian poet of the time. Majid discovered that Brodsky had adopted a technique which had him concentrate in his verses on nouns, and to minimize the use of adjectives and adverbs. It made his poems dense and palpable like a thick steak, not airy like an omelette. He started to examine in his own compositions if the same approach could work for him. But at that time Majid was disappointed and surprised when the news of Brodsky's death met with such a tepid reaction in Russia. The newspapers barely covered the story of his death, the *Kultura* state television station did not have any special programs dedicated to his poetry. There were no public memorial meetings, no public readings, no public grieving, no calls for a hero's burial in the pantheon cemetery of either St. Petersburg or Moscow, no calls for a memorial statue to be erected to him. The public reaction to the news of his death was met with almost universal indifference. The only public discussion that showed any emotional reaction to the Brodsky's passing was the news that he had requested to be buried in a cemetery for non-Christians in Venice. And this discussion was dominated by those who felt that Brodsky was a traitor to Russia for the effrontery and desire to be buried in a foreign cemetery. But Majid grieved. As did many other poets around Russia, most especially those who of his friends in the circle of the old Akhmatova who had stayed behind. Later Majid noticed with some irony that in 1997 on the one year anniversary of Brodsky's death there were public memorial observations and celebrations for the great poet held around Russia. But in the meantime, his collected works continued to be published for the first time in Russia. Majid's eulogy was published in the late spring of 1996 in *Literaturnaya Gazeta.* (Apparently they had not gotten instructions banning Majid's works, or they narrowly interpreted them to be only for political verse.)

Russia no longer loves its poets
They expelled him into howling exile
Neither at home nor abroad could they silence him,
They banned him, but they could not silence him.

A master of his craft his words
Resonate with truth emotion
And a profound love of the Russian word
He had a profound love of the Russian word.

They said his voice should not be heard, a parasite,
But he was heard from the furthest Arctic wastes
His words aimed like arrows at us
His words struck us like arrows aimed at us.

He refused to be silenced and he sang
Of Pushkin's oppressive city, even on the street corners
He would recite to the dim-witted and shuffling crowds
He refused to be silenced and so he died, struck down.

Although small and outwardly quiet
He was a giant who walked through the land
With the towering command of Peter on his steed
His range and insight struck one and all.

And where his words most struck their target
They reverberated, the arrows stuck fast:
From Michigan's sandy taiga and lake shores
To Sweden's granitic coast they heard him loud and clear.

But in his homeland, in grey Piter, the gaping crowds
Ignored him still, preferring the bombastic versifiers
Few were the lovers of Russian verse who loved him
Who called him—who begged him—to return home.

Condemned by the state he was reviled by his people
No one read his verse, he's too difficult they said
No one heard his verses, he's a foreigner.
Unacclaimed in life he lives and now lies dead abroad.

Russia threw away its greatest poet and his words
But in exile his salvation was another poet in exile
And his words were saved by foreign devotees
Because Russia no longer loves its poets.

1996 was the year scheduled for presidential elections and Yeltsin was hoping to get re-elected but his reputation had suffered badly from the economic hardship and his odd and often drunken behavior in the previous five years. At the beginning of the year it looked as if he might lose to the communists, his most feared and despised opposition. So Pavel Jastrzebski who was already working in the Kremlin for Yeltsin re-assigned Majid to work alongside him there until at least after the elections. It was a tough campaign as President Yeltsin was immensely unpopular following such a prolonged period of economic hardships and uncertainty, not to mention the unpopularity of his war in Chechnya. For Majid it was difficult because the campaign was run by the re-election committee which strictly controlled the flow of information and statements from the Kremlin, and because he had to deliver presidential promises and pledges about the war which were clearly meant to be ignored or broken after the elections (and were). And then again this was a time when public speaking by the country's leaders reached its very nadir. Yeltsin was a bumbler, often drunk, and he made a number of clumsy bloopers which have become famous for their clown-like inelegance and stupidity. His less clear statements were always finished with a smirk and his friendly, slurred "You git it?" His Prime Minister, Smugleekin, was even worse for making often incomprehensible utterances which left everyone wondering what he was addressing or even if he was not suffering from dementia. This left it an exceedingly difficult challenge to be a public spokesman for these men. Even trying to decipher what Yeltsin wanted to say and re-phrasing it so it was clear and comprehensible was a task. Close to the election date, Majid found he was only following instructions from the re-election committee, which meant he had almost nothing to do if the re-election committee did not dictate to him a statement to give to the press.

One fine day in late May there was a strategy meeting to be held in the Kremlin and while the participants including Majid were gathering outside the Presidential administration offices on Ivanovskaya square three black Mercedes drove up almost together and disgorged three beefy black suited gentlemen who briefly and stiffly huddled together. Majid almost immediately recognized them as three well known military men who were veterans of the Afghan War and conflicts in the former Soviet Union since 1991: General Lebed, General Grachev, the Defense Minister, and the unlikely General Rutskoy (but perhaps Majid was mistaken in his view of this latter as Rutskoy remained a political enemy of Yeltsin at that time). But then a strange thing happened: The three of them appeared to mount three heavy warhorses and then took off their black sharkskin jackets which revealed gleaming chain-mail vests on their chests. They wore Persian style iron helmets—the ones with sharp peaks on top, Iranian inscriptions around the brim, and with chain-mail ear flaps—and one, who looked like Lebed, bore a long, heavy *kontos* lance, the second held a broad sword, and the third, who was slighter than the others and resembled Pavel Grachev, held a bow. They rode straight up to Majid, and Lebed, the stern thick-necked hero, in a deep voice boomed out, "And which way shall we lead our brave Russian people?" Hero Grachev pointed up decidedly without conviction, while Hero Rutskoy—the one with the bushy moustache—pointed to the left, and finally Hero Lebed pointed to the right, squinting hard to the horizon as if he heard enemy hordes approaching. "There are treacherous enemies everywhere, especially the Communists!" boomed out Hero Lebed. He beat his chest. "But we must make peace with our Muslim neighbors." said Hero Grachev, diffidently. "No, we must bring back the Soviet Union. Death to the enemy serpents!" boomed Hero Rutskoy. "Only that will end all our ethnic and sectarian bloodshed." They advanced upon Majid and Ilya Muromets, that is Hero Lebed, leaned forward to Majid and in his deep gruff voice said to him, "Young poet, you must employ your lyre and verses to uplift our people." "Yes," said Alyosha, that is Hero Grachev, "and you must eulogize me and my exploits." From out of the administration offices rushed a crimson clad strelets in a black peaked cap clutching a battle axe, who looked just like General Korsakov, head of Yeltsin's bodyguard service. "This way heroes, great and powerful," he said directing them with his battle axe. Alyosha addressed Strelets Korsakov, "You must beware of conspirators from within. There are those close to the Tsar who would try to overthrow him!" "Come now, we must warn Tsar Boris of the perils confronting us!" shouted Ilya, Hero Lebed. And the three trotted off on their stallions to the back of the palace, with the crimson clad Korsakov running along behind them. Once inside the conference room, Majid did not see the three heroes again. Not long after Yeltsin won re-election, as improbable as it seemed through most of the year, General Lebed arranged a cease-fire peace with the Chechen separatists. Majid was so pleased he wrote an encomium to Lebed. He was naïve enough at the time that he thought the issues had been settled and peace would last, but less than four years later he was disabused of those conclusions and war broke out again.

During this assignment to the Kremlin, Majid began to apply himself seriously to improving his spoken English. This was useful he thought even though his main tasks for the Yeltsin presidency were to communicate with the Russian press corps. He spoke some English but his main exposure was reciting English poetry such as Yeats, or the metaphysical poets, or Shakespeare so he was not fluently able to conduct much of an English language conversation. He continued these efforts right up until his death. After Yeltsin's re-election in June, Majid left the

Kremlin and resumed working as a consultant for the other company clients of *Yasnost*, and as a consultant he picked up where he had left off with most of the clients that he had had in 1995. It was at the end of the year that he began reading and translating the poems of Heinrich Heine. He was especially struck by *Dichterliebe*. Ironically it was just as he began studying Heine's works that he finally got a hard copy of the poems of Theophile Gauthier, which had so enthralled him two years earlier. He had looked and looked around the bookstores and libraries of Moscow and could not find any of Gauthier's poems in the original French, but at the end of 1996 a foreign contact he had met at one of his clients informed him of the new internet bookseller, Amazon, still at that time in its early days. This expatriate was getting lots of books through Amazon.com, delivered reliably, and she showed Majid how he could get this book delivered to him in Moscow. It came after only six weeks in the middle of the winter, delivered reluctantly after spending some time in Russian customs, but arriving in perfect shape. Majid was amazed at this technological advance—by that time he was also becoming proficient at the use of his computer and especially of the internet—and found the only difficulty he had in the future in acquiring other books was that he did not at that time have his own credit card. (But it was not too long after that that he was able to get a credit card from his now growing account at the Tar-ry Bank (*Degtembank*).) So he split his time for several months working on the early poems of Heine and the book of collected verses of Gaulthier which had come to him from France via the US by Amazon. He translated most of the poems from *Dichterliebe* (A Poet's Love) into Russian that year, a time when he did not have much love, and he submitted it for publication in 1998. He made an effort to preserve their poetic rhythm and metrics as well as to keep some of the rhymes.

Overall, the year 1997 was a good year for Majid. He gave another recital in a medium sized theatre on the shady Boulevard Ring in the late spring. It was packed with poetry lovers, mostly young women.

Anna was not in sight, but Liza was there with her mother and they gave him a very large bouquet (worth a small fortune) at the end of his performance. Also at the end of the performance when the scrum of admirers surrounded him Lara reappeared after an absence of almost five years. They began seeing each other again after that and she became his sexual partner again not too long afterwards, she moving in to his large apartment and acting like an adopted cat. The affection was greater than before but they were not in love with each other it was clear and after a few months Majid invited her to leave his bed and his apartment. Indifferently Lara again left him for someone richer, someone who had a nice car; it was her strategy in life. From that springtime recital there were reviews of his poems in the literary journals, and they were very favorable. Later, when he was on leave from his job at *Yasnost* that summer, he spent three weeks living at Bella's dacha at her invitation. It was a very relaxed time when he composed a number of poems and began work on a verse translation of Shakespeare's MacBeth (which he finished a few years later). But her attempt at match- making between him and Liza was not successful. Also that summer there was finally a major effort to memorialize the life and achievement of Brodsky made by his surviving friends. This entailed a large memorial service held in a big hall in the center, where those that knew him recalled key events in his life. All of the poets that Majid knew were there in the hall, Voskreshensky, Krivonosov, Rheiner, Bella, Gangnus, and many he did not know. There were readings of several of his poems and a performance of a moving piece for quartet. As part of the observations, *Kultura* aired a film that Brodsky had done on one of his visits to Venice as well as a film that had been put together in the months since his death. It highlighted key moments in his biography including some of his activities in America, interviews with poets who had known him, and it featured readings of a number of his poems, some even by the poet in the years just before his death. Ironically it was just a couple weeks after these memorial events that Okudzhava died abroad in pain and isolation in a Paris hospital. Majid hadn't seen him in more than a year as he had been very ill in the last two years of his life. Unlike Brodsky, his body was brought back and was given a public hero's funeral. There were copious outpourings of memorial observations and TV reprisals of films and recordings of the Moscow hero. His recordings in various second hand shops and book stalls sold out within days.

A small incident occurred that summer which left a lasting impression on him. He was a passenger in a car driving outside the city in dacha-land with Igor at the wheel. Igor, as was his wont, was chattering away about plans and rumors when Majid, still a nervous passenger looking out the windshield and holding on to the dashboard, saw in the street a couple hundred meters in front of them a man step out into the street in front of white car and then fly into the air like a contorted gymnast doing a flip. He had been hit and thrown by the car through the air. "Did you see that, Igor?" Igor had. "That man was hit hard." Igor slowed down as the approached the stopped car and then came to a stop, as is required when in Russia you have witnessed an accident. Jumping out of the car was a traffic cop. Crumpled and bleeding on the street was the body of the hit man, lying in such a twisted way that it was certain he was not alive. The traffic cop had hit and killed the man. He signaled with his arm to them and shouted as he glanced at the body, "Keep moving. Don't stop. It is just a drunk who fell." He motioned on the cars behind them also. "Well, I'll be." said Igor as he slowly pulled his car around the accident and drove off. "The traffic cops are supposed to protect pedestrians, not run them down like that." The image of the broken and twisted body of an older man lying in his own pool of blood on the asphalt was one that stayed vividly with Majid for years afterwards.

After the summer one of his oil company clients took Majid to an investors' conference in London which as part of its efforts to make a stock offering on the London exchange. This time—only the second trip abroad for Majid—he had lots of work and he was required to making a presentation in English and answer questions in English. The preparations for this trip were made by the client's investment bank and he worked closely with the Moscow-based bankers in advance of the trip. That was when he met and fell in love with Irina (or Ira - pronounced Eera—as she was called by her friends and almost everyone.) He worked closely with her for several weeks before they went to London and in London it seemed he never left Ira's side. Unlike in Vienna though, there was no free time for Majid to explore the city or view its cultural treasures, although one of the events put on for the conference was to go to Covent Garden for an evening at the opera. From the dates when Majid was in London it must have been the opera *Iolantha*, the story about the blind but beautiful princess which was transformed into one of Russia's most beautiful operas by Tchaikovsky and which Majid's client company was sponsoring there in London. Majid sat next to Ira and became enthralled by the aroma of her perfume (it smelled a little like rose and citrus blossoms, but Majid could not tell for sure and he did not dare try to smell her neck), and the romance of the story on stage. But how could he take the scales off of Ira's eyes and make her fall in love with him just as Iolantha did with Vaudemont? Irina was a beautiful Tatar girl with long straight black hair and a large and ready smile, who also happened to be brilliant, as she had studied finance at university and foreign languages, but she was not struck by Majid particularly and did not know then that he was a poet. He did not solve the problem of attracting her in London. He began only afterwards in Moscow to try and win her heart, but he had the difficulty of not seeing her often. As he was busy during those four days and as in typical fashion London was dark, seemingly dirty, crowded and its skies overcast, chilly, and usually spitting rain, the city did not make a favorable impression on Majid, at least not in comparison with Vienna. But the trip inspired several more poems from Majid in which he wrote down later that autumn his emotional responses to London and especially to Irina. Further in that year in the early winter a publisher agreed to print a new collection of his verses, which included some of those London poems and some which were evidence of his new found attraction to Irina conflated into the person of Iolantha.

Back in Moscow, with his normal work resumed with other clients, he did not have much opportunity to see Ira, who was not one of his clients. There was nothing to do. He had to call her and ask her out on a date. But he did not know what she would like, in fact he did not know very much about her at all and so when he called her he was almost as surprised at himself as she was in getting his call. So after some clumsy minutes he finally managed to invite her to join him at dinner. He thought Sirens would be nice: The seafood restaurant with the live fish in aquariums under the glass floor and with erotic paintings on the walls of sirens and mermaids calling sailors to their deaths. The same restaurant that Anna had invited him to a few years earlier, where she had begun her seduction of him. He later thought that that was an appropriate place because they had oysters on offer, and he had read that oysters acted as aphrodisiacs (although he was unclear whether the effect was just on men, or on women as well). She agreed to his suggestion and they agreed to meet there. He went there by metro and she drove herself after work. When he arrived she had not arrived yet and was still not there by the appointed meeting time. After she was about 45 minutes late he decided to call her on his new piece of technology, a mobile phone (she of course, as did all the investment bankers, had her own). There was no problem, she apologized; first she had to stay a little longer at her work than she had planned and then she had become stuck in traffic gridlock and was still 15-20 minutes away, if things began to move. As it was, she was another 35 minutes away and she arrived flustered, agitated, and full of apologies and explanations. At the dinner, over cod and king crab legs, Ira revealed a bit more about herself. She had not known before that Majid was a published poet; she said she never read poetry and didn't go to recitals either. She had of course read some Pushkin in school in Moscow when she was young, but then it was a general requirement. She was not it seemed impressed that Majid was a poet; it seemed to her it was like saying you had brown hair or having learned to speak French. She had studied English in school and university and went often to London on work and on vacations. Her dark eyes often fluttered at him, and he concluded that it was a sign that she liked him (only much later was he to find out that she wore contact lens and they—not coyness—caused the rapidly blinking eyes). She wanted white wine with dinner and so although it was not his custom to drink with meals, they finished off a bottle. He became drunk, she only seemingly a little more at ease and responsive with him. He asked her if she liked concerts. She said that she liked to dance, so they agreed to go to a club after finishing dinner, although Majid told her he did not know how to dance at all, having never done it. She said there was nothing to it, and she turned out to be right. The nightclub was loud and crowded. Once dancing, Ira lit up, smiling much more than previously in Majid's presence, and displaying a very vigorous style and athletic movements. Majid felt intensely self-conscious and awkward on his feet. He was following her movements, but usually lagging her. He was dripping with sweat as the club was muggy and the music blaring. They took a break for some refreshment; Ira ordered a sweet cocktail and he had a coke. Her face was beginning to show a blush even though her skin color was almost olive colored. After another round of dances, a tall, blond, skin-head approached her. "Out of my way runt," he said as he brushed Majid to one side. "Dance with me girl. You look really hot." Majid stepped between Ira and this interloper. "She's dancing with me." "I told you to get lost, you effeminate twit." And he addressed his words with a slight push to the chest. Majid tried to react, to resist, but the interloper actually wasn't alone. Two of his confederates held Majid back by the arms. Majid noticed that his assaulter had a small dark blue tattoo on his hand at the joint between his thumb and pointer. "Leave him alone, you goon." shouted Ira. "I won't dance with you." "You need a manly man." By now the other dancers around them had stopped and crowded around, as it looked as if a fight were about to break out; something they wanted to see. Majid was still struggling with the two holding him back. He shouted out, "Is it so manly to act like an onager in rut, or like a shaved-headed baboon running from hyenas". The interloper did not know what an onager was. "Get away from us." Ira now screamed. The beefy bouncer handling door and face control was heading toward them from the door. He loved fights, he loved bashing unruly clients, and he was good at it. The crowds meanwhile had pushed in closer on all of them. "Leave him alone," again Ira screamed moving to push at the unwanted guest. This latter, looking at the coming conflict and seeing a second bouncer heading his way through the crowds which had now enitrely stopped dancing, decided it was better to retreat, and as he spun away to make his departure he smashed Majid hard in the gut. He hissed, "you little prick." and he made off. His comrades dropped him like a sack of flour on the floor. His head took a hard knock on the floor as he landed. It took Majid some time to recover, or to even realize where he was. Not since he was a picked-upon boy in his schooldays back in Ufa had anyone hit him, and even then never so hard. Some crowd members picked him up and hauled him to a table away from the dance floor. Ira stuck with him and a waitress came over to see if he needed any help. The little bit of alcohol he had drunk with dinner combined with the body blow was enough to keep him unclear. He was faintly aware of the waitress's copious cleavage quite near his face, and Ira stroking his arm and saying something solicitously. Had he vomited? He wasn't sure, but he had that sour taste in his mouth as if he had. His shirt was torn, or so it seemed. Finally his breath came back and his vision cleared up. The music was thunderously pulsating just as was his head. Then he was aware that Ira was speaking to him, with a very concerned expression on her face. "Let's go, Slava. I'll drive you home if you like." She did and she dropped him off at his house with a small kiss from behind the wheel. "I enjoyed myself." she said. "In spite of that gorilla."

That 'gorilla' was not so unusual in everyday Russian life, although that one in the disco tech did not in the least resemble a gorilla; for one thing he was not particularly big or powerfully built, maybe only three inches taller than Majid. And in addition he was fair skinned, blond, and wore his hair cropped short as if he were a new army recruit—and that is why his like are called skinheads. And like the skinheads in Germany, he was a nationalist, not knowingly a neo-Nazi, but an ultra-nationalist who along with the scores of other young men openly espoused political ideals like the national socialists and especially carried out on the streets their racial hatred of Chechens, Azeris and other dark skinned Caucasians, Jews, and Central Asian migrant laborers. Later in the decade they would extend their hatred policies to include Muslims of any origin. Many of these young nationalists had served in the army where they had learned how to fight and use firearms, although many had before their army service been small time criminals and hoodlums. And this unorganized grouping of nationalist youth (for nearly all of them were under 35 years old) had as their spiritual and political leaders two very different but powerfully spiteful men who both sprang from the underbelly of the internal security services of the former Soviet Union; one was a radical writer and poet named Benjamin Lemonsky and the other was the leader of the national liberal socialist party who had been for many years an agent provocateur for the KGB, named Tikve Vladvolzhen. This latter, Vladvolzhen, had become in the years after 1992 the public political leader of the nationalists. He did not outline any concrete political agenda for the future of Russia but he espoused Russian nationalist views and specialized in public vituperation and profanity laden calumny laced with hatred. Most of his outbreaks in the Duma and on the election campaigns were staged to appeal to those seeking to assert their machismo and power, to a less educated group of young men who did not have many opportunities for working and did not want to join the serious criminal gangs but instead moved about in hoodlum gangs. Vladvolzhen was one who used violence and preached violence. Even in the Duma he would assault his political opponents. He gained his greatest infamy when in front of the TV cameras he bashed a woman parliamentarian in the face because she had called him a low life (and she had bested him and humiliated him in debate). And in the mid-1990s the targets of this violence promoted by Vladvolzhen were young men from the Caucasus, and especially Chechens. Around Moscow, as Majid took his long walks around the city, it became clear to Majid that there was a running battle going on where small gangs of nationalist young men, usually skinheads, would prowl around looking for small groups of Caucasians to assault. The press, both the newspapers and TV, made a feast of detailing the low-grade warfare of knives, bats, brass knuckles, and air pistols that occurred in the bedroom neighborhoods on the city outskirts, grim, concrete high rise ghettos which had years earlier been divvied up between various ethnic groups with Russians left in the in-between neighborhoods. Unemployment was high for all these different groups so the nationalists had a ready pool of recruits. The press showed weekly deaths of Caucasians in these neighborhoods, as well the daily results of knifings of Russian youths. It was in this background that Majid witnessed an incident by a gang of hoodlums. He was riding on the metro and standing not far from him were two youths who were discussing music (one was carrying a cello case). They were dark haired Armenian boys and they were talking loudly.

Three skinheads walked through the corridor of the wagon and tried to get past them and shoved and cursed the two. One of the two Armenians, who Majid had heard from the discussion was named Arkay, answered back, saying something like 'take it easy, I'm getting off at the next station'. The skinheads shouted louder, hurling insults and calling Arkay a big-nosed Azeri bastard. The train stopped and the doors opened and Arkay (but not the cello player) step out with the skinheads trying to hustle and push him out, shouting at him. The leader of this little band of hoodlums looked like almost all other skinhead nationalists, blond, short hair, and Majid noticed a very common small black tattoo in the joint between his thumb and index finger, almost a mark of man who has served in the army or in prison, or both. The doors closed and as the train started again Majid could see that the three hoodlums had surrounded Arkay on the platform and were shouting, spitting at his face and pushing him from all sides. The train rolled on and Majid lost sight of the Armenian. Later that evening Majid saw on the TV news that there had been a stabbing murder on the metro platform (the same one where Majid had seen this incident) of a 20 year old Armenian conservatory student and the assailants had run off and escaped. The student had bled to death on the platform before help could get to him. It was upon hearing this that Majid realized that this was Arkay that had been murdered by those same hoodlums he had seen. And then the thought struck him: It could just as easily been him who lay on the platform bleeding to death from a stab wound to the heart, because he realized he looked a lot like Arkay (he didn't have a big nose but a straight long one) and the skinheads in that metro wagon at that time had been looking for a fight with anyone who looked even remotely like the hatred Caucasians. He became aware then for the first time that he was target just as much as any Chechen or Azeri or Uzbek youth getting around the capital city. And slowly he realized that no one would come to his assistance if he were assaulted just as no one had come to the aid of Arkay; whether or not this lack of help was due to the general fear crowds have of getting entangled, or to gross indifference, or Majid thought—and this was worst of all—to a widespread feeling by the Russian population that this was the sort of punishment that men from the Caucasus deserved. After that incident and sudden awareness Majid began to hold Vladvozhen in contempt and he would always cast a wary eye on any young Russian man dressed in a white tee shirt and with very short cropped hair. The low grade war in the ghettos of distant Moscow bedroom neighborhoods carried on, and unlike a murder in the open on a metro platform in the city center, this war largely did not make the news, except when a large number of fatalities resulted or when a number of skinheads were murdered by the enemy gangs.

Over the next year, the relationship between Majid and Irina blossomed slowly but steadily. They went out together initially on more dancing dates, but not at that same club where he had been assaulted. Dancing was important to Ira. It was clearly a release of her suppressed erotic energies and once on the dance floor, even surrounded by many other dancers, she led Majid through a series of jerks and contortions, humping and bouncing—often touching him, embracing him and then spinning off—so that he concluded she wanted desperately to make love to him there on the floor. He liked it very much; he especially liked how her breasts flounced wildly about when the dancing was especially rollicking, and when she threw her long black hair around her head. It was a strange introduction to her, as at the bank she acted like a soft-spoken librarian. There had a few dates at restaurants, and a couple where they went to classical music concerts and once more to an opera; *Eugene Onegin* in this case. Ira seemed to like him; after a few dates they began holding hands as they strolled along the boulevard grit paths after dark. It was only after half a dozen or so dates together that Ira asked Majid if he would recite a poem for her. He recited two, but although she paid close attention to him and was staring hard at the middle button of his shirt trying to concentrate on the meaning of the words, she did not really understand if the poems were good or not, nor if she fully understood the sense. But she did not ask for him to explain. She sometimes would talk to him about financial issues and her work at the bank, but that did not interest Majid much either. He could only relate the financial movements in Russia's markets when they were told from a personal point of view—the actions of the oligarchs or the decisions of key investors in trying to gain control over a company. It was only after several weeks that he was surprised to learn that Ira had been married before—for less than two years—when she was 19, and then divorced. She did not talk about it at all, except to say it was a youthful mistake, and she had never seen her ex- even once in the subsequent seven years. Then one evening in the fall, after dancing until they both were soaked through, they embraced and kissed, and perhaps after that point it seemed Ira began to love Majid. In the winter one evening after a date she accompanied him back to his apartment and they made love that night, and stayed in bed making love until they had to have something to drink and some breakfast the next morning. At the end of the weekend of making love, they both felt a deep, physical bond, something had changed inside them. Ira was unlike any of Majid's other lovers. She had swarthy skin, not the pellucid white skin of Russians—the look almost as if she was sun-tanned or had spent long hours in the suntanning beds which were all the rage in Moscow then. Caressing her tanned skin, smooth and blemishless, Majid thought he could feel the sun of the sun in her. She smelled faintly of musk. Finally, they had to separate on Monday to their respective places of work, but they did so very reluctantly and they spent the working days that next week frequently speaking to each other over their mobile phones and hoping to rush the day until they could get together again and fall once more in each other's arms. The next month and a half ran by with a continuous rush of passionate love; they were perpetually coupled until, during the work days they would be exhausted and feeling the glow and soreness of love. Ira brought her clothes over from her parents' house and moved in with Majid. The intensity only finally tapered off when they had to stop to clean up after themselves, stacks of dishes, clothes, and sheets, but they were a pair by then. Majid was so pre-occupied that he was unable to compose any poetry in that period, at work he felt like a zombie. Ira said work was hard for her as well. It was then made even more difficult when after living together as lovers for six weeks they had to separate, because her work assigned her to go to London for a week. He felt that entire week as if a hole had been punched through him, he was always missing her, and they both spent a fair sum of money talking when they could on their phones. But she came back, and he met her at the airport and rode back with her to his apartment. She brought all kinds of gifts and specialty items for him and they resumed where they had left off. There was little time in the next coming months for them to establish a steady routine because she again had to travel to London for a week, and he also had to fly out of Moscow to his clients' on several occasions, usually for only a night or two. But when they were both in Moscow they would count the minutes until they could re- unite at Majid's house. They would often eat dinner out at a restaurant of café because they left no time to shop for food. And they went only once more to a dancing club. Eventually she moved all of her wardrobe and shoes to the closet in Majid's room. Toward the end of that year as the winter darkness spread chill and gloom over the city, they even planned on going on a foreign beach vacation together, someplace where it was warm and sunny and they could spend all day together. It did not matter that Majid did not know how to swim (in fact he was a little bit afraid of the water) and that he had no summer or beach clothes. They spent all of one Saturday shopping for their vacation needs and swimwear and then flew off to what to all appearances seemed to be a 10 day honeymoon. They took a charter package tour to the Dominican Republic and fell in love again. Ah love.

It was into the mid-winter of 1998 that Ira and her Slava finally began to settle into routines as if they were a newly married couple. Neither of them could cook much of anything, but they tried. They regularly would go out to eat evening meals in a neighborhood restaurant. They bought a washing machine for their clothes. Their dress shirts and blouses they sent out to cleaners. They still regularly went to out to dance, occasionally to a concert. They had their own bathrobes and toiletries. Neither of them was at all sporting so they passed on cross country skiing weekends or ice skating in one of the city's many rinks. But Ira came to like her Slava's commitment to long strolls, even in the winter, and they would often walk arm in arm through the dark icy nights under the stars, and later in the spring under the blossoming trees. She went to the recital he gave in the late winter of 1998 and she was so filled with pride to hear her lover recite his own works to a large hall of eager fans that she almost could have burst. With his complete pre-occupation with Irina in the evenings after work, his work on poetry slowed down considerably. But he still managed some composition and some translation. He would recite for her as he composed and ask her opinion. But most evenings of most days were dedicated to Ira. Eventually they talked about getting married officially. And after some months living together they finally agreed they would. She was enthusiastic about the proposal, and frankly he was excited by the prospect as well. The next step was to reserve a time at the bridal registry office for a simple ceremony. The nearest Saturday that they could get for their ceremony was in early June so they took it and spent most of five months as affianced together. He even got her a ring, but he could not do that without convincing her to accompany him to the jeweler's for a fitting. He bought her a small brilliant. Later in the spring he bought himself his first car—a small dark green Ford. His mood made a dramatic shift as is clear from a poem he drafted that year.

I was that Arab lost in the sandy wastes
Salt and sand crusted round his eyes
His tongue swollen from thirst so no words
Could convey his songs, his skin was blistered.

The last brackish drops of water consumed
His head athrob from the merciless sun
Seated on the deflated hump of his mount,
Near death, at the end of his strength, hope.

When suddenly on the distant sky,
What did he espy but a fata morgana
A spot of cool greenness reflected up high
His heart beat faster for one more time.

A chance vision telling him there was hope
In the parched desert beyond the heat haze
He rushed forward and then appeared a lake:
Alas, this was but a deceitful mirage.

But it was not a mirage, it was you,
Irina, an oasis in a cruel
Desert land. You are the fountains
And jasmine gardens in my life.

This poor Arab rushed into this lush landscape
And drank deeply of its fresh waters
Yours kisses were like restoring cold wines
The fluttering of birds like your softest sighs.

The gently clapping banana blossoms
Are your gay laugh and sweet song
Dappled shadows of palms are your dark locks
Silver mint flowers are the delicate scent of your breath.

In the still cool shade of the oasis, I loved you.
I rolled in your clear springs as if
In your tend'rest embrace. I drank my fill
I wrapped myself in your perfumed moist folds.

In this oasis you caressed my brow
And refreshed my heart
You have given me your love and new life,
Irina, my odalisque of the desert springs.

In June 1998 his translation of Heine's *Dichterliebe* was printed in the *Znamenka* (Banner Street literary journal, a Soviet era literary journal which had made the transition and now published uncensored and innovative works by young writers, its chief editor was a Mr. Churbanin who had also made the conversion from a Soviet literary bureaucrat and gate- keeper, to a modern progressive editor with taste and now had close relations with the Gorky Institute). It came out at about the same time Majid and Ira wed, and as it was a collection of love poems it was a very appropriate wedding gift. He did not earn very much at all from this, but he had not expected much as poetry occupied a second rank in the journal. Neither was there very much critical comment or attention paid to it. Lyric post-Romantic poetry just was not in vogue at that time. Nevertheless he decided to translate the entire collection of Lyrical Intermezzi from which this excerpt came so he continued. He had really begun to love Heine's verses—so simple, direct and musical—*Wenn ich mich lehn' an deine Brust, kommt's über mich wie Himmelslust*—and by now he was keen to hear Schumann's version performed in concert. He liked them so much that he wanted to continue to translate the entire collection by Heine. Perhaps society was not really interested in poetry in this period as there was a profound financial and political crisis developing since the beginning of the year. Oil prices had fallen and state debts had blown up out of control. In March, Yeltsin had dismissed his long serving tongue tied prime minister, Victor Smugleekin and at the same time, but unrelated, Majid's patron, Jastrzebsky was fired abruptly from the presidential administration. Their wedding was a small affair attended by Ira's family and friends, and only Igor Formico attending from Majid's side; neither his mother nor the Buterbrodskys could come from Kazan. But the event was overshadowed by the palpable fear of another round of economic hardship, which put a damper on the celebrations. After Majid and Ira came back from a short wedding trip to Paris—the city of Light and Love—Ira came home from work one evening and began to tell him of the seriousness of the financial crisis and the expectation that the ruble was going to crash. They concluded that there were going to be economic hard times again, but neither of them projected on how such a crisis would affect them nor what to do, if anything, about the looming threat. Investors were pulling money out of Russia so fast that the stock markets were collapsing and the Central Bank had run through its foreign hard currency reserves. She told him how after the IMF had sent Russia emergency support funds to the tune of $5 billion, someone or some group had stolen them. But for this breathtaking theft there were no political consequences, perhaps suggesting that everyone got paid off.

As has so often happened in Russian history, August was a disastrous month, and in the year 1998 Yeltsin must have thought that it was in his cards for things to blow up if for no other reason than it was August. And this August was the time when everything snapped at once. The ruble lost two thirds of its value against other currencies. Many workers went out on strike for six months without pay, and many others lost their jobs. Everyone who had hard currency debts found they were underwater (so to speak). Fires broke out in many parts of Russia because of the heat. Officials had to come back from their vacations. And many of the Russian banks declared a default on their foreign borrowings and then shuttered their doors claiming bankruptcy, when really it was a convenient cover to steal the depositors' money. Which meant vast numbers of Russians suddenly lost all their savings. Majid was one of these victims, as Degtem Bank one of Russia's largest, where Majid had his principal deposits, closed claiming bankruptcy saying all its depositors would lose their money, but meanwhile its owner-director, Mr. Smolnov, absconded with hundreds of millions of dollars to London. Millions of Russians around the country fell victim to the same maleficence, and those that did not lose their deposits saw their ruble depreciated and their buying power greatly reduced. By September, the investment bank where Ira worked saw no future in Russia securities so they dismissed her, along with many other junior bankers, and shrank their business. It was less painful for the senior bankers who were foreign: they merely sent them back home. It was a hard time, and although Majid kept his job his income (of course he still earned next to nothing for his poetry) fell as a couple of his clients canceled their contracts as they decided they did not need the services of *Yasnost* in that time of economic crisis.

This was the year when Majid started working on one of the major themes of his future poetry: the greed and the attendant thievery which ran throughout Russian society. He had of course witnessed and heard lots of stories about this, grand theft of tens of millions of dollars by the ruling elites, the bribery and kickback gains of the all-powerful *chinovniki* who could block any endeavor, any project if they did not get a large illicit payment in cash, the Duma deputies, Vladvozhen for one, who openly demanded cash contributions from any petitioner wanting a meeting with them, the flow of funds through money laundering schemes, the protection racketeering which had driven Aram out of the country One of the alarming news stories of the spring of that year was the arrest of a property registrar, who upon inspection by the police was found to have a closet full of shoe boxes, everyone stuffed full of large denomination ruble bills. This *chinovnik* was to be prosecuted, but before he could be brought to court, the prosecutor found that the police had lost the evidence of his filthy lucre—in other words the ill-gotten cash had disappeared in many other pockets. The chinovniki claimed piteously that he was being political persecuted, unjustifiably.

But it was after Majid bought his car and started driving it he noticed an entirely different layer, the "background noise" of small time theft. He had to pay a number of small bribes in addition to the requisite fees to get his car inspected and registered in a timely fashion (that is, to get to the head of the daily line to apply for the process, to convince the inspector to look at his car on that day and not at an unspecified future day, to confess that the condition of the car—it was new—was up to acceptable standards, and to get the documents attesting all this printed and delivered to him). Once he was driving he found he was frequently stopped by the traffic police who demanded $10, $20, even $50 for them to overlook the flimsiest of contrived infractions. This occurred so regularly and at so many different points that he had always to carry in the car a stash of cash, dollars preferred but large note rubles would work too, just to be able to drive around town and, in the summer, around dacha land. He discovered that everyone he talked to about this faced the same dilemma and resorted to the same solutions. During the months after his work leading up to his London visit, his clients' auditors would tell him horrifying stories of the ways that the companies had to mask their bribes, protection money payments, and managerial theft within their accounts. It seemed in the business world everyone had the same problems. It was so widespread it was as if for companies the primary criterion for choosing an investment project of any size was the need for a manager to get a percentage pay-back from giving out the contract to the vendor or supplier or contractor. And then, when goods or equipment were purchased, allowances had to be made for the theft of critical parts or pieces which was made during shipping and delivery. Losses en route for the delivery of fuels by his oil company client were many times higher than the industry norms in the rest of the world because of skim-offs done by managers or "friends" of managers. More immediately, Majid one morning in the dirty, wet spring of 1998 went out to drive his car to his office and he discovered that his windshield wipers had been stolen (somehow using the more familiar term equivalent term of 'were pinched' made the theft seem more trivial or less serious). And not long after that one evening at the end of his work day he was dismayed to find his car would not start and sounded as if the battery were dead: he discovered that overnight someone had broken through the grill and opened the hood and stolen his still new car battery. He could not believe that someone would do this in broad daylight and that no one noticed or interfered in the theft. He was advised by his work colleagues, who thought Majid rather naïve, that this problem was so endemic that he had to have installed an elaborate car alarm system that would both sound off shrilly and block the engine if anyone so much as lightly brushed the car while walking by it. (Why, they were amazed, that Majid even dared to park his car out on the street.) One day that spring one of his friends who ran a tourist agency complained to him that he was robbed on the street in traffic when the thief boldly opened his car door and snatched his briefcase full of customers' tickets and passports off the passenger seat and ran off before he could react; he had forgotten to lock his doors while driving. Majid listened wide-eyed and registered that he needed to follow the same practice. But it was the August collapse and the attendant grand theft that brought the issues together for Majid into one systemic societal disease. About a month after the crisis broke out and closure of the Degtem Bank, the Central Bank announced that it had negotiated a system by which depositors could recover a small proportion of their savings. Smolnov stated that he owed his depositors 'dead donkeys' ears'. So Majid went to collect his donkeys' ears to add to his collection of useless items he had picked up over the years in Moscow—it took a lot of document submissions, many repeated visits to different branches of the closed bank, and time. He never did collect his entire allotted recovery amount in rubles from his savings. What he got he put into the state-owned central savings bank. Mr. Smolnov never did face criminal prosecution, but then he lived very comfortably in England with many bodyguards protecting him and his family and his living donkeys.

The response to the August crisis revealed another very disturbing trend to Majid (and many others). It was the beginning of the return of the rule of the KGB in Russia. A small group in the press noticed this creeping takeover and their background articles stoked the discussions that people around Moscow had, through meetings of friends and colleagues in the new coffee shops now sprouting up around the city, through the traditional discussions at the kitchen tables between friends, and for the first time, through internet networks. This encroachment was spotted by the appointments of former KGB people to key ruling roles in Yeltsin's government, people who had no previous public political roles. It started with Stepoffshin being given the role as head of the department of the interior, which ran both secret police service and the public police. He had previously been the head of the Internal Secret Police, but had been dismissed after the massacre at Budyonnovsk. He had done nothing that would have gained him credit to expunge his earlier disgrace. But was most alarming and noticeable of this new trend was when Yeltsin appointed Evgeny Upriamikov as the new prime minister right after the crisis broke. This elderly man—who had been many years as a KGB agent in the Middle East—was a strange appointment as his attitudes and political directions were completely at odds with Yeltsin's. His appointment was so out of sync with Yeltsin's views it seemed as if he had been hoisted on Yeltsin to take over and re-set the government's direction. And in the months that followed Upryamikov appeared to be heading away from liberal democratic politics and market economics. All this distressed Majid. And the situation got worse when seemingly out of nowhere, Yeltsin appointed a virtually unknown St. Petersburg spy, Sputyanin, to be his new interior minister. What Majid was most concerned about was that if the secret police and ex-KGB men came back in to run the government, stern controls of public expression and censorship would return not long afterwards, the freedoms which had briefly flourished after the demise of the Soviet Union would shrivel up and be swept aside like so many dead flowers in an untended garden.

At first it was the monasteries
Which seized the products of the land.
In the name of God, they seized the land.

Then it was the Church that claimed the souls
And tied live souls to the lands the Churches owned
The peasants to the lands belonged which the Churches owned.

Soon the tsars required the labor of men and women
And tied poor peasants to lands given to nobles
These poor people became the slaves of ignoble nobles.

A serf had no rights to live or to own or to be free
He could flee to Turkic lands, but the state
Chased him through all time, he was owned by the state.

Alexander freed the serfs, but poor men remained enslaved
In the army they had to serve a lifetime in penury,
In the city sweatshops they had to serve a life in penury.

Revolution brought no freedom, now the state
Owned the people, their ev'ry movement and thought
Working as prisoners without hope or thought.

And so Russians are forever enslaved
They have no free life, because they belong not like men
To God or the state, like chattel, not like men.

But think not that chains and bonds are enough
To enslave us, the thoughts and words must be controlled
Serving God, tsars, and states, our thoughts and words.

So books are burned and banned, free speech
A chimera, words must also be enslaved.
A slave of the state cannot have his own words.

The enemy of the state is the serf who speaks his mind
So through all time they must repress the poet:
Silence him, ignore him, burn his words, the repressed poet.

Chapter Four

Majid had reached a pinnacle of his career by his thirtieth birthday in mid-1999. He had published four collections of his poetry in Russian, and one in Tatar, and in addition his translation of *DIchterliebe* had been published in a literary journal and over the previous ten years more than two score of his poems had appeared in other journals. He was acknowledged as a poet of great promise, a prodigy, the leading young poet of Russia, and his works seemed to be popular. Up to then his recitals had been well attended and the demand for more appeared to be strong. Certainly there was some considerable jealousy beginning to emerge within the community of poets, mainly those of the generation before his and his father's generation, poets who had suffered repression and had not been published in their formative years because of Soviet restrictions. But his future looked good and he was hard at work on a number of projects. He was deeply in love with the beautiful Irina, his wife, and she loved him and even was beginning to like his poetry. He had money and a job, which was well paid but not so demanding that he could not continue to compose verse both in the day and in the evenings. With a new wife, it is understandable that his output of poems diminished somewhat, but that is an experience that has occurred with other great creative artists, such as composers, poets, novelists over the years, especially those who could not earn a living wage from their works.

The financial crisis was not prolonged and in total it did not do too much damage to Majid's well-being. He and Irina had plenty of money to live nicely, he was not hungry again—many people were, especially pensioners and others on fixed low incomes—and they were still able to enjoy going out occasionally for dinner or dancing. Most important for everyone was the recovery of the oil price which saw a rapid rebound in the general economy in 1999. By the summer, Irina was re-appointed to her job in the investment bank because business had returned. So they had enough income to contemplate a foreign vacation in the south of France.

But politically Russia was slipping backwards. In the past several years of peaceful coexistence between Russia and Chechnya a civil war had blown up based on a new phenomenon, Islamic fundamentalism. This movement led to a great radicalization and fragmentation of the society, and the fighting became more tribal and savage and the fundamentalist leaders claimed that an Islamic state would take over the entire Caucasus. At the same time, the takeover in Russia of the government by former KGB officers, continued; Yeltsin seemed to have lost his direction and leadership of the government. First Stepoffshin replaced Upryamikov and then Sputyanin replaced Stepoffshin, which looked like a steady progression of the more secretive, more inscrutable and more autocratic personalities taking control in turn. Very little at all was publicly known about Sputyanin except that he was a KGB officer from St. Petersburg who was mentored by Andropov and took the latter as his model and inspiration of what a proper KGB man should be. Of course Majid was well aware that it was largely due to Andropov's sponsorship and prompting that the USSR invaded Afghanistan and stayed at war there for a decade. And Andropov was the first KGB man—the so-called guardians of the communist party during the existence of the USSR— who himself became the leader of the communist state; just as in Rome the praetorian guards became the emperors whom they were sworn to protect. With Andropov as his admired mentor it seemed clear that Sputyanin would not be a democrat and would not foster the further development of a civil society. As things developed after Sputyanin was appointed prime minister, he seemed to be the prime mover behind the throwing out the 1996 peace settlement and re-opening the war against Chechnya. And from the beginning of Sputyanin's rule, Majid had a terrible foreboding of the beginning of a police state. This suspicion became the basis for much of Majid's explicitly political poems over the coming two years. But he also became more politicized by his appointment as the press spokesman for the ambitious Mayor of Moscow, George Puddle, who by early-1999 saw that Yeltsin was on his last legs and that presidential elections—which he felt he stood a good chance at winning—were slated for the next May. George Puddle needed the complete apparatus to appear presidential and to be a serious candidate, even before official campaigning started. So, he needed a press spokesman and public relations director to communicate his views as a national leader—not merely as the mayor of Moscow—on legislation, on foreign affairs, on social development to the public. Through connections the mayor's office found Majid who still worked at Yasnost, and who looked eminently qualified (they had already decided that they did not want Jastrzebzky for the position because he presumed too much an independent political identity and he had represented Yeltsin over too many years). So the mayor invited him to his office on Tverskaya Avenue to meet him and to interview him. Majid did not know how to prepare for the interview and he approached it with some trepidation, which was made worse by the amount of security checks he had to pass through at City Hall on the way to Mr. Puddle's office. After the first check point and security screening at the entrance which was manned by armed military police, there were several other security check points on the way up to the office. These were manned by very big, strong looking men all dressed in identical black suits and black ties—men who scowled at Majid, examined his passport closely, looked at his mobile phone, and patted him down for weapons before sending him further. The mayor greeted him standing in his office, taking him in his large pudgy hands with a bracing handshake, a combined pout and smile on his jowly face. Majid had seen Mr. Puddle on TV of course but he was still surprised to see how short and round the mayor was; even dressed in his dark gray suit the mayor's a large rotund belly protruded noticeably. And he was a lot shorter than he appeared on TV. He wore a broad tie which seemed to choke him, and he was very bald. But what was most surprising to Majid in that first meeting was that Mr. Puddle was soft spoken and warm, contrary to his demagogic demeanor in public outings. It was the first of many times that he was to see Mr. Puddle put on or take off his political "public" costume. In the interview Mr. Puddle had Majid sit opposite him on the formal table which was pushed up against the main desk to be shaped like a T. This was a mark of familiarity for Majid as, from Soviet times, visitors would be seated on the upright of the T and the senior official would be distant and unreachable, seated behind the safety of his imposing desk. But what most set Majid at ease was that Mr. Puddle was short, not taller than Majid. The interview went conventionally, "I need someone to make public statements to the press and to make press releases about policy aims and achievements." "You have been highly recommended to me for your work with X Company and Y Company." "Did you study public speaking in university?" "Can you improvise press statements on short notice?" "You realize of course that the main focus of your press duties will be in support of my national ambitions?" And it went on that way for 40 minutes or so. But the interview in its length was all for nought; Mr. Puddle had decided to hire Majid from the moment Majid spoke his first words to him. Once more Majid's magic voice tone and way of speaking had won over an adherent. Majid confessed that he was not aware of the mayor's positions about many issues, but even this did not deter Mr. Puddle in hiring him. He needed a spokesman who conveyed trustworthiness and sincerity. Finally, as Mr. Puddle began to wrap up the interview he turned on the charm offensive. "I understand you are a poet. Isn't that right?" Majid embarrassed answered him affirmatively. "Then perhaps you could share with me some of your poems? Maybe you could write a paean to my favorite creature, the honeybee?" Majid agreed, but added that he did not know much about bees. Mr. Puddle volunteered to educate him about bees and honey, his favorite hobby. And thus Majid was hired. In the coming months he eventually came to understand that Mr. Puddle was very much unlike the person he had his first impressions of; he came to understand that the mayor was a desperately ambitious and greedy man, that he had a volcanic and volatile temper, and that he had profound contempt for many people around him and especially his political rivals, a contempt which he was not afraid to share. He displayed this contempt in part by being treacherous and deceitful in his dealings with his lieutenants. But Majid also learned that a lot of Mr. Puddle's motivations came from a deep and bitter insecurity about his height, something that had trailed him from his youth and from his early career as a model Soviet Communist worker (he wasn't model or the ideal; being short and pudgy from his earliest youth with a funny low pitched raspy voice he had frequently been the butt of savage jokes—a little like the young Majid).

Majid had scarcely started working for Mayor Puddle when the slow burning Islamic civil war in Chechnya exploded into active war, literally bombs exploding. The second round of war between Chechens and Russia was to be characterized by the new use by the Chechens of terrorist bombs, both booby trap mines and for the first time suicide bombers, while Russian forces unveiled their latest thermobaric bombs with their awesome blast and high temperatures. And the Islamic fanatics began with the intention of taking the fighting to areas outside of Chechnya and with a general plan to take the violence to the heartland of Russia. These were undoubtedly a primary reason for the replacement of Stepoffshin with Sputyanin as prime minister. Immediately after the appointment of Sputyanin, who had long organized a plan to invade Chechnya and eliminate the Islamic radicals, there occurred several massive bombings of residential houses in various parts of Russia. Sputyanin claimed that they were terrorist attacks by the Chechens and they were a casus belli for Russia to throw out the cease fire and attack. Majid, along with many other close observers of the war and the advance of the KGB in the Russian government, suspected that these bombings were staged provocations. These suspicions grew stronger in September of that year when a small group of internal secret police (now called FSB) were arrested as they were in the process of planting large bombs in another suburban residence. Sputyanin and FSB authorities claimed it was a training incident intended to demonstrate the public's vigilance. This was ludicrous; but it did not matter as the Russian invasion and bombing went ahead almost as if on schedule, and the vast majority of Russians accepted them as bombings of the Chechens which justified war. This time, the second war in Chechnya, the Russia forces attacked with greater vehemence and with massive aerial and artillery forces. The press coverage was extensive but it occurred with long time lags and it omitted videos of the bombings. Once more Majid was overwhelmed with despair by the fighting and killing, especially of the civilian deaths in the capital city of Grozny and in the surrounding villages. But he also noticed that the general public in Moscow did not seem to care very much at all, except for the nationalist groups which stepped up their calls to punish the "darkies" from the Caucasus, especially Chechens. But it was the bombs were most horrible. The bombings, which occurred throughout the summer of 1999 and later, were especially horrifying because so many of them were targeted at non-combatants—innocent women, children, and older men in their homes and in their towns and cities. Throughout the last half of 1999 Majid was tormented by frequent awful nightmares of bombings, of people being obliterated by blasts, of residential buildings exploding and collapsing on their residents.

In that late summer when Russia was churning with war, Majid received a letter from Avram from Israel. He had not heard from Avram for a long time and Avram conveyed the important news that he had found his fortune and was enjoying life in Israel. When he had arrived he had first tried some odd jobs, but then he decided to reproduce what he had started in Moscow in the early 1990s. He founded a coffee shop in Tel Aviv which sold lattes and expressos but also sold bags of roasted coffee beans or ground coffee. At first his business developed slowly until he re-branded itself as a Russian coffee bar with tea (sold from samovars not tea bags and served with raspberry jam), a sort of Israeli Starbucks with Russian branding. This immediately attracted the custom of the by then large Russian immigrant community and Avram's business—as well as his social integration into the community—took off with a huge success. He even engaged the recent Ethiopian immigrant community by using their contacts to import quality Arabica coffee from Ethiopia which won him more customers. His original shop was soon too small, and he began to open new outlets in Tel Aviv and then in Jaffa, Haifa, and other cities where Russian immigrants had settled in large numbers to where at the time of this writing he had a chain of 23 coffee bars and shops. And he was rich. But he missed Russian culture and although he could get several transmissions of the leading Russian television broadcasters he longed for Russian song, verse, and symphony. And he concluded his letter by inviting Majid to come to Tel Aviv and give an evening long performance of his poetry, all expenses paid plus a generous honorarium. He even suggested that Majid might do a separate program of poetry reading of his and other recent Russian poets, like Brodsky for instance. Majid phoned Avram (this was another technological advance in Russia—the inexpensive calls put through the internet) and had a three hour talk with Avram—it was like a refreshing balm to talk with Avram after so many years separation. Avram was still an irrepressible character and even over the lines Majid could feel his affection for him. They agreed that Majid would give a recital of his own poems in early October which Avram would arrange and advertise.

Irina and Majid flew down on the appointed date leaving behind a sodden, dark and gloomy Moscow and landing a few hours in the brilliant—no blinding—sunshine and bracing warm salt air of Tel Aviv. But Majid's first welcome to Israel was more than a little chilly. The passport control agent, speaking to him in Russian, immediately harped on his name. "You're a Muslim, aren't you?" "No why do you say so?" "From your name." "My father was Muslim, so I was born with a Muslim name, but I am not practicing." "You don't look Russian. Do you come from one of the Muslim republics of the former Soviet Union?" "No, I am half Tatar, half Russian. I grew up in Tatarstan, which is not a Muslim republic. But I live in Moscow, with my wife." "Do you support the Chechen separatists?" "No." "Ever been to Chechnya?" "No." "Have you ever visited any other countries in the Arab world?" "No." "What are you coming to Israel for?" "A friend who lives here invited me to give a poetry recital." "Who is that friend." "In Hebrew?" "No in Russian." "What is your profession?" "I am a poet." "That's not a profession." "Maybe not, but it is my calling." "So can you recite for me one of your poems, right now?" Majid was a little surprised by the request, which was expressed in a very hostile tone. "So it will be in Russian." "That's fine. I will understand it."

> *"The Russian lived on the margins between the open steppe,*
> *Wild and endless, where only tall grasses rustled,*
> *And the dark pine forests where shadows hid the*
> *Sly wolf and rapacious bear*
>
> *Death came from the steppe on war horses*
> *In a land built of wooden huts, fire was the enemy*
> *Or from the west armored knights bore down*
> *On the harassed Russian quaking by his church."*

"Fine that's enough." "But it's not finished. Wouldn't you like to hear the whole poem?" (The poem was written in ABAB rhyme, iambic hexameter, and was 100 stanzas long.) "No, that was enough. It sounds nice enough, as poetry goes." "Do you like Russian poetry?" "No, I never studied it in school." "Did you like my poem?" "I don't know, I could take it or leave it." Finally, after more questioning, the agent let him into Israel; wishing him success with his recital, but still sounding skeptical. Ira was waiting for him beyond the passport control booths, bemused. And then they were in the big halls leading to the baggage claim. Even before he had left the airport, Majid was aware that he desperately needed a pair of good sunglasses. And then when they stepped out of the airport to be greeted by Avram, tears came to his eyes, not for a sudden flush of affection for Avram but because the sun burned his eyes almost shut. But after adjusting to the light he was overwhelmed by the lush tropical landscaping around the airport, flowers in bloom in the trees and on the verges, oranges hanging on the trees, and the smell of hibiscus. And warm; it was a paradise that he had never expected. Avram ignored Majid's wonder and kept talking excitedly. He was very taken by Irina and addressed her with all kinds of attentions and familiarities. He drove them to the beachfront Hilton Hotel where he left them, recommending them take a long walk along the beach and to swim in the mid- afternoon before the sun got too low. He would meet them in the hotel lobby just after sunset and take them out on the city. They did go into the sea, which was warm, but Majid did not know how to swim so he only waded in the water. But the currents along the coast were strong and tugging at his legs and they knocked him over once. It frightened him tremendously and he left the water, to the distress of Irina. Still feeling afraid, he thought about the death by drowning of Percy Shelley, the horror of being overcome by rough seas, and he felt how humiliating it would be to come to Israel to give a poetry reading and to drown in the seas right next to where he was to recite.

The next day Majid and Ira went to see Avram's coffee shop. It was a large traditional café with large windows facing the seaside. There was a crowd of consumers, some reading the Russian newspapers which were hung on the walls, and some in shorts and loose tops just hanging around. Majid noticed quite a few young men whom he thought resembled him in statue and in the face. He asked Ira if she noticed that as well—"Yes, some very sexy looking young men. But they are mostly darker than you." And the coffee was not bad at all—better tasting than the weak coffee served up at the new Moscow chain of coffee shops, called Coffee "Chaos". After a day out touring old Tel Aviv and Jaffa, Avram dropped them back at their hotel and invited them to be ready at seven to go together to the hall. When they arrived at the hall, Majid was surprised and flattered to see that more than five hundred people were in attendance in the audience. Avram introduced him as Slava Khairulin, the leading poetic voice of the young post-Soviet generation and one of Russia's greatest poets since the late Yosip Brodsky. Majid had prepared about ninety minutes of declamation. But he also had a few poems on paper in back up in case he needed to recite more after he was finished with the first ninety minutes. He presented a different collection of poems from the previous four years, but also introduced a few quite recent lyrics he had worked on that year. He decided it was timely to recite his banned poems from 1996 about the first Chechen war. In addition, he recited a new poem that he had written earlier that summer in reaction to some of the nationalist rant against Caucasians and the new wave of anti-semitism.

I write my hymns of praise and admonition
For my Tsarina who is German, but in Russian,
My odes could not exist without my Volga homeland
Anacreon may be my model but I created new lines.
I see the Russian condition through different eyes
My ear hears Russian verse with a foreigner's discernment
My odes are richer because of my origin.

Tatar I may be but the home of my songs is in Russia
My sounds are Russian words
And the rhythms rise from the Russian soil.

From the beginning my noble blood gave me an entry
To the richness of the Russian past.
A product of the Lyceum it gave me a classical grounding
My nanny atuned my ear with her fairy tales.

So I create a new language, a new music
And drape it in the rich tapestry of Russian
My words are forged in sounds of the forests.

African I may be, but the soul of my songs is in Russia
Yes my skin is swarthy and my hair is dark and curly
But from the cradle I had a different ear, hearing my own bylina.

I am a lover of Russian women, young and old
And I bring my artist's eye for the curve of a lip
A gracious leg or refined bust to the form of word,
Which captures a primeval moan—love of my mother tongue.

Perhaps poetry should begin as a moan in my mother tongue
And although my visual home is Odessa and Marburg
My mother tongue is Russian, my words resist the steel boot.

Jewish I may have been born, but the flow in my speech is Russian
The sounds of my words come out of a native impulse
And the rhythm arises from a Russian energy.

I speak to you with the howling of the wind on the steppes
The wind which blows over all of Russia
My verse arises from the warmth of a spring sun
And the merriment of the chastushka.

I sing of Russian love and sorrow, the Kama's
Steely grandeur and the hope after suffering.
My poems are compiled from a myriad of dreams.

Tatar I may be, but Russian blood flows through my veins and my verse
The sounds of a liberated Russian people vibrate in my songs,
And the rhythm of a new Russia can be heard in my modern voice.

It matters not if he is Polish, no harm
If his name is Mickiewicz or Khodasevich.
No harm if a poet be Jewish or Tatar

Indeed better a poet be African for his rhymes.
All see the world differently and hear an unfamiliar sound
In their verse, and so by they fertilize the Russian word.

[This poem was very difficult for me to translate because there were layers of meaning in the words, and allusions to the poets he portrays. Of course he speaks as if the poets Derzhavin, Pushkin, and Pasternak were living in the present day, and interestingly he has elevated himself to the same level as these past masters. This poem appeared in a collection he published in 2002. I could not find any record of the reaction of the audience members to it when it premiered there in Tel Aviv. Perhaps the references were too obtuse for the audience to recognize whom he was talking about. And I am certain they did not know that he referring to himself in the last ten lines.]

Majid noticed that the audience that evening was quite different from the ones he had performed for in Moscow. The crowd was much older, there was a lot of white-haired people and was hardly any young people or teenagers. The usual throngs of well-wishers off stage after he finished did not include the usual fawning, and admiring young women trying to paw at him. The only loving looks from a young woman were Irina's who was beginning to really adore listening to her Slava recite. Avram offered an explanation. "Most of these people left Russia ten to fifteen years ago, so most of the children did not have any Russian schooling where they would have been introduced to Pushkin, Lermontov, or Blok or Tsvetaeva. If they were old enough, the only schooling they've gotten is in Hebrew which as I understand does not include much poetry of any sort in its curriculum. The young people therefore only have the chance to speak Russian at home or in public social gatherings but in school they speak Hebrew. So they probably prefer rock music concerts to Russian poetry. But the adults who immigrated got good Soviet doses of Pushkin and Mayakovsky in school, and went to recitals by Gangnus and Vozkresensky. And that is why they ache to be immersed again in the rich waters of Russian verse. But I expect that this is a dwindling market in the coming years. Of course I studied poetry in university and I thirst for good Russian poetry, so I especially loved hearing you recite." The rest of the evening Majid and Irina spent with Avram and a group of his friends who had also attended the recital at a restaurant which had an open hearth fireplace in the middle of the room. The conversations were lively and noisy but Majid was enthralled by the smell of the grilling meats and the warmth from the fire. They flew back to Moscow the next day. Avram saw them off at the airport promising them another engagement in a year or so.

The fall of that year was supposed to be the peak of Mr. Puddle's national run for the presidency. He had linked his Fatherland party in a political union with a party led by the former prime minister, Mr. Upryamikov, and the two of them had planned an intensive major national campaign from the beginning of September for the scheduled parliamentary elections in December. This would be followed by Mr. Puddle's campaign for the presidential elections which were due in May 2000. And initially when the two allies plotted their strategy in the summer, the auspices were very favorable. The sitting parliament had even tried to impeach President Yeltsin. But the sudden and unexpected appointment of Sputyanin as the new prime minister and especially the explosive opening of a second war in Chechnya, which for most of the population was even more unexpected, made the outlook for Mr. Puddle and Mr. Upryamikov suddenly less promising. Nevertheless the fall was intensely busy and Majid made a large number of press releases and statements outlining Mr. Puddle's positions often trying to repair or refine the manner of Mr. Puddle's often clumsy or offensive public or off the cuff expressions of his views. In spite of the efforts it remained difficult to ascertain what political positions, beliefs, and directions Mr. Puddle and the Fatherland party wanted to promote. Majid in this time also gave interviews to members of the press or political observers. One of these in particular stuck in Majid's memory. It was an interview with a man named Bruce Chatka, who said he was third secretary in the political section of the U.S. Embassy and he even had a business card with a gold embossed eagle on it to prove it. Mr. Chatka, who was a blond haired man about Majid's age, came into the small meeting room in the mayor's office all smiles and manly, friendly bustle. Too much smiling, thought Majid; he looked like a horse trying to smile or raise its lips. He began his introductions and background statements in fractured Russian, but within two minutes, asked if Majid could continue in English, which he said he could. Mr. Chatka then began his questioning abruptly, "So Mr. Puddle wants to be the next president of the Russian Federation?" "Yes, he is preparing to submit his name as a candidate for the next elections which, as you probably know, are next spring." "Well, I can tell you for sure Mr. Majed (he mispronounced his name), that Mr. Puddle will be sure to lose the upcoming elections because he has the wrong ending for his last name." Majid was unclear what Chatka was talking about. The latter smiled even more pronouncedly. "You see, since Mr. Yeltsin has come along, the ruling elites in Russia have been '*-ins*' and not '*-offs*'. Get it? Mr. Yelts-*in* and Mr. Sputyan-*in* or for instance Mr. Smugleek-*in* and not Mr. Pop-*off* or Mr. Roman-*off*, or Mr. Brezhn-*eff*. Now this is too bad for Mr. Puddle because he is an '*-off*' and so is Mr. Upryamik-*off*. So he does not stand much a chance of winning, now does he?" Majid could hardly believe his ears and thought he was talking to an imbecile. "Excuse me, you're saying that someone with my last name, Khairul-*in* (changing the stress to the last syllable to conform to Mr. Chatka's pronunciation) for example just by its spelling qualifies me to be in the ruling elite?" "Well, yes, that is how it now works here in Russia. A poor Mr. Bolban-*off* off in the provinces doesn't stand a chance to make it." Majid paused for a moment, thinking of the Jewish last names of so many of the filthy-rich oligarchs, and then asked, "And where does that leave the poor '*-skis*' or '*-men*'?" "Oh don't worry, Mr. Kairilun (he mispronounced his last name) I am saying this only partly in jest. You don't think American Kremlinology is really so simplistic, do you?" "I assure you I know nothing about American Kremlinology." (Now he was sure he was talking with a fool.) "Tell me, Mijed, Mr. Puddle is really a communist, isn't he? If he is elected president, he will start to re-nationalize everything that has been privatized, right?" "No, of course not. He is not a communist and he does not want to see the return of the Communist party to govern in Russia. He supports the market economy, but with economic safeguards for ordinary workers." "Then why has Mr. Puddle been the leading opponent to the national program of privatization of state owned assets here in Moscow, and why has he blocked it whenever he could?" "He has only blocked the insiders' privatizations which has been the way that Mr. Yeltsin's government has conducted privatizations." "Ok, so Mr. Puddle is a closet-communist." "I am not sure what you mean." "I mean he secretly still believes in the Communist dogma about property." "I don't believe so." "Fine, then. Another question. If Mr. Puddle is elected to be president, will Russia continue to view the United States as a friend in international affairs?" (Majid was wondering how to suffer fools who ask such questions. He was also thinking of how to terminate this interview.) "There are no friends in international affairs, only allies, and partners, or opponents." Majid spent the next few minutes trying to extricate himself from the interview. "Are there any questions you have about Mr. Puddle's concrete positions?" When Mr. Chatka finally left—again all broad smiles, and familiarity and vigorous handshakes Majid concluded that it was much easier addressing the specific questions politely put by Russian journalists. At least with that bunch he could be sure that their minds were mostly focused on the buffet table of canapés rather than the details of policy.

Majid was very busy with his day-time job as the press secretary for the mayor's office. He often returned to his home in the late evening too tired to do any work on his poetry or translations or readings. He no longer had the energy and stamina that he had had only a few years earlier. He often sat in sessions late into the evening in the mayor's office at that T-shaped table with other political advisors and observed deliberations and discussions about events and how to respond to them. And he sometimes saw events unfolding that directly had an effect on the mayor. One day in that late fall, there was a sudden bustle in the corridor around the mayor's office. The security chief, Mr. Nockhimoff, was rushing about, the bodyguard detail were slamming doors checking the offices one after another. One of the deputy mayors came up the stairs and rushed to his office in the arms of his bodyguard. People were emerging into the corridor out of curiosity. Majid was among them. Someone whispered, "They shot at Mr. Orkhonashvili's car." (For that was the name of the deputy mayor for special projects who had been rushed to his office in the arms of his bodyguard, shaken but not shot.) "His bodyguard was killed." "Who would do that?" "It was an ambush, not even a kilometer from here." Mr. Nockhimoff carrying a walkie talkie was trying now to calm the people and shunt them back into their offices. Majid heard him say, "They were shooting more accurately today. Lucky for Orkhonashvili to escape with just glass shards in his hand." Of course it was even more fortunate that he had a heavily armored Mercedes. Somehow the news escaped city hall and Mayor Puddle who was at that time out at a campaign activity was likewise ambushed—not by assassins but by journalists—as he made his way back to city hall later in the afternoon. "Who could have done this horrible act?" they asked. "Was it a gangster hit?" "Why would anyone want to assassinate Mr. Orkhonashvili?" And this is when Mr. Puddle improvised his famous comment in answer to the latter question, "Maybe it had something to do with the business he is in." (Said disingenuously as if Mr. Puddle had no idea what Mr. Orkhonashvili did in his position as deputy mayor for special projects—projects like building casinos and hotels and collecting large kickbacks, not to mention the rebuilding the Christ the Savior Cathedral which was still underway.) Nothing came out of the incident. Mr. Orkhonashvili carried on in his shady duties. The city conducted a large funeral for the slain bodyguard (who had absorbed six bullets that had broken through a window), and opponents of Mr. Puddle in his quest for the parliament and presidency made a large clamor of how the incident demonstrated the criminal and corrupt relations of Mr. Puddle's government.

During this hectic political season Majid continued to compose poems and he called on Igor Formico to see if he could book a recital before the end of the year. But Igor was unable to find any spark of interest for a poetry recital during this highly inflamed political season; no theatre wanted to put on a poet who might declaim controversial political positions, and no auditorium or hall manager thought that there was enough interest in poetry in general. He offered a poem for publication to *Literaturnaya News* and they told him that he would have to wait before they could publish it, perhaps in the new year after elections. The general political tensions of this season had as a fiercesome backdrop the ever more savage warfare in and around Grozny in Chechnya and this background even was interrupted by the first terrorist bombing in the streets of Moscow (which made all the news) as well as the introduction of innovative small bomb explosions which killed anonymous businessmen and bankers (which really did not make the news). This innovation in the latter spate of perhaps six bombings was that they were achieved by sophisticated small limpet type bombs which were stuck onto the roof or hoods of the victim's otherwise well-protected Mercedes as they passed through traffic and were timed to go off within five minutes. With this background noise but without any immediate prospect to recite his works, Majid carried on with his projects. He was nearly finished with a Russian translation of Heine's *Lyrical Intermezzo* and he was writing a long poem based loosely on the career of Gabriel Derzhavin. The year ended with a serious setback for Mr. Puddle and Mr. Upryamikov: in December their newly-forged joint political party lost in the elections for the parliament, or that is they came in third behind the party of power which was the puppet of the president and prime minister. This was a huge disappointment for Mr. Puddle and had tremendous impact on the mayor's office. But even worse was the bombshell news on New Year's Eve when President Yeltsin announced with apologies that he was stepping down immediately and that he was appointing to take his place as acting president, the shady prime minister—and the man that Majid already feared and distrusted—Mr. Sputyanin. The KGB had returned to power in Russia—some said that they had never left power—the rule of the police state was about to begin, and democracy and civil society were bound to fail. These fears were shown to be justified in the new year when presidential elections were announced for March, instead of May, and almost at the same time the Kremlin began to twist Mr. Puddle's arm trying to convince him not to run. They used every trick in the book, so to speak; they claimed Mr. Puddle's party was not legitimate, that he did not have national representation, that he had illegally obtained funds for campaigning which would disqualify him. But the Kremlin also used its black arts. It threatened Mr. Puddle with criminal prosecution for multiple cases of corruption. They threatened him and his wife for theft of state funds, and they suggested that his life would not be safe if he insisted on being included on the ballot. By March, Mr. Puddle, looking very glum, caved in and announced he would not run against Mr. Sputyanin for president and would instead he would join the latter's political party and support him for president. By March, this capitulation by Mr. Puddle, humiliating as it was to choose between life in prison, assassination, or running for president, was complete and for several months Mr. Puddle very uncharacteristically went silent in public. Sputyanin won the presidential elections almost by acclaim. It was not exactly an uncontested election; there was a token Communist Party representative and a flunky, someone who was even more unknown and unrecognizable than Sputyanin who ran against Sputyanin. But the dashing of Mr. Puddle's ambitions to run for president—and he was in 2000 a very credible candidate in an open political contest—raised the question of what more there was to do for Majid within the mayor's office, and for the first half of the year 2000 he was expecting to be dismissed at any time.

Although Mr. Sputyanin as an acting president and then as the sole candidate for president made promises to raise the power of the state and end the war in Chechnya promptly. Neither of these things happened in the dark year of 2000. Instead there was immediately after Sputyanin's access to the Kremlin a noticeable increase in the militarism. The ordinary police forces started carrying more often and more openly Kalashnikovs, and the soldiers from the special operational forces began to patrol the city of Moscow in twos and threes armed with high powered rifles with several bullet clips, full body armor, helmets, and stun grenades as if the war was going on in Moscow city. That included the neighborhood where Majid and Irina lived. It seemed strange to see these big men strolling around trying to look conspicuous when instead they looked like they were trying to figure out whether to shoot the little old lady at the bus stop or not. The Duma, and especially members of Vladvozhen's party started calling for the "masculinization" of the TV program; the need for more heroic manly war films (which the Soviet Union had produced in surfeit) to be broadcast in place of all the effeminate TV soap opera serials and especially the advertising for women's sanitary pads. (They succeeded in driving these latter off the air.) Vladvozhen even brought a real kalashnikov into the Duma and posed with it to show how manly and aggressive he was, and he was recorded as saying he was ready to shoot any Chechen that he saw unlike many of the sissies in the Duma at that time. And it became clear that's Sputyanin's war in Chechnya was conducted not by the army—which with its poor underfed and undertrained recruits was too unreliable and cowardly—but by the special commando forces of the KGB (okay, so it was the FSB at that time). These forces were brutal and ruthless in their means. And that meant that Sputyanin had to hide the most serious offenses and "war crimes" from the public, something which could only be done by banning journalists from reporting about the war, especially video journalists. This marked the beginning of the "secret" campaign of journalism suppression and censorship. Sputyanin likewise began to replace the Yeltsin era oligarchs with his own cronies and supporters, the "power men" (or *siloviki*) by putting them in charge of state-owned enterprises or administrations which had their own armies or militias. But in spite of all the outwardly increase in the security atmosphere and militarism, suicide bombings conducted by Chechens and other disgruntled Muslim fanatics, came to Moscow in earnest starting shortly after Sputyanin became president, that is in 2000. There was a suicide bombing in the underground passageways of the metro conducted by a very unmanly young women (this was determined by putting the pieces and scraps of her body back together), and then there was another on a train station platform. People in Moscow were outraged, but after the initial shock they carried on as if nothing particularly untoward had happened. After all, these attacks were the justification and raison d'etre of President Sputyanin's war in Chechnya. And not all that many lives were lost it could be said. In the first bombing, only five people were killed (not counting the bomber whatever her name was) and two dozen injured, and security forces were able to arrest two Dagestani men within a couple days, saying they were relatives of the bomber who were present inexplicably in Moscow and were thus accomplices of the bomber. In the second bombing, 8 people were killed and three dozen injured, and they were all evacuated quickly by the emergency services and looked after carefully in Moscow's hospitals (there was never any word whether accomplices were arrested later). But the news stories did not tell everything: most of the terrorist bombings occurred in the Caucasus, and especially in Chechnya and Dagestan in 1999 and 2000 and most of these were not widely reported. Bombings especially suicide bombings were a ghastly new weapon of the desperate Chechen Islamic fundamentalists and independence fighters and most of the victims were not Russians or Russian armed forces, but they were usually civilian non-combatants from those regions around Chechnya.

That summer, as Majid felt a threat to his income and Irina also did not feel secure in her job, the two of them decided not to travel abroad for vacation. Instead they spent two weeks out at a rented dacha in a pine forest not far from Peredelkino outside of the heat and swelter of Moscow. These two weeks allowed Majid uninterrupted time to work on his verse projects. It was then that Majid learned two things about Ira: One that she dyed her hair black, which he discovered when he caught her in the act of dying her hair. She informed him that all the women of Russia, even the very young teenage girls dyed their hair. He had suspected that those women he saw with ice blond hair, or the cotton- candy colored pink and orange hair-dos, or those old ladies with lilac colored coifs could only get those results through hair dyes of extreme strength, but he had not imagined that every female he saw used hair dyes. But once told by Ira, he noticed it everywhere. Hair colors that were not natural and uniform in extreme. He wondered, if all the young blond women in Moscow use hair dye or bleach to achieve that tint, what was the natural color of the hair of Russia's women? Second, on a warm summer's evening when a cloud of midges were shimmering in the air like the lightest of sheer silk scarfs, Ira told him that she was two months pregnant and expecting their first child in the next year. Majid was so pleased by this news—he almost did not know what to do. For the first time he was going to be a father (at least consciously knowing he was going to be a father as he still didn't know about his first son). But of course a poem was called for. He even gave it a title, which as we have seen was contrary to his usual practice.

The miracle

It is hard to understand the miracle
Of how God fashioned man from a blood clot,
Or how out of the turbulent embrace of passion
A spark could be struck that starts a life.

But miracle it is that has sprung from our love.
I look at you, and see you transformed
From your vulva to the slight swell of your belly
The landscape has changed, as it has in your eyes.

There is a new pulse racing inside you
I place my ear to you and hear its faint motor.
What wonder, what a joyful sound it is,
Growing fast from an inchoate lump.

How have we done such a thing? I do not know
Such a marvel that will bear our mixed
Vital and secret codes. It can only be
Said that this is the glory of a miracle.

During this summer he finished his long poem on greed and theft in the life of Gabriel Derzhavin. It was written as an ode to the events of Derzhavin's life in his scramble to get to the top of Russian society. He wrote it in Alexandrines in homage to Derzhavin's own famous style, and like the earlier poet he introduced a number of innovations into the meter and into the use of more contemporary words. He even sometimes contrived new rhyming pairs. It is a poem of 420 lines written in stanzas of four lines each. As it was a long poem, he found that it was difficult to find a literary journal that was ready to publish it. They all advised him to publish it as a stand-alone book, perhaps with a few other poems added to give it the necessary length for a publishable booklet of poems. In his life he never found time or the venue to give a public recitation of this poem, which has come to be known as *Derzhavin's Grief.* But some of his friends say that he recited it to them one evening in a private gathering at Bella's house in Peredelkino. They related how, Majid took more than two and a half hours to recite it to them, but that even though he held a sheaf of papers with the printed-out verses, he recited it almost entirely from memory, stopping only occasionally to take a sip of water. Sadly, it appeared as a small published booklet just days before Majid's death; so that he never witnessed the reaction to the poem nor the important message he had wanted to deliver.

Derzhavin's Grief tells the stories of Derzhavin's efforts to make money, any way he could; his adventures, and mostly his misadventures when it came to making money during his life. These at the beginning of his life entailed gambling and swindle deals masquerading as investments. Majid lays out that Derzhavin was good at cards—using his strong memory he was in effect a card counter—which gave him tremendous advantages over most of the other players he encountered who were barely literate or numerate. But Derzhavin in this poem is shown as a young man who was not above cheating to get ahead. Majid lays out further a sad litany of instances when Derzhavin was himself swindled and even robbed of the money he had won. He lost money that he had borrowed from his mother, who had in turn squeezed her serfs on her estates to get the funds, and sometimes his relatives stole the money from him. In some respects Derzhavin is portrayed as mostly an honorable man in that although he often fell in with greedy swindlers with harebrained schemes to make big money, he often thought of his loses as debts that he should honor. Majid portrays Derzhavin's earlier motivations as being driven by greed, but that eventually he began to make his money from his services to the tsarina and the state. But the portraits Majid makes of Derzhavin's relatives and colleagues and friends show people who were strongly driven by grasping, unrelenting greed in all of their activities; unmitigated greed that often drove them into criminal activities and into prison. Even in Derzhavin's later state service he was not above pocketing some state funds for his own gratification. After Derzhavin loses his first beloved wife, he chooses a second more for the financial improvement that she brought to his life than for his love. Majid closes the poem with the ironic reflections of the elder Derzhavin who expresses some regret for the financial excesses he had committed in his youth and remorse for some of the harm he inflicted on those around him. But Majid does not attribute any bitterness to Derzhavin's character toward those who had swindled him or stolen funds from him. It seems that Majid had relied primarily on Khodasevich's biography of Derzhavin, but he inserted his own views about the rampant financial swindles and greed of the principal players of that day and age. And Majid is more judgmental than Khodasevich. It is clear that he sees greed and all the crimes—great and small, petty and vicious—that greed inspires as one of the major failings of the Russian people.

Mr. Puddle felt strongly about the glorification and beautification of Moscow. And one way this was manifested was by his commitment to commissioning statues and monuments out of the city budget. A lot of these commissions went to Mr. Puddle's buddy, a ham-handed sculptor from Georgia who was also short and squat like Mr. Puddle and who was also given to bombastic artistic statements. Ironically the cultural heroes that were celebrated by this program were so often representatives of the culture and excellence of St. Petersburg and not Moscow, take for example the wretched monstrous statue of Peter himself which the mayor and his Georgian buddy plopped in the middle of the Moscow River. Or the sickly statue of Alexander Blok, who was about as Peterburgsky as you could get and champion of Symbolism which nobody seemed to have practiced in Moscow, or likewise the equally sickly image of Dostoevsky (another denizen of St. Petersburg) taking the place of Lenin's head in front of the State Library named after Yves Desange (eh.. Vladimir Lenin). But in those years of 1999 and 2000 when Majid began working for the mayor's office, a couple new statues were erected which Majid took notice of. First there was the statue of the very obviously consumptive Anton Chekhov which was erected by an already dead artist on the site of the famously stinky former public toilets on an obscure corner of Tverskaya Ulitsa not far from the Moscow Arts Theatre where Chekhov's first works scored their biggest hits. And then there was the statue of Puskhin and his wife Natalya gracing a waterless fountain in the center. The couple are depicted as if the pair were being ushered into a ball to be presented to the Tsar, hand in hand, but their arms spread wide so that Natalya's big hoop dress does not knock over the slight poet, about to bow or curtsey, it is not clear. In the summer of 2000 when it was erected, Majid made a point of walking over to this statue (the first of several more of the Puskhin couple erected in those years) to make a homage to the great poet. It was only a short walk from the Moscow City Council which is the mayor's office. On an overcast and cool evening after work, Majid walked over to the newly unveiled statue. When Majid arrived there he was surprised by what he saw. The statues were bronze finished in a buffed gilding material. They were lifesized, meaning the size of Majid, and so they appeared on their pedestal to be small. And they were not made to look sickly, consumptive, suffering, corporeal, or anything other than happy. (Perhaps this reflected Soviet attitudes to these cultural heroes: all of the artists involved in the statues mentioned above were products of Soviet arts training and in Soviet times Dostoevsky, Chekhov and Peter and their works were all openly denigrated and pushed into neglected shadows.) But not so Pushkin. And the artist apparently had spent some effort to capture a close likeness of the couple, based on the most well-known portraits made at the time of their lives, instead of trying to twist their faces to represent some underlying emotions, illnesses, or suffering. Majid spent several minutes staring at the statues, first at Alexander Sergeivich and then at Natalya Nikolaevna. Then he walked around their pavilion looking at them from all angles until a strange thing happened. Natalya—or we could be so bold as to call her Natasha—let go of Alexander's hand and turned on her pedestal to face Majid, smiled faintly at him, and then with both hands lifted the hoops of her dress just a little, revealing her dainty ankles, and she gingerly stepped over the borders and came down off the pedestal. She walked up to Majid and looked him in the face, then looked over his shoulder, as if to make sure no one was staring at them, and then looked quickly back at Alexander and back full into Majid's face. "Slava, I have to tell you, I find your verses to be very nearly perfect and as good as anything as my husband's over there." She nodded her head a little bit at the statue of the singletary Pushkin now. "And I must confess to you, I find you much more attractive than him. Your skin is fairer, for one thing. And you have such lovely, long eye-lashes." She flashed her eyes at him and blinked them several times in a coquettish manner, then smiled again. "But now my time is short. I have to tell you. Look closely at my face, study it closely and remember. This is not the same cute face that Brullov painted. The next time you see this very face—not gilded bronze obviously—this will be the woman that you marry. And you should ask her straight- away to marry you and to do so as soon as is possible." Majid of course was stunned that a gilded-bronze statue of a famous—but now long dead—beauty should be addressing him and commanding him to marry her. He could only mumble out, "But I am already married." To which the re-incarnate Natasha answered curtly, "You won't be at the time you see this face next. Now remember, what I told you. And please help me to get back up on my pedestal." She offered him her hand and with the other took up the hoops of her dress and again gingerly hopped back up to be at the side of Alexander again, whose hand she promptly took into hers and she nodded quickly at Majid and then turned her frozen gaze once more forward toward the on-coming reception. That beautiful small face was seared into Majid's memory and the experience of the vision disturbed him in a way that his earlier visions had not.

It was a warm, late summer morning in early September when the cool night air raises large pillows of fog on the Moscow River, after normal life resumes on the streets of Moscow, that catastrophe struck Majid. Irina was still employed by the investment bank that had hired her back only 10 months earlier and she had an assignment that morning to go to a breakfast investors' meeting at the rather frumpy grand old National Hotel, just a prodigious stone's throw from the Kremlin walls. She arrived at 8:15 by the metro line whose exit discharged right onto the main entrance to the hotel next to the big plate glass windows inscribed with the hotel's name in gold which the re-developers had placed rather tastelessly in the ground floor fronting less than 12 years earlier. The subject of the day was non-ferrous metals mining company that was seeking to expand its shareholders numbers and attract more outside investment. The presentation was in a second floor private dining room which had a buffet breakfast laid out on a separate table displayed with white linen, chafing and serving dishes, fine silver, and stacks of china from where the bankers and company representatives took their breakfasts before sitting at a long table. The presentation and questions and answers took little more than an hour and a half, and Irina stepped out promptly when this was finished and moved quickly down to the front foyer to get to her next appointment on time. She was putting on her lightweight raincoat, at a little after ten, in this large foyer next to the door standing in front of the plate glass window when a huge explosion occurred right in front of it. The concussion sent glass and shrapnel through the foyer and the blast wave knocked Ira to the floor along with a couple other people and hotel employees who were unfortunate to be there at that moment. The entire room and the reception area were "de-peopled" in just a moment and filled instead with thick angry clouds of white plaster dust. Some alarms went off in cars parked outside, and further inside the hotel security alarms were also whining. There were small flames creeping up on the drapes. The bomb had blown in from outside. Ira was unconscious, and unknown to her, she was bleeding to death from the glass shards which had torn through arteries in her neck and upper arms and face. It took several minutes for the hotel security staff to come to the foyer room to appraise the damage (the security staff at the front of the hotel had also been knocked to the ground) and to see if the humps of white bodies on the floor were living. It took twenty-five minutes more for the first aid responders to arrive and pick up the bodies. Ira was taken to an emergency hospital only six minutes away, but by the time emergency doctors could look at her she was already dead, never having known what had hit her. The suicide bomber, for it was a suicide bombing, was a young women not even Irina's age and she had apparently stood against the plate glass window on the outside sidewalk while wearing a 18 pound vest bomb padded with nails which police coldly reported had the explosive equivalent of three sticks of TNT. Not much of the bomber was left, nor the car next to her, but police told the world that she was the widow of a Chechen terrorist who had recently been killed in an attack by Russian special forces, therefore it was a vengeance attack. They could not explain how so much high powered explosives (this had not been a homemade bomb of detergents and fertilizer) got into Moscow, nor how a young woman who obviously was heavily dressed in her bomb vest went unnoticed and could set off her bomb while leaning on the plate glass window when the hotel was so well supplied by security men, including two at the door not 12 feet distant (who by the way were only slightly injured). All this later reported in the police investigations did not concern Majid one jot. For it was his Ira who was the only death from this bomb (other than the bomber herself who remained anonymous) and it was Ira who could have been saved if someone had come to her aid earlier and tried to stop her copious bleeding. But response in these cases is often too little, too late. Irina was one of a dozen bodies taken to the emergency hospital, although she was the only one to die. Another dozen or so were treated on the site for minor cuts and wounds, including four who had the misfortune to be walking nearby on the sidewalk. Unfortunately for Ira and Majid, the blast had also separated Ira from her purse, and it was covered under a very heavy coat of plaster. The plaster dust was cleared away in only a few days and a large plywood sheet was hung in the place of the plate glass window.

As part of his regular daily routine to track the day's news coverage, Majid had gone to the press room at 11 am that morning to watch the TV news broadcasts or to read the running news wire. He was immediately alarmed by the hot breaking news—there had been a bombing at the National Hotel about an hour earlier, some casualties, but details would be coming later, the TV broadcasters announced. (This meant that their video cameras had not gotten to the hotel yet and there was no information to report. What would news be without a video clip, even if it is only a talking head in front of the news site?). Majid knew that Ira had gone to the National for her breakfast meeting. And he also knew that she would be finishing around 10 am when it was reported the bomb purportedly went off. He immediately called her mobile phone which, of course, did not answer, even after he let it ring many times. He rightly feared the worst, and he immediately set off for the hotel, which is not even 700 meters down the hill from the mayor's office. What he found there was pandemonium, but he could not get anyone to tell him if Irina was inside the hotel. There were by then ambulances, fire engines, and police vehicles all around the hotel and even the traffic on the main thoroughfare next to the hotel was blocked off. None of the ambulances were driving off, although there were a few victims seating on the ground being administered to by the medics. After some frantic efforts to get past the blocking line of policemen, he was able to reach a medic and ask him if he knew if there were any deaths, and where injured victims were being taken. The harassed medic did not know, but knew that victims in need of emergency medical treatment were being taken to the "Sklif", as it was familiarly called by the ambulance crews, the venerable Sklifosovsky emergency hospital as it was more generally called, which lay about a mile away (or about three metro stops—except that neighboring metro entrance was closed to both those wanting to get into the metro and passengers wanting to emerge from the metro.) There was absolutely no one at the hotel who would, or could, tell him anything about the victims and most importantly whether Ira was one of them. If anything, many of the responders reacted to Majid suspiciously, from his looks apparently, looking like a Muslim or even possibly a Caucasian man, albeit slight of build. So by the time Majid reached the admitting room of the "Sklif", he had reached a level of distress that was inconsolable and irrational. He could scarcely express his worries and what he was searching for. Everyone there was either too busy, too indifferent, and too officious to listen to Majid describing his Irina and whether she was there after the bombing attack. No one wanted to tell him anything about any of the people that had been brought in from the National Hotel—as if it was classified information. While he was pressing to get information in the hospital, Majid continued to call Ira's mobile phone which continued to go unanswered. It took most of the day to finally get through to someone who was willing to tell him that there had a young, unidentified, dark-haired woman who had been admitted from the bomb blast, and that she had died. But then there was the bureaucratic blockage that kept him away from identifying her: because she was unidentified and how could he prove to the nurse that he was her husband and next of kin. His internal passport showed he was married to Irina, but she herself had been admitted unconscious (if not already dead) and without her own internal passport. They needed affidavits, certificates, notarized permits, and other documents to establish that he had any right to know anything about anyone who had been brought into the hospital. He called to Ira's bank, and they confirmed that she had gone to the breakfast meeting (or at least that she was supposed to have gone) and she had not returned to the bank offices that day. They also told him of the breakfast's organizers. He called them and discovered that she had signed in when she had arrived there and was indeed at the event, although no one knew what had happened to her when she left or at the time of the blast. Finally after much delay and putting together the story of Majid's relationship to Irina (he needed to produce a number of photos of her) he succeeded in getting permission and early in the evening, the morgue department let him in to identify the unnamed victim of the suicide bomber. He did not really see her. He knew instantly it was she. He recognized her hair, the shape of her head, her feet, the small mound of her lower torso, but he did not see her; he did not look into her face. There were too many tears in his eyes to see her, to look into her peaceful face or to see the wounds left by the shards of glass. Her neck had been badly disfigured by the cut from a large piece glass (which had been removed) and there were a number of other much smaller pink lines where wounds were.

Irina's violent and sudden death and the dehumanizing, bureaucratic steps Majid had to take to reclaim her body and then bury it was like a violent kick to his viscera; it literally knocked the poetic voice out of Majid. His despair was so great it reached into his gut and pulled out the poetic voice that had sustained him since he was a little boy. He had no words. Poetry and rhymes no longer made sense to him in such circumstances. His grief, once he had gotten over the tears and inner wailing, silenced him. He could not imagine how a poet could write or find any words or appropriate sounds to convey the music of such grief and misery. Over the following seven months he was as if transformed into a zombie. He did not recite, did not draft any verse, translate, or even read other verses. He even ceased writing letters. He went to work, but at the end of each day, or week he could not remember what, if anything, he had done during the time that he was in the office. Nothing around him seemed to matter anymore.

So there was a long period of silence in our hero's life biography where no poems or verses came to light. His grief persisted and his isolation and loneliness grew. It is interesting to speculate as to what it was that broke this silence and assuaged his profound grief (if indeed his grief was ever assuaged in the short remit of life left to him). Through the next year, Majid continued to find offense at the extent to which Sputyanin began increasing the trappings of a police state while also escalating the brutality of the war in Chechnya. But although he had written a number of political poems in 1999 and 2000 opposed to the increasing involvement of the KGB in Russian government and society, in the years following Irina's death he ceased writing such verses. There were no public performances that he gave for a period of more than two years. There was increasing censorship and review of literature being published, especially that which was critical of Sputyanin, who quickly installed his confederates, the siloviki in many of the critical "power" segments of the government. He also began re-nationalizing or closing down the press which had very briefly tried to sound an independent voice opposed to the president's policies. As best as I can understand it, something happened in late 2001 which shook him and restored his poetic muse. He had spent that summer at Bella's house in

Peredelkino and those around her tried hard to encourage him to return to composing verse. He remained through that summer a listener only, listening intently to other's poems recited there, to the lively discussions about versifying and the debates about the future directions of Russian society under Sputyanin. But he did not contribute and he did not work on anything. He did not even take any notice of Bella's daughter, Liza, who was still attractive and young after graduating, and who tried to be compassionate and friendly with Majid, but who no longer attracted him at all. It occurred to him that perhaps he was finished, that he was like the poet Blok, about whom Khodasevich said, that when the muse inside of Blok expired the man outside began to die. In that fall, two events occurred however which turned Majid back on. One day, out of the blue—or as the Russian expression goes, like thunder occurring in a clear sky—he received a letter, an old-fashioned conventional, written on letter paper. The address on the envelope had been to him care of the Gorky Institute and they had forwarded it to his address. It had taken ironically more than a year to find him and be delivered. In the letter, a man introduced himself as an Irish poet, living and working in the U.S., who had studied Russian in his university years specializing in Russian poetry. He claimed he already had acquired some reputation and had published two volumes of his own poems. This poet, named Plaivy, who claimed he loved especially the poetry of Pushkin and Tyutchev and Tsetaeva, had found a volume of Majid's poems and claimed he was extremely impressed. He had then searched for more of Majid's works and was able to procure three of the four volumes of verse which Majid had published in the previous 12 years. He concluded his letter with the statement that Majid's poetry was the greatest literary work of the past two decades coming out of Russia. His aim in writing to Majid then was not merely to praise Majid's poetry, but to ask his permission to translate his poems into English and publish them in a volume, side by side with the Russian originals. He was planning to print the poems in English and Russian through the Pushkin Renaissance Publishing House, in the U.S., a recognized organization that already was the leading publisher of Russian literature outside of Russia itself. Majid was astonished. He could hardly believe it. As a post-scriptum to the letter the poet included a reference, saying that if Majid was interested he could find a selection of Plaivy's own original poems, in English, on his internet website. Majid looked up the website, and sure enough, there were a dozen short English poems posted on it, written in a very modern style in blank verse, but with crisp and rhythmic line construction. They were good poems; he enjoyed their sound as he recited them out loud from the website. He took out the four little volumes of poems that he had published and began to look through them again, fondly reciting some to himself as if they were long-lost dear friends. Some of the poems now went back twelve years. Majid then wrote a short letter in English to Plaivy and sent it through the internet mail to the address that the website indicated. This way began a correspondence which lasted for the remaining years of our hero's short life. It was not long afterwards that Majid called Plaivy and the two had a long talk that was the beginning of a long-distance friendship. During that conversation Majid agreed to Plaivy's proposal to translate into English and publish 46 poems from the three most recent volumes of Majid's printed works. This project was not finished in Majid's lifetime nor even when I began this biography some years later and it is now scheduled to be published in the next Fall. [It was Plaivy, by the way, who first introduced me to Majid's poetry and steered me to this project.]

Also late in that year, Igor Formico called him and invited Majid to a lecture to be given by the older poet and leading literary critic Igor Grachkov on the topic of the fate of poetry in Russia. The lecture was given in the blue hall of the Central House of Writers. All 350 seats were taken in the hall and more people crowded in as the lecture began. Grachkov started with the theme that the Symbolists were the beginning of the end for Russian poetry, just as the modernists in the West had killed poetry in the France and the English-speaking world.

He claimed that the Symbolists sought to objectify poetry and made verse more obscure and highly referenced to outside materialist realities. This had the result that poetry became impossibly obscure and filled with so many allusions that no one could understand it when listening to it, poetry could only be understood as a written text which had to be carefully parsed and studied to undercover its meanings. The spirituality, inner emotions, and music of words—which were vital for poetry—were thus driven out. And the result was that the necessity of recitation fell away. This trend was actually helped along by the Soviet cultural authorities which drove poetry from the public sphere when and wherever they could. Grachkov said that not everyone was like that—Pasternak and Akhmatova were exceptions—but even the poetry of Brodsky presented the listener with enormous challenges and lacked all spirituality and humanly feeling. He made the claim that even when Brodsky recited, his verse sounded more like a medical diagnosis then a euphonic statement of inner feeling. He recited a few lines as an example. Majid looked over at the "dean" of Russian poetry at that time, Valery Reiner, and saw deep scowls disapproving shaking of the old man's head. Grachkov then took up the Soviet contribution to the demise of poetry. He pointed out that Soviet cultural authorities from the earliest sought to control poetic discourse because they feared it so much. They looked to control poets and to do that they banned their recital and publication unless the poets became raw eulogizers of the state and state policies. Furthermore the Soviets insisted that poetry must speak to the lowest common denominator and be manly, optimistic, forceful, and in a word, bombastic. Mayaskovsky was the greatest example of this ideal; Yesenin was an example of a better poet who tried but could not comply with these Soviet standards and so he killed himself. Thereafter until after the death of Stalin, Soviet censors did everything to silence real poets. It was easy to do—they denied them the "air" of public recitation and publication. Only beginning in the 1960s did they allow the so-called dissidents—poets born in the 1930s—to perform. Ironically he said they were descendants of Mayakovsky in their style and poetics, their bombast and declamation, but once the object of their opposition was removed, their poetry has evaporated. All other poetic diction went underground or was driven out (as in the case of Brodsky). The Russian public over a huge period of time became unaccustomed to the poetic word, to the euphonic conveyance of inner and spiritual meaning and beauty. The combined forces of the objectifiers and Soviet repression had driven poetry out of existence as a spoken art form to the point where it had become a merely written art form—and so it was dead. The irony of this, he claimed, is that the membership of the newly founded Russian Poets' Society and the annual reward winners of the previous last few year demonstrate this: it is entirely made up of the generation of the 1930s—old men whom no one has ever heard giving public recital of their verses. (There was at that point a large outcry throughout the hall, as a goodly number of those same poets were in attendance, including Reiner.) Grachkov then concluded his speech by saying that this lamentable condition is now continuing as the young poets also choose (voluntarily) to forego public declamation and recital. They write academic verse and they mean for it to be read. And their vehicle of choice is to publish on the internet. They do not address other young people and so they have no audience, anywhere. This means that Russian poetry, he concluded, will become as Anna Akhmatova had said in one of her earlier verses: "No one will want to listen to our songs." Grachkov then surrendered the podium and sat to one side. A maelstrom of anger broke out in the hall, denunciations rained down on Grachkov, those old men whom Grachkov had attacked stood up and shook their fists in the air in fury—looking liking so many white-haired pensioners protesting the delays in their pension checks. The scene was cacophonous but Majid looked at it and recognized Grachkov's point: the audience was entirely comprised of elderly men (and a few elderly women) trying to look bohemian, but mostly appeared old and dowdy. All the young people, he realized were next door in the cinema hall watching a Hollywood block buster movie in translation. Majid began to feel the anger from the hall was striking at him as much as it was lashing out at Grachkov, the heated discussions around him were cries of inner anguish trying to deny that they had been silenced, suppressed and muffled through so many years. These were people who had tried to live as poets but they had merely carried on and survived through uneventful lives as quiet automatons until they were old, without memories and without voices or songs. As Majid turned to leave the hall still resounding with angry hecklers and offended cries, someone he did not know shouted out while shaking his arm at him—"Look there, that's Sasha Khairulin! He's not from the 1930s generation! He's a young poet that speaks out! There is still some living poetry of the spoken word." People turned toward him. Then someone else started to shout: "Recite! Recite!" and then another, "Declaim us a poem, Sasha!" Majid was stunned and felt like a deer caught in the headlights of an oncoming car. "Recite! Recite!" People began to chant the words, as if through their vented anger and chanting they could coax verse from him on the spot. Majid fled from the hall, embarrassed and fearful, angry and confused. He rushed outside and began to walk rapidly toward the Boulevard Ring. He decided to walk the mile and a half back to his apartment and soon was walking at a rapid march pace. Much of the route he took is park land, heavily treed and quiet in this cool evening of late autumn when the falling leaves click and scrabble in the wind. After only a few minutes he found himself reciting under his breath verses which fit the pace of his march and which vented his flustered feelings of anger and fear. The words repudiated the idea of the death of Russian poetry and conjured up the image of an angry prophet expounding on what people should do to avoid damnation and certain death. The sounds—for he was declaiming quietly but out loud as he marched—were rhythmic and emotional and he repeated and reworked them to the beat of his marching so that by the time he arrived back at his empty apartment he had composed most of the stanzas of a poem. He spent the rest of the evening pacing around his study completing the poem and was done with it well after midnight. He then stopped, stood upright and began to recite the entire poem out loud, and satisfied with the resulting verses, he wrote them down, dashing off the 32 lines in no time. It was the first original poem that he had composed in more than 13 months. And it was to be the first of a rash of poems he wrote in the next year. Unfortunately, this poem was never recited publically, nor was it published during his lifetime; he came later to consider it an inferior composition. The text, which had the title The Death of Sweet Words, was found among his personal papers after his death, still in its original paper form.

After these two incidents, Majid re-discovered his "voice" and was resurrected as a poet. He began composing poems again and at a prolific rate, as can be judged by the output of the period from late 2001 through to early 2003. He resumed work on his poetic translation of Macbeth and he started in 2002 work on translating the French Phedre into Russian alexandrine verse (this was unfinished at the time of his death). It was only a few days after Grachkov's lecture and Majid's poetic march back home, he came up with the idea that was to possess him for the rest of his life. He thought that the best way to publish his poems in the manner in which they were best delivered—by his own recitation—would be to make video films of him reciting them and then to upload the videos to the internet, to a website dedicated to his verse, where interested "poet-ophiles" (*stikhi-lyubiteli* in Russian) could view the poet reciting his verses the way they were meant to be delivered. He did not know if the internet could do that at that time. He was not very familiar with the internet, or its offerings, or its technical limitations—but he was determined to find out if it would be possible. He was particularly inspired by the two films which had been made of Brodsky reading his poems in a church in Venice not long before his death. These had been shown on TV as videos and in cinemas as regular short films. So why could they not be shown through the internet? Majid thought about this project all that next week, and finally called his dynamic friend Igor Formiko to discuss the plan and how it might work. Typical of Igor, from the start he was greatly enthusiastic, and although he too did not know much how it would work on the internet, he knew some programmers who probably did. Igor said that the first step in such a program was to select the poems to be filmed and begin putting them on digital video. Igor knew of lots of people who had camcorders and he would ask them if they would be interested in filming a library of Majid's recited verse. First Majid needed to select the poems to be recited and filmed and then to make them accessible he needed to give his poems titles. In the winter of 2002, Majid and Igor started this project. The programmers they had talked to all suggested that for technical limitations each video should be less than five minutes long and that titles would be written in through the video cam. Through the remainder of that winter and into the spring, Majid recorded 18 short recitations of his verses. This library was already well beyond what their selected programmer thought was feasible to put onto a website in those early days of internet websites featuring film clips. But Igor found a programmer who began work on the program code that would enable video clip down-loading and viewing to run through the internet. This latter specialist was a young man—almost ten years younger than Majid—and he said that as for himself he did not especially care to listen to poetry, whether in live performance or through film. But he did like the concept of down-loadable video clips, especially if they were of jazz music clips. He though that could make a business so he felt his work for Majid would help him in develop the same capabilities for his favorite jazz music. Of course, Majid needed to pay this young man for his efforts, and this young programmer, even though he was getting paid for what he liked to do anyway, took his time at drafting the code for the website. It became a considerable expense, and there was no chance, it seemed at the time, that he could make any money from the site. You could say the programmer dawdled as a way of stretching out his payments, although there were some real technical challenges which he had to overcome in the work. He did not finish with a "beta" version until the next September, but this beta version of the website could only accommodate two short video clips of three minutes each. They launched this website in October that year, and the programmer pledged to work on the capabilities so that a much bigger selection of Majid's video films could be put on the web. This latter work stretched into 2003 and even beyond so that Majid's poetry website grew slowly as well as its capacity—but it was from the beginning seen for what it rightly was: a significant innovation in the way poetry was delivered and shared. By the time of his death, Majid's website presented the interested viewer with a selection of 25 poems on video which our hero had composed and published in the previous twelve years. They all featured the face and voice of Majid—dressed interestingly enough in a redingote which looked a lot like something Pushkin might have worn in his day—reciting with his inimitable inflection and hypnotizing intonation the poems which he liked best (and which were on clips of less than six minutes each). The programmer put into the website a counter which recorded the number of viewers who looked at the site and recorded the numbers of times poem videos were viewed online. According to Igor, the response to the website and the number of "hits" on the site and "views" of the poems ran into the tens of thousands. Majid's "virtual" audience was sizeable, but not vast—his reputation established but he was not widely renowned. But this counter demonstrated that he had a following of people who liked his verses.

During the course of this work on this poetry website in 2002, Igor also managed to find a theatre manager who was willing to stage a recital by Majid. This was scheduled for late April and by that time Majid had already composed a number of new poems which he was eager to present publicly. But one he did not recite was a poem that he had worked feverishly on in the late winter of 2002. It was an attempt by Majid to come to grips with the grief he still keenly felt over the death of Irina and his unborn child; an attempt through verse to address his feelings which had tormented him in the previous 20 or so months.

He put a one word title on the page when he printed it: *Grief* (which in Russian is a word *gore* which looks and sounds a lot like the word *goret'* which means to burn or it could be related to the word *izzhora*, which is the burning of acid reflux).

I thought I saw you in your usual chair
Curled up as you often were, reading a book,
But it was only a wishful memory of you.
Instead there is an empty place in the chair.

Again I thought it was your gentle caress at my arm
As we strolled under the lindens, leaves tumbling
Down, but it was only the touch of a crisp leaf
Next to me, with the breeze there was only an empty space.

With a flash, a blast, glinting of shards of glass
You have left me—for good—in a cloud of dust
And I am bereft of all love, your gaiety
Snatched from me, there is only an empty space left in me.

Such pain this sudden emptiness. It is as if some
Cruel god reached down into my viscera
With red hot tongs and snatched out my heart
Tore out my voice and poured in molten lead

Which burns to this day, casting a hollow
Space where once beat my heart. Inside of me
The burning lingers, I am blistered and as if dead.
And I can only hear the roaring as in hell.

If only I could chase after you as my
Own beautiful Beatrice, too soon taken away
But the empty bowels of hell do not hold you,
Oh no, neither Virgil nor Dante have I as guides.

And my songs are not so sweet as Orfei's
That the gates of the afterlife would open to me
Another view of you, my dearest Eurydice.
If there is a heaven for pure souls, you are there.

But such consolation does not ease my suffering
Nor soothes the burning pain, nor fills the empty spaces
In my life that one vengeful blast created.
I will forever feel this burning within.

He could not declaim this poem without tears coming to his eyes or a tightening in his throat choking off his voice. He could not hope to be able to deliver it in a public recital. It was another poem of his that remained un-published in his lifetime.

The recital turned out to be a disappointment for Majid. Not even half of the theatre's seats were sold, that is fewer than 200 people were in attendance. Igor had advertised this recital in the press as well as in the literary journals, and he even posted announcements of the recital on the internet on several cultural websites. He sent notices to the Gorky Institute of Literature and to the *Kultura* television station for them to announce the recital on their daily events calendar, but they did not post it. The audience appeared to be a mixed group of students, bohemian looking young people, and a number of elderly poetophiles. He did not notice that Reiner was in attendance, nor did he see Bella in the back of the hall in her black cloak and sitting in her wheelchair (but she slipped out quietly at the intermission and did not tell him that she had attended: at that time she was suffering and could only get around in a wheel chair). He did not feel that he connected well with the audience—people were not looking at him intently as they had in past recitals. Their response to his poems was muted, or so Majid thought. Afterwards Majid was not mobbed at the foot of the stage by young women admirers as he had been in previous years. Igor tried to put a good face on the result but Majid could tell that he was disappointed by the turnout as well. Even the theatre manager as he was paying Majid his share of the night's take, half apologized by saying, "Not much demand for poetry for poets, I guess. Art for art's sake, that sort of thing. We see it in theatre plays also." In fact, everyone was noticing the sharp decline in interest. Two months after Majid's lukewarm reception at this theatre, the elder statesman of the 60s generation, the outlandish Yevgheny Gangnus—the poet who in his time during the Soviet stagnation gave recitals to stadiums full of cheering fans—learned the same thing. He gave a recital, which was well advertised, to a mostly empty hall. He was hurt by the reception: Gangnus got larger audiences in the halls of the universities in America where he spent much of his time teaching those days than he did in Russia these days.

The recital was the first time that I heard Majid declaiming his poetry live. I found it was an amazing performance. It gave me the opportunity to introduce myself to Majid in person and to ask to interview him with the idea of building a biography and also to uncover more of his as yet unpublished poems.

It was about that time that Mayor Puddle opened a new installment of his program to beautify the city through statuary. In the Swamp Place Park, he attended the opening of an installation sculpture called Children are victims of Adult Sins by an expatriate Russian sculptor who was a leading social critic. Majid was amongst the official delegation at the opening. The sculpture is an allegory comprising a number of large iconic bronze figures of distorted creatures personifying human vices, among them alcoholism, theft, prostitution, greed, violence, graft, war and so on who were threatening two innocent children standing in the center of this group of grotesques. The mayor, ever displaying his favorite pose of hypocrisy and ignoring the fact that he had been often accused of many of those same vices, gave a moralizing speech saying how important it was that children be protected from vices. There was a small crowd in attendance and after a short ceremony (at which the artist did not attend because he was still wanted for libeling several leading politicians including Vladvolzhev with his pointed satirical artistic creations) everyone rushed away save for Majid who took a longer look at the sculptures. He was especially impressed by the long pointed noses and long needle like fingers of most of the personifications. On all of the faces there were malign and baleful expressions. It struck Majid as the first truly poetic and accurate sculpture that Mayor Puddle's program had erected over the prior decade. He thought that there was salient irony especially as the two small children standing in the middle of circle of vices (think of Hansel and Gretel) were the most inappropriate of all the symbols in this sculpture as this was the peak moment when hardly anyone in Moscow or Russia at large was having babies at all, and the resulting demographic crisis had even reached the attention of Sputyanin, who took time off from his conduct of the war in Chechnya to address the demographic crisis (especially the lack of babies) as one of the most important tasks of his administration. Almost the next day criticism of the sculpture began to fly into the mayor's office and make the rounds of the press and internet discussion sites. Some of the national politicians even detected that a few of the faces of the personified vices resembled them too much and threatened libel suits. There were even some critics of the composition who felt that because the artist lived abroad he should not have won the commission or because he was ethnically Caucasian, and not Russian, conflating all Caucasian peoples with the Chechens he was an enemy of Russia. This uproar took about two weeks to die down; the mayor decided he did not need to even acknowledge it, so Majid had no public statements to make about the statue. And in any event, Mayor Puddle told Majid that he didn't like the composition very much, and he liked the artist even less. No need to give either of them any more celebrity. Almost a month after the opening of this installation, it was in the news again. This time, in the early morning as the local emigrant laborers who were cleaning up the park, one of them noticed that the two small statues of the children and maybe one or two of the vices had been hack-sawed down and carried away. This was a time when exceedingly high commodity prices for non-ferrous metals (especially copper and bronze) combined with continuing pressing poverty incited the more daring to steal metals from almost any unprotected public source, such as public bronze statues, or copper or aluminum cables, electrified or not for their scrap value. This controversial installation was not the first in the city to be victimized (nor would it be the last). Ironically the statues taken were the ones that were the easiest and quickest to saw down with an electric hacksaw: besides the two innocent children, the thief or thieves took the personifications of theft and war—all easy enough to chop off at the ankles. The marvel of the incident was that no one saw or heard the bold thieves as they were sawing away though the night, undoubtedly casting off cascades of bright sparks. After that incident, it was decided to encase the allegorical installation inside a heavy iron bar fence which was padlocked every evening and not opened again until late in the morning. This lent it the sub-title which was one of the personified vices—willful forgetfulness of vice.

It was not long after the incident at the Swamp Place Park, when Majid was in Mayor Puddle's office along with the mayor's principal political advisor discussing the formulation of a statement to be given on the mayor's behalf on one of his new policy initiatives. The group were sitting around the T-shaped table in the mayor's office, which overlooked the heroic statue of one of Moscow's early princes, Yuri the Long-Armed, who by all claims 855 years earlier had founded Moscow. Mayor Puddle often looked out his window fondly at the statue, his namesake, imagining himself as Yuri the Long-Armed in chain mail on a stallion. But the mayor mistakenly thought the epithet the Long-Armed, meant something like the justice giver, while in his lifetime Yuri was given this epithet because he was an encroacher, he was constantly seizing unlawfully other princes' lands and cities. So contrary to what Mayor Yuri Puddle wanted to believe, his namesake was Yuri the Encroacher. In the middle of these discussions, the door to Mr. Puddle's office flew open and a big, agitated man rushed in. It was John Fawn, the managing director and owner of the city's large building company, Doomstroi. "Yuri Ivanovich, we simply cannot progress on our project. We are blocked everywhere!" he exclaimed angrily. Mr. Puddle stood up and glowered at Mr. Fawn. "What do you mean, barging in here so rudely? Can't you see I'm busy." "Your building department informed me that they are issuing a fine on us for not advancing our project in Chisty Prudy. This is unfair and unjustified." Mr. Fawn was referring to a building project which the mayor had started several years earlier to renovate the residential buildings of the inner city. This project had entailed auctioning off the rights to rebuild clusters of large residential blocks located in specific neighborhoods. Doomstroi had won one of the neighborhood groups. The tricky part of these contracts was that the winning construction firm had to evacuate the residents and re-locate them to residential towers located in the outer suburban—and less desirable—neighborhoods of Moscow. This was not so easy, as many of the residents of these older dilapidated residential buildings were elderly and had lived nearly all their lives in their apartments in these buildings. The project had been controversial from the start and had caused a lot of heartache among those being evacuated for the brutal way that some of the contractors dealt with them. "This is not fair. We cannot start on this one building on Smoked Fish Street because there is one little old lady who refuses to move out and will not take our money or our exchange apartment we're offering her. She's refused already for four years. We can't start building until she's gone." The mayor was by now also angry. "What floor does this dandelion puffball live on?" "The fifth." "In that case the solution is simple. I'm surprised at you—you're a tough nut in most of your business dealings, and you can't handle this one old lady?" Mr. Fawn fell silent. "Come now, Ivan Ivanovich. Haven't you ever heard that frail old ladies often die from falls? Especially falls down stone staircases? Isn't an accident like that something that you can make happen?" "I suppose so." "So then, do it, and stop bothering me with your little problems. The sooner you get this straightened out the sooner the fine will be lifted. Now get out." Majid was dismayed. He had just witnessed the mayor counsel one of the city's most brutish builders to commit murder so he could carry on with his construction. How could this happen? Majid could not believe the heartless cruelty of the mayor. But there was big money in all this and the raw greed was nowhere so evident as it was in construction. Only the week before in a press conference, Mayor Puddle had baldly stated that he considered his number one priority was to look after the economic well-being of the local construction industry. Even Mr. Puddle's political advisor thought that that was an unfortunate blunder to state in public, putting the interests and economic well-being of the city's residents in a lower position of importance. The incident and the exchange between Mr. Puddle and Mr. Fawn enraged Majid and as he left the mayor's office, he began to think of a response. And of course that came in the form of a poem. A short satiric epigram in this case, really just a lampoon. [I've translated it as best I could trying to preserve the levity in the verse.]

Yuri the Long-Armed sits
   On the back of his fiery steed
Looking out over his broad domains
   He stretches his mighty arm and says, 'Law'.

Yuri the Short-Legged sits
   His big belly extends o'er the edge
Of his big puddle, his bulging eyes
   Look out for storks and he says, 'Kwakit'.

His long sticky tongue shoots out from
   His fat lips, eating all bugs
In his boggy realm, his long
   Sticky fingers steal everything, and he says, 'Kwakit'.

He is the top predator on his perch
*   Save the sharp-beaked blond stork*
Who lives down the street.
*   He dreams He is a knight only his fiery steed,*
But he can only say 'Kwakit'.

He put this poem on his website where it was noticed by some of his fans who liking it then spread it through the new social networking sites on the internet. It spread like wildfire and soon the whole city it seemed was laughing at the pudgy, greedy Mr. Puddle—the chief bullfrog who said 'kwakit'. Mr. Puddle, himself not an internet networker, never knew. Those few in the office who saw the unattributed verse on the internet, snickered at him but never told him that it was circulating. If he had known, Majid knew full well that Mr. Puddle had a volcanic temper and that he would strike out at those who mocked him. If he had known that it was Majid who wrote the lampoon, he would have fired him immediately and perhaps sued him for libel. No one in Russia can tolerate being insulted or mocked—for an exceedingly proud people that is the worst of offenses.

About a week after this incident, Mr. Puddle invited Majid into his office. The mayor was still unsuspecting of the existence of the lampoon, but Majid entered with some trepidation. Mr. Puddle got right down to business. He needed to make a press statement addressing the problem of adult children knocking off their elderly parents so as to accelerate the time when they could inherit their parents' apartments. "This is a serious problem. Greedy people, who do not think twice about killing their mothers or fathers by pushing them down the stairs, for instance, so that they can get the apartments, modernize them and sell them for a large profit. These past few years as the privatizations have continued and market values have risen, we've seen a strong and steady increase in this incidence of patricides or matricides. And I think it is fair to say it is all within the family, greedy children without scruples." The announcement would be a new regulation that inheritances of apartments where an elderly parents/owner died suddenly in an accident would be held up for at least a year, maybe longer, until the criminal investigative commission was assured that it was not murder for self-benefit by younger family members. Mayor Puddle wanted Majid to draft the press statement. He should coordinate it with the people in the legal department who were drafting the new regulation. About a month later, much to his disgust, Majid called a press conference and made a brief statement about the new policy on privatizing and inheriting apartments in the city. At the same time Majid was instructed to draft and issue a press statement about the celebrations that would occur in September to mark the 855th anniversary of the so-called founding of Moscow by Mr. Puddle's hero, Yuri the Long-Armed.

Through the summer and fall of 2002, Majid continued his routine: soporific work in the mayor's office as a press spokesman during the day, walking the 3 kilometers to his apartment, eating out for dinner, and then all evenings working on either new verses, translation or reading poetry. He was busy but still he was beginning to feel lonely. Once a week he would meet with Igor after work at a sound studio and would record himself on video reciting one of his poems. These sessions took much longer than he expected—usually three or four hours but he enjoyed the activity. He was building up a library. Less often he would consult with the programmer about the progress in building his video website. It was during this period that he continued working on Macbeth—he finished the new translation in the darkest days of the winter of 2002-2003—and he continued the work on a new Russian verse translation of Racine's Phedre. He only rarely saw people, his social life was minimal but it did not bother him. In the summer of 2002, he again spent two weeks at Bella Akmadulina's house in Peredelkino. People there noticed that he seemed less aloof and sad then the year before, but for those with longer memories he did not have his usual sunny disposition of earlier years. The atmosphere that summer was dismal; the weather sultry and humid. Bella herself was feeling weak and broody, and liked to stay in her wheelchair letting her husband take care of her needs. Liza did not stay there while Majid was visiting, so he did not see her. Okudzhava of course had died, and Voskreshensky had had a mild stroke and was confined to his house so he stopped visiting there altogether. It was difficult for Majid to work on his own poems at Bella's house that summer, so he kept at his translation work and after two unsatisfactory weeks he went back to his stifling apartment. Toward the end of the summer he got an unexpected invitation from Valery Reiner at the Gorky Institute. In it he asked if Majid, as an honored graduate of the Institute, could come in the fall to the Institute to give a recital of his recent works to an assembly of students of poetry and a few honored guests. [I was one of those honored guests, and this was the second time I saw our hero Sasha Khairulin perform his poetry live in front of an audience.] Majid accepted and prepared a short program for a 45 minute recital. He did not know what to wear. He didn't want to wear the jacket which looked like a redingote (which for the video clips had been the idea of Igor Formiko) so he finally settled for an open white shirt with a gray jacket and black slacks. He remembered the time only a few years earlier when all he had was shabby old clothes and scuffed up shoes for one of his earliest public recitals. Now at least, his clothes were clean and new. At this recital Majid arrived early and Reiner greeted him warmly, saying he was so glad that Majid had accepted the invitation and that he was keenly looking forward to hearing for the first time Majid's poems recited. He briefly mentioned that the new Association of Russian Poets would very much like him to join their association before he showed Majid to the small hall. This time it did not matter the size of the audience: it was a command performance and was obligatory for the Institute's first year students. But the little lecture hall was packed. [I had arrived early and had a seat in the very middle of the hall with an eye level view of our hero when he stood.]

The hall normally held 90 auditors but on this fall morning standing room only does not express the crowding: there was twice the capacity crammed into the room, people standing leaning against the walls, students sitting on the corridor stairs and seated on the skirts of the podium. Reiner introduced our hero as Slava Khairulin, Russia's greatest living young poet, a successor to Joseph Brodsky and a man with a voice that reminded him of the greatest poets of the Russian nineteenth century. Reiner even confessed that he found Slava's poems were better than his own. Then Majid recited seven poems—all from memory—with pauses only for the audience to applaud or to take a sip of water. He was standing through the entire performance. This audience reacted very warmly and effusively to Majid's verses. I myself was bowled over by his intonation and concentration. I can only use musical terms to describe how he used inflections, crescendos and de-crescendos, accelerating and then slowing to fit the meaning or the feeling of the line, his use of alliteration to add another dimension of meaning to the words he so carefully picked. His performance was mesmerizing. It was hard to imagine that interest in poetry was declining in Russia from the reaction of the audience. But as I said this audience was custom picked, and a specialist audience if you like. Mr. Reiner told me himself afterwards that interest in poetry was waning and in the previous decade schools had cut the study of most of Russia's poets out of their curricula, and there were no more regular poetry recitals in schools, or yearly public declamations of classic Russian poems, like the one Majid had given when he was a young boy. Young people were not discovering the joys of Russian poetry nor the treasures of Russia's leading poets until them came to literature departments of universities like his.

[Plaivey was absolutely right about Majid. Here was a genius of the Russian language, in the same mold as Pushkin himself. I was overwhelmed by the sounds of his verses. I confess that I did not understand everything he said. Listening to poetry in a foreign language is like listening to opera in a foreign language: unless you know the words well already in advance you miss a lot. But then I understood the phonic meanings even when I did not catch or understand the literal meanings so well.

There is another, deeper meaning to the phonics of words and word arrangements that are sometimes greater in import than the literal: just listen to Dylan Thomas reciting his works to understand what I mean. I have to also admit that I was playing a digital voice recorder recording the entire recital, even though I had no permission to do so. And I noticed there were several others amongst the students who were doing the same thing and openly held up their handheld recorders.]

Majid was very pleased with the turnout for his recital and for the warm applause. There was even one student who presented him with a copy of a volume of Majid's published poems, asking if Majid could put his autograph on the cover page. That had never happened to him before. But the euphoria he felt after the recital quickly faded away on his walk down the leafy Boulevard Ring when he realized that the next day was the day in September two years earlier when Irina was killed in the suicide bombing at the National Hotel. Crisp yellow leaves were tumbling off the linden and horse chestnut trees and they reminded him of the coming death and desolation of winter. He fell into despondency over the following two weeks when again he could not find his voice.

It was not long after that that there was a surprising and daring raid on the small town of Malazdok located about 50 miles outside of Chechnya and led by one of the more extreme Islamist separatists. It was not clear what the objective of this raid was. It was not purely a terrorist action, as the small band of Islamists took 200 people hostage, but it included some acts of savagery which appeared to be vengeance when they bombed a barracks with its complement of 60 soldiers and security forces. This group was surrounded after a day by Russian special forces, but then the special forces were betrayed by locals and most of the band was able to escape after inflicting more than 350 casualties, mostly non-combatants, on the local population and the soldiers with only a small loss on their side. This raid was an outrage against all civilized values and Sputyanin was especially outraged that these terrorists could move so far and so freely outside the boundaries of Chechnya. He concluded that they had the tacit support of the local governors of the provinces neighboring Chechnya. The raid and its tragic outcome became the pretext for President Sputyanin to suspend democratic elections of governors. From then on he extended his autocracy with a program he called 'vertical democracy', but which was dictatorship or the extension of the police state directed by Sputyanin. For Majid, and for many other Russians without a voice, it was the totally wrong and unjustified reaction, and it was the beginning of a process of steadily stripping away the rights of Russian citizens and dismantling of the constitution which Sputyanin was committed to. Majid composed a short poem of protest to the decision. He did not support in any way the vile attack on Malazdok, but it was a political poem which was highly critical of Sputyanin's quest to enslave the Russian people. He sent to his friend Valery Polasky an editor at the Literary Gazette, but after only two days, Valery called Majid and explained to him that there was a censor's proscription on publishing any political poems by Majid, and there had been for a couple of years. The editors considered his poem was too political to print. He apologized but there was nothing that they could do for him with that poem. But he assured him that if he had any other poems that were not political they would be eager to receive them and print them. As a result, this particular poem remained unpublished and was presumed lost because Majid had printed it and sent to the Gazette the only paper copy. But by a strange twist of fate, Valery Polasky continued to try and get the poem into publication. At that time the Literary Gazette published editions of its journal in several different countries, including the U.S., the U.K., and Israel, where there were sizeable Russian populations. The editorial board decided that the ban on Majid's political verses did not extend to these foreign editions, and so Valery got the editorial board to accept the poem for publication in the Israeli edition. Ironically it finally appeared in the monthly Israel edition only in the week after Majid's death in 2003. [This happened to come to my attention only a few weeks ago as I was finishing this biography of the poet so I don't have it here and haven't been able to translate it.]

Late in the fall of 2002, Majid began work on a subject that he had long mulled over—it became his final masterpiece, The Ballad of Salavat. It is a verse narrative that has been likened to Pushkin's Eugene Onegin both for its structure and rhyming patterns, although it is not nearly as long as Pushkin's work. It has only 144 stanzas rhyming AbAbCdCdEE and is written in iambic tetrameter. Although it seems it is probably not the finished work that Majid had conceived of, the works stands as completed. He had stopped working on it before his murder. It is a masterpiece of contemporary Russian poetry, and it is slowly finding recognition throughout the country as such, although there have not been any live performances of the poem as of yet. It was published in this final form about three months after Majid's death. The poem tells the life story of the historical Salavat, or more properly, Salavat Yulaev, who Majid was convinced was a Tatar knight, even though in Soviet times, the Bashkirs claimed him as one of theirs [and continue to vigorously to this day]. Salavat was a very young man, but quite cultivated, when he went out in revolt in support of his father who had been swindled by Russian interlopers in the steppes of what is now Bashkiria. His father protested by joining in the Pugachev peasant and cossack revolts against the Russia authority of Tsarina Catherine. He was captured by deceit and along with his father lashed, and dragged in chains across Russia to the far western port city of Rogervik on the Baltic Sea of what is now Estonia. There he spent the next 25 years of his life in isolation, penal servitude, and sadness dreaming of his life on the warm open steppes of his childhood home. The poem focuses however on Salavat's efforts as a poet in his ample free time, and even quotes some verses from the Tatar (translated into Russian) that Majid purportedly attributes to Salavat. In this literary effort Majid has Salavat develop into an important Tatar poet whose works caused a problem for the governor of the penal colony because Salavat used so much paper and ink. The poem ends with Salavat repeatedly petitioning Catherine over the years and eventually establishing a correspondence with the poet and senator, Derzhavin—who had been so instrumental in suppressing the

Pugachev revolt—who pleads on behalf of Salavat for his release. It is to Derzhavin that Salavat sends his corpus of verses that he had written over more than 20 years, and it is Derzhavin who ensures that they survive. In the end Catherine agrees to be presented with a resolution for clemency but she dies before it can be signed and enacted. As the new emperor, Pavel, comes to power and resolves to undo so much of what his mother achieved or stood for, he orders the release Salavat at once, but the decree freeing the now worn down, broken-hearted and sick Salavat arrives in the middle of a howling winter after many days on the hard icy post roads. When the prison warden goes to inform Salavat of his liberation he finds he is already dead, sitting at a writing desk, frozen, as is the ink in his inkwell.

Although he had already spent four months working on this ballad, Majid began working furiously to finish this poem from January 2003 when he got a sudden premonition of his own imminent death. It was a bitterly cold winter and on the morning of the 25th of January, the mercury in the thermometers in Moscow fell to -34 degrees celsius. It was his 34th birthday and he was all alone in his apartment. The cold was seeping in through every crack, the windows rattled, and the heaters—which ordinarily over-heated his place—were straining to keep the apartment warm. In the entire Moscow region, electricity was going out because of the strains on demand from electric heaters, tram lines were freezing up, water pipelines were bursting even when two meters underground. Many people did not go out; but they huddled around their burning gas stoves in their kitchens. Majid was alone in his apartment, no plans for a birthday party, no desire to go outside to work, no incoming phone calls wishing him many happy returns. Instead he was thinking about how he was approaching an age in life when many of Russia's most brilliant poets had prematurely died. Gogol had been 42 when he died sick and alone. Pushkin died when he was only 38—of course the wound from his duel hastened his death—but Yesenin lived to be only 30 when he hanged himself,

Mayakovsky killed himself at the age of 36, Delvig lived only 32 years, Lermontov also dead from a duel at 27 years, Blok who lived only 40 years died of depression. Mandelshtam lived longer—all of 47 years—but he like the young Gumilyov at 35 years of age were done in by Stalin's henchmen. Majid could not help but think that he was in a perilous age in his life and that like his hero, Salavat, he was alone and cold with his verses going unheard and unread. The life of a poet in Russia was cold, lonely, unhappy and unappreciated—and short, and on this day Majid felt this particularly keenly. On that depressing morning—of course that time of winter is the very darkest when day time hours are barely six hours long and when the darkest of clouds sit only a few hundred meters above your head effectively blocking out that little bit of daylight—it was all Majid could do to boil himself some tea. There was nothing in the cupboard to eat—not because he was poor as he had been 12 or more years earlier, but because he had been too indifferent to the demands of going to the store to buy some food. Finally around midday he decided to dress up warmly and go to work. At least there, at his office he could get a nice warm lunch in the cafeteria. Fortunately, his apartment and the mayor's office were neither far from metro stops so he did not get too chilled through, although his shoe soles were thin and did not protect his feet from getting cold. The deep cold had emptied out the city it seemed. But once inside the city hall which was filled with warmth, Majid began thinking how the current cold snap—and this was to be only the coldest day of a ten day cold spell—seemed to be appropriate to the sufferings and hardships that Salavat faced in his prison barracks for so many winters on the howling windy Baltic. He thought how Salavat must have sat there in Rogervik looking out at the blinding ridges of solid ice lying on the sea—which looked a little like the snow-covered steppes of home—and must have wondered where he would go if he stepped out and crossed the ice. Finland? Sweden? Ah if he only had the strength. Of course, Majid accomplished nothing in his office on that shortened dark day and he reversed his route back to his apartment after five hours. He threw himself into writing his ballad, sitting under a blanket at his desk, often jumping up and pacing the room to recite under his breath the next verse or two to see if they fit. He did not even notice that he did not have dinner that night. He worked late into the night, and even when he went to bed in a half sleeping state his mind took in the sounds of the winds which were blowing outside and rattling his apartment windows to be the frigid Baltic winds blowing through the prisoners' barracks in long ago desolate Rogervik when Salavat sat there.

But the next day things turned completely around. It was only -18 degrees Celsius when Majid woke up to shower and shave, and by the time he left his house, even though it was still dim and murky outside, it was already -14 degrees. Before he 3left, he checked his inbox on his electronic mail and there waiting for him was a long letter from Avram. And it started with birthday congratulations from his émigré friend. By this time, Majid wrote and received nearly all his mail electronically and only sent letters on paper to people who did not have computers—like his mother in Kazan. Avram was apologizing for not keeping in touch for a long time and wanted to repeat the invitation to Majid to come to Israel to give another recital in the coming months. Again his offer was that he would pay for Majid and Ira's airfare and stay in Tel Aviv (he did not know about Ira's death in a bomb blast) and he would guarantee a good enthusiastic, attentive audience, plus an honorarium. This was the perfect birthday gift for Majid (although he had to sadly inform Avram of the circumstances of Ira's demise) and he quickly wrote a short acceptance letter and pledged to write him more at length from his work computer. They later agreed that a date in March would be ideal and could be arranged without too much difficulty. It would be a welcome relief also from the cold.

Then later that day in the office Majid was called to come to Mayor Puddle's office. He had not been in for several weeks to see the mayor. When he got to the outer foyer reception that was when he first laid eyes on the beautiful Natalya Kudryasteva, a new girl in the office and

Mayor Puddle's new personal assistant. He was thunder struck. There was something so familiar in the face—he had seen it not long before he thought. At that moment he could not linger and try to learn more about her; she did not stand up from her desk when he went in. But he did introduce himself (as Slava) and got in reply a modest introduction from Natalya (who was called by everyone Natasha). She was not entirely new in the city hall as she had worked in the office of one of the deputy mayors for a couple of years, but she had started working for Mayor Puddle only at the start of the year. As it was, the business that Mr. Puddle wanted to see Majid about was trivial and the meeting lasted not even five minutes. When he passed back through the outer office, Natasha was now standing away from her desk, and Majid saw that she had a stunning figure to match her beautiful face. They looked at each dumbly for a few moments—what could he say?—and then embarrassed by his obvious display of being attracted he quickly ducked out of the office into the outer corridor. He paused just steps away at the top of the grand staircase to catch his wits. And that was when he recognized where he had seen Natasha before. This new girl in Mayor Puddle's office was the spitting image of the vision he had had of the sculpture of Natalya Goncharova when not long before she had stepped off her pedestal and addressed him. And he recalled that she—the statue—had very explicitly said that when he next saw her, he must ask to marry her. He became very excited. But he did not have to wait long, only a few hours later he saw her at the lunch canteen and asked if he could sit with her. She was quite willing to let him sit with her and talk with him, and he thought she was fluttering her eyes at him flirtingly (he learned later that she was self- conscious, embarrassed, and wore contact lens which made her bat her eyes uncontrollably when she was feeling self-conscious). She was a little shy at first, but soon she was talking to Majid as if they had long known each other. He learned that she was from a provincial city in the Ural Mountains, that she had gone to a technical university there and had studied economics, that she was 27 years old and unmarried, but had been married for less than a year while she still was in university, and that she lived with friends with whom she had moved to Moscow three years earlier. Majid told her that he was a poet from Kazan and Ufa. He could not get over how much her face looked like the statue of Natalya Goncharova standing on a pedestal on the Boulevard Ring—of course without the gilded bronze complexion. She had a spade shaped face with a little chin, a long straight nose just slightly turned up at the end, light brown hair worn short, pouting lips red with lipstick, eyes lined with black kohl and she was quick to smile at him which revealed pearly white teeth. As they stood up and picked up their lunch trays, he noticed that she had a small bust and very small waist. What Majid did not realize then, and never did clearly understand, was that Natasha, except that she wore eye makeup and had short curly brown hair, looked almost identical to the younger Anna Gorchitskaya who had seduced Majid more than 15 years earlier. As she was moving away, Majid became even bolder and blurted out an invitation asking her out for dinner that same evening. Natasha accepted, almost cheerfully it seemed. As they left the canteen together, his eyes were fixed on her shapely bell-shaped bottom in her black tight-fitting skirt. He was completely charmed, and aroused at the same time. They agreed to meet at the inside foyer at the main door at six-fifteen that evening and they would walk to the restaurant. By the time he had gotten back to his office, he was so excited that he was unable to do anything the rest of the dark afternoon. He could not bear the wait until their appointment by the exit door. He had not felt so elated in more than two years. He thought of which restaurant to take Natasha to, either the hole-in-the-wall restaurant called the Cheese Hole where he particularly liked the food, or the new more romantic and attractive restaurant (and more expensive) called the Cosmos Cow. Unbeknownst to Majid on that cold dark afternoon in the center of Moscow, Natasha was equally aroused and excited. She later confessed to him that she had fallen for him, love at first sight, and was dying to see him again after work hours. He was like a prince that she had dreamed of when she was young, a dashing romantic poet, some one that she had fallen in love with years before as an ideal image of a man. At the appointed time, finally, Majid met her at the outer doors to the city hall. They were both dressed in their heavy coats, she in a black wool knit cap with a matching long scarf. She looked so different to him cloaked in her heavy winter clothes and long coat; they made her seem small and insignificant and they hid nearly all of her most alluring features. But her smile was still quite visible; it was broad and gleaming. Majid felt a little awkward at first on how to greet her. But he quickly took her by her shoulders as if to hug her and gave her a small kiss on the cheek and they stepped out into the cold night street. He had decided to go to the Cosmos Cow, which was a twelve minute walk up toward Pushkin Square. She almost at once put her arm into his and snuggled against him as they walked through the wafting frosted vapors of the crowded streets as offices spilled out their contents at this quitting time. Majid spoke excitedly about his projects, his video recordings, and his goals, he felt foolish that he did not let Natasha speak much, but she encouraged him onward with pointed questions about poetry, for instance, even though she did not know much about Russia poetry or any other. They walked closely together, she snug against him, and he becoming more aware of her small body against his. She was about Majid's height, but slender. She wore high black stylish boots which accentuated her small feet, shapely ankles and calves. There was no snow on the sidewalks, but he listened to the gentle crunching of their feet on the salt and grit which had been spread against ice. As they were walking he became aware that he could feel her presence but he could not see her except for her feet and ankles. Not long before reaching the restaurant, on an impulsive whim, Majid pulled Natasha with him into a small flower kiosk. "So how about some flowers for you?" he asked. "No occasion, other than our first date, and I'm so glad to meet you." Natasha's first reaction was to resist, along the lines of 'no, you shouldn't buy me flowers', but instead she said, "How very sweet of you." And he bought her some yellow chrysanthemums- which of course were very much out of season—wrapped in pale blue cellophane. With this bouquet in her arms Natasha had to release his arm so now he could turn his head toward her as they walked and look at all of her. He could see that her cheeks were quite red from the frost—both were exhaling heavy clouds of frosted vapor with each breath. In the restaurant, they sat opposite each other at a small table tucked in an obscure warm corner of the place. A waiter brought a tall vase with water for Natasha's mums. They looked deep into each other's eyes, lots of smiling. Majid told Natasha a lot about his childhood in Ufa and Kazan, his relationship with his father and with the Buterbrodskis (he left out his sexual affair with Anya). She spoke about her older married sister and how she looked up to her, but she was really talking about how much she wanted to have a family like her sister. Neither of them noticed their dinners—it was good food, but not good enough to distract them from each other. Two hours flew by, as if in a trance, the coffee and dessert dishes long since cleared away, and the waiter idling about impatiently. But it was a cold winter night in mid-week so there were no lost clients or crowds of diners waiting at the door. Majid and Natasha talked on over empty water glasses and the table seemed to be shrinking as they grew closer. Natasha thought Majid was the prettiest man she had ever met. He had long dark eye lashes and dark wavy hair that contrasted with his white skin on his face. She was completely overwhelmed by his gentle and sincere manner and madly in love with him and his good looks by the end of the dinner. And then for the next twelve hours or so everything rushed by with an intensity and pace that was dizzying and hard to remember: Leaving the restaurant, walking arm in arm to the bus stop, deciding to go together to his apartment, tossing the bouquet to the floor of his apartment, hugging and kissing in the entryway even before the coats were off, dancing in close embrace, more kissing, undressing, making love in the living room, moving to the bedroom, making love again, waking for water and the conveniences, then making love again, and waking slowly in mid-morning with faint daylight coming into the room, making love again, professing their love to each other—until finally Majid posed to

Natasha the imperative, "Marry me, Natasha. Be my wife." She did not use words to answer one way or the other, but she accepted. They were still in a cloud of feelings and confusion, which often accompanies a long night of passion, when they dressed again and went back to city hall later that morning. Natasha indeed had accepted Majid's proposal to marry him and in the days that followed she moved her personal things in with him in his apartment, and they set up house together. He had to buy food to stock the refrigerator—which he had not done for some time—and tea and coffee for the evenings. The conversations in the weeks that followed as February cast its white gloom on the city were still intense and full of emotions, feelings, memories, plans, and promises. They went together to the wedding bureau and reserved a wedding date for April, enough in advance so that she could invite and ensure that her mother (her father, Rustam, had died from alcoholism when she first went to university just before she got married the first time) and her sister and her family could come from Uzhinsk. He also invited his mother and the Buterbrodskys to come to their wedding. Once officially registered, Majid insisted on buying an engagement ring for Natasha to replace the ring that she wore on her middle finger of her right hand as a reminder of her divorce from her first husband. Natasha grew ever more in love with her Slava, and her excitement about the coming wedding grew steadily.

For his part Majid threw himself even more intensely into poetic composition. At his office, there was almost no work to be done for Mayor Puddle who was at that time in a muddle in his life's objectives and ambitions, thwarted everywhere by Sputyanin. Majid spent most of the working day working on his Ballad of Salavat and on other poems which came to him. Evenings he spent talking with Natasha about plans and aspirations, but he also spent a couple hours versifying and reciting under his breath. When he was working Natasha would sit with him and watch him or read. He would declaim for Natasha when he had a finished stanza or when he wanted some outside critical appraisal.

It turned out that Natasha had a good ear for poetic diction and she gradually came to appreciate the unique talent of her Slava in shaping and putting words and sounds together. On a couple of occasions she accompanied him to the room where he was making video films of his recited poems. His recording project was moving along satisfactorily, but Kozlorodov, the programmer putting together the website with video links, continued to protest that he was having difficulties which only more pay could remedy. Majid told her of his upcoming visit and recital in Israel and he insisted that she accompany him there. This proposal also pleased her as she had never been outside of Russia before and the prospect of a warm weather visit abroad during the winter was enticing. The days (and their nights together) flew by for Majid in a dizzying crush, and his mind was flooded with ideas and rhymes. In March just before their trip to Israel when he was preparing his program to present to the Tel Aviv audience, the director of the Moscow Artists Theatre called him and informed him that they had decided to perform his translation of Macbeth in the Fall season and that they would sponsor the printing of this version. But then he added that the theater critic whom they had consulted, Vladimir Zastoyov, while overall liking the new translation and its poetic feeling had a number of quibbles with Majid's translation and had even stated that in some places the translation was mistaken. What if Majid could make some changes? Majid reacted immediately. He would not allow nor make any changes. "After all, they say that both Shakespeare and I are geniuses." he told the director. "Who is this Zastoyov that anyone will ever remember one word of his views or opinions?" And that ended the issue there. The play in its Khairulin version was later to be acclaimed as a brilliant and fitting Russian poetic rendition of Shakespeare's and thereafter was everywhere adopted and accepted as the standard. It is unclear whether critics ever picked up on the intention that Majid had in selecting and giving a more forceful translation of Macbeth: he was consciously thinking of Sputyanin as a Macbeth—in much the same way that Pushkin had landed on Boris Godunov as a metaphorical stand-in for Nikolai the

First—the tyrant and usurper and you can see that many of his verse translations bring that aspect to the forefront. But about all this Majid was to never know. The next day, entirely as if nothing had happened with the news of Macbeth, Majid and Natasha at the lunch break walked down Tver Street to the Manezh Square and bought their air tickets to Tel Aviv. They did not need to get visas as Israel had shortly before dropped the requirement for Russian citizens to have visas in order to enter Israel. Majid composed two new poems just in the week before they flew, and he prepared them to deliver at the recital which was scheduled to be two days after their arrival. Avram met them at the airport. He had changed a lot since Majid had previous visited and his appearance alarmed Majid. Avram's curly orange hair which from university days was always a wild tangle of fur was now mostly gone and he had a bald pate surrounded by neatly trimmed hair on the sides but the orange color had grown darker and was flecked with white and gray. He had grown quite plump and the skin on his face and neck sagged, although he was still tanned. But his garrulous and friendly character and his unbounded enthusiasm still shone through. "Well, after all, we are growing older. It should happen that way. You have your beautiful women to help keep you looking young." said Avram, as he stooped to kiss her hand. "So what you see is the result of hard work and hard eating and drinking. And I plan to make you partake in some of that hard eating and drinking while you're here." Avram reported to Majid that the recital was going to be packed as demand was stronger than even he had anticipated. "I hope I don't disappoint then." said Majid. "You? Never. You could recite poems by Pushkin and the crowds here would love you for it and believe they were your poems." said Avram laughing.

"It would be more satisfying if I recite my poems and they believe that they are Pushkin's." As earlier, Avram had made all the arrangements for their stay and entertainment. Again they stayed on the beachside hotel so they directly went out onto the beach. Avram had recommended that while the outside air and sun were warm the water was perhaps still too cold for swimming. Majid passed on the swimming but Natasha eagerly went into the surf and came out spluttering and her limbs all in goosebumps. She said gasping, sputtering and laughing all at the same time, that the water temperature was no cooler than usual swimming temperatures in Russia during the summer, but it was still good to have a big towel to wrap up in straight after leaving the water. Majid could not help admiring her figure in the tight swimsuit; her figure and silhouette reminded him of a film scene of the young actress Chulpan Khamatova which had stuck in his mind. He loved Natasha and he could not take his adoring eyes off her during the entire time they spent on the beach. They later met for dinner at a seafood restaurant outside of old Jaffa, but the evening air was too chilly to eat outside and Avram brought along a few friends and his current girlfriend (all emigrants from Russia) and they sat in a small, white washed room with stained curtains warming the place with their conversation. Avram said he was planning on opening one of his coffee bars in Brooklyn, New York. He thought that with the substantial Russian Jewish diaspora living in Brooklyn his business would do well. And he thought there would be the same strong demand for top Russian poetry there as well. But that just as in Israel it was a demand that was sure to decline in the future because the demographics were against poetry; and the young children of those emigres were not studying in Russian and in many cases not learning or speaking Russia. "Listening to poetry," said Avram, "appears to be an activity for the elderly, even though the best poetry was produced by the young." Sadly young people did not appear to think of poetry as entertainment and it was entertainment that young people sought if they ever turned to books, whether literature or poetry. Ironically, those were almost the exact words that had been used by the publisher that Majid had approached not long before with the proposal to publish his Ballad of Salavat. "You can't sell books and you can't push them out to the book stores unless they are perceived by young people to be entertainment that can rival electronic video games or MuzTV. Poetry doesn't sell. Even classics. I'm pulling titles out of my catalog all the time these days. Book stores are closing." The next evening, just as Avram promised there was a large auditorium in the middle of Tel Aviv filled with middle aged and older Russian speaking Israelis all eagerly waiting to hear the genius of contemporary Russian poetry Slava Khairulin reciting his own verses. Of course many were in attendance who had attended four years earlier, but that did not matter, the program comprised an entirely new array of poems. Majid was warmly received and there was strong applause between each poem—once again he delivered the entire program, over seventy minutes, from memory. And in this program he felt at liberty to present some of his political poems of the past three years. Some like this one expressed his condemnation of the presidency of Sputyanin. It has come to be called *The Tsar* and it is interesting that it appeared in Russia through the social networking websites not long after he first performed it there in Israel. Majid never did try to publish it, nor any of the other political poems. There must have been in that audience reporters who collected some of the poems and reported back to authorities in the Kremlin on their content.

The Tsar has returned—what is to be done?—
Or better were we to say the autocrat?
Or to say the head of the Cheka
Has returned as head of state?
And he has immediately gone to war
Against separatists and against Russians.

He has set himself up as above the law
Although as Tsar he is not God's appointee
His oprichniki run through the streets
In black Mercedes with howling dogs' heads.
His racketeers have seized national assets
Their militias also prowl the streets, unchecked.

He is not a believer in constitutions
Nor in that Western import: democracy.
Civil society is not for him
Public discussion and social freedoms he disdains.
He believes only in manly strength, and projecting violence.
His word is the only law and he will brook no opposition.

As Tsar he does not seek the people's will
He will lead by oppression
And he will choke out those who voice
A different direction from his own power vertical.
How long before he re-opens the gulags?
Not long now before he enslaves us all.

The Tsar has returned. He will crush us.
No one invited him, he usurped
His power by secret threat and coercion.
Russia is sure to suffer under his boot.
While he struts his power as if he were an immortal
All the world should tremble—as do we.

The Tsar has returned.
Long live the Tsar.

One member of the audience afterwards came backstage and introduced himself as a Russian émigré poet and literature critic named, Samoel Katzenellenbogen. He appeared to be in his fifties, maybe early sixties, stout and short, white haired and he was bursting with excitement: "I am so glad to hear your verses, Slava. Wonderful, sublime, beautiful, lyrical! Not since Brodsky, has Russia produced such a poet, such poetry! Bravo. Bravo." Others were also praising him, but in the crush Majid was only looking for Natasha who, when she finally came backstage and moved through the throng surrounding him, gave her fiancé a big hug and kiss. Avram was in the crowd and was also beaming with pride that this was his friend from Moscow. "Such declamation!" said one of the audulatory crowd. "And to think he gave the entire program from memory." Avram cut in: "Your greatest pianists give hour-long solo concerts all from memory—why should it be so different for a poet?" The evening ended in a dinner reception party at one of the hotel restaurants where a lot of well-wishers gathered to congratulate Majid. They stayed late into the night drinking to Majid's health and happiness, and to his poetry. Natasha was burning with pride and admiration while Majid could not tear his attention from her. She did the drinking for both of them.

Once back in Moscow, Majid decided one evening to take a long detour route with Natasha to walk by the statue of Natalya Goncharova Pushkina, the one that had spoken to him in a vision almost three years earlier. He was curious to see if the vision would return, and he wanted to see how close the resemblance between his Natasha and Alexander Sergeivich's Natasha was. And if his Natasha would recognize that resemblance as well. They were again dressed in their winter coats and boots, the ones that made Natasha look much stockier than she was and made them both seem shorter than in the summery weather of Israel. They both still had some of the golden sun of Israel emblazoned on their faces, clear that they had just returned from a sunny clime. The winter nights had grown shorter and it was now staying light until after the end of working hours so that when they reached the statue of Russian poetry's most famous couple, standing in front of the church where the real couple actually got married almost two centuries before, it was still the dim light of a twilight spring evening. The air was frosty and the vapor from their breaths still came out in white puffs. But when Majid and Natasha reached the statue, Majid was thunderstruck in horror. There were workers and scaffolding all around the place where the statue had stood. They were in the process of removing it from its pedestal. Another few minutes later and Majid would have missed seeing it altogether. And why were these workers removing this recent embellishment of the city's parks? Majid did not need to ask. As the workers carried the statue off and onto a frame of wooden pallets, he saw the reason. Someone, a metals thief, had sawn off Natalya's outstretched arm. In front of the entire city, under the street lights at night, or in broad daylight—it had to be a daring, and desperate thief who could so quickly saw off an arm and dash off to his scrap metals dealer in the open. Markets for scrap metals were now at an all time and metals theft was again a perilous problem in many parts of the country, especially perilous where live power lines were being salvaged for their copper or aluminum cables. "Can you imagine anyone so base and desperate that he could deface this monument to beauty and art, just for a few kopeks?" he wondered to himself out loud. "I wanted you to see this monument of a poet's love to an immortal beauty. As a testament to our own love." Natasha not understanding said, "It's alright, Slava. Our love does not need a testamentary monument made of brass." She paused, "It's such a disgrace that someone would disfigure this statue, like the man who slashed the Mona Lisa." (Natasha did not know about the metals thieves or the incentives for their thefts.) Majid remained shaken throughout that evening by the sight of Natalya being carried off horizontally missing her right arm.

Back in Moscow there was another individual who throughout that winter also was paying close attention: unwanted attention to Natasha. He was one of Mayor Puddle's bodyguards named Boris Emelianenkov. He was a towering, ham handed shaven-headed goon from Siberia who had been previously in his career a professional mixed martial arts boxer who had had to retire earlier because he had had one concussion too many. Under his black suit jacket and white shirt he was covered in tattoos, but only a small tattoo of the Cyrillic letter B appeared on the joint between his thumb and forefinger. He, like many in the Mayor's office, found Natasha irresistibly attractive, but unlike others he could not restrain his desire to let her know of his attraction. At first he would come and stand next to Natasha's desk and loom over her for long stretches of time, saying nothing pretending to watch what Natasha was doing. But even before Natasha and Majid had left for Israel he had begun to edge closer and begun to say things, like 'Doll, you're so beautiful.' 'Don't you want to kiss me?' 'Hey beauty, give papa a small kiss.' Into March these statements, menacing and unwanted, could be dismissed by Natasha telling him 'get lost' or 'go stand somewhere else' and Boris would. But it was still annoying and harassing to Natasha and she reasonably felt it was threatening. After Majid had bought her an engagement ring which she wore to the office, Natasha told Boris that she was going to be married and would he leave her alone. But Boris was not the brightest bulb in the chandelier and Natasha's statements did not deter Boris's advances which occurred as much as three times a day. Even before leaving for Israel she had told Majid and after almost two months of this harassment she had complained to the head of the bodyguard contingent, one Mr. Dantezov, about Boris's objectionable behavior and asked that Boris be positioned somewhere else. Dantezov brushed off her complaint as unjustified, "You mean a pretty girl like you doesn't expect to receive the attentions of red-blooded men? You attract him. You should feel complimented." Nothing happened to Boris. Then only in the week before their departure as the first warm streams of March begin to suggest spring, Boris became more assertive and more menacing. He switched to the imperative, 'Give me a kiss, girl.' And he started using extremely crude, vulgar language, 'Hey bitch, give me a kiss.' 'Let me stroke your redbud tits.' Natasha found this harder to deal with and had to be much more forceful her in protests. She told Majid again about the harassment and he spoke to Boris in the outer corridor, but politely, telling him to leave his fiancé alone and to stop harassing her. Boris' first reaction was to deny that he had ever said anything to Natasha and besides he told Majid, 'What business is it of yours?' Of course, Boris did not think he was harassing her and he was utterly surprised and dumbfounded that Natasha and Majid were a couple. "How could a doll like her ever hook up with a squib like you?" Boris said and then ignored Majid. But for the rest of the week before their departure Boris kept quiet and spent less time in the fore-office. This harassment started again almost as soon as they had returned. Boris again began to sidle over to Natasha's side of the desk and would hover over her, even after she invited him to stand on the other side of her desk. He arched his neck and loomed over her trying to look down the front of her blouse. The vulgarity returned at once but was even more menacing. "Give me a kiss, babe, and I'll give you a fuck you'll not forget." She screamed at him and he was like a rock. Majid went to Dantezov and complained in the strongest terms that Boris had to be removed, that he was a menace and threat to Natasha. But Dantezov again brushed off Majid's concerns, saying that there was nothing he could do. That the Mayor had to have a bodyguard, and such a bodyguard had to be posted near the Mayor when he was at work. And he was sure that no harm would come to Natasha. But he then sent Majid off with a non-committal, "I'll see what I can do. Tell Natasha not to take him too seriously." That was no palliative at all. Natasha had to stand up without looking at him every time Boris started to walk over to her side of the desk. That stopped Boris at first, and he would retreat. But after a few days he would stand where he was, almost blocking her, and he began to harangue her again. 'Give me a kiss. You'll remember it.' 'You want me to stroke your tits, don't you?' Natasha would respond forcefully, "Get out of my way and shut your foul mouth." But that only worked for a few hours at a time. Boris came back at her, 'How could you agree to marry that little dick? You need a big dick, like mine.' On one day, exasperated, Natasha got up from her desk and rushed into the mayor's office. The surprised mayor, who was talking with some colleagues, looked up and asked if there was anything she needed. Natasha retreated, but decided that she needed to complain to Mr. Puddle about Emelianenkov and to ask for him to be relocated, or she would have to resign and leave city hall. In tears she later that evening told Majid about the incident. He said he agreed with her, namely that she should tell the mayor or resign, but he also told her that if she felt especially annoyed or threatened that she should call him and he would come straight away. She had a one number speed dialer and Majid was top of her dial list, so that was feasible. Little did she know that she would need to use this method so soon afterwards.

It was now early April, snows in the city had mostly melted to the point that there remained only black greasy piles of ice where earlier snows had been thrown to the sides of roadways and footpaths. The grit had not been cleaned from the streets or sidewalks, while the mornings often had icy patches. It was on this day, that Boris made an advance that went too far. He again began to creep over toward Natasha, who was trying hard not to take too much notice of him, but he had a big grin on his face. When he got close, he said, "So princess should see what a real man is all about and what you will be missing." In a flash with one hand he unzipped his fly and his half erect penis flipped out of his open fly. "So suck my real man." And he started to approach closer. Natasha gasped, jumped up, and reached for the phone, shouting at the same time, "Get back." She had dialed the quick dial to Majid's office before Boris could react. "Help, Slava. Come at once!" Boris was trying to wrest the phone set from her hand, but he was also trying to put his penis back. "Help!" she shouted and she jumped to put the desk between her and Boris. Boris was fumbling, and in confusion did not know whether to advance on her or retreat from the office altogether. His first instinct was to grab her and hit her, but he could not reach her and both his hands were occupied with his wayward penis and his fly and zipper. Majid opened the door and came in running. Natasha hopped behind Majid. "That's it Borya. You've gone too far. Natasha go in and tell Mr. Puddle what has happened. Borya, step outside." Accustomed to meekly obeyed stern commands, Boris did so but at the same time in his head he heard an invitation to fight. Majid followed the bodyguard out into the corridor by the top of the grand entry marble staircase. He did not really know what he would tell Boris. The notion that Boris had disgraced Majid and dishonored Natasha crossed his mind. He would challenge Boris to a duel—what an improbable idea. He began to angrily address Boris, "Your behavior is un…" Before he could finish his words Boris's giant fist had lashed out in one of his favorite killer blows straight into the middle of Majid's face, throwing his head backwards violently and completely lifting and knocking Majid off his feet backwards. He flew head first down the stairs and rolled clumsily down all 28 steps to the bottom landing where he stopped in a disjointed pile and began to bleed. Even before Majid stopped rolling there were witnesses who saw his fall. At the moment he stopped at the bottom, Natasha came to the outer door looked around and screamed when she saw her Slava. Her scream attracted others who came out of their offices to see what had happened. A security guard down the corridor who had half seen what had happened came running and shouted at Boris, who was standing dumbly at the top of the stairs looking at Majid's body and feeling contented that he had delivered the right blow: he had done well what he had always had been trained to do.

It is unclear whether the solid blow to Majid's nose killed him instantly— as seems to happen far too often in the cage boxing matches in criminal districts of cities around the world—or whether Majid died when his neck was broken in his violent tumble down the staircase. At any event, his body was lifeless and broken when Natasha and others got to it, and he never recovered or reacted again to any outside stimulus. When the ambulance crew arrived, they pronounced him dead already. City Hall put out the story that died from an accidental fall down the stairs—his neck was broken after all—and that was the end to the matter. The story was not reported. Boris was not dismissed.

And indeed that was the end of the matter. The life of the brilliant young Russian prodigy and poet came to a sudden and untimely (and violent) end, just as his father's had. And except for the understandably distraught and grief struck Natasha few knew or found out the story. Word of his sudden death did not get out.

Few came to mourn him, and so the career of our hero, Russia's greatest young poet of the past 170 years, was eclipsed, cut off in his prime, as in a cliché is too often said in Russia these past 20 years. His musical talent for putting Russian (and Tatar) words magically together is silenced forever, although with Natasha's help we are getting a large volume of his unpublished works collected, printed and published. How many poems were lost with him, never written down, only resident in his memory. We'll never fully understand where this enormous talent came from, his acute ear, his prodigious memory, the wonderful sonorities. His legacy is still being judged and assessed, but the judgment is that Russia lost one of its finest. Igor finished the work on the website showing Majid's video recitations and so we have a record of many of his shorter poems and that enchanting lyrical voice will live on. With time there will be more flowers put on his grave stone in the future than were at his funeral, but for now we can only lament.

A year or so before his death Majid wrote a premonitory poem, part of which I offer in this translation.

> *Those who die young should be heroes,*
> *Heroes inspire us and lead us through darkness*
> *And only heroes can challenge death for us.*
> *They give us hope and reconfirm our love.*
>
> *When the young die, unknown and unheralded*
> *It is bitter and tragic, a close-felt sadness.*
> *The sour smell of a mound of fresh turned earth*
> *Covered with cedar chips soon sinks into oblivion.*

Orfeo Dichter 24
January 2007

Orfeo Dichter is a literary critic and Professor of Russian Literature at the University of Indianopolis. He also teaches at the University of Wallonia in Brussels. He is from the Italian speaking region of Switzerland, and speaks English, Italian, German, French and Russian fluently. In addition to this biography, he has written extensively on Russian poetry and published biographies of the poets Gavrila Derzhavin, and Yevgheny Gangnus, Petro Leporiti, and Alexander Pushkin. He met the poet Majid Khairulin three times at recitals of his in Russia and has arranged for the printing of his complete collection of Russian and Tatar poetry at the University Press. He collected the materials for this biography from his six long interviews with the poet, and with the key people in his life. And he consulted the many letters that Majid wrote to his mother, to Anya, to Avram, to Formico and to Innokenti.

www.ingramcontent.com/pod-product-compliance
Lightning Source LLC
Chambersburg PA
CBHW041750310726
48978CB00011BB/377